She was sudd
(oddly) of her
uncomfortabl
somehow she
watching her.
pleasurable s
heard the two
was conscious of greetings being exchanged.
Someone came near to her (she could hardly
breathe), a voice said, 'Hannah'.

She looked up. It was Samuel. He was smiling at
her, but almost at once the smile seemed to falter.
Had he sensed that it was not *his* face she had hoped
to see when she raised her eyes?

Also by Helen Cannam
in Sphere Books

A THREAD OF GOLD
A KIND OF PARADISE

HELEN CANNAM

A High and
Lonely Road

SPHERE BOOKS LIMITED

A SPHERE BOOK

First published in Great Britain by
Sphere Books 1990

Copyright © Helen Cannam 1990

Printed and bound in Great Britain by
Cox & Wyman Ltd, Reading

ISBN 0 7474 0234 5

Sphere Books Ltd
A Division of
Macdonald & Co (Publishers) Ltd
Orbit House
1 New Fetter Lane
London EC4A 1AR
A member of Maxwell Macmillan Pergamon Publishing Corporation

For my parents, with love

ACKNOWLEDGEMENTS

The characters and events in this book are all imaginary, as are the two places I have called Hollinthwaite and Thornside, though any one who knows the Dales is welcome to speculate as to where they are situated.

Like anyone with an interest in the traditional way of life of the Yorkshire Dales, I must acknowledge a debt to the many writings of Marie Hartley and Joan Ingilby, and in particular their fascinating work on the old hand-knitting industry.

I should also like to thank Linda Vickers of Tow Law for so patiently instructing me in the use of a spinning wheel, and answering my many questions about sheep and wool; Mrs Micklethwaite of Lanchester, for showing me how to knit with her grandmother's knitting sheath; and Mary and Michael Crompton of Ireshopeburn for providing an enjoyable day's instruction in the use of a handloom and much valuable information on the early textile industry.

Any errors of fact are, of course, entirely my own.

PROLOGUE

In the hollows the snow still lay deep, frozen and glittering in the low afternoon sun; but on the road, which ran over the highest and most exposed ground, the wind had thinned it, and tramping feet and horses' hooves had quickly worn a narrow uneven path that threaded its black way across the whiteness of the moor. Yesterday, in the first warmth of the season (they had thought the thaw was on its way), it had even melted a little, exposing the stony earth and the coarse faded grass; but at nightfall had frozen again to a ringing shining hardness on which the steady old pony – his shoes sharpened before the winter storms – slithered a little as he plodded homeward with the two riders on his back. Now and then John Burton would lean forward to run a calming hand along his shaggy neck and murmur some soothing phrase – 'Nigh on home now, lad. Quiet now, steady. Thou'lt have us safe soon enough.'

An icy little wind rose with the sinking of the sun, penetrating even John's heavy coat and the thick cloak worn by his wife Agnes, who rode pillion behind him. The two grey figures huddled closer, seeking warmth.

'Be glad to be out of this,' John said with feeling.

'Aye.' There was no need to say any more. The horse plodded on, past a gaunt and solitary inn, desolate now in winter when the drove roads – as this was – were empty. A little further on they glimpsed a cluster of rough single storey buildings, marking one of the many lead mines which burrowed into the fells, and soon afterwards the track dipped into a narrow valley, its contours sharpened by the water that once had rushed down to free the lead ore for the miners and then subsided again to a gentle moorland beck, at present laced with ice along its bank.

The horse splashed through the water and then, more slowly, followed the road up again. Here, from the summit, briefly, they had a clear breathtaking view of the folded hills of Swaledale, purple-shadowed beneath snowy tops turned to rose by the setting sun, all arched over by a sky of opalescent green.

'Not far now,' said John with satisfaction.

The downward track slanted across the dale side towards the dusky land of meadow and pasture, farms and little villages that bordered the river Swale, whose rushing waters could be heard clearly now that they had dipped down out of the wind. They reached the road that ran along the north side of the dale and turned the horse's head to the west.

Half a mile on, and the glow of the lights – dim and uncertain, but heartening all the same – marked out the houses of Hollinthwaite, strung along the road where the land was high enough to be above flood level. Only dimly now could they make out the low stone buildings, ling-thatched, dotted here and there with those cheering rectangles of light; but they did not need to see to know each one, as surely as if every line were clearly visible.

A narrow lane ran at right angles to the road, hemmed in by the walls of the adjoining houses; and up this they turned, passing the simple Friends' meeting house where, each First Day, they met with other Quakers from the district. A little further on, the village ended where a beck ran down from the moor, forming a natural boundary. The horse plodded through it, and then on past Low Farm, whose slated roof and extensive outbuildings declared a prosperity superior to that of most of the houses in the village. Old Mary Harker was on her way back across the farmyard, having barred in the hens for the night. She saw the

Burtons coming and paused to wait for them to pass, a black bony figure, still but for the incessant movement of her hands, busy with the inevitable knitting. The click of the needles joined the other gentle sounds of the winter's evening.

As they came alongside the farmyard wall she called out, 'How didst thou find thy sister?'

John Burton reined in the horse. 'Well enough. She has kindly neighbours.'

The old woman nodded. 'Aye well, that's something. She had no bairns, had she? They can be a comfort when a woman's left.'

'It seems we're not a family for bairns,' said John quietly. Mary scarcely seemed to hear him, for she went on, 'Not that I had as much – though maybe that's just as well, as it happens.' She broke off, and said quickly, 'I'd best get in. There's no one to keep an eye on the little ones.'

The gravity of John Burton's expression increased. Agnes said with a sad note in her voice, 'How is she today?' It was clear to them all that she was speaking of young Ann Gayle, wife of Joseph Gayle who owned Low Farm, who had been ailing ever since the birth of her second son some months before. Mary, a widow without ties, had come to Low Farm to care for the troubled family.

Now she shook her head. 'Failing fast. She'll not linger more than a day or two more. Poor bairns, they'll be motherless soon.' Then she became brisk again. 'I must go in. I daren't leave young Robert alone for more than a minute, not when there's no one to mind the baby. You'd think he blamed poor little Samuel for his mother's illness. He'd do anything to hurt him. More than once I've only just got there in time. And of course Joseph'll not leave her bedside, not as things are. I've to do everything.'

Despite her claim of urgency, Mary seemed inclined to go on talking indefinitely. At last John interrupted her. 'We'll not keep thee then,' he said, and she remembered her responsibilities and left them.

John and Agnes went on their way in a silence deeper than ever, because it seemed as if death was all around them.

A quarter of a mile further on, where the track rose steeply again, they reached the long line of High Farm, sheltered by a plantation of ash and birch, only the stone porch, chimney stack and glazed windows marking out the human living quarters at one end from those of the animals at the other.

A neat gate in the dry stone wall admitted them to the yard, and there John halted again to allow Agnes to slide slowly and stiffly from the horse.

'I'll go and stir up the fire,' she said, and her husband nodded (there was still just enough light for her to see him do so) and turned the horse towards the stable.

Agnes walked as briskly as her cramped limbs would allow across the frozen earth towards the house end of the farm. The indoor cat came to meet her, curling itself about her ankles, purring a greeting. Agnes, warmed by a sense of homecoming, paused – as she always did after one of their rare absences – to gaze at the house, the weathered stone, the mullioned windows, the carving over the porch: 'J.B.A.', and a date, 1668. The A stood for Ann, and the John Burton who had built the house ninety-six years ago had been her own John's grandfather; but Agnes liked to think all the same that the initials in some way marked the house as theirs too.

The cat, scampering ahead, reached the porch; and there, abruptly, came to a hissing halt. Tail erect and bushy, ears laid back, hairs a little bristled along its back, it stared into the blackness before it.

'What's up, puss?' Agnes, conscious of a faint anxious tremor but no more, stepped forward; and then she too halted.

What was that sound? It was like nothing she could

4

remember hearing before; it was wrong, unearthly, out of place. The wind in the trees, the splashing of the little waterfall in the beck behind the house, the cry of sheep on the fell, the gentle stirrings of the animals in the barn, the rustling, somewhere, of a mouse: all these were normal, constant sounds, a part of their life at High Farm. But not this – not this faint wailing cry, uncanny and inhuman.

Agnes shivered, and turned to see if John was coming; and was relieved to see him emerge just then from the stable. 'Dost hear it?' she called softly. He came to her quickly, listened, and then took her hand in his. They stepped forward.

The sound came from the darkest corner, just inside the porch, where something glimmered faintly in the shadow; and it *was* human after all. Agnes paused only for a moment, and then gave a little cry and stooped to gather it into her arms, murmuring softly in a confusion of concern and dismay and tenderness.

John stood in silence and watched her, his wife, his childless wife, rocking the tiny wool-wrapped bundle in her long-empty arms, her head bent over the small crumpled face, her voice softer than he had ever heard it, murmuring on and on.

'Best bring it in out of the cold,' he said at last, and put an arm about his wife and steered her forward. He lifted the latch, opened the door, ushered her in; and then left her to find her way to the settle by the kitchen hearth while he stirred the glowing peats to life, and poured milk for the cat, and barred the door, and lit the rushlight to bring a hesitant illumination to the simple, spotless room. 'It'll need milk,' he said then, and put some in a pot to warm over the fire.

'Best mix it with water. That's what my mother did, when her milk wouldn't come for our Jane.' The infant, momentarily silent, began to whimper again, more loudly than ever, as if returning warmth gave power to its lungs. Agnes rocked it. 'Poor little mite. Who would do such a thing – leave it like that, in this cold?'

'Some desperate soul,' said John gravely.

'Aye. She must have been desperate. Unwed, I suppose, and the man left her. We must see if there's been talk.'

'Best not, perhaps. She'll be wanting to hide her shame, not flaunt it. Maybe we'll hear, maybe we'll not. We must wait and see.'

His wife looked up then, and John saw that the strong plain angles of her face had been suddenly transformed, lit with an inner radiance. 'Aye. And meantime it's mine – mine and thine, to care for.'

John came and sat beside her, looking down at the wailing infant, his expression thoughtful and touched, just a little, with something of the same radiance. 'The Lord's gift to us, given into our care, for a time.' His voice was full of wonder. He put out a hand and slowly and very gently ran a finger down the soft pale cheek of the baby. 'Maybe it's what we've waited for all these years – why there were none of our own.'

Agnes smiled at him. 'Could be. That could well be it.'

CHAPTER ONE

They had been baking all morning. The fire was stoked to a red glow beneath the bakstone where the havercakes cooked, one after the other, and its heat filled the kitchen. More than an hour ago Agnes had opened the door into the yard, letting it stand wide so that the clear March air could flow in. But somehow it seemed to make little difference here by the hearth where they were working.

Oatmeal from the meal ark, salt and water; mixed to a stiff dough, rolled out, carried to the bakstone; cooked one side, turned, baked a little more; set to dry on the cake stool – and then the whole process began again, over and over, as it would until they had enough havercakes made to stave off hunger through the approaching lambing time.

Hannah, carefully packing the first havercakes – dried and cooled now – in the basket where they were to be stored until needed, was uncharacteristically silent. Concentration explained part of it perhaps, Agnes thought; but very likely the child was simply too hot to waste her energy in her usual chatter. Agnes paused for a moment, rolling pin motionless beneath her hand, and watched Hannah, as she did so often, conscious of the warm glow of happiness somewhere about her middle which the very thought of the girl brought to her. Twelve years she had been with them now – twelve years since they had returned from the family funeral to find the tiny creature abandoned in their porch. It seemed like yesterday, yet every day of it brought a new joy, and never once in all that time had Agnes or John known a moment of regret.

Hannah did not seem to know she was being watched, as she carried the cakes from table to basket, reaching, walking, bending, with a lovely unconscious grace, absorbed in the task. Then, abruptly, in that odd way she had sometimes, she came all at once to a complete halt, half way between basket and table, and stood quite still, like a bird poised for flight.

'Oh!' The cry was full of wonder, and so was her face, all the gravity and exertion gone from it. She looked enraptured. 'Listen – listen there!'

Agnes listened, and after a moment heard what she supposed had caught the child's attention – the long rippling call that returned every year at this time. 'The curlews are back,' she said matter of factly. Then she smiled. 'Thou hast worked hard, lass. I reckon it's time someone cast an eye over the sheep, just in case a lamb's come early. Take thy knitting with thee.'

Hannah always seemed to display her whole soul in her smile: it was dazzling, and irresistible. She gave a little skip, pushed her knitting into her pocket, and ran towards the open door, to be brought to a halt by Agnes's quiet, 'Hannah!'

The child shot a swift smiling glance over her shoulder and took the last few steps to the door at the approved sedate walking pace, calm, controlled, demure. She passed through the dazzling rectangle into the aromatic brightness of the farmyard, which smelt of pigs and horses and chickens and dung, familiar good smells overlaid with the sweet fresh indefinable scent of the wind from the fells.

Her clogs splashing through the mud (it had rained yesterday), yet somehow light-footed all the same, she slithered out into the lane. Only there did she remove the knitting from her pocket, tuck the supporting sheath into her belt and set her fingers working with the long curved needles – no danger now of dropping the wool in the dirt. She did not look down at her busy

8

hands, or at the pale coarse yarn which ran through her fingers, or at the stitches running rapidly from one needle to another. She had no need to look, for she knew the work was going exactly as it should, automatically, neatly, as, stitch by stitch, row by row, the stocking took shape below the needles, as it did whenever her hands were not occupied with some other necessary task.

She was running again now, as fast as the increasing slope would allow, past the point where the stony track became a mere impression in the grass; by the side of the vast enclosed field where the village cows grazed in the summer months, and the small solid stone barn where, at present, their own two cows were housed. Here, by the wall that marked the edge of the open moor, she paused and looked back the way she had come, her eyes tracing a path over the crowded roof tops, across the dale road, on to the fields – meadows for hay mostly – which bordered the river. There were just a few where, later, crops would be sown, and her gaze found its way unerringly to the small neat rectangle of their own land, where she could just make out her father's figure, dog at his heels as always, plodding slowly along behind the horse-drawn plough as it turned the earth, ready for the sowing of the oats. She watched him for a little while, taking pleasure in the straightness of the furrows, the slow rhythm of the work; yet conscious all the time of the lovely call of the curlew, overhead and behind her, up there above the fells.

At last she turned and went on her way. When the bird fell silent she began to sing herself, letting her voice run up and down, here and there, just as it pleased, and then gathering it at last into the rather more solemn notes of one of the knitting songs, which were the only songs she knew, since Agnes and John forbade any other kind of singing (and were even a little doubtful of so obviously useful a form of music).

But there was no one to hear her now, and the impulse to sing was too strong to be resisted.

She reached the summit and there, silenced by breathlessness, she paused again. She looked around her, into the valley, its depths hidden now; and then over the fells, bronze with last year's bracken, deep brown where heather and bilberries grew, dun with the coarse moorland grass, though here and there a touch of new green hinted at growth to come – all that sombre grandeur laid out below the jubilant blue of a sky clear of any but the faintest wisps of cloud, soft and light as sheep's wool caught on a bramble. To the east, the horizon was marked by the drove road, on which the only traffic was a string of five packhorses, the bells on their harness just faintly audible. In two months' time the drovers would be back again, plaid-draped figures whom Hannah loved to watch as they tended their lumbering herds of cattle. Then she would know it was summer.

To the west, where the land dipped a little, was the heugh where the Burtons' small flock of sheep would be found – most of them anyway. There were few who wandered away from the place, and even those almost always returned before long. There the lambs were born, there they grew and in time bore their own lambs; they knew it was where they belonged. Singing again, Hannah began to run towards it, her feet finding their way with the sureness of experience over the tussocky grass and the scrubby plants of heather and bilberry, dodging the most marshy places (she had only once lost a clog, watching appalled as the orange-brown peaty ground closed over it, too late to save it).

Here on the fell the wind was fresh in spite of the sun. It tugged at the heavy creamy folds of her skirt, the exquisitely white ties of her cap, the less spotless linen of her apron. She loved the feel of it on her cheeks; but then she loved everything about these high places – *everything*.

She could see into the hollow now, sheltered a little, sunny, full of good grass and the sweet plants the sheep liked, already reviving after the winter. The little flock – thirty of them – were scattered over the hillside, heavy slow creatures at this time of year, close to lambing, with their fleeces almost full grown; but for all that they still had the wild look of their kind, the fierce black and yellow eyes alert in the black faces beneath the curled horns. She looked about for the two black ewes, kept because their wool was useful for making a contrasting pattern in undyed gloves and caps. She had a special liking for them; they were different, handsome and distinctive. She saw one, far off and . . .

She halted, ceased her singing, felt her mouth stretch in a wide happy grin in tune with the pleasure that filled her. Then she gave a joyful skip, called 'Samuel!' and ran towards the thin figure seated on a rock across the hollow. The sheep scattered as she ran, but she saw only the boy, who had looked up and was grinning at her, though his hands (like hers) continued to work at his knitting. Like her, like all the Dales' children, he had learned to knit from his earliest years, as naturally as he had learned to talk and walk and do all the other things necessary to a normal existence.

As she came up to him he said nothing, only nodded and shifted to one side a little so she could sit down on the rock.

'I saw thee go past when I was baking,' she panted. 'I thought thou might be here.' Then she added, 'At meeting yesterday, thy Dad said thou had cold. I thought maybe thou wouldst be sick for ages, like Friend Garnett.' He was the scholarly old Quaker who made a small living teaching many of the Hollinthwaite children, Hannah and Samuel among them. For some time now he had been laid low following a neglected cold that had led to an inflammation of the lungs.

'I'm well now,' Samuel told her. 'It was just a cold.'

Indeed, though his voice sounded thick and muffled, he looked healthy enough.

Reassured, Hannah relaxed. 'Curlew's back,' she said. She could trust Samuel to share this particular delight, as she could see he did from the enthusiastic way he nodded.

'Aye. It's been calling all morning . . . There are catkins on the alders by the beck.'

'Oh,' said Hannah, and smiled at him all the more, so that he would see that she appreciated his pleasure. She knew how interested he was in growing things of every kind. When he had enlarged further on the qualities of the catkins, and their purpose, she said, 'I've to look the sheep over. I'd best do it now.'

He walked with her as she found a high place from which to see them, and began to count, as she had heard her father do so many times, 'Yan, tan, tethera . . .' The knitters used the words to count stitches too, so she had learned them almost as soon as she could talk.

'There's some of our ewes got in amongst,' Samuel said, and pointed. 'That's one. Thou canst see the brand.'

She began again, and then walked down into the flock. They came towards her now, recognising a friend in the quietly moving figure. It was then that Samuel exclaimed, 'I nigh forgot! I've this for thee.' He thrust a hand into his pocket and pulled something out and held it towards her. Hannah stared at it for a moment, and then gave a soft cry of delight and took it, holding it gently, wonderingly, in her hands.

It was about ten inches long, shaped like a goosewing, made of a glossy, richly coloured wood, and carved all over, on every inch of its glowing surface, with an exquisite and intricate pattern. The carving seemed to run endlessly, seamlessly over it, without a beginning or an end, yet when Hannah looked at it closely she saw a wonderful wealth of detail: a flower here – a wild pansy, a cinquefoil, acutely observed, perfect in

12

every detail; an animal there – a lamb, new born, with long uncertain legs, a ladybird, a hedgehog shuffling through meadow grass. How could anyone cram so much into so small a space, and yet make of it, not a confusion, but a satisfyingly ordered design?

'It's beautiful!' she murmured at last, and he coloured with pleasure, though she did not see him do so, for she was too busy admiring the object. 'Where didst thou find it? Didst really buy it just for me?'

'I didn't buy it. Father gave me the wood – it's cherry, from the old tree in the orchard.'

'*Thou* didst make it? All thyself? Thou didst carve all this?' Her tone mingled disbelief and amazement, and this time she did look at him.

Rosy with gratification, he nodded vigorously. 'All of it. Thou likest it?'

'Yes – oh, *yes*!' She continued to trace lines and curves with her fingers, as if she could not touch it enough.

'It's to use,' he reminded her. 'For thee to use.'

Momentarily, she looked as if she did not understand him. Then she grinned suddenly and glanced down and pulled from her belt the old knitting sheath that John Burton had made for her when she first began to knit. She held it beside the other, comparing them. The basic shape was the same, but there any resemblance between them ended. Her father's was smaller, a child's sheath, fast being outgrown, as he himself had said more than once. It was without ornament, a simple and functional object, smooth and stained from long use. Samuel's gift was a joy to touch and see, made not just with love but with a rare skill. Hannah slid it into her belt, slotted the end of her right hand needle into it and began to knit. It felt strange at first, even a little clumsy, so much bigger was it; yet very soon she began to feel as comfortable with it as if she had been using it all her life. It was not just beautiful, then; it was also perfectly suited to its purpose. She raised her eyes to Samuel's watchful face

13

(he looked just a little anxious) and smiled all her delight at him.

'I wanted to have it ready for thy birthday, but it took too long,' he explained.

'That doesn't matter,' she said. Because it was such a pleasure to use, she went on knitting with it, putting John Burton's old sheath away in her pocket. She would keep it, for that too had been made with love; but she was glad that its smallness made it right for her to put it aside.

After a moment, Samuel said, 'Is it really the day thou wast born, the day they call thy birthday? Or is it just the day thou wast found?'

She frowned a little, with puzzlement. 'Found? What dost thou mean? It's my birthday, the day I was born – the same as thine, the same as everyone's.'

'But how do they *know* thou wast born then?' he persisted. 'Maybe thou wert two days old when thou wast found. Or six, or more —'

'Why dost thou keep saying "found"?' she demanded, quite clearly failing completely to understand him, even to make any sense at all of what he said.

'Thou wast found, wast thou not?'

She grinned, blushing a little. 'Under a gooseberry bush? Thou canst not believe *that*, Sam Gayle!'

'Course not.' He reddened too. 'Thou wast born to thy mother like everyone else. Only no one knows who thy mother was.'

Hannah stared at him. She was conscious of a strange choking sensation, as if her heart had grown and grown and, in its frantic thudding, threatened to cut off all the air to her body. She said mechanically, 'Agnes Burton is my mother.' But she sounded as if she no longer dared to be sure of what until now she had never even thought about at all, since it was so much beyond question, the most sure and unvariable fact of her whole existence.

Yet Samuel persisted, shaking his head, though there was some hesitancy in his expression – but she sensed that was from something other than doubt as to the rightness of what he said. It came rather from the realisation that he was in fact intruding upon her something of which (to his astonishment) she had heard nothing until now.

'She's not. Thou wast found in the porch.' Then, defensively, he concluded, '*Everyone* knows that.'

She continued to stare at him, but said nothing, because she did not know what to say. How could it be true? It was some fairy story, made up to tease her, if not by gentle Samuel, then by some other more malicious person. She was the child of her parents – of that quiet, hard-working couple who cared for her so lovingly – born in their solid bed upstairs, with its much-washed linen curtains; just as nearly every child was born in its mother's bed, when the time came.

Yet here was Samuel trying, or so it seemed, to hint that this was not so, that she was in some way strange and different, not like other people. How *could* it be true?

Her fingers knitted on (as his too were doing now), but her frowning, puzzled, frightened face continued to stare at him, trying to understand.

'They never said. It can't be right,' she objected at last.

He was silent then, his consternation clear enough, not because he believed what he said to be untrue, but because she did not know what he had been sure she would know; and he was the one who was responsible, clumsily, for breaking it to her. She saw all that on his face, and her heart went on thudding and thudding inside her with fear and dismay and bewilderment, while she waited for him to speak again.

'I thought thou knew,' he said then, quietly, slowly, with obvious reluctance – and a note of pity too, which she found the worst of all. 'I thought they must have told thee, when everyone else knows. I've heard Father talk of it often, and Mary.'

His father – whom he knew to be so, with certainty, as she had known (still knew, surely?) that those two people who lived with her at High Farm were her mother and father. It was she who, sometimes, pitied Samuel and his brother Robert, because their mother was dead and they had only awkward, gossiping Mary Harker to turn to in her place, while she had mother and father both. They *must* be her parents; it could not be otherwise; Samuel must be wrong. He had made some dreadful mistake.

She felt resistance rise in her, denying the truth of all he had said. It was just a piece of idle gossip, just the kind of thing Mary Harker would say, not giving a thought to its effect on anyone. The look of uncertainty on Samuel's face – that came not from regret, or concern for her, but from the realisation that he might after all be wrong. He was beginning to see his mistake, but he would not admit it. Suddenly furiously angry that he should treat her so, should threaten her happiness, she sprang to her feet.

'Mother says gossip's wrong, it's hateful, it's poison! She's right, she is that – and thou hast listened to it, Sam Gayle. It's poisoned thee and I'll not speak to thee again, not ever!' And then she turned and ran away from him down the long slope, stumbling now as she had not done on the way up, and only just saving her clog in time from the sucking softness of a peat bog.

It had never seemed so far back to High Farm, but she got there at last, startling the hens into squawking agitation as she ran across the yard, to come thankfully to the heart of the house: the kitchen with its fire in the great hearth over which a porridge pot burbled comfortably, while Agnes Burton – her mother, her dear, safe, loving mother – stirred serenely away. Everything was exactly as it had always been.

Agnes looked round at the sound of the clogs on the flagged floor, but there was scarcely time for a smile to lift the corners of her mouth and light her eyes before

16

Hannah was beside her and had clasped her in a fierce and desperate embrace.

Agnes laughed softly, with concern rather than amusement, for she had glimpsed the tense pallor of the child's face before it was pressed against her breast. Carefully, she laid down her spoon and then, without hurry (she never hurried) she put her arms gently about the girl. 'Well now, Hannah lass – what ails thee?'

The small face was raised to hers. 'Thou art my mother, art thou not? No one else but thee?'

There was a tiny scarcely perceptible pause, just enough for a quick sharp indrawn breath but no more, before Agnes said soothingly, 'Of course I am, lass. Who else?'

A faint tinge of colour touched Hannah's face – with relief, Agnes realised; though it only increased her own misgivings.

'I knew it!' cried Hannah. 'It was just gossip, like I said. Folks shouldn't gossip, should they?'

More troubled than ever, Agnes pushed back the stray wisps of hair from the girl's forehead. 'Indeed they shouldn't, lass.' She resisted a strong impulse to leave it at that, and instead pursued, 'Who's been gossiping now, then?'

'Samuel.' Hannah bit her lip. 'I mean . . .' She bent her head again and Agnes held her close and wondered if the child could feel how fast her heart was beating beneath the heavy layers of homespun and linen.

'We'd best have a talk, my lass,' she said then, with sudden resolution. She had known it would come one day. A part of her had hoped she might be spared, though she had never really believed that was possible. Indeed, she was even a little surprised that it had not come before, and had found herself wondering, now and then, if Hannah had learned the truth long ago and had simply accepted it in an untroubled way, as a not very interesting fact. But she had sensed that she was deluding herself.

Now it had come, as it was always likely to do, unexpectedly, without warning. Had they done right to keep it from Hannah? Would it have been better if she had grown up knowing the truth from the first, so that it might have become as much a part of her as her present false assumption that it was Agnes who had given birth to her? Perhaps. She did not know, and in any case it was too late now for regrets.

She steered the child towards the oak settle whose high back screened the hearth from the draughts, and sat down there with Hannah beside her. She put an arm about the girl's shoulder and laid her own red, work-worn hand over the long pale fingers, and said comfortably, 'Now, lass – what's Samuel Gayle been saying?' Oh, how hard it was to keep that calm and tender note in her voice!

She could see that anxiety had begun to return to Hannah, as was only natural when the first reassurance had been followed by this sudden new gravity on Agnes's part. The girl looked up, her dark brows drawn together slightly in a frown of unease, and said in a tone that mingled indignation and distress, 'He said thou weren't my mother – that thou found me in the porch.'

There was a little pause, and the distress deepened on Hannah's face, and then Agnes spoke very slowly and carefully, considering every word. 'I am thy mother, Hannah, just as surely as my dear John is thy father. God sent thee to us to bring joy into our life, and indeed thou hast, from that first day.' She saw the smiling relief on Hannah's face and knew she could not leave it there. But it was with great reluctance that she added, 'I am thy mother, because I have cared for thee and loved thee and watched over thee from the very first – and if that is not what makes a mother, then I don't know what is.'

Hannah was not a stupid child. On the contrary, her quickness of perception sometimes startled John and Agnes. It was only for a moment that her face showed not just relief but a relaxed and sighing delight. The next instant Agnes saw that the full implication of what she said had reached the child. The relief faded, and the delight; pain darkened the eyes raised to hers, and Hannah burst out sharply,

'Then thou art not my mother!' She pulled her hands free and drew back into the corner of the settle.

Hurt, distressed, Agnes reached out to stroke her cheek. 'I told thee, lass: I'm as truly thy mother as anyone ever was.'

'But thou *didst* find me, didst thou not? Samuel was right!' The anguish in her voice was almost unendurable to Agnes, but she knew that she had long ago reached the point beyond which there was no turning back. The years of unruffled happiness, of safety, had suddenly retreated; they were far off now, and a great unbridgeable gulf cut her off from them, and Hannah too. Agnes had to go on and hope that somehow at the end the child would emerge calmed and reassured from the tempest that had so suddenly broken around her.

Hannah tossed her head free of the caressing hand. Accepting that rejection, Agnes let her hand fall and – in spite of the involuntary trembling of her voice – said as quietly as she was able, 'Aye, we found thee. God gave thee to us, our very own bairn. We've been thy mother and father from that day – thine *only* mother and father!' She said these last words with great emphasis, almost with severity, as if it was something against which there could be no argument – nor could there be, she firmly believed.

'But there was another mother, wasn't there? My *real* mother.'

Agnes had not thought words could hurt so much. She had thought herself strong, able and ready to

19

understand Hannah's needs, to give her all the love and consolation that she needed. Yet this simple assertion of what was, practically speaking, undeniably true seemed almost like an act of betrayal. She had to fight an impulse to cry out angrily from the depths of her own pain. Instead, she said very quietly, 'I'm thy real, true mother, lass.'

Hannah shook her head fiercely. Agnes saw that she was not far from tears. When she spoke again the words were forced roughly from her. 'No, no – thou art not! There's someone else. Who is she, my mother?'

Agnes thought of the unknown woman who, for whatever reason, had abandoned her infant, and so relinquished all claim to motherhood; the woman of whom she had not thought at all for many years. What right had she now to intrude, to come between Hannah and Agnes, who was in every true sense her mother? How could Hannah even think she mattered to her in any way? Hurt, resentful, angry, Agnes pressed her lips tightly together. It was becoming more difficult every moment to remain calm and loving and reassuring. Yet perhaps, if she were to tell the little she knew, that would be enough. Hannah, learning the truth, would be content, and come, like Agnes, to put aside any thoughts of the shadowy woman who had given her birth.

'We've never known, Hannah,' Agnes said. 'We never heard. It's my belief she's dead. Maybe it's best that way. She doesn't matter, poor woman, not to thee. She only gave birth to thee, that's all, nothing more. Thou wast just like a little motherless lamb. God gave thee into our care, just the same as we put orphan lambs to the ewes that have lost their young. That's all thou dost need to know.'

Hannah opened her mouth to protest, and then closed it again. Agnes's expression, like her tone, warned her to ask no more questions, to let it rest at that. There was a point beyond which sympathy and tenderness and patience would fail her, and Hannah did not want to risk reaching that point. Agnes had scarcely ever been really angry with her, but those one or two rare occasions were etched indelibly, and painfully, on Hannah's memory. Each time, they had brought with them a sense that she had somehow failed Agnes, in a most serious and hurtful way. She had been forgiven, of course, and readily, once her penitence was clear, but what remained was a lingering sense that Agnes's anger was dangerous and might, in certain circumstances, be difficult to reverse. Besides, what more was there to ask, if her mother – the woman she called her mother – knew little more than she did, perhaps no more at all?

It was such a tiny thing, the knowledge that Agnes had kept from her, which now had become a part of her too. A tiny thing – and yet everything. Because of it the whole world was different.

She sat very still, with her hands clasped lightly in her lap and her head bent. She sat much like this every First Day, for the two long hours during which meeting lasted, outwardly quiet and calm, whilst inwardly she would be fighting all the impulses to fidget, yawn, chatter, laugh, get up and run about; terrible, at times near-irresistible impulses, which would set a sensation like an ache running through her limbs and her resolutely upright body.

It was like that now, except that the impulses so fiercely held back were different ones, a confused mass of impulses she could not begin to disentangle or respond to. Somehow sitting still was the only possible solution, the only course of action that did not threaten incalculable dangers.

She did not stir when Agnes cautiously reached out again to stroke her cheek; and when, a moment after, the familiar arms drew her near and closed about her, she allowed herself to be held, and hugged and caressed and kissed, and sat limp and submissive while

21

tender little words were murmured over her. They did not really reach her; some black horrible thing kept them from her. Suddenly desperate to escape from it, she clung to Agnes, saying nothing, trying simply to shut out everything that had happened since she ran out on to the fell.

'I am thy mother; John is thy father.' The words went on and on, repeated endlessly, echoed in her brain by a meek little voice that woke no response in her, but did somehow shut out the other things she did not want to think about.

The consoling voice ceased at last, to be replaced by the sensible, practical, everyday voice, reminding her that there was still today's knitting to be finished. 'Thou hast not turned the heel yet, lass. See here —'

Hannah looked at the work Agnes had retrieved from where it had fallen on the floor (she could not remember dropping it) and now held up for her attention. Without a word, she took it into her hands. She felt calm again, exactly as she always did: the quiet, obedient, hard-working child who was daughter to John and Agnes Burton. Nothing had changed after all.

But when she set her fingers to the familiar task they would not do as she wanted. Her heart began to thud so fiercely that it set her body trembling and her uncontrollable hands fumbled, jolted the needle from the sheath, dropped the wool. She kept missing stitches, so that she had constantly to stop and retrieve them — she whom Agnes always said was one of the best little knitters in Swaledale.

She was glad when Agnes went to collect the eggs (the hens were beginning to lay again after the winter) and left her to watch the pot on the fire. She was sure that she would get on better without those anxious eyes watching her all the time.

Then she wished Agnes had not gone, for in her

going she seemed to take with her all the safe ordinariness of the room. It looked no different. There were still the great beams overhead, worn and blackened, hung with dried bunches of herbs and the rack on which lay the joints of bacon left from last November's pig killing; the pale plastered walls, unadorned by pictures or ornaments; the great arch of the hearth within which the fire burned below the bubbling pot; the simple furnishings – settle, dresser, table, benches, stools, the meal ark where oatmeal was stored, the wall cupboard for salt and spices, the one armchair, the carved and polished grandfather clock, John's pride in which was the nearest he came to un-Quakerish vanity; the worn flags of the floor, swept and sanded each week, so that they squeaked beneath her clogged feet. She knew everything that was here as well as she knew herself – better perhaps, for she could see them whenever she wished. Everything was solid, familiar, unchanging.

Yet she felt as if she were standing on some surface that might at any moment tremble and split beneath her feet, to let her fall into some dark nothingness without end. Indeed, it had already been shaken, and the cracks and fissures shivered unseen but tangible wherever she trod.

Before today, she had not thought very much about anything. She had done what had to be done, spoken or been silent as seemed best, welcoming or simply accepting the daily tasks, the people she met, the different activities dictated by the day or the season. Sometimes she had done things that John and Agnes did not like, but she had not worried about that very much. Doing wrong sometimes was a part of life, as was being forgiven, and knowing that John and Agnes would go on loving her, whatever she did. Now she knew what she had never recognised before, that she had been happy. At the same moment she knew that she would never be happy like that again. Worse, she

23

feared that she would never again be happy in any way as long as she lived, that always and forever she would feel as she did now, alone and threatened and very, very frightened.

The trembling had eased just a little by the time John Burton came in, and she was knitting efficiently again, her eyes on the simmering mixture in the pot, watching it yet not really seeing it, and certainly feeling none of her usual eager anticipation of the forthcoming meal. She was not in the least hungry, though it was a long time since breakfast.

She looked round as John crossed the room. She saw at once that he must have met Agnes outside, and that she had told him what had happened. He had a solemn, important look on his smooth rosy face, and came to kiss her as if it were some special day, though when he spoke his words were nothing out of the ordinary.

'How goes it, lass? That's a grand stocking thou art doing there – a good neat heel. I couldn't have done better myself.'

It was a long speech for John Burton to make, and the stocking was no different from any others she had made in the past months. She smiled faintly and said nothing, since she could think of nothing to say. She saw his eyes move from the knitting and sharpen suddenly, as his attention was caught, genuinely so this time.

'What's this, then? I've not seen thee with this before.'

It was the sheath, the beautiful sheath so lovingly carved by Samuel. She had forgotten all about it until now; his kindness and his friendship had been blotted out by what came after, almost as if they had never been. She felt herself colouring, and knew it was with shame at her own ingratitude. She remembered the things she had said to him, in her anger and hurt. Yet he had told her the truth after all, and she had run from him as if from an enemy.

'Didst thou have this from Samuel Gayle?'

It seemed he had known that Samuel was making it for her. She supposed that was why he had not made her a new sheath himself, once the old one was outgrown. She had wondered about it sometimes.

'Aye,' she said, and took it from her belt so that he could see it better.

For a moment, watching his face, she was afraid that he disapproved. It was after all a very elaborately decorated object for a simple Quaker to use, a vain and worldly thing; except that it was not, she knew it was not, for the beautiful thing so lovingly made was good, not shallow and frivolous like the distracting vanities one ought to avoid. This was like the heart-stopping call of the curlew, or the loveliness of a primrose or a rainbow, a miracle of creation to be enjoyed in all its wonder.

'It's a fine thing,' said John slowly; and 'fine', she knew, was not a term of approval. Then he looked at her anxious face and smiled. 'It's fit for its purpose too. A kind gift. See thou does good work with it.'

She knew that this too was part of the strangeness and uncertainty of today. At any other time, John Burton might have made more of an issue of it. They were loving, her parents ('We *are* thy parents, lass!'), but they were uncompromising where the demands of their faith were concerned, and expected her to be the same. It was something she had always accepted without question. But she knew somehow that this matter of Samuel's gift would have been different, that she would have fought them to keep it. It was fortunate perhaps, if anything about today could be said to be fortunate, that John was more than usually indulgent towards her.

The rest of that day seemed to Hannah a little like one of those horrible dreams in which the most ordinary and commonplace of surroundings are somehow shot through with terror, a dreadful, pervasive, inexplicable terror from which there is no escape. Perhaps it

25

was not quite terror that she felt, as she moved quietly and mechanically through the remaining routine of the day, but it was certainly a frightening strangeness, as if she no longer quite belonged.

Once that afternoon she thought of Samuel, and wondered whether to go and make her peace with him and thank him properly for his gift. Then she knew she could not bear to go outside. She shrank from seeing anyone or anything. It was hard enough to endure this house and the two people who lived here with her; she had no courage to face anything more. When some of the neighbours came to gather about the fire with their knitting, as they often did of an evening, she made her escape before ever they were admitted, glad that John and Agnes understood enough to accept her quite genuine excuse of a headache.

Even so, it was a long time before she slept that night, in her narrow little bed under the rustling heather thatch. She was very tired, more tired than she could remember ever having been before in all her life. She was certainly too tired to think clearly or coherently, even had she wanted to do so. She lay in the dark remembering what Agnes had murmured to her before she left the room downstairs: 'We are thy father and mother, Hannah. We love thee just as much as we always did.' But it brought her no comfort. She could think only that if things were as they had always been, then Agnes would have had no need to say that. Real fathers and mothers did not do so. Misery and fear, unfocused and amorphous, worried at her weary brain, keeping sleep away until at last, defeated, they gave in.

When she woke as usual at dawn, there was an instant of near normality, when she knew it was time to get up, and felt nothing. The next moment, terror clutched at her, cold and black and horrible. She knew there was something dreadful from which sleep had sheltered her, which now she must face again. She shut her eyes and tried to go back to sleep; and then she remembered.

Strangely, remembering was almost a relief. It was bad still, but not quite as bad as that first terror had suggested. In fact, lying on her back thinking, 'Agnes and John Burton are not my parents. I was found. I do not know whose child I am,' she felt very little emotion at all.

She rolled over and slid out of bed and dressed. What had changed, after all? She was still Hannah Burton; John and Agnes still looked after her; today would be just the same as every other day. She had learned a small fact she had not known before, which everyone else had known for years. That was all. This morning, after breakfast, she would go and see Samuel and put things right with him. Then she could forget all about it.

Samuel was not at home. 'He's gone for the rest of Alice Blakey's knitting. It wasn't all done yesterday.' So Mary Harker told Hannah. She seemed inclined to talk further – neither Samuel nor his father had much time to spare to listen to her, so she was liable to seize on anyone who called – but Hannah, not in the mood for casual talk, quickly made her escape.

Alice Blakey's cottage was the last building at the west end of Hollinthwaite. Hannah set out down the lane and along the stony rutted earth of the village street. She realised then that she had been wrong. Certainly, the surface of her life was unchanged: the village, like High Farm, looked exactly as it had always done, and indeed she felt more cheerful than she had last night. But something was different all the same. Within her now was the knowledge that some unknown woman, and not Agnes, had given birth to her. That woman might still be alive somewhere; most probably she was a Daleswoman; she might even be someone Hannah met almost every day, or at least from time to time. It was not unknown for pregnancies to be kept secret until the very last moment. There was stout Elizabeth Alderson who had not even known herself that she was pregnant until the labour pains began.

There were not many people about today. Now and then a neighbour called a greeting, or Hannah would glimpse a woman, here scattering grain to the hens, there cutting a cabbage in a garden or scolding a child. Each time, she thought, 'Is it her?' Each time, she studied features and figure, seeking a resemblance.

She knew she was not like Agnes or John. She was tall for her age, and thin and her hair, thick and wiry and curling out of control, was very dark. She knew her hands and feet were long and narrow, not like the broad strong hands of John and Agnes, those two sturdy, brown-haired people, who resembled one another more than she resembled either of them. Odd, she thought now, that she had never found that puzzling. But then she had never seen herself in a mirror and rarely gave any thought to her appearance.

She looked about to see that no one was looking and then she stopped and turned to stare at her reflection in a nearby window. The room inside was dark and empty, but even so the reflection was distorted and uncertain; it told her little more than she knew already. She was tall and thin, pale, with dark untidy hair constantly escaping from the neat white cap. That was all.

She walked on. She saw no one who looked like that, nor could she remember that anyone she had ever met had just such hair, allied to such height and such long slender bones. For the first time in her life, she felt acutely conscious of herself. She was no longer a Hollinthwaite girl, walking along her village street. She was a stranger, odd, different, set apart; she no longer quite belonged. Did people stare at her and wonder whose child she was? Had they always done so, ever since she was a baby? She felt that they were doing so now, with every step she took.

28

She was glad when she reached Alice Blakey's cottage and could turn her mind to Samuel. She was about to bang on the door when she saw him crouched on the bank a little further up the road, gazing intently at something. She let her hand fall and went to him.

Evidently what interested him was a clump of primroses, still just in bud, for he was kneeling beside them with his head bent. He did not immediately look up, though she knew he had heard her coming. She knew too that he was not seeing what she could see: a cluster of nearly-opened flowers, delicate and pretty, which brought a lift to the heart. What he saw was quite different, both more and (somehow) less than that. He saw the exact spearhead shape of the leaves, with their long central vein tapering towards the tip and their crumpled surface, and the way they grew from the base of the plant. He saw the tiny fine hairs on the short purplish stems, and the way the delicate green six-pointed sepals still protected the furled creamy yellow petals. She knew that was what he would see, because often he would show some plant to her, telling her about it, while his eyes shone with enthusiasm. It was this same keenness of observation that made it possible for him to carve the flowers and animals on her knitting sheath in such loving detail.

He did look round at last, and she knew then that he had remembered yesterday, and how they had parted. He smiled, but hesitantly, as if not quite sure how she would respond, and he stood up rather awkwardly, waiting for her to say something.

'Thou wast right, Samuel,' Hannah burst out almost at once. 'I shouldn't have flown at thee like that. I'm sorry.'

He stopped smiling altogether. 'I shouldn't have said owt. I didn't know thou'dst not been told.'

'I had to know some time. Now it's done.' With that, Hannah's tone made it clear that the subject was at an end. Their peace was made. She said next, touching the sheath at her belt (she was knitting as they talked, as usual), 'I didn't thank thee for this, not as I ought.'

'Thou didst like it. That's enough for me,' said Samuel happily. 'I'm going home now. Art thou coming?'

She glanced at his empty hands. 'Did Alice Blakey not have the work ready?'

He gave a little cry and clapped a hand to his forehead. 'I forgot. Oh Hannah, I'm glad thou art here! What Father would have said . . .'

'What he always does,' Hannah retorted with a sudden grin. 'That thou art a daft dreamer with no sense in thy fat head.' She had heard him often enough, so she knew.

'Aye,' Samuel agreed, a little sheepishly.

They called at the cottage and collected the stockings, promising to bring eggs and cheese as payment, as agreed, and then set off together back along the street – Samuel, Joseph Gayle's son, who belonged, and that strange Hannah Burton, who was not really a Burton at all.

After a brief silence, Samuel said casually, 'I'm to go away to school at the back end.' His tone was neutral, as if he was not entirely sure what he thought of the prospect.

Hannah came to a halt. Perhaps, two days ago, it would not have hurt so much, to think of Samuel going away. Now it was yet another fissure threatening to open beneath her feet. 'Thou'lt go to Sedbergh then?' she asked, quietly enough.

He nodded. 'Aye.'

'And lodge with thy uncle, like Robert?' Robert, three years older than Samuel and Hannah, was a remote figure who had gone away long ago and rarely returned even in the holidays. It must have seemed a convenient arrangement, for him to lodge with his uncle William, a prosperous hosier in Sedbergh, but William Gayle, who had no children, had grown fond of the boy and Robert of him, and somehow bit by bit he had become more William's son than Joseph's. Joseph, preoccupied with his business, had not seemed to mind his son's absence very much, but Hannah could not bear to think that Samuel might be lost to her in the same way.

'I don't know,' Samuel said. 'My uncle's been poorly this winter. And ...' He hesitated, then went on, 'There's a hosier Father knows, a convinced Friend, too – I could stay with him. From things Robert's said, Father has cause to think my uncle's ... Well, he married out, when he wed his second wife; and that's not all, I think.'

For a Quaker to marry a non-Quaker was a serious matter, as Hannah well knew. It led inevitably to exclusion from membership of the Society of Friends. She had seen it happen amongst their own neighbours, more than once; it largely explained the dwindling numbers at meeting.

But today it was not the question of Samuel's lodgings that concerned her, only the simple fact that he was going away. The autumn was a long way off, of course, but even so a great heavy weight of depression settled itself inside her.

She parted from Samuel at Low Farm and walked on alone, over the stepping stones and up the hill. A lapwing passed overhead, its wings moving with a slow heavy beat. Further off, the curlews were tumbling and calling, just as they had yesterday. Then, she had heard them with a pure and simple joy; now she felt something quite different. The sound was lovely still, lovely enough to make her catch her breath, but it seemed to have acquired a desolate, heart-breaking note that brought the tears rushing to her eyes.

She remembered then how she had run singing on to the fell yesterday. Did other Quaker children sing like that, she wondered? Did they ever have the same longing to indulge in that forbidden activity? She thought probably not; she had never heard Samuel sing, or any other of the few children who came to meeting. Maybe when – if – people heard her sing, they thought, There's that queer Hannah Burton: what dost expect, from a foundling?

She did not feel like singing now. She did not at the moment think she would ever feel like singing again. The world had not changed; it was she who was different. Or, rather, she had always been different, it was only that she had not known it until now. She felt even that it was only now, since yesterday, that she knew anything. Something had begun yesterday, like a new life starting; only it felt more like a death. From that point she had to find her way, step by step, like an infant walking alone for the first time. She could not remember what that had felt like, but she thought it must have been pleasanter than this. The worst thing was the feeling that she was cut off for ever from the happy years that lay behind her, by the great gulf of yesterday, and that from now on she was entirely alone, stepping from an unknown past into a future she could not see, which might hold all kinds of unimaginable terrors. She knew she was no longer a little girl. The trouble was that she did not yet know what she had become.

CHAPTER TWO

i

'What now?' Robert drew rein and looked impatiently round at his brother, who had halted his own beast some way back and was now kneeling on the ground, examining intently something in the grass beside the road.

'I *think* it's a purple orchid – no, I'm almost *sure* it's a purple orchid!' Samuel's voice was high pitched with excitement. 'They like lime, thou knows. Is this ground limey?' He began to scratch with his nail in the earth.

'Damn you, Samuel – come on! It'll be dark soon!'

Samuel, startled, looked up.'Not for hours yet . . .' he began, gesturing towards the brilliant blue of the sky and the high hot sun. Then, observing his brother's thunderous expression, he said meekly, 'I'm sorry. I'll come,' and remounted his horse.

They set off again, Robert glowering ahead of him, Samuel occupying himself, as he always did while travelling, with the inevitable knitting. After a little while Robert glanced over his shoulder. 'Dost *have* to do that?'

'What?' Samuel asked, puzzled, and also a little alarmed. He had a healthy respect for Robert's rages.

'That damned knitting! I can't stand it – click, click, click all the time. I hate it, I tell thee!'

Samuel stared at him. 'But . . .' he faltered. 'Everyone knits, always . . .'

'I know. That's what I can't stand. At least Uncle William left it to his workers. He didn't expect his own family to waste their time on it.'

'It doesn't waste time, it uses it,' Samuel pointed out;

33

but, with some signs of reluctance, he put the knitting away. After a short time he said gently, 'Thou must miss Uncle William.'

Robert frowned the more, and Samuel wished his clumsy attempt at sympathy unspoken.

'What if I do? I can't mend it. He's dead.' Then he added, in an unusual burst of confidence, 'What I wish most, is that he'd hung on till I was twenty-one.'

To Samuel that seemed a strange view of things. To wish a loved person were still alive, that was one thing; simply to wish he'd hung on a little longer was quite another matter. 'Why?' he asked. 'What difference would that have made?'

Robert's look was full of contempt for someone so unable to see the obvious. 'Because then I could have had the money straight away, of course. As it is, I've two whole years to wait.'

'Oh,' said Samuel. 'I see.' His tone suggested that he rather wished he did not. 'What wilt thou do with it – the money, I mean?'

Robert shrugged. 'Who knows? Use it to get away, I reckon – *right* away. No more sheep, no more wool and knitting and stockings, no more never-ending talk of the hosiery trade. No more tedious men and plain women. A bit of life, that's what I want.'

'Oh,' said Samuel, who had no particular love for the hosiery trade himself, but could not envisage ever wanting to leave his beloved Dales, or the people who lived in them; one person in particular —

'Father's expecting thee to stay,' he remembered suddenly. 'He wants thy help with the business.'

'He'll get it,' said Robert brusquely. 'I can't lay my hands on Uncle William's money until I'm twenty-one. I might as well make the best of things in the meantime.' He grinned suddenly. 'Who knows? Maybe I'll do so well at home I'll make our fortune.'

Samuel tried to throw off the depression that had settled on his spirits at the thought of an energetic

Robert taking command at home, as he surely would. Their father might be a strong character, but Samuel suspected he would be no match for his eldest son. All the peaceful years of Robert's absence, during which Uncle William had doted on him and the brothers had met, in passing, only at school – well, that was at an end now. The only consolation was that when Samuel returned to school after the holiday, Robert would no longer be there to lord it over him and lead the other boys (with whom he was universally popular) in goading his shy younger brother. Even Samuel's many scholastic achievements had seemed like failures under Robert's scorn.

And of course there was Hannah, to sweeten his homecoming. He let his thoughts dwell on her, and felt comforted and almost happy.

ii

All day Hannah had been helping John Burton and Joseph Gayle to dam the beck just above High Farm, where a small natural pool already existed below the little waterfall. The men brought stones and sods of earth, and Hannah packed them together to form a bank at the lower edge of the pool, widening and deepen it and at last stopping the flow of water altogether, but for a tiny controlled trickle. Every year, when sheep washing time came round, she helped them to form the washfold, and by now the two men respected her practical skill enough to leave the building work to her.

By late afternoon the work was done. Joseph Gayle stood looking at the dam, his face full of satisfaction. Then he glanced at John Burton. 'I'll say this for thy lass: she's worth four of my Samuel.'

Hannah was sorry to hear that, for Samuel's sake (especially as he was not here to defend himself), but she could not help feeling proud all the same. Samuel's father had not finished, either. He went on, 'Thou'lt never feel the want of a son, with a daughter like thine.'

The words brought a familiar pang to Hannah. She glanced at John Burton's proudly smiling face. He has no daughter either, she told herself; only me. It was a depressing thought, taking the edge from her pleasure in the day's work. But then that was how it had been during the past four years, since she had first learned the truth. The knowledge had lingered on at the back of her mind, like the dull ache of a decaying tooth, to flare up suddenly now and then, without warning, in a sharp stabbing pain. She bent down to push a sod more firmly into place; quite unnecessarily, but she was afraid they might see something of what she felt in her expression. The next moment, she realised that their attention had left her altogether.

'Well now! Here are thy lads, home at last!' That was John Burton. Hannah straightened and turned round to see where the two men were looking.

The newcomers were just passing High Farm, making their way up the track to where their father was working. There was Samuel, of course. He had not changed at all that Hannah could see. He was a boy still, thin and awkward, carrying himself as if he was always a little afraid of where his next step might lead him. There was none of that defensiveness about his companion, at whom Hannah looked next. Her initial glance became a longer scrutiny, full of lively interest.

So that was Robert; Samuel's brother, whom she could scarcely remember, who would be back at Hollinth-waite for good now. He was no longer a boy, but a man, young and vigorous, and at first she could see no likeness at all between him and Samuel. Then, as she stood quietly waiting and watching, there beside the dam, a little screened by the two older men, she saw that there *was* a likeness; but it was scarcely more than that of a shadow to its object. Both wore the sober Quaker dress, of course, the severe grey coat and broad-brimmed hat. Both were tall, but Robert's height was matched by breadth and an air of alertness and energy. Both had brown hair, but Samuel's fell straight and heavy about his face, while Robert's curled crisply, lit with gleams of bronze and gold. Robert's face was all strong lines, square and firm and assertive; Samuel's somehow lacked any definition, an infinitely forgettable face, without marked characteristics. Both had brown eyes, but Samuel's were quiet and dark and soft and, lately, needed the aid of spectacles; Robert's were bright and quick – and had come unerringly to rest on Hannah.

She was suddenly acutely conscious of him and (oddly) of herself too. She felt her colour rise uncomfortably, and looked quickly away, though somehow she still knew quite well that Robert was watching her. It was a strange and not wholly pleasurable sensation, yet undeniably exciting. She heard the two older men moving, stepping forward, was conscious of greetings being exchanged. Someone came near to her (she could hardly breathe), a voice said, 'Hannah.'

She looked up. It was Samuel. He was smiling at her, but almost at once the smile seemed to falter. Had he sensed that it was not *his* face she had hoped to see when she raised her eyes? She hoped not, for he was like a brother to her, a part of her family, with as much right to claim that link as anyone, and she was glad to have him home again. Even so, for the time being it was Robert who had all her interest and nearly all her attention. Samuel was, she realised, saying something complimentary about her appearance, which surprised her a little, but she scarcely heard it. She did not exactly watch Robert, but she did glance his way now and then, and always when she did so found that his bright eyes were looking at her, even though he was, apparently, talking to his father. Joseph Gayle's face was full of a wondering pride, as well it might be, to see his son grown into so splendid a young man.

'I'm that glad to have thee home again, lad,' Joseph

Gayle was saying. It was, for him, an unusually emotional observation, expressing far more than it would have done on the lips of a more demonstrative man. He clasped his son's arms and held him like that for a moment before letting his hands fall again. 'Well,' he went on, his voice still gruff with emotion. 'Thou art back in time for sheep washing.'

'So I see,' said Robert, with just the faintest trace of something that might have been amusement or might have been derision.

'Aye. Work starts tomorrow. They'll all be here first thing.'

'Then we'd best be getting home,' John Gayle put in. 'It'll be an early night for the lot of us. You'll look in on us on your way? Agnes will want to see you.' That question was addressed to the two brothers.

'Why not?' returned Robert easily, and they all began to make their way back down the hill.

Agnes was just returning from the evening milking as they reached High Farm. She swung down the backcan in which she had brought the milk from the cow pasture, and Hannah went to take it from her and carry it to the dairy, leaving Agnes free to greet the new arrivals. Hannah did not look behind her as she went, but among the general murmuring she could hear Robert's voice clearly; it was deep and rich and resonant, and seemed to set all kinds of odd vibrations running through her. Naturally enough, it was the older brother who talked most, because it was round him they all gathered, since it was so long since any of them had seen him. Samuel had after all been absent from Hollinthwaite as little as possible during the years of his schooling.

Hannah placed the can on the stone floor of the dairy and made her way to the kitchen, from where voices – *that* voice – now came. In the doorway she paused. Robert was still quite clearly the centre of attention, talking with great expression and lavish gestures of the hands. He is so *alive*, Hannah thought. Beside him, everyone else seemed somehow diminished, touched with a certain drab greyness, which of course had nothing to do with the sober clothes that all alike wore. It was not surprising that Samuel should be hanging back a little, apart from the others, saying nothing. Hannah had a feeling that so it had always been when his brother was at home, that she was seeing something often observed in the days before Robert went away to school, but long forgotten. There was something so naturally assertive about Robert that it was inevitable that he should dominate; his return after a lengthy absence had nothing to do with it.

She went to stand beside Samuel, who at once turned with a look of thankfulness and smiled at her. 'Busy day tomorrow,' he murmured.

She did not want him to talk to her, because then she would not be able to hear what Robert said, but she could not hurt his feelings by ignoring him. She smiled vaguely and nodded, and hoped he would leave it at that; but instead he looked about the room and then said softly, 'Where's the clock gone?'

She glanced towards the corner where, until this year, the grandfather clock had stood; and, momentarily at least, forgot all about Robert. 'The Justices' men took it.'

Samuel looked distressed. 'For the tithes? That was a heavy fine.'

'Aye. It wasn't the value, though.' Even now she could not think of John Burton's distress without pain. The annual visit from the Justices' men had been a part of her life for as long as she could remember, and accepted as such: an unpleasant necessity, like the snow in winter. Since no convinced Quaker would pay the tithes demanded by the established church, then inevitably the Justices of the Peace would order the seizure of goods, in lieu of tithes. So, each year, hams and cheeses and stockings and sometimes household

39

goods would be carried away. Sometimes the bailiffs were grim and silent; sometimes they looked as though they were sorry for what they must do, and tried to make it as painless as possible. This year they had been of the former type, and had taken only one thing, the grandfather clock that John Burton loved so much. Hannah knew that, true to the demands of his faith, her adopted father had long ago suppressed his disappointment and accepted the loss; one ought not to value worldly things, after all. But for her . . .

'And what didst thou think of it all, Hannah Burton?'

She had not seen Robert join them. The others had begun to discuss tomorrow's arrangements, and he had seized the opportunity to wander over to them. He must have heard enough to know what they had been talking about.

Hannah coloured, but found courage enough to look at him. 'It's wrong, I know,' she said, 'but I was angry.'

She was surprised to see an approving grin on Robert's face. 'Well done, Hannah Burton!' he said. 'I knew thou wert a lass of spirit!'

'It is the injustice of it,' she explained gravely, as if in spite of his approval she felt the need to defend herself. 'Why should we have to pay tithes to a church we're no part of? Why should they have a right to take our goods, because we refuse to do what is wrong?'

'Why indeed? And why do we always stand meekly by and let them do as they please, without a word of protest?'

'It's better now,' Samuel pointed out. 'A hundred years ago we'd have gone to prison.'

'Oh, wonderful!' said Robert with heavy irony. 'Progress indeed! What sticks in my gullet is the humiliation of it. I remember well enough how I used to feel when they came – the shame, the futility too. I suppose I'll have to get used to it again.'

'What did Uncle William do then?' Samuel asked curiously.

'Paid his tithes, of course. But then he was disowned, as thou knows. No point in empty gestures for him. But if a man's going to refuse, then he should be ready to get angry and fight. All that meek obstinacy is not for me.'

Hannah could not quite approve of what he said, but it struck a chord in her all the same. Meekness might be a virtue (as she was always being told), but it was not one that came readily to her. Besides, she had never before heard anyone question these accepted values, and Robert's audacity excited her. And not just his audacity, of course.

'Come then, lads. We'd best be getting back before dark. Mary will have supper ready.'

Samuel turned to go, but Robert lingered just a moment longer. He bent his head towards Hannah and asked softly, 'How old art thou now, Hannah Burton? Sixteen?'

There was something in his eyes that seemed to stop her breath. Unable to speak, she could only nod.

'Thou wast a bairn when I last saw thee. Thou art a woman now.'

It was a compliment, she could see that, but it left her so confused and overcome that she could think of nothing to say in parting that he would remember her by, or think of with approval. When he had gone, she was annoyed with herself that she should have been so stupid. But there was nothing she could do about it now. At least, she supposed, she would see him again tomorrow. The thought filled her with both delight and trepidation. The hours that must pass until then already seemed interminable.

iii

High Farm and Low Farm always washed their sheep together, and most of their neighbours came to help, just as John Burton and Joseph Gayle and their families would go to all the other sheep washings in the hamlet.

41

At dawn Hannah went with John and Joseph (the boys were not there, she was sorry to see) to bring the sheep from the fell to the folds by the beck, their walls newly repaired for the occasion. It was there that, very soon, the men of the hamlet gathered. Hannah's place now was in the kitchen, where Agnes was already at work making a good mulled ale, with milk and eggs, to fortify the men in their chilly task, and gooseberry pies and curd cheesecakes for the feasting afterwards. There was already an unaccustomed noise and bustle in the kitchen, as many of the village women came to help, bringing with them laughter and talk of a kind not often heard at High Farm – many of them were not Quakers or, by marriage, had relinquished their membership.

Hannah always enjoyed the liveliness and good fellowship of sheep washing time, but today her thoughts were outside with the men, and she went from one task to another scarcely noticing what she was doing and what was said to her, or even, sometimes, what she said in reply. Was Robert out there now? Would he be helping to toss the sheep one by one into the dub formed by her sturdy dam? Would he take his turn in the ice-cold spring water, rubbing the tarry salve from the fleeces so that they were fit for shearing? Or was he a stranger now to his father's way of life, after so long in his uncle's more urban establishment? She did not think Robert would take part in something just because it was expected of him, yet Joseph Gayle was full of hopes for his son's return, seeing him as a partner in the business for which one pair of hands was never enough. He had recognised long ago that Samuel would make neither a hosier nor a farmer: 'Though what he *is* good for, the Lord alone knows,' Joseph Gayle would add, with a melancholy shake of the head.

'Hannah lass, stop thy dreaming and take this ale up to the washfold. Jane Alderson will go with thee.'

Hannah turned at Agnes's amiably scolding voice,

and smiled at the sturdy girl a little younger than herself, who was already grasping one side of the handle of the pot in which the ale had been warmed with the whisked eggs and creamy milk. Hannah took hold of the other side, and together the two girls went out into the June sunlight.

It was very hot today, baking hot, the light dazzling on pale stone and hard earth, the sky so brightly blue that it almost hurt the eyes.

'I'd fancy that job today,' said Jane, nodding towards the busy throng of men moving among the noisy agitated sheep. One man, his turn at the washing over, was just clambering out of the beck, shivering in spite of the heat, his clothes drenched and heavy, the water pouring off him. Hannah just had time to think: He *is* there! when Robert said, 'I'll go in next,' and began to pull off his shirt (he was already coatless). There was a chorus of protest from the men:

'Thou'lt catch thy death, lad!'

'Not in this heat – the water's that cold!'

'Nay, lad, keep thy shirt on!'

But Robert had already leapt in, joining the other man whose turn had come.

Beside Hannah, Jane murmured, 'Look at that, Hannah Burton! *That's* a sight worth coming for!'

Hannah did not need to ask what she meant. She could only agree, though she could not possibly have put the thought into words. Robert's appearance there in the water completely deprived her of all power of speech. She could not remember ever having seen a man stripped to the waist before; if she had, he had looked nothing like Robert, or she could not have forgotten. All that breadth of shoulder ...! The strong muscles moving beneath his taut gleaming skin, he reached out to grasp a sheep by the forelegs as it landed in the water, rubbed its belly and tail, turned it and dipped its head and then let it swim free to the further bank. Hannah could not take her eyes

43

from him. She scarcely knew where she was going, except that it was nearer to him. He might have been naked, from what she could see, with the water to his waist—

'Hey, watch out!' She had tripped, and some of the ale had spilled. Jane, glancing at her, giggled. 'I'd say thy mind's not on the job. Didn't I say it was worth coming for?' She made a rueful face. 'I reckon thou hast more hope than I have.'

Someone came to meet them and take the pot. 'Allow me.'

Hannah, startled, looked round. 'Oh! Samuel! I didn't see thee!' She was too conscious of Robert to notice Samuel's hurt; not that he would have dreamed of bringing it to her attention. With a kind of melancholy resignation, he accepted Robert's ascendancy as something as natural and inescapable as the coming of the day. He had not exactly anticipated it, as he looked forward all the way home to seeing Hannah again, but now he was confronted with it he knew he could not fight it. The worst of it was that it was only now he was with her again, and saw her spellbound by Robert, that he realised that what he felt for Hannah was more than just brotherly affection. At the moment when he recognised that no happy outcome was possible, he found that he loved Hannah; that he had always loved her.

He carried the pot to the men, and those who were at present unoccupied brought their tankards and beakers. Jane, laughing and joking, served them. Hannah stood by with her eyes on Robert, as he stooped and stretched with vigorous energy in the icy water. She would have liked to stay until he came out, but there was work to be done back at the house, so at last, reluctantly, she left. She was the more disappointed because he did not even appear to have noticed that she was there.

About two days after the washing, the sheep were sheared. Once again the neighbours gathered, this time at Low Farm, where the sheep were brought down to the folds by the farmhouse and John Burton and Joseph Gayle and the other men set to work on the clipping.

Hannah was there too, wrapping the clipped fleeces as they fell from the shears, working with a dexterity born of years of experience. First she laid the fleece flat, then the legs were folded in, before the wool was rolled up from the tail end; finally the neck was twisted round the whole and tucked in, to make a neat parcel.

Robert came as well – Hannah knew that at once – but he had no skill with the shears. Instead, he directed the carrying of the wrapped fleeces to the woolroom nearby, where they were to be sorted and stored, until required by the men and women who would card and spin and knit them into stockings and caps for Joseph Gayle to buy and resell. The High Farm fleeces were laid aside separately, so that Hannah and Agnes could card and spin them at home during the next few days, to supply their own requirements through the coming year.

Hannah was glad that she could wrap fleeces by instinct, for it meant that while her hands were busy her eyes could stray, furtively, now and then, to Robert. She wondered if he had been deliberately avoiding her since the day of the sheep washing; certainly he had paid her no attention then or afterwards. He was always, so Samuel said, 'riding on business for my father'.

Yet here he was today, working near her and coming often to take a fleece from her hands. Their eyes would meet, and sometimes his fingers would brush hers, just for a moment. Did he too feel that touch like fire in his veins? she wondered. He gave no sign of it, looking as assured, as fully in control of himself as ever. Not once did he make any obvious move to be near to her or speak to her, more than necessity demanded. It was tormenting, when she wanted so much to see some sign of the attraction that Jane Alderson swore he felt for her.

He did talk to the men working with him, lightly for the most part, joking with them, laughing about some piece of gossip. Sometimes, briefly, he would be more serious for a moment. His voice – light and laughing; graver and more resonant – seemed all around her, and a part of her too, closer even than the continual bleating of the sheep, keeping her nerves and senses in constant life.

They broke for ale and a rest, stretched on the grass in the heat; it was hot today too. Someone was saying there had been riots in London. It seemed a supremely trivial matter, as did the war with the American colonies, which they began to talk of next.

'One thing, so long as the armies are busy, they'll need stockings for the soldiers,' said John Hird, who, like Joseph Gayle, was a hosier.

'Not from me, they won't,' said Joseph gruffly.

'Why not, then?' Robert demanded. 'They don't make war with stockings.'

'Armies make war, and they can't take the field without stockings. Thou knows that.'

Hannah, who saw every fleeting expression on Robert's face, noticed the sceptical look that passed across it, though all he said was, 'Uncle William made his money by army contracts.'

Joseph Gayle frowned. 'Thou knows what I think of that.' It was a warning to drop the matter or risk a fiercer argument, and Robert clearly took it. He let his companions move on to lighter matters, and fell silent. Hannah, half glad, half tremulous, saw his eyes move and come to rest on her face. They looked grave and thoughtful. She knew she coloured, and she bent her head so he should not see it.

46

The end of sheep clipping was a time for celebration. Everyone was welcomed to the kitchen of Low Farm, where hams and cheeses, mutton pies and gooseberry tarts, curd cheesecakes and havercakes were spread out for all to enjoy, with lavish quantities of ale to wash them down. The Quakers amongst the company sat together a little apart from the rest, whose uninhibited talk and laughter was not quite seemly, though at clipping time Joseph Gayle tolerated a good deal that he would otherwise have forbidden beneath his roof. Hannah, with a silent Samuel beside her (she supposed his thoughts were out on the fells with the plants he loved so much), was conscious only of Robert, a little further off, nearer to the noisier company. Unlike the other Quakers, there was nothing withdrawn or set apart about him. His bright brown eyes darted quickly here and there, full of laughter, coming briefly to rest, from time to time, on her. She wished she were near enough to talk to him, though what she would have talked about she had no idea.

There was a sudden stir of excitement far off near the door, an intensification of talk and laughter; the next moment, almost all the younger members of the company (except the Quakers) had gone out into the evening. Then, clearly into the sudden hush that filled the kitchen, came the sound of a fiddle, vigorously playing a dance tune. Before she knew what was happening, Hannah found that her feet were tapping to the rhythm. She even ceased for a moment to think of Robert. The music seemed to tug at her senses, calling her to come and dance. She thought she had never wanted anything so much.

Near her, Joseph Gayle began an animated discussion about the quality of this year's fleeces, in which the others soon joined, as if by doing so they could somehow shut out the profane sounds. Hannah realised suddenly that Robert was no longer in his place.

She glanced quickly round, and then was aware of someone behind her, bending to murmur in her ear.

'It's hot in here, Hannah Burton. Shall we step outside?'

It *was* hot; but she knew that was not why she slid from the bench, glad that no one appeared to notice (Agnes and John because they were deep in talk, Samuel because he was lost in some world of his own), and went with Robert, her heart beating fast with delighted excitement.

It was warm outside too, the air heavy with the odours of sheep and wool, but there was a reviving freshness about it as well. The sun was low, the depths of the dale already full of shadows, but here on the grass beside the beck the light shone full on the fiddler and the colourful moving patterns of the dancers, vigorous and breathless and full of laughter.

Hannah stood still. Oh, how she ached to dance! But she must not, she knew she must not. She wondered if Robert felt the same. She was about to glance at him, when she became aware of his fingers touching hers, and the next instant they had closed about them, holding her hand in a firm grasp. She could not move then for several moments, because beneath the still surface of her body fire ran through her veins from his touch with such intensity that she felt consumed by it.

She looked round at last, and knew that he had been watching her for some time, as he was doing now. His eyes looked very dark, his expression grave.

'Thou wouldst like to dance?' His voice was unusually soft.

'Yes,' she whispered. 'Oh yes – but we must not!'

A smile hovered briefly about his mouth. 'No, we must not,' he agreed, and she wondered why she felt so disappointed, or what she would have done if he had answered differently. Then, suddenly very grave again, he studied her face intently for a moment before saying, 'Thou art beautiful, Hannah Burton.'

She stared at him, high coloured, breathless, her eyes wide with wonder. 'Beautiful! Me?' She would have thought he was teasing her, except that his face held no hint of laughter.

'Didst thou not know that?'

She shook her head.

'Hast thou ever seen thyself?' When she simply looked puzzled, he added, 'In a mirror.'

She was surprised he should ask. What good Quaker home possessed such a thing? 'Of course not.'

He pondered for a moment, and then said peremptorily, 'Come with me!' and led her towards a door at the stable end of the house, near the woolroom.

Inside, it was dim, for there was no window and the light from the door did not reach the furthest corners. Hannah saw only a disorderly jumble of objects, clearly stored here because there was no room for them anywhere else. 'Wait here,' Robert commanded. 'I'll get a light.'

She waited, alone in the doorway with the sound of the music enticingly in her ears, wondering (with some excitement) what was going to happen. Robert quickly returned, with candle and tinderbox, which he set down on an upturned barrel while he lit the little flame. Then he took her hand again and raised the candle and led her on into the room, which proved to be bigger than she had thought.

Someone, long ago, had discarded a long mirror, left perhaps by some unenlightened ancestor of Joseph Gayle. Robert turned it to face them and rubbed the glass with his sleeve and then set Hannah before it and held the candle high. 'There! Am I not right?'

Hannah stared at the stranger who looked back at her. She saw a young woman, in much the same way as, every day, she saw her neighbours and family and friends, except that this was a new face, a new form, to be assessed and responded to. This woman was tall and very slender, her head held proudly on a long

49

neck above a crisp white collar, which contrasted with the familiar undyed homespun gown — she knew that well at least. The simplicity of the clothes served only to emphasise the lovely line of the pale oval face, the straight nose, the clear dark brows, the exquisitely formed mouth, soft and yet firm, neither too small nor too large. The eyes were wide, fringed with long dark lashes, deeply blue like the sky as dusk merged into night. She was a creature of the night indeed, skin clear and pale as starlight, the hair, curling irrepressibly beneath the sober white cap, as densely black as the deep-shadowed corners of wood or farmyard. Below that proud head the creamy greyness clothed a body that was long, graceful, gently curved. Yes, Robert was right: she *was* beautiful, this young woman gazing wonderingly at her from the mirror.

It took her some moments to realise that this, now, was Hannah Burton, her very self, the individual she had known so intimately all her life, suddenly taken a separate and startling shape before her. She had known, painfully, that there were gaps in her knowledge of herself, an incompleteness she could never hope to fill unless she were one day to find who her parents had been. Now she realised that there had also been a gap of whose existence she had been wholly unaware, until now, when this new piece of knowledge slotted into place, making her just a little more complete than she had been before. The knowledge of this stranger in the mirror, who was herself, was something she would henceforth carry with her always.

She turned to look at Robert. Somehow, conscious of herself, she saw him more clearly too, in the light of her new self awareness. She saw the strong face starkly lit, deep shadowed between the cheekbones and the square jaw, the eyes, glittering in the candlelight, watching her with her the intentness she had noticed before. 'Well?' he said. 'I was right, was I not?'

She coloured, but could not quite bring herself to

admit her agreement. She knew now, though, what it was that made him look at her like that: her beauty, awakening admiration and interest. She felt an odd sensation, as if something inside her was turning right over. It was not entirely a pleasant sensation, for it brought with it an indefinable ache for something she did not understand.

Robert said no more, but instead put out his hand, and very gently, with a kind of experimental softness, touched her cheek. She shivered, not from cold, but because of the turmoil his touch had set going inside her. It was not fear, though she had an uneasy sense that there was something here to be avoided; that now, at this moment, she ought to turn and run from this place and from this alluring young man. There was something in what she felt that was like the call of the fiddle, enticing her to some wild abandonment that was far removed from all that she had ever learned to recognise as good; only her response to Robert was stronger by far than anything the music had drawn from her, and, she knew, infinitely more dangerous.

She did not move. She felt him spread his fingers against her cheek, running them down it caressingly. She felt her breath come fast, with difficulty, through parted lips. She saw that his mouth, too, was a little open. It held her eyes, a perfect mouth, neither too full nor too thin. She knew it moved nearer, towards her own. Her heart was beating so fast that she could scarcely breathe at all.

Robert's fingers slid along her cheek to her jaw, and into the thickness of her hair and the gathered stiffness of her cap, drawing her closer. She closed her eyes, shutting out all the warning voices, and the next moment felt his mouth reach hers. Soft at first, exploring, and then coming to rest, firmly, pressing hard, so that something burst inside her, releasing a tumultuous torrent of feeling like nothing she had ever known or imagined possible.

At her sides her hands tensed and then raised themselves and found their way somehow, by no deliberate choice of her own, about his neck. She was aware, as if from a long way off, that he put down the candle; and then his arms went about her too, pulling her near. Everything she had, all she was, all she felt, was centred in that kiss.

It seemed to go on for ever, and yet to be ended in the tiniest interval of time. Robert drew away. Then his arms fell to his sides, and Hannah felt suddenly bereft. She found she was trembling. Her breathing was still much too fast, like his.

He turned to take up the candle, avoiding her gaze. She saw the way his head bent on the strong neck, the supple power of the wrists showing beneath the plain white bands, the breadth of the shoulders, which she had seen gleaming and muscled at the sheepwashing. She knew then that what she had given him just now was more than a kiss, that in giving it she had given herself, and that because of it she would never be the same again. She was also afraid. What if he did not feel about her as she did about him? What if he should despise her for surrendering to him so readily? Yet what could she have done but that, when she had been taught from infancy to be open and sincere in everything?

'Let's go back,' he said. He extinguished the candle, so she could not see his face to judge from it what he thought of her now. She thought, I cannot bear it if he does not care. She knew now that what had woken in her on the day of his return, and burst into fiery life as he kissed her this evening, could find fulfilment only in him.

This is love, she thought, as they stepped out into the sunlit yard.

CHAPTER THREE

i

'We're going to Thornside cattle fair tomorrow,' Robert had said yesterday, as he leaned on the farmyard wall to watch Hannah, who was carrying a pail of whey out from the diary to the pigsty. 'Mary Harker too. Wilt thou come?'

Hannah had opened the pigsty and poured the whey steadily into the trough, and only then, when the pig's excited squealing had subsided, did she try to reply. By that time she had herself sufficiently under control to say calmly, 'If I'm allowed.' She had known, however, that her face betrayed all her delight at his request.

They had gone indoors and Agnes, applied to, had said with equal calmness, 'If that's what thou wouldst like.' Her expression had given nothing away. Hannah wondered sometimes how much Agnes and John knew of what she felt for Robert, if indeed they knew anything at all.

Now it was dawn, and outside Low Farm the sturdy galloways – large shaggy ponies bred for strength and endurance – were standing saddled and ready, one each for Robert and his father, one on which Hannah would ride pillion with Mary Harker, and the pack-horse laden with stockings and caps and gloves for Joseph Gayle's stall at the fair.

Little was said as the company met and mounted. Even Robert was subdued, and did no more than nod at Hannah and offer her the glimpse of a muted grin. The light had a uniform greyness, so that everything seemed somehow colourless and without feature. It was, Hannah thought, as if life had not yet been breathed into the still landscape. So must the world have looked in the moment before creation.

In silence they set out down the lane, the horses' hooves sounding loud on the scattered stones underfoot; past the meeting house and the silent cottages; along the street, where one or two early risers paused to watch them go and waved perhaps, but did not speak.

Just beyond the village, the drove road branched to the left, through the meadows, and they went that way, crossing the river at the ford. The road, wide, pitted by the summer-long movement of the cattle upon it, turned steeply up the southern slopes of the dale, between neat stone walls, past solitary barns and plantations of birch and holly and mountain ash, and on into the open where only the grim and secretive settlements of the lead miners relieved the desolation of the landscape. Yet it was here, as they came within reach of the highest point, that Hannah became conscious of a change in the light, a new brightness and warmth. She glanced over her shoulder, and then she called, 'Wait! Oh, look! Please look!'

They all halted, and turned to look where she pointed; to the east, where the dark line of the hills was edged with a rim of gold, which stretched long fingers out in all directions over the shadowy valley. The next moment the sun slipped into sight, and wherever they looked the land was suddenly alive with colour – the purple and bronze and green and gold that patterned the fells, the dale burning with the fire colours of the autumn trees, wherever the sunlight touched them. Hannah felt she could have sat there for ever gazing at it. Delight and wonder filled her, brimful and overflowing. She did not just see, she *felt* the loveliness of it all, as an experience beyond words which she would always remember.

She wanted everyone to feel it too, or if not everyone, then someone. With reluctance, and yet eagerly, she took her eyes from the scene and turned them on

Robert; and found he was looking not at the landscape but at her, in that intimate way she had begun to know very well, but also with a hint of gentle amusement. She found, faced with that expression, that she could not after all tell him what she felt. She did not want to risk his laughter, however kindly it was meant.

'Can we go now?' he asked teasingly.

She saw that his father was more than a little impatient at the delay, and could only say, meekly, 'Aye, of course.'

She tried not to feel disappointed at their reaction, at Robert's in particular. To console herself, she glanced once more at the loveliness of the sunrise before they reached the summit and the dale disappeared from view. After all, she thought, I know I am not like everyone else. I mustn't be surprised if they do not feel as I do.

She had thought that in Robert she had found another outsider, someone who, like her, chafed sometimes at the earthy practicalities of life at Hollinthwaite. In part at least it seemed that she had been wrong. But then he was no foundling, but a Hollinthwaite lad by birth, rooted there for generations. She supposed that was something no one could ever take from him. To him there could be no magic in what was in his blood.

Where Swaledale was wild and yet intimate, a dale of swift water and birch trees and deep narrow valleys, Wensleydale, seen at last spread before them as the road dipped steeply down from Thornside common, was all spacious grandeur. The river Ure snaked wide and silver through the fertile meadow and pasture that bordered it. Across the width of the dale the land undulated, forming gentle lesser hills and valleys, green and wooded, between the high splendours of the fells that bordered it to north and south. Far off, a glimpse of shining water between two hills marked the lake of Semerwater. A knot of pines on a round hill, cloud shadows moving swiftly over the gentle greens of the autumn fields, scattered farms and barns, a network of stone walls, here and there a hamlet nestling grey and secure in some sheltered hollow – it was a whole world in one, this great dale, a small universe. Hannah, who rarely visited it, never came on this view without a surge of excitement, as of an explorer sighting new lands. A glance at Robert brought an answering grin, as if this time he knew exactly how she felt. Her spirits rose.

Thornside, built on the hillside before the land levelled out towards the river, was a town of peatsmoke and angled roofs, thatched and slated, of stone houses of every possible shape and size. The buildings crowded this way and that in every available corner on both sides of a street that curved its way down by market place and church on to the turnpike road that linked the dale with the greater world outside.

At the very edge of the town the riders came on a drove of cattle, filling the road from wall to wall with a bellowing, surging mass of animals. Behind them the drover in plaid and bonnet called to his dog, moving the herd steadily forward. He looked surprisingly calm, Hannah thought, for one responsible for such unpredictable charges.

'I knew we'd be late,' said Joseph Gayle gruffly. Then he commanded, 'This way!' and led them into a lane that wound its way round the backs of houses – close-packed, often ruinous, huddled about tiny ill-smelling yards, where hens scratched and scruffy children played and women sat knitting or spinning; past neat vegetable plots, pigsties and stables; past malodorous dyeshops, where the stones were stained startlingly blue and red; past the nauseating stink of a tannery, and sheds where the gentle rhythmic clatter of looms filled the air; and back at last between two substantial houses to the seething clamour of the market place. Here men and women shouted above the bleating of sheep and the lowing of cattle and the endless clatter and roar of hooves on cobblestones. Here the smell of animals and dung, and of the tarry wool of the recently-salved sheep, overpowered all the human smells of the town. Here it was hard to believe, in a scene of such apparent disorder, that any buying or selling could ever be done.

Somehow they pushed and shoved their way to the stalls, set a little apart from the animals, where other goods were sold, and where Joseph Gayle laid out his wares on a stall between that of a weaver (heavy with bales of coarse cloth) and that of a milliner, which had on it more different styles and sizes of hat than Hannah had dreamed were possible.

'Get the horses down to the mill,' Joseph commanded his son, as soon as the packs had been lifted from the animal's back.

'Come with me,' said Robert, with a glance at Hannah. She did not wait for permission or encouragement (she did not think Mary Harker had heard what was said), but took the reins of two of the horses in her hands and followed Robert, who was leading the other two, into the crowd.

More than once she almost lost him – it was a good thing she was tall, she thought, or she would certainly have done so in that crowd. He led the way down the hill and round a bend in the road where, suddenly, there was space, and everything seemed extraordinarily quiet.

It was not absolutely quiet, of course. Far from it, for the din of the fair could still be heard: the clatter of clogs on cobbles as townsfolk – and those from farther afield – hurried to buy or just to look, the thud of horses' hooves, the rattle of cartwheels; and the normal town sounds of men and women and children at work or play in the houses and alleyways of the town. But they could hear their own footsteps now, and the sound of the horses, and if they spoke they could be heard.

'Where didst thou say we were going?' Hannah asked, a little breathlessly, having hurried to walk alongside Robert.

'Thornside mill. To my Uncle Samuel. We can stable the horses there. He'll be expecting us. There's not much stabling left in Thornside today.'

'I did not know thou hadst an Uncle Samuel.'

Robert shrugged. 'He's old and lives alone. Keeps himself to himself.'

'With all the people coming to the mill? He'll not find that easy.'

'He finds it only too easy, I'm sorry to say. Thou'lt see soon enough. He's had bad health, and there are two other mills near Thornside, both doing well. He's not kept up, that's all. And he doesn't care.'

It sounded discouraging, but even so she was not quite prepared for the scene of decay that met her eyes when at last they came to the end of the tree-shaded lane – gloriously gold and red and copper and bronze – that led from the Thornside road to the mill.

The mill stood alongside Thornside beck, which tumbled down a rocky cleft between the tree-covered banks that sheltered the northern side of the building. Soon, Hannah thought, there would be little left to shelter, for the mill showed signs of fast returning to its natural state. Walls and roof (slated, so once money had been spent on it) were green with moss and lichen, and the mortar had crumbled away, leaving great gaps in the stonework, in some of which stray weeds had taken root. The little kiln, where once oats had been dried, had long since collapsed altogether. The mill race had silted up and was choked with weeds, and only a trickle of water seeped along it now, with no effect at all on the millwheel, whose metal parts were badly rusted, the woodwork broken in many places. Window and door frames were splintered and rotting, and more than one door in the mill or outhouses hung half off its hinges.

The wooden gate that led into the nettle and grass grown yard was held permanently open by a rowan sapling of several year's growth, and in any case it was clear that any attempt to close it would cause its complete disintegration.

Yet it was a lovely spot. The land sloped gently up to the north beyond the beck, where a neglected field enclosed by a stone wall formed the mill garth, long unused for any purpose. To the south a small wood bordered the outbuildings. It grew below the level of the yard, so that over the tree tops there was a clear view of the dale beyond, the pattern of fields, the shining river, the gentle hills, and far off, hazy in the morning sunlight, the blue line of the fells, beyond which lay Wharfedale and Littondale and many lesser hidden valleys.

Hannah returned her gaze to her immediate surroundings, where Robert was investigating the possibilities of what, she supposed, passed for a stable.

'It's worse than I remembered,' he said with disfavour. 'But it will have to do. At least it's not raining.' He led the horses to the least ruined part of the building, and even managed to find hay for them, and a bucket in which to bring water from the beck.

'It's so *sad*,' said Hannah with feeling, as they rubbed down the horses. 'Such a waste.'

'Thou art right. That is precisely what it is. When I think what it could be! Uncle Samuel isn't even liable to tithes, thou knows.'

'Why ever not?'

'The mill belonged to one of the abbeys round here, hundreds of years ago – Jervaulx, I think. I don't know the rights of it, only that no one who has it must pay tithes so long as he's here.' He moved on to the next horse, stooping for a fresh handful of straw (as fresh as the supply they had found would allow) with which to rub down the rough sweaty coat. 'It's not just that, either. Thou saw the beck out there – running well even after a dry spell. It hardly ever gives out. There are mills doing well in much worse places than this. When I think what it *could* do —'

'But thou said there were too many other mills,' she pointed out.

'Mills don't have to grind corn. They can full cloth, and other things too.' He straightened and shrugged. 'Still, it's none of our business. Hast done? We'd best go and find my uncle.'

Beyond the stable, on the most level and sheltered part of the mill's land, a neat wall enclosed a large garden. Pushing open the gate, they found it an extraordinary contrast to the neglect outside. Here, everything was in perfect order, leeks and cabbages marching with mathematical precision, carrot tops in a green and feathery line, onions well grown and ready for harvesting, gooseberry bushes and raspberry canes carefully tended, and not a weed in sight. It was clear enough where Uncle Samuel's heart lay.

He was digging potatoes at the far end of the plot, stooping now and then to lift the tubers and rub the earth from them before placing them in a basket. He did not appear to have heard anyone coming, or perhaps he deliberately ignored them until he could do so no longer. Then he thrust his spade into the ground and came to meet them – a thin, bent figure in neglected Quaker dress, with no hint of a welcome in his expression. He looked Hannah over, heard Robert's introduction and explanation with complete impassivity, answered the subsequent inquiries about his health with uninformative brevity, and then said, 'I'll be getting on then,' and returned to his potatoes.

Robert grinned at Hannah. 'That's it then. Let's take a look at the fair.' He saw her nod an enthusiastic agreement. He realised that her eyes were different today, bright and sparkling, like a beck beneath a summer sky, with none of the deep, dark, sombre quality they usually had. On a sudden impulse, he reached out and took her hand, and together they ran towards the fiery tunnel of the lane.

There he halted, the better to look at her. She was breathing fast – from the running, of course; but not just from that, he knew. He felt a sudden longing to seize her in his arms and kiss that lovely pale shining face, all over ... Deliberately, carefully, he stepped forward, leading her on at a steady walk towards the road, where the presence of others going to Thornside would make any such display of passion impossible. She was a respectable girl; and, besides, it was not what he had planned. In any case, there was a pleasure of quite another kind in walking about Thornside Fair with the loveliest girl in the Dales at his side, gazing at him with such brightly adoring eyes.

In spite of the apparent chaos, some buying and selling had already been done. They met two men coming from Thornside, driving cattle and sheep before them, with that rosy, rather smug look about them that suggested satisfaction in a good bargain made, and very likely sealed in an alehouse afterwards. In the market place it was easier now to move amongst the diminishing herds; and other attractions had sprung up to tempt those who had completed the day's business with time to spare – or perhaps these other activities had been there all along, hidden by the animals. In a back alley to their left a cock-fight was in progress. Robert, fascinated, longed to join the shouting excited men and women, but one glance at the stricken look on Hannah's face warned him that he would be wiser to go on. There was a wrestling booth too (that did not interest her either), and a dancing bear which rather aroused her pity for its sad condition than awoke any delight in her at its skill. There were stalls selling ribbons and chap-books and other knick-knacks, but he did not risk them either; he suspected that her obedient Quaker spirit would be unmoved by their charms. Nor was she thirsty, though a booth selling ale stood at every corner.

There was also Blind Tom, who had turned up at the clipping and was here now, playing his fiddle, as if his very soul was in it, for the red and perspiring dancers tripping and stumbling their way through a succession of country dances.

Not dancing either, Robert suspected, with a furtive glance at Hannah. Then, at one and the same moment, he remembered the clipping, and saw her face. She'd had just such a look then, all eager longing, poised, as if her feet ached to dance. He glanced quickly round. It was the most public of places, but he saw no one he knew, and his father's stall was some way off, just where the road swung round up the hill. With such a crowd in the way, it was unlikely he would see. Robert tugged at Hannah's hand. 'Come!'

She gasped and opened her mouth as if to speak; but she came. He left her no time to protest, swinging her at once into the jostling apology for a circle just forming before them.

He had danced before, now and then, at his uncle's house. He danced well and learned quickly, as quickly as any of the dancers here. It was Hannah who amazed him. He knew she had never even dreamed of dancing before, yet here she was glancing at the dancers' feet, alert for the least sign of the next step, and picking up the pattern of the dance in no time at all. She was soon dancing with a graceful lightness of step that put to shame the clumsy efforts of most of those about her, as if the music had somehow caught her and filled her and told her exactly what she must do. Robert could not take his eyes off her. She was exquisite, like a rare flower in a cabbage patch, the most beautiful creature there, all lissome lines and graceful movements, all parted lips and sweet, happy glances. Whenever the dance brought them together, he touched her hand with a caress, let his arm rest just too long about her waist, felt the fire of her nearness fanned to a white heat in his veins.

The last triumphant chord vibrated through the air. Here and there a boy and girl, breathless, laughing, aroused, ran quickly down the lane past the church-yard, seeking privacy. Robert slid his arm about Hannah's waist. He felt her droop against him, and the throbbing of her body beneath his touch grew wilder than ever. He bent his mouth to her forehead. 'This way,' he whispered.

The lane was quiet, the wood on the slope beyond it quieter still, though little furtive sounds told of other couples together in some secret place. Robert found a narrow path, and at its end a glade, where dense undergrowth screened them from view. He halted and turned her to face him. She looked up at him – not far, for she was tall for a woman – her face touched with colour, her lips parted, her eyes now very soft and dark. He brought his mouth down on hers, felt the little shock that ran through her, intensifying as he slid his hands over her body. He had kissed other girls before, but he had known nothing like the fierce desire he felt now. It seared him through and through; it urged him on, so that he moved her steadily back to where a tree barred their path, pressing her against its trunk, and his body on to hers. He raised his hand to her throat, caressing the soft white skin, seeking a way beneath the heavy unyielding fabric of her bodice. How could such snow pallor inflame his senses like this? He wanted her as he had wanted no one in his life before. He was nineteen, nearly a man; he had never had a woman, and it was this woman he wanted, here and now. She wanted him too. He felt it in the way she responded to him, the melting of her body against his. If he were to press her to the ground and take her it would only be to give her what she ached for. 'Oh Hannah!' he whispered fiercely. He thrust his tongue into her mouth and fumbled for the lacings of her bodice.

Then through the tumultuous fire of his feelings for her shot a cold, sharp, warning voice. No! Not now, not yet! He forced back his head, eyes closed. He thought, 'Is this really what I want?' His blood throbbed, Yes! Yes, go on! The voice in his brain, cold, unmoved, persisted: Get her pregnant, and where are you then?

She was his neighbours' daughter. If she fell with child by him, there would be no escape. He knew there would be no one else he could blame, and he had no money (yet) to allow him to run away. He would find himself forced into marriage, and that would be that: the end of all his hopes. It was not that marriage to Hannah was unthinkable. One day, perhaps, who knew? But marriage to anyone, now, would be a grim prospect. To be trapped at nineteen; children, ties, all that marriage meant ... He shuddered, and the fires recoiled and lost their force. This was no part of his plan, not at all.

He opened his eyes, pulled himself away from her, drew a deep breath. His hands moved to her arms and held her there, at a safe distance, he hoped. Hannah gave a little cry. Her eyes flew open, and he saw the sense of loss in them, and of rejection. In him, matching them, was the sharp ache of unsatisfied desire. It made him cold.

'We'd best get back,' he said brusquely, and let his hands fall. He turned and began to walk quickly away. She had to run to catch him up, though she said nothing. They walked on in silence, not looking at one another. At his father's stall he said, 'Stay here now. I've someone to see.' And then he left her, without a backward glance. In that moment he almost hated her, because she had roused his desire but could not satisfy him.

He went back to the mill and saddled his pony and rode at a heedless pace to an inn on the edge of the neighbouring village of Hawes. He had called here once on business for his father, and found the land-lady's daughter (clean and presentable enough) more than willing, had he chosen to make use of her. Today he did choose. It did not take him long to get her into the hayloft, and even less time to have what he wanted from her. He paid her for it afterwards, because he wanted her to have no claim on him, though he knew quite well that he was certainly not the only man to have enjoyed her favours. He was sorry she was not Hannah, but the short excursion had served its purpose and he rode back to Thornside in a happier frame of mind. He was able to greet Hannah – her expression anxious and relieved at once – with all his old easy affection, restoring the strained links between them at once. But he had learned a useful lesson today. He would be more careful in future.

ii

For a long time that night, Hannah could not sleep. She lay staring at the faintly discernible outline of the window, and its view of stars bright in a velvet-dark sky, but she saw only Robert's face, close to hers, with desire in his eyes, and lips that eagerly sought her out.

On the whole she had not enjoyed today. Not that she had been unhappy. Sometimes she had even been deliriously, ecstatically happy – in the dancing, for instance; when he put his arms about her. On the other hand, perhaps 'happy' was the wrong word, even then. It had been something much more intense than that. Happiness was a simple and comfortable thing. What she had felt then, what she felt now, was neither simple nor comfortable.

She knew quite well, in essence if not in detail, what would have happened under the trees, had Robert not put an end to it. Her body ached still, ached agonisingly, for what it had longed for then. There was a great dark chasm inside her which she feared would never be filled or satisfied. Yet she ought to be grateful to Robert – no, she *was* grateful. She had let him go much too far as it was; other men would have had their way without a second thought. She was astonished, looking back, at the strength of her own feelings, and at the way they had overcome all the promptings of her conscience. Robert, because he cared for her, had saved her from herself. She could only be tenderly grateful for that care.

Unfortunately, gratitude was not enough to still the ache that tormented her. She wanted Robert, and she could not stop thinking about him. It was an agony beyond words. She did not think it would ever end.

She closed her eyes and thought of the way his hands had touched her, imagining what might have happened next. She found her own hands were exploring too, as she wished his had done ... In sudden shame, she forced them to her sides. Robert had been strong, for her sake. She must be strong too.

She opened her eyes again and sought out the brightest star there beyond her window, and fixed her attention upon it. It was like the light that shone to guide her, pure and clear and uncompromising. She saw it illuminate the path along which she must walk and from which she must never turn aside: a straight path, silver in the light, running like the drove road across the darkness of the high moor, where the wind cooled all the wayward passions and impulses of her flesh. She imagined herself walking on that road, braced against the siren voices from the dark, her eyes on the light. It was quiet, but for the sound of the wind; the air was sweet in her nostrils; the silver light lay soft on the road, and a sense of peace filled her through and through. Soon she drifted quietly into sleep.

The following evening, John and Agnes and Hannah took their knitting to the house of Richard Thwaite, farmer, and elder of the Hollinthwaite meeting house, where they gathered with other neighbours – all

Quakers tonight to work by the light of the peat fire. Only John Burton had the benefit of a rushlight, for, a fine reader, he had been asked to read to the company from his favourite work, the Journal of John Woolman, an American Friend who had visited Wensleydale a short while before his death some years ago. Most of those present had made the journey to Countersett meeting house to hear the visitor speak. Many, like John Burton, had been moved and inspired by the man, and his words of gentleness and love. Hannah, who had been only eight then, had stayed at Low Farm in the care of Mary Harker. John and Agnes had told her all about it afterwards, and she had heard John Woolman's writings read so often that she felt she knew the man as well as she knew her closest neighbours. Like John, she loved him for his concern for the negro slaves, the Red Indians, the oppressed of every race and creed and colour; his anguish at the suffering of any living creature; his witness against the human greed that he saw as the cause of that suffering. Tonight, like the others, she listened quietly, and wished she too could have heard him. More than that, she wished she had his compassion, and courage, and strength to do what was right even when it meant opposing (however gently) the wishes of one's friends.

Later, they walked home in the dark with Mary Harker, John lighting their way with the lantern. Hannah, tiring of their neighbour's incessant talk, fell behind a little, so that she could concentrate on her own thoughts. She did not come up with them again until they reached Low Farm, where John went to exchange a word with Joseph Gayle, and Mary kept Agnes talking at the gate, and did not see Hannah coming towards them in the dark. Mary's voice, full of low-voiced indignation, broke into Hannah's sober reflections.

'. . . dancing, Agnes Burton! Dancing, I say!' Hannah, suddenly uncomfortably certain that she knew the subject of this particular piece of gossip, stood quite still. Mary went on. 'I saw her with my own eyes, her and young Robert together, tripping round in all that heathen crowd. Quite shameless about it too, from the look of it. I thought thou shouldst know.'

'Didst thou?' returned Agnes, in the neutral tone that Hannah knew meant she was angry, but was trying hard to control it. Hannah hoped very much it was Mary who had angered her, and not her news.

'It must grieve thee, I know,' their neighbour went on, apparently unperturbed. 'After all thou hast done for her, and thy man too. Thou couldst not have done more, no one could. But that's the way it is. Blood will out, when all's said and done. She's not of thy getting – it was bound to show one day. Bad blood is bad blood, and there's nowt thou canst do about it.'

'Nonsense, Mary!' retorted Agnes briskly. 'There's no such thing as bad blood, and thou knows it. She's as much a child of God as thee and me.'

'Well, I know that, of course.' Mary Harker sounded very uncomfortable, Hannah was pleased to note.

'It's not bad blood,' concluded Agnes. 'It's young blood. We were all young once.'

If Hannah had thought (with relief) that this was the end of the matter, she was wrong. She was in bed and about to extinguish the candle, when Agnes came into her room and sat down on the edge of the bed, in what seemed an ominously grave manner.

'Hannah,' she said quietly. 'Thou knows I don't give ear to gossip, not as a rule. But I heard something tonight I want thy answer on. Thou knows I'll trust thy word, whatever thou sayst.'

Hannah, reddening a little, raised her eyes to Agnes's angular face. 'I know. I heard. Mary Harker told thee – about the dancing at Thornside. It's true. I did dance.' It would not have occurred to her to lie, but she was distressed all the same to see the hurt that passed over Agnes's features.

'Thou said nowt last night.'

Hannah coloured more deeply than ever and shook her head. 'I knew thou wouldst not like it.'

'I like it less that thou didst keep it from me.'

'I know. I am sorry.' Then she went on earnestly, 'I did not *feel* it was wrong, truly I did not. It was such a little thing, jumping about to music.'

'It is vanity, Hannah. It takes thy thoughts from where they ought to be.'

It had certainly done that, Hannah acknowledged, remembering what had come after. She felt ashamed that she should have no intention of telling Agnes about that particular episode. She told herself that it would hurt Agnes too much to know of it.

The next moment, she wondered if Agnes knew everything anyway, for she said, 'It's not just the dancing. Thou wert with Robert Gayle, is that not so? Alone with him?'

Hannah nodded, conscious that her fiery colour probably told Agnes far more than Hannah wanted her to know.

'He's a good lad, and our neighbour's son. I've nothing against him. I know thou likest him, and one day maybe we'll be glad of that, thy father and I. But thou art too young yet by far to be thinking of such things. It's not good to be wed too young. Besides, Robert's not settled yet, nor ready to be. Let things go too fast, and thou couldst find thyself where no lass would wish to be — where none of us would wish thee to be. Let him be thy companion and neighbour, just as Samuel is. But watch that thou dost not let him be more to thee, not yet awhile. Best not to allow thyself to be alone with him, if thou canst help it.'

Hannah accepted the warning meekly, knowing quite well, not only that it was given in love, but that it was wise advice. She had learned that herself, yesterday.

Yet all the same a part of her did not want to be wise or heed any warning. That rebellious part of her nature wanted to abandon all caution, all constraints, and give Robert all he might want and more. It was that part of her which had set her feet dancing yesterday, without one single twinge of conscience; and led her to sing when no one was by to hear; and filled her with excitement at the worldly bustle of a fair. It also made her increasingly impatient with the endless routine of her life, so that sometimes she longed to break free from it.

Was Mary Harker right after all? Was there bad blood in her – the same hot, impulsive blood that had led her mother to ruin, so that she had been forced to abandon her child to hide her shame? Might the same thing happen to her, if she were not very careful? She wondered if any true child of Agnes and John Burton would have felt as she did. On the whole she doubted it. Other Quakers were tempted sometimes, even the very best (like John Woolman), but she had never heard of any as headstrong and wilful and rebellious as she felt herself to be. Could someone like herself, of such unpromising origins, ever be truly content with the life of ordered simplicity and seriousness that inevitably lay before her? Unless, of course, Robert could share it with her. She was sure that would make all the difference.

CHAPTER FOUR

i

Samuel no longer looked forward very much to going home, especially for the long summer weeks that lay before him. True, it was preferable to school, though that was better now, since Robert had left. But, of course, Robert was now at home all the time.

There was no escaping him. He was always there, talking, laughing, keeping everyone busy with his commands (for Samuel or Mary), or his ideas (for his father, though even they were only commands in disguise, if Joseph Gayle would only see it). When he was not actually present, he was never out of anyone's thoughts. Joseph Gayle was constant in his praise. The dour old widower seemed to have taken on new vitality since Robert came home; every sentence almost was peppered with his name, spoken with a shining pride that lit his eyes too. Robert had such a good head for business. There was always some scheme he had in mind. He was always eager to be busy, never idle; not, implied Joseph Gayle's tone and his expression, like his dreamy, inadequate younger brother. Robert was the son any man would have prayed for.

Then there was Hannah – but Samuel tried not to think of her; that hurt too much. It might be inevitable that Robert should take his place there too, but it did not make it any more bearable.

No, on the whole, the nearer he came to Hollinthwaite, the more depressed he felt.

It was Robert who came first to meet him as he turned into the yard at Low Farm and dismounted. His father followed soon afterwards, and Mary too, wiping her hands on her apron and beaming at him.

Robert clapped him on the shoulder. 'I do believe thou hast grown, brother,' he said cheerfully. There was something more than a little patronising in his tone, but then there always was, where Samuel was concerned.

Samuel smiled feebly and turned to unbuckle the saddle bags containing his few belongings (mostly books).

Joseph Gayle clasped his hands and said, 'Come in, lad. Tell us how thou hast been,' which at least was a warmer welcome than he had expected.

He went in and Mary brought ale and havercakes and cheese, and gooseberry tarts, and they all sat about the table – all except Mary, who waited on them, and then stood knitting by the fire while they talked.

Joseph questioned Samuel closely about his last term at school, and even expressed a modest pleasure at prizes won in several subjects. Samuel was astonished. Joseph had never shown much interest in his academic achievements, even before Robert came home – at Christmas and Easter he had not even bothered to ask how his younger son had done. Samuel, wholly unused to being the centre of attention, found it all more than a little disconcerting, particularly when his father concluded with an affectionate pat of the hand and a gentle, 'It's good to have thee home, lad.'

'More hands with the sheep washing,' Robert put in briskly, rather in the tone of one trying to restore common sense to a regrettably emotional discussion.

Samuel hated sheep washing. The weather was almost always cold (and if it wasn't, the water invariably was) and as a consequence his bones always seemed to ache for days afterwards. Besides, he did not enjoy large and convivial gatherings. Before Robert came home Hannah's presence had always made it bearable, but he knew where Hannah's attention would be this year, as last.

'We begin Second Day,' Robert added, as if anxious to rub it in, Second Day being the day after next. Then he said, 'Oh, by the way, Father, I've sorted the stockings for the carrier. I put today's lot with them.'

'Not Alice Blakey's, I hope. Thou knows I put those by.'

'Ah!' said Robert, with a look of self-congratulation. 'Thou wilt have no need to do that any more. I have solved that little difficulty for thee.'

Last time Samuel was at home he would have expected his father to beam with pleasurable anticipation at such a statement, eager to know more. Now, Joseph Gayle did not smile at all; in fact he looked rather grim, and said guardedly, 'Oh?'

'Aye,' said Robert, quite untroubled. 'Told her we'd no more need of her services. An honourable retirement, I said.'

'Thou didst *what*?'

Robert met his father's furious glare with a steady gaze. 'Thou heard.'

'I thought maybe I'd heard wrong. I hoped —' He struggled for words through a rising fury. 'That thou shouldst *dare* take it on thyself! What right hadst thou to meddle, without a word to me?'

'Are we not partners?' retorted Robert serenely.

'Thou art a lad of twenty! I am thy father! Thou dost nowt without my authority, *nowt*, I tell thee!'

'All that fine talk about a man's head on a boy's shoulders – what's become of that, then? What about thy trust in me?'

'Thou knows I did not mean this.'

'Why not? Oh, come now, Father, Alice Blakey's been past doing good work for years now. She's nowt but a burden – thou hast said it thyself. All those stockings thou canst not sell —'

'I can give them away, when there are folks in need.

73

They're not past wearing, and it keeps an old woman in victuals.'

'Charity! That's what it is. If thou must give away thy goods, then give them – but thine, not mine. We're running a business, not a benevolent institution.'

Joseph Gayle's expression was grimmer than ever. 'Dost give no thought to an old woman's pride? So long as she can knit, she can keep herself. Let her do it until she dies, if she's able. I'll not be the one to tell her she's no use any more.'

'No. I've done it. So that's that.'

To Samuel's appalled astonishment, Robert sounded utterly unrepentant.

'Thou hadst no right!'

'Thou hadst need of my help with the business. Thou hast it. But thou hast it on my terms or not at all!'

The argument continued, growing more bitter and furious by the minute. Samuel caught Mary's eye, and saw that she had a resigned, incurious look. Was it possible that this kind of thing had become commonplace? It seemed hard to believe that things could have changed so much in just a few short months. Yet . . .

He hated to hear people quarrelling. He pushed back his stool and stood up. 'I'm going out,' he said. No one appeared to hear, but he went all the same, thankfully drawing a deep long breath of the evening air as he closed the door behind him.

He did not cross the beck. Over there was Hannah's house, and he did not want to risk meeting her; though briefly the question flickered through his mind – might she be different too? Might she even have come to dislike Robert?

That was too much to hope for, so he turned the other way, along the lane and on towards the river. He crossed at the bridge and followed the drove road up the further slope of the dale. He walked quickly, feeling the strain fall from him a little as he went. It always helped him, when things got difficult, to walk alone on the fells.

He was only a few yards up the hill when he heard someone running behind him, gaining on him quickly. A voice called, 'Samuel!'

He knew that voice, with its note of command; instinctively, unable to help himself, he halted and turned round. His next instinct was to run on and hide – in the barn up there on the left perhaps, or in the wood near it. But it was quite obvious that Robert had seen him, and he could not hope to run fast enough to escape his brother altogether. He would only look foolish. So he stayed where he was and waited for Robert to come, and tried to suppress the rage in his heart at this intrusion on his solitude. Robert *was* his brother after all. Besides, he had never in his life thought to challenge Robert's wishes, however inconvenient they might be.

It was clear that Robert was still in a state of furious anger, even after running most of the way from Low Farm. He was gasping for breath, but his eyes glittered, and as soon as he was able he burst out, 'Didst thou hear that? The stupidity, the blindness – I would not have believed it of him! Now he wants me to go and tell her it was all a mistake! I told him: 'I will not – not so long as I have breath in my body!' Why should I humiliate myself, when I *know* I'm right? All that talk we've had to listen to, about "Business comes first," or "There's no place for bad work in my business." Then *this* happens! He's in his dotage, that's what it is. God, it's time I took over, high time!'

'I thought that's what thou hadst done,' said Samuel mildly. He did not think there was any point in telling Robert precisely what he thought of his action. Robert probably knew anyway, and did not care.

'It's what I've *tried* to do. I *hate* this place – *hate* it and loathe it! They're so narrow, so blinkered. They see no more than is in front of their noses – and God knows that's little enough!'

'Father's done quite well out of it, in worldly terms, if that's what thou hast in mind,' Samuel pointed out.

'In Hollinthwaite's terms, maybe. When I think what he could have done – what *I* could have done! When I first came home, it was different. He couldn't listen to me enough. He backed me in everything. Thou wilt have heard him often enough. Then the moment I truly start to do something, this happens. It's not the first time neither. He's not had a good word to say for anything I've done, for weeks now.'

'I think,' said Samuel cautiously, in the little pause that followed, 'that maybe he doesn't really put business first, or only in a manner of speaking. Thou canst not be a Friend and do that. Hard work and honest dealing, that's one thing. But an old woman in need – well, she has to come first, in the end.'

Robert shot him a contemptuous glance. 'I wish thou couldst hear thyself! How can something come first "in the end"? Anyway, either business comes first, or it doesn't, and if I'm to make anything of my life, then it *must* come first. How else will I ever get away, from the small mindedness, the boredom, all of it!' He swung round suddenly and looked back the way they had come.

It is beautiful, Samuel thought: the mist rising along the river, the sun rosy on the tops. He heard Robert spit out his opinion of it all. 'Look at it, just look – a desert, a prison! Who would *choose* to live in this wilderness?'

Samuel said nothing, but he no longer felt any pleasure at all in the climb. There seemed no point in prolonging it. 'Let's go back,' he said.

On the way down, Robert said casually, 'I want Father to send me to London. I've told him so.'

Samuel thought fleetingly of Low Farm without Robert, and his heart leapt. But he only said cautiously, 'London? What wouldst thou do there?'

Robert shrugged. 'I don't much mind, so long as I'm there. Uncle John might take me on. Who knows, he may have a real businessman's mind. In any case, it would be something to do until I come into my money at twenty-one.'

'That's a year away.'

'A whole year! I'd go mad, staying here until then. No, I must get away.'

'Dost thou think Father will let thee go?'

'I put it to him,' said Robert brusquely. 'He refused. Point bland. But with thy help . . .'

Samuel resigned himself to hearing what role Robert wanted him to play. He knew he would do it, because he always did. This time it might even be to his advantage in the end.

ii

It was a beautiful day, so Hannah took her spinning wheel out on to the grass beyond the farmyard. The curlews called overhead, larks sang, the beck chattered gently alongside, and the rhythmic whirr of the spinning wheel merged easily with the natural sounds. After a little while Hannah began to sing too, softly and without words, the line of her voice weaving here and there through the other sounds.

Today's batch of wool had been carded yesterday, to disentangle and straighten the fibres a little. Now she had only to take a soft oily handful of the wool, twist a length to thread through onto the bobbin, set the treadle working, and pinch and tease out the wool as the wheel did the work. It was a task to occupy the hands and not the mind. Her fingers knew instinctively what to do, to ensure the most even yarn, with just the right degree of twist to it, for the knitting afterwards. Meanwhile she could look around her and sing and think of Robert, as she did almost unceasingly, as she had done ever since he came home just over a year ago.

She knew all was not well at Low Farm. Samuel, whom she rarely saw, had taken to going for long solitary walks – to seek out plants that interested him, he said, but it was clear he was also escaping the strained atmosphere at home. Whenever she saw him she thought he looked deeply unhappy. She rather missed his gentle friendship, but then she had little time for it now, since Robert came home.

Robert for his part said little to her about his disagreements with his father, though from hints he let fall sometimes it was clear enough what the trouble was: the son thought his father too unadventurous, the father thought his son too rash. It made her uneasy. She had thought Robert happily settled here in Hollinthwaite; now it was clear that he was becoming increasingly restless and discontented. She wanted him to feel, as she did, that any kind of life was bearable, so long as they were together. At least she was quite sure that in her company he was able to put all his troubles aside. He made it clear enough that then he thought only of her.

It made up for everything, to love and to be loved in return. For her, these days, all she did and saw, every part of her life, was transformed by joy, because Robert loved her. He had not told her so, not in so many words; but he did not need to. He sought her out on every possible occasion, openly and publicly, so that everyone knew she was his choice. There could be no clearer indication of his feelings for her. What was more, their two families accepted the situation too, and approved of it. She knew they must wait some years yet, but one day, inevitably, they would marry. No problems of disownment there, in the uniting of two staunchly Quaker families.

From here she could see the whole of Hollinthwaite going about its daily tasks. Clipping had been finished two weeks ago, so that it was spinning and not knitting that occupied most free moments now, for the women and girls at least. They sat in groups in yards and gardens, or before their front doors, singing and chattering above the incessant whirr of the wheels.

The very youngest children carded the wool for the spinners. Near them, little boys knitted the yarn that was already spun, pausing to play at marbles or giggling at some small boys' secret talk. The men knitted too, as they leaned on walls and discussed the weather, the price of wool, the good points of a foal newly born to a favourite mare. Very soon, in a week if the weather held, it would be haytime and every man and woman and child would be put out in the fields getting in the vital crop. That was a time for lads and lasses to eye one another, seek a greater closeness at the breaks in the work, plan who to partner at the haymell, when all was safely in the barns. Hannah smiled to think her choice was made, and his; all those anxious concerns were behind her for ever – it did not even matter that they would not be dancing.

And there was Robert now, striding up the slope towards her with his long powerful stride. Her voice swelled into a last joyful cadence, and fell silent. She hoped he had not heard her singing. She was never quite sure how far his toleration went for any un-Quakerish behaviour. There had been the dancing at Thornside, of course, but since then he had been assiduous in his attendance at meeting and unfailingly correct in his behaviour towards the elders and other members of the Society.

He had heard her. As soon as he was near enough, he grinned and said, 'Don't stop. Thou hast a fine voice. I love to hear thee.'

She coloured, with pleasure rather than shame. 'Dost not think it wrong?'

'Why should I?' She did not know what to say to that, but evidently he did not really expect an answer, for he went on, 'I must speak with thee. It is important.'

Her foot stilled, and the wheel fell silent. She felt suddenly afraid, though she could not have said why. Robert looked perhaps rather graver than usual, but not significantly so. Besides, what made him grave might just as easily be a pleasurable thing as an unwelcome one. His eyes were bright enough, after all.

He sat down on the grass beside her. She never ceased to find pleasure in the way he moved; whatever else was in her thoughts, a part of her noticed such small things, all the time. She waited for him to speak.

He grinned up at her, and happiness banished all the gravity from his face. What he had to say *was* pleasurable then! She felt her heartbeat quicken, as if in anticipation – but it could not be that, surely? Not yet . . .

He cleared his throat, and then said suddenly, 'I'm to go to London.'

It was nothing like what she had been expecting. 'London? What for? How long wilt thou be gone?'

He shrugged. 'Who knows? That depends how it turns out. I'm to work for my uncle John Gayle. He has a large hosiery business there, as thou knows, I think.'

'Aye.' She could not take it in. She had expected nothing like this. Robert going away, indefinitely – *was* that what he meant? She looked at his excited face. That could not be all of it; he could not look like that, if he was leaving her. 'Dost thou want to go?' she asked, knowing quite well it was a foolish question.

'Of course. There are no prospects for me here.'

No prospects, when she was here? Could he really mean that? Was he not rather coming round to saying something else, which he was afraid might prove hard for her? She knew she must reassure him. 'I tell thee, Robert – I shall be happy anywhere, so long as thou art there.'

She spoke very earnestly, with great gravity, and watched for the happy relief to light his face. Instead, he looked puzzled, and then frowned a little. 'I know thou wilt,' he said. Then he added lightly, 'When I've made my fortune, then I'll come for thee.'

Again, she could not quite take it in, and she seized on the inessentials. 'But thou hast a fortune already.'

'Uncle William's money? That's a pittance, by London standards at least. Besides, I can't lay hands on it yet. No, I intend to do better than that for myself, somehow.'

'But why? What use would it be to thee, to have a fortune?'

'Freedom – that's what money buys. That's what I want: my freedom.'

Hannah felt cold. He had said nothing about her, about his family, or Hollinthwaite; only about freedom, and she sensed uneasily that freedom, as he used the word, excluded all those other things. But if she did not speak out now she might risk losing everything, just for the lack of a little boldness. 'Take me with thee!'

He smiled at her, tenderly, but with a little distance in the smile. 'Thou knows that cannot be. Thou art too young yet, and so am I. I shall come back for thee one day, I promise thee.' There was an unmistakable note of finality in his voice.

She stared at him, stricken, unable to speak. He stood up and took her hands and pulled her to stand beside him, and then he put his arms about her, stroking her hair, her body, everywhere, with consoling caresses. 'Come now, Hannah my lass, thou hast courage. Thou art strong. There will be no woman to match thee, even in London. I shall have to come back for thee. Time will pass fast enough.'

She pressed her face to his shoulder and wept, and he tilted her head back so that he could kiss her. All the careful restraint of the past year was cast aside. He kissed her fiercely, urgently, with all the passion he had for so long kept at bay, and she found herself forgetting her misery in responding to that kiss.

But he was still very far from allowing his feelings, or hers, to take control. After a time he gently put her from him. He said quietly, 'Dry thy tears, Hannah. We've some days yet. I shall go the moment the hay's in, but I shall stay until then. Let's make the most of it.'

She obeyed him, because what he wanted must always come first with her. But later, awake in the night, she stared in anguish at the stars and thought, 'How can I ever live without him?'

CHAPTER FIVE

Meeting was nearly over, but – as usual – no one had
been moved to speak. From outside the clear windows
of the meeting house came the soft rushing of the
wind in the trees, the singing of the beck, the more
distant sounds of sheep bleating on the fell, a dog
barking. Inside, the simple bare room was still, the
silence disturbed only by the slow ticking of the clock;
the faint rhythmic sounds of breathing, enlivened by
an occasional sigh or even, now and then, a snore;
the shuffle of feet on the boarded floor; the swish of
woollen cloth against the wood of a bench, as someone
shifted his position; the dry, persistent, irritating noise
of Martha Storey's cough. Samuel, who had closed his
eyes in an attempt to shut out intruding thoughts,
admitted defeat and opened them again. They came
to rest, inevitably, on Hannah.

It struck him again, as it had when he first came home
some weeks ago, how thin she was, and how deeply
her eyes were shadowed. Where now was the lovely
carefree seventeen-year-old from whom Robert had
parted two years before? The familiar anger against
his brother flared up in him. How could he, who had
the inestimable, miraculous good fortune to be loved
by Hannah, value that gift so little that he could not
even keep his promise to write to her? One single
letter had she received since he went away, and that
one short and uninformative and sent only a few weeks
after he left home. Samuel, returning for the Christmas
holidays after Robert's going, had seen how the brightness had left her. The next time he came home he
knew hope had gone too. She had become tense and

even irritable, always busy, not because it was what was needed (though it generally was, of course), but because it helped to stop her thinking. He saw that, from the way she rushed into everything with a fierce and restless energy.

How long would it take, he wondered, before she would begin to accept that Robert would not be coming back to Hollinthwaite at all? She would have to accept it one day, if she was ever to be happy again. Was there any remote possibility that she would come then to love Samuel instead, now that he had returned home for good and was available for her to see and talk to whenever she chose? On the whole he thought that was too much even to dream of in his more fanciful moments.

Meeting must be at an end, for Hannah was rising to her feet, and so were others round him. Men replaced their hats, everyone shook hands, and then there was a gentle murmur of talk as the small gathering made its way to the door. By not attending, Samuel had missed his opportunity. His way barred by two substantial farmers, he glimpsed Hannah ahead of him, stepping out into the sudden summer shower that had swept down on them from the fells. She would hurry home as quickly as she could, and he would be unlikely to catch up with her now.

By the time he emerged from the meeting house, Hannah had indeed gone, and Agnes and John too. So had his father and Mary Harker. They left him very largely to himself these days – not out of respect for his approaching adulthood, but rather (as he knew only too well) because they dismissed him as a dreamer living in a world of his own, and thus not worth wasting time on. He did his best to help with his father's business, since that was expected of him, but he knew he fell constantly short of what was required. Joseph Gayle was a grim figure these days, more dour than ever, a thoroughly disappointed man. With reason, his younger son had to admit.

The rain came down in great swathes across the dale, driven by a gusty wind that rocked the heavy summer foliage of the trees and sent shredded handfuls of leaves and twigs scattering across the fields and the road. Samuel clapped his hand to his hat to hold it in place, and ran as fast as he could up the lane, splashing in newly formed puddles, slithering in the mud. Round the corner, running with bent head, he collided with a tall cloaked figure, walking so slowly that she was scarcely moving at all.

'Oh, I beg thy ... Hannah!' He came alongside her, casting a sideways glance at her face. From her withdrawn expression, he wondered if she had even noticed the collision, though she did turn her eyes briefly towards him. She did not smile. 'Thou hadst best hurry,' he said. 'Thou art soaked already.'

She shrugged rather hopelessly. He saw then that her lower lip was trembling; she was very close to tears. On impulse, deeply troubled, he reached out and took her hand, clasping it warmly in both of his.

'Hannah, what is it? I cannot bear to see thee so sad.'

She halted, and simply stood looking at him, saying nothing. It was clear that if once she tried to speak she would lose all control.

'It's Robert, isn't it?'

She nodded, pressing her lips tightly together. Then she began, 'Not just ...' and stopped again, unable to continue.

'Thou hast not heard?' She shook her head. 'No more have we,' said Samuel. 'Not a word, since his twenty-first birthday.' They had thought he would come home then, if only to see to the arrangements for claiming his inheritance, but he had simply concluded them all by post, through a lawyer hired in London. Soon afterwards, they had heard he had left his uncle's house for an unknown destination. Whether or not there had been a quarrel they did not know, but it had been clear they had not parted on good terms.

'Uncle John's still heard nothing either,' said Samuel. He stroked her hand, his eyes never leaving her face; behind the rain-spotted spectacles they were full of concern. 'There was talk that maybe he'd gone abroad.' He did not want to console her with false hopes. Since he did not believe that Robert would ever choose to return, it would be better if she accepted it as soon as possible. But he wished there were some way of taking the pain from it all. He longed to hold her in his arms and kiss away the sadness from her face, but since he knew that would not help at all he did not do it.

Hannah's mouth moved silently. She was, Samuel thought, trying very hard to control herself sufficiently to speak. She did so at last, saying in a voice harsh with unshed tears, 'It's not just that – it's other . . . Samuel, I just don't belong . . . I don't know who I am . . . without Robert, I am nothing . . .' She gave up the struggle and broke off.

'Thou art our dear Hannah Burton,' he reassured her.

She shook her head. 'No, not Burton.' Her voice came now in a near-whisper. 'If I knew . . . But I don't . . .'

That old business, he thought sadly. He had supposed she had long ago ceased to think of it. Had it simply returned to trouble her, because she was so unhappy in other ways? Or was it that she had carried that burden with her ever since – blundering fool than he was! – he had first forced the truth upon her? He hated to think she might have borne so much unhappiness for so long. He felt helpless too, because he could not comfort her in this either. 'Hannah, thou knows they love thee, Agnes and John – more than thy own real mother ever could, or thy father, whoever they were. We all know thee as *their* child, no one else's. No one will ever know who thy mother really was.'

'*Someone* must know,' she whispered.

'If it was anyone near, we'd know by now. I tell thee,

it's my belief it was some passer-by, a gipsy maybe.' He was not sure if she would find that consoling, but it did indeed seem the likeliest explanation. He knew he was not alone in thinking that.

'Then ... If thou art right – I'll never know.' She looked stricken rather than comforted by the thought.

'That's what I said. Thou must learn not to think of it.' He felt they were going round in circles, achieving nothing. By now the rain was not simply dripping from the rim of his hat, but running down his nose and inside his collar and into his shoes. Hannah must be even more wet than he was. 'Best get home,' he said gently. 'Thou'lt catch thy death.'

She looked at him as if seeing him clearly for the first time, and the faintest glimmer of a smile touched her lips. 'So wilt thou.'

He supposed that if his appearance amused her he should be glad. It seemed a long time since he had seen her smile. 'Come then,' he said, and tugged at her hand. Together they ran over the sodden ground to Low Farm, where she left him. He watched until she had reached the gate of her own home, then he went in to the dim and gloomy kitchen.

John Burton met Hannah at the door of High Farm. 'Lass, where hast thou been? We thought thou hadst come on ahead. Look at thee – thou art wet through!' He took her cloak as she untied it. 'Get thee upstairs and out of those wet things, my lass. Then in by the fire and get a morsel of hot porridge inside thee. Hurry now!'

She smiled faintly at his anxious concern, and hurried upstairs as she had been told. She changed into dry clothes, her eyes on the drenched landscape beyond the window. It seemed only too well in tune with the dreary turmoil of her own feelings.

What she had said to Samuel was quite true, though she knew she had not put it well, because she did not know how. Robert had given her life a purpose. He had come to Hollinthwaite just as she had begun to feel restless, even a little bored, by the endless, unchanging routine of her days. And she, who had never felt wholly a part of this place since her childhood ended, had found that she did after all belong. As Robert's lass she had found the whole meaning of her existence; she had discovered herself. Then he had gone, and very soon she had realised she had been deceived. If he had loved her once, it had not survived his going. She remembered then that he had never in fact declared his love, in so many words.

The days had taken on a dreary sameness. She wandered through them like a sheep astray in a winter storm, not knowing where she was or where she was going, lost in a featureless waste. There was no one she could turn to for comfort, though she tried to tell Agnes and John and Samuel what she felt, but none of them really understood. How could they, when they only knew what it was to be rooted firmly in a place and a family, secure and safe, certain of who you were and where you belonged? However much they might try to understand, they would all believe she was making a drama out of nothing.

She went down to the fire and the hot porridge and the attentions of the two kindly people who seemed to have nothing at all in common with her. They might have been strangers, for all the closeness she felt to them now. In truth, they *were* strangers, to whom she was a changeling creature who had been thrust into their care in the oddest circumstances, whether they chose or no. She had thought sometimes that she might be the bastard of some fine lady, born and disposed of in secret so as not to sully the family name. Such a child might well have instincts at variance with the quiet and modest life of Agnes and John Burton. Or if Samuel was right and her mother had been some passing gipsy woman (and that seemed only too likely), then no wonder she was so ill at ease. Gipsies liked to dance and sing; they loved and hated with equal passion, they could not bear to be tied or penned in – they had to live free, or die. Her gipsy blood (if such it was) would never be content within the walls of High Farm, unless she were to have Robert's love as its focus. But she knew now that was impossible.

The rain was not a shower after all. It lashed the dale all afternoon and for most of the next day. By the following morning, when it ceased, the beck had become a roaring torrent.

'Just when I've to ride to Thornside,' John Burton grumbled mildly, when he came downstairs. 'It'll be hard going.' He had planned to take their last two months' knitting – six dozen pairs of stockings – to market there.

'Leave it this week,' suggested Agnes. 'The stockings will take no harm.'

'Best not,' said John. 'That barn wants mending before it rains again. Dick Alderson said he'd do it next week. But we've the stone to get and he'll want paying.' So, he implied, they must sell the stockings to pay for the repair.

'I'll go to Thornside for thee,' Hannah broke in. She had a sudden longing to get away – anywhere, for however short a time, even to Thornside with its poignant memories.

John shook his head. 'Not alone, lass. But I'll be glad of thy company, if thou wilt ride with me.'

So she rode pillion behind him on the laden pony. They had to take a long way round, because the river ran too deep and fast for them to risk crossing by the ford; the nearest bridge was some miles away to the west. Everywhere, the road was strewn with the debris of the storm, and in the steeper parts the whole surface had been washed away.

Just beyond the ridge on the dale's southern edge the land sloped into a little valley, deepened by lead mining, where the road crossed a small beck. Today, even before they came within sight of it, they heard the water roaring. Reaching it, they found that the harmless little stream had become a fiercely flowing river.

John drew rein at the water's edge and looked at it doubtfully. 'We'd best find another way,' he said.

Hannah slid down from the saddle, pulled off her clogs, hitched up her skirts and took a cautious step into the water. Even at the edge, where it overflowed the bank, it was well over her ankles, and she felt its power. She nodded. 'It would be safer, I think.'

They rode downstream, looking for a better place to cross. At one point, where the valley widened, the water seemed to flow more slowly, and it was clearly shallower. 'We'll give it a try,' said John. He patted the pony's neck. 'Thou art a good, sure-footed beast, art thou not, lad?'

The animal made steady progress to the centre of the beck. What happened next Hannah did not know, then or afterwards. Perhaps the water was much deeper there than they had thought, perhaps the force of the water was too strong for the pony; perhaps he simply slipped on a slimy rock and lost his footing. Whatever it was, with a sudden whinny of terror he fell and was swept sideways downstream with the fierce current of the water.

'Hannah!' John cried.

She clung to him, but the water dragged them apart, drenched her clothes to a great leaden weight, closed cold and fierce about her. Rocks battered her, bruised her. She could not breathe. 'It is not happening, it is not real!' said her brain.

Then all at once she realised she had come to a halt. Some obstacle — a rock probably — had caught her, holding her momentarily still. By some miracle her head was free of the water. It just gave her time to drag herself to a shallower place and then to the bank, where she lay bruised and exhausted, face down on the wet grass, too stunned to think.

She began to shiver. Then she thought, 'Father!' She forced herself to her feet and stared up and down the bank, and the stream that was no longer a stream. There was nothing – nothing but wet grass and rocks and wildly rushing water. Then something caught her eye downstream, something black, struggling and heaving . . . the pony! She ran.

She knew he was past help. He did not, of course. His eyes on her, he tried again and again to rise out of the icy imprisoning water. But she could see from the angle of his legs that they were broken, and he was too heavy for her to move. Sobbing, she knelt down and held his head and made meaningless little noises, scarcely audible above the roar of the water, while her eyes scoured its cold surface for any sign of life – human life. She knew she had no choice but to leave the pony to his fate. 'I'm sorry,' she wept, and slowly stood up.

A sound caught her ear – a shout, she was sure it was a shout. It came from where the valley curved to the left, the beck with it, and disappeared from view. Relief swept her. 'Father!' she called, and ran as fast as she could – though she stumbled often – to where the sound came from. A few yards more, and she could see.

Three men – lead miners, from their rough appearance – stood in an agitated group at the water's edge, dragging something to the bank. Hannah came to a halt, panting, exhausted. Every last ounce of strength poured from her, leaving only just what was needed to keep her on her feet. Her eyes took in the little scene, without really registering it, or not at first. It was a man they had taken from the flood, a big sturdy man, balding, with grey hair and a coat of undyed cloth. He lay as still and lifeless as the rocks that littered the bank.

Her lips formed a word, as if the meaning had

reached them before it reached her brain. 'Father . . .' she whispered. She took a step forward, then another, unsteady, tottering.

One of the men saw her and came running and put an arm about her. He was dirty and stank of stale sweat and other things, but his arm was strong and with his help she reached that motionless figure. There he let her go and she fell on her knees and touched the wet, still face. It was cold, very cold, the features a little distorted. 'Father!' she cried to it in a despairing whisper.

She felt a hand on her shoulder. The man had dropped to the ground too, and put his coat about her. 'He's gone, lass,' he said. His voice was extraordinarily gentle for one so rough looking. 'It's my belief his heart gave out. He don't look drowned. He won't have felt much.' The hand patted her, a little clumsily. 'He's safe with the Lord, lass. Safe with the Lord.' He said it as if it were a refrain, to be sung in a harmonious repetition. It sounded soothing, but did not reach beyond the numb surface of her mind.

'Best get them home,' said one of the other men. 'Where art thou from, lass?'

For a moment she could not answer that. There seemed to be only a terrifying blankness in her head. Then she remembered, though it was just a word seized out of nowhere. 'Hollinthwaite,' she whispered.

'Right then. I'll get a beast for to carry thee – and one for thy father.'

Through her numbness, her sense of being caught up in an appalling nightmare, she knew they were extraordinarily kind to her, these three rough men. Lead miners had a reputation for wildness, and they looked wild enough. But they lifted John Burton's heavy body with great tenderness and laid it in as seemly a manner as they could over one of their ponies, covering it with a rough blanket they brought from somewhere. Then they lifted her onto the second pony and all three went with her upstream to the road. 'We'll see thee safe home,' they assured her.

They passed her own poor pony, his struggles almost at an end. One of them went to look, and did something she could not see and came back, saying, 'He'll suffer no more.' She sobbed again then. What was wrong with her, she wondered, that she could weep for the pony, but felt nothing at all, only a chilling numbness, when she looked at John Burton's shrouded body?

The men talked as they went, quietly and gravely, with obvious regard for her feelings. They told her they were followers of the Reverend John Wesley – 'the people they call Methodists'. They had heard him preach nearly ten years ago, and it had changed their lives. 'He's the first preacher ever had a thought for the likes of us,' one of them said. 'The dregs of the earth, that's what we are, to most religious folks.' He must have looked Hannah over and drawn his own conclusions from her appearance, for he said next, 'Thou art a Quaker, lass?'

'Aye,' she said, automatically. The talk seemed to flow round her, meaningless, yet soothing too. At least it prevented her from thinking about anything else – if she had been able to do so; and she was by no means sure of that.

'Big in lead, your people. The London Lead Company has a good few of the mines round here. Not where we work, though. Good to their workers, they say. The company's Quaker-run.'

'Oh.' She wished the journey was at an end, though not because there was anything to look forward to on reaching home. She gave no thought to what awaited her there. She was conscious only of being horribly cold and bruised, and of aching so much that every movement of the pony seemed to send pains shooting right through her; and of wanting to sink unhindered into some kind of oblivion.

Once in the village, there were incessant questions

from neighbours. She was thankful that her companions did all the talking, so she need say nothing.

At Low Farm, Mary Harker called out something from the farmyard, and one of the men went to tell her what had happened. The other two led the ponies on ahead, over the beck, up to High Farm, left little more than an hour ago. It felt to Hannah as if she had been away for years; in fact even now it did not feel like coming home. It was all too unreal for that.

In the farmyard she was fleetingly conscious of Agnes coming smiling to the door. 'What's this then —?'

After that there was a confused moment. Agnes ran. There was an exchange of words, and then a horrible silence. And then a cry of such unendurable anguish that Hannah thought it would be seared on her memory until the day she died.

Agnes's sobs went with her, as hands helped her to dismount and steered her up the stairs to her room. There she was undressed and put to bed and given something to drink that took the pain from her bruises and made her drowsy, but did not bring her the longed-for unconsciousness.

She lay there through the dragging hours of that slow dreary day. She was aware of much coming and going downstairs, of low voices and weeping. The neighbours would be there, of course, offering all the help and comfort they could, both practical and emotional. Twice, Agnes looked in on her. Hannah closed her eyes and pretended to be asleep, though she saw enough to know that Agnes never ceased to weep. She knew what the older woman wanted. She wanted to take Hannah into her arms so they could weep together for their loss, and perhaps find some comfort that way. But Hannah had no tears to shed for John Burton, and no comfort to offer. What right had she to weep after all, who was no daughter of his? Must Agnes not feel she had nothing now, when there was no one left to her of his flesh and blood? She knew she ought not to feel like this; she knew Agnes would not. But she could not help it. Perhaps it was a part of her gipsy heritage, not to share the normal human affections which bound people together at times like this, and helped them to learn to live again. The worst of it was that though she could give no comfort, she ached to receive it – only she did not know how that could be done.

CHAPTER SIX

It was a bleak winter that year for the two women left to manage alone. They had help from their neighbours, of course, whenever possible, but that could not compensate for the loss of John Burton's strong arms and kindly presence about the place.

Hannah, forcing herself to a quick recovery – she shed few tears, unlike Agnes, who cried often for months afterwards – found herself taking charge. She arranged for Joseph Gayle to buy the stockings they knitted. They might make a little less profit that way, but there would be no more trips to Thornside market because a bill must be paid. She took him the fleeces she had left from the clipping and asked him to find spinners to prepare the yarn for her, so that she would have more time for the work that had to be done. When Agnes, in her moments of deepest unhappiness, seemed ready to give up, it was Hannah who decided what was to be done next, and did it, who cooked the meals and made her eat, who planned ahead for the two of them.

But she did not talk to Agnes more than necessity demanded. When the widow began to speak about John – as she often tried to do at first – Hannah would change the subject or leave the room. They were not companions but strangers, living under one roof. Once she heard someone say to Agnes, 'It must be such a comfort to thee, to have Hannah about the place.' Agnes had made some safe and non-committal reply; Hannah had felt herself pierced by guilt. She knew she was doing wrong. It was only that she could not do otherwise. Something seemed to have dammed up all her capacity to feel, something with roots that went far back beyond the horrible day of John Burton's death.

She could not even bear Samuel's gentle and sympathetic presence. After one or two sharp rebuffs, he gave up and left her alone. He was not in any case a man who believed easily that he could be of much use to anyone, however much he loved them.

The next spring, just before lambing, they woke one morning to a heavy dove-grey sky, touched with a hint of rose, from which already a few thin flakes of snow were falling. It had been freezing for several days before and the ground was like iron, and dry. Today there was just a little increase in warmth, and the wind was beginning to rise.

'We're in for a storm,' Agnes said, in the expressionless tone she used when speaking to Hannah. She had learned from miserable experience that emotion only repelled the girl.

'I'll bring the sheep down before it gets going,' Hannah said, practical as ever. It was what John Burton had always done, when a storm threatened at this time of year.

She put on her cloak and took John Burton's stick and called the dog – he was beginning at last to accept that his master had gone for good, and that it was Hannah he must serve now. Together they set out, bent against an increasing wind and ever faster snow, up the slope to the fell.

It did not take more than an hour to reach the heugh and gather the sheep. They huddled together, shivering and bleating, watched by the dog, while Hannah counted them. She counted once, twice, three times. There could be no doubt: six were missing, a black one among them.

The snow was swirling now, harsh and stinging on her face and her fingers, where the mittens ended. She could see no more than a few yards ahead. Already the ground was white, only the most prominent tussocks still showing brown and dun.

She looked about, told the dog to stay where he was, walked from side to side of the heugh, and to the highest point above it. The wind dragged at her clothes, bitterly cold. There was not the slightest trace of the sheep, only white on white wherever she looked.

The dog might well find them, but if she set out with him the rest of the sheep were in danger of scattering in the storm, and any lambs coming early might well be lost. She would have to get them safely into the fold by the farm before she looked for the others. She retraced her steps, calling to the dog to drive the sheep ahead.

It seemed to take hours, though she supposed it was not really so long. But in a landscape made feature-less by the snow, where all the familiar landmarks were obliterated, there was only instinct to guide them, until they reached the barn and the wall of the cow close. Even then, they might almost have been any-where. Hannah was glad of the dog's intuitive sense of direction.

When the sheep had been safely penned in and fed with hay, Hannah looked into the kitchen to warm herself briefly by the fire. 'I'm going back up,' she said. 'There are six missing.'

Agnes protested, but – faced with the cold stubborn-ness of Hannah's expression – soon gave up. Hannah put on a warmer pair of gloves, pulled her hood over her head, called the dog again and set out once more on to the fell, the stick in her hand.

She knew before she reached the top that she had been foolish to come. The snow was thick underfoot now, and in this wind was drifting fast. She had seen little before; now she saw nothing, only that impene-trable, terrifying whiteness, where land and sky merged into a formless swirling of snow. The dog plodded courageously on bedside her, miserable but resigned. Every step took a tremendous effort of will and energy.

She had come, so she would not turn round. Besides, they must not lose the sheep, if it could be helped.

They passed the barn – recognised only because its stone wall loomed up just two inches from Hannah's nose – and were out on the open fell, where even in clear weather the landmarks were few, and those largely close to the drove road, which was marked at intervals by pyramids of stones. Hannah scanned the ground as she went, not only because a familiar rock might show her she was on the right path, but also because she could make no progress at all with her head raised, so great was the force of wind and snow.

She thought at last that they had reached the heugh – no, she was as sure of it as she could be. There was the rock that had been Samuel's favourite vantage point. A drift concealed it, distorting its shape, but it was there somewhere, she was sure. Or was it?

She called as she went, the call the sheep knew: 'How, how!' But the wind instantly whipped the sound away, and she knew she would not hear even if a sheep were to bleat suddenly beside her. The only hope was that they would stumble on the animals by chance, or that the dog would sense their presence beneath a drift, as a good sheepdog could.

She did not know how far she walked. She had long ago lost all sense of time. To walk in the heart of the blizzard was to be without boundaries of any kind, of space or of time, without guidelines. She even ceased to think, of why she was there, of the sheep, of anything. She was walking mechanically, one foot then the other, on and on. When, as sometimes happened, she found herself in deep snow, she would retrace her steps and take another way, avoiding the drift.

She did not feel particularly cold, though she had done at first. After a time she even began to feel pleasantly warm – from the exertion, she supposed. Certainly she felt tired, with a drowsy tiredness which, she knew, would very soon force her to cease walking.

Her pace grew slower and slower. One step, two, three . . . The snow was growing deeper the further she went. It would soon be to her waist. Another drift. But it was soft and yielding. If she lay down now, it would close around her, warm, safe, holding her in sleep. She fell forward, face down, and was vaguely surprised to find she did not feel cold at all.

The dog barked sharply just beside her. She felt his nose pushing urgently at her shoulder and her cheek. She wanted him to stop, to let her sleep. He persisted, obstinate, agitated in his barking, nuzzling at her.

From somewhere – she did not know where, for she had been conscious only of drowsiness like a soft wool filling her brain, wool soft as the snow about her – a thought burrowed into her mind. Talk heard often enough, among farmers in winter time: 'If thou art lost in snow, keep on, find shelter. When thou art warm, that's the time to watch out.'

I must get up, she thought then: If I stay here I shall die. She was not sure why that should force her into action. The thought of dying here as she was now, feeling so comfortable, so drowsy, was pleasant enough. Yet some will not to give in must have reasserted itself. With a tremendous effort, a painful effort, she forced herself to her feet.

It was quite senseless anyway, in this waste of snow, to think she would be more likely to survive on her feet. The dog barked encouragingly and went with her as, with weary stumbling slowness, she trudged her way out of the drift, back, round, on and on. Sometimes he ran a little way ahead, so that she thought she had lost him. Then he would come back and bark, waiting for her, his eyes alert on her face. As soon as she reached him, he would run on again. After a time she realised, dimly, that he was leading the way, though to what she had no idea. Probably he had not either. She supposed it would do no harm to follow him. On and on and on in the endless whiteness . . .

Something had changed. There was no longer simply a blur of white, enclosing her. Before her, just a little way ahead, she could see something dark, something grey, a background for the swirling snow. It was a strange sensation, suddenly to be faced with a barrier, to realise that the world had not all turned to limitless snow.

Another step, and she could put out a hand and touch it. It was hard, unyielding. She could support herself on it. A building, her slow brain told her at last. She groped her way step by step along it. The dog ran backwards and forwards beside her, watchful and excited.

The wall disappeared. She reached out into emptiness. Then she realised she had come to a corner. She tried to move on, but a great wall of snow barred her path: another drift. She stood staring at it, hands on the wall, and thought, I can't go round it.

She looked about for the dog, but he was nowhere to be seen. She thought she heard him bark somewhere far off, but she could not be sure. It was silly, so near (she supposed) to shelter, but she knew she had reached the end. She could do no more. She knew that in a moment she would fall again, and this time she would not get up.

She was not very clear about what happened next. Everything was blotted out completely for a little while. Then she was confusedly aware of the dog barking again, and of voices this time, ordinary human voices, near at hand. She thought, I'm at home – he's brought me home! She felt herself being lifted, awkwardly, and carried some distance. There were odd noises which she was too weary to identify. She had no intention, either, of opening her eyes. She did know that the light went, a door closed, and with an extraordinary suddenness the roar and chaos of wind and snow were shut out. There was another interval of blankness then, before she became aware of anything again.

This time her sensations were clearer and much less pleasant. Pain first, the horrible ache of feeling returning to chilled limbs. She was shivering violently too, though she had been well wrapped in something thick and dry. Under the wrapping, she lay on a hard surface, of wood she thought. She heard no voices, only the crackling of a fire and what might have been the dog panting. Someone was rubbing her hands.

She opened her eyes.

After the constant whiteness it seemed very dark. In fact there was not much light in the room. There was the fire in a vast hearth, near which she lay on what seemed to be a settle, and a small window far off across a wide expanse of not very clean flagged floor, on which stood a large table, benches, many stools. In spite of the fire there was a general smell of damp and dirt, some of it coming from the woman who was kneeling beside Hannah and rubbing her hands.

Hannah studied the anxious face, or what she could see of it in the firelight. Not a young woman, she decided, but not particularly old either. She saw a weak chin and prominent teeth and a thin nose, and wispy brown hair beneath a dirty cap. She thought she might have seen the face before somewhere, but it was not the kind of face one would remember in any detail, if one had simply seen it in passing. On the other hand she knew everyone within miles of Hollinthwaite, or so she had thought. Could she have strayed so far from home?

With an effort, she found the words and forced them out. 'Where am I?'

The woman continued to hold her hands, though she ceased her rubbing. Hannah had the impression she was oddly agitated about something. Perhaps she was moved at having rescued someone from the storm.

'Drovers' Inn, Hollinthwaite moor.' Her voice sounded a little tremulous too.

Not so far then, thought Hannah; and no wonder

she did not know the face. She had probably seen the woman in passing, but the inn was a lonely and unprepossessing place, and she had never had cause to halt there. Though today she could only be heartily thankful that the dog had brought her to it. She was trying to frame suitable words to express her gratitude, when the woman spoke again.

'Thou art Hannah Burton, art thou not?'

She was surprised, and then remembered how near home she was, and ceased to be surprised. But before she could reply, a door banged shut somewhere – it sent a gust of cold air sweeping across the room – and a man came into view. He was broad and quite tall, and looked a little unsteady on his feet. He must, Hannah supposed, be the man who had carried her in from the snow; the woman did not look large enough or strong enough to have done so.

'She come to then?' The man asked. He did not sound particularly concerned. He came nearer. 'Aye. I see she has.' He stood looking down at Hannah, in no very friendly manner. He was, she saw, rather older than she had thought at first, very much older than the woman.

'Canst take a little broth?' the woman asked, in a gentle and tentative tone which contrasted strikingly with that of the man.

'Aye. I thank thee,' said Hannah. At the same moment the man said,

'Canst pay for it?'

'Father!' the woman protested with faint indignation. As well she might, Hannah thought. She was shocked herself by this evidence of ruthless commercialism, but she simply said, 'I'll see thou art paid everything thou art owed, when I get home.'

Clearly struck by the way she spoke (after all, strange young women did not usually speak in so familiar a manner to older men), the man looked at her. 'Hm. A Quaker, if I'm not mistaken. I suppose that means I can trust thee.' He turned to his daughter. 'Thou hadst best get a room ready. The way it's going out there she'll be here for the night.' When the woman hesitated, glancing towards the pot of broth hanging over the fire, he said brusquely, 'Go on – thou heard me! Get on with it!' He raised a hand to her, and the woman flinched and then scuttled from the room. Hannah, who had never in her life had a hand raised against her, felt another sense of shock. She watched rather apprehensively as the man went to the fire and ladled broth into a bowl and brought it to her. He stood by in silence while she ate.

Afterwards, she felt much better. The pain in her limbs was subsiding, and she shivered only a little, now and then. But she felt weary beyond words and she was glad when the woman came back to show her to her room. It took all the reserves of strength left to her, and the support of the woman's arm about her, to get her up the stairs and into the curtained bed, between sheets that were none too clean but had been well warmed. She fell asleep almost at once.

She was disturbed much later by sounds from some-where downstairs. A scream first, shouts, crashing and banging, feet running and running, more screams. She lay rigid, unable to remember precisely where she was or why, appalled by those dreadful noises in the dark – for it was dark, with the not-quite-complete darkness of a snowy night.

Then she remembered. She sat up. What terrible thing could be happening? She thought of the man with his hand raised to his frightened daughter. Was that it? What was he doing to her?

There was a scratching noise on the floor and some-thing loomed up at the edge of the bed, something she sensed rather than saw. Her flesh crawled; until she remembered the dog. She reached out and felt the wet nose on her hand. She was so thankful for his familiar companionship that she put her arms about him and buried her face in his wiry coat. 'Oh, Fly,' what must I do?'

The noises continued, the screams worse than ever. If some terrible crime was being committed and she had not even tried to prevent it, how would she feel in the morning?

She slid out of bed, pulling a blanket about her, since she had no idea where her clothes were (she seemed to be wearing a nightgown of some kind, rather too short for her). 'Stay, Fly!' she commanded. Then she crept on to the landing.

It was intensely dark there, though a gleam of light from below showed her where the stairs were. She groped her way towards them. The noise grew louder. It was clear it came from down there, from the kitchen perhaps. She felt her way with her bare feet, step by step, very carefully and slowly.

Below was a large room – the inn parlour – lit by a lamp and a fire that was almost out. As she descended further she saw that a door led from it into what she supposed was the kitchen; and the noise was indeed coming from there.

Then, just as she reached the foot of the stairs, there was a final crashing sound, and then silence.

She halted, listening. Only a clock ticking, and the rattle of the snow on the windows. What had happened? Should she just go back to bed, and hope that was the end of it? She would very much have preferred to do so. She was cold and frightened, but some more courageous impulse told her that first she must make sure that all was well.

She crossed the room and pushed open the door.

The kitchen was a scene of chaos. Chairs and stools were overturned, and one of the benches by the long table; plates lay shattered on the floor; objects of all kinds – clogs, pots, half a loaf of bread, a lantern, a poker – lay in the most unlikely places. On the settle the man lay slumped, head back, mouth open; he was snoring loudly. His daughter was making a reluctant attempt to tidy up, righting a chair here, retrieving a knife there. She straightened as Hannah stepped into the room, stared, and then coloured. 'Oh! Thou shouldst not be here! Thou wilt catch cold. Go back to bed!' She came to Hannah, ready to turn her to go back the way she had come.

'I heard shouting,' Hannah said. 'I thought something was wrong.' She glanced at the man. 'Is he —?'

'Drunk,' said the woman. 'Dead drunk. He'll be like that until morning. Then he'll come to with a bad head and a worse temper.'

Hannah transferred her gaze from the father to the daughter, and saw that there was a swollen bruise on the woman's cheek, and an ugly gash over one eye. Her gown was torn too, as if rough hands had caught at her. 'Thou art hurt!' Hannah cried compassionately. 'Oh, I wish I had come sooner!'

The woman gave a grim little smile. Her grey eyes had a bleak look in them. 'Then thou wouldst have got it too. No sense in that. I'm used to it.'

Hannah's eyes widened. 'Is he often like that?'

'Often enough. Monday nights, always, when he's been to Middleham market. The snow stopped him today, so he got drunk here instead.' She laid a hand on Hannah's shoulder. 'Get back to bed,' she said with great gentleness, as if she was deeply sorry that Hannah should have had to learn that such scenes as this ever took place. 'Go and have thy sleep out.'

'I'm well rested, I thank thee,' said Hannah, and indeed she did feel quite well, fully herself again. 'Thou shouldst put something on that cut. What hast thou got?'

'Water,' said the woman, then went on bitterly, 'brandy, ale, wine, whisky, gin: take thy pick.' Again the soft note returned to her voice. 'No, Hannah Burton, thou art kind to think of it, but take thyself back to bed. Or hast thou need of something? Art thou hungry?'

Hannah realised she was certainly hungry, but she had no wish to have this poor battered woman waiting on her, as would certainly happen if she were to admit to her hunger. On the other hand, she could not bear the thought of leaving her alone like this. What must it be like to live with a man who got drunk and beat you? She knew such things happened, but she had not come so close to them before. It was worlds away from the quiet orderly life at High Farm, the gentle kindliness and courtesy of Agnes – and John. Abruptly, she found that tears were starting to her eyes at the thought of him. All these months, and she had not wept . . .

She gulped and forced herself to concentrate on the woman.

'Let me help thee. I am not tired.' She bent to pick up a few pieces of a broken plate, white patterned with blue, from the floor near her.

The woman came and grasped her hands. 'No, no – thou must not! Please!'

Hannah stared at her, startled by the urgent pleading of her tone. As if sensing the girl's surprise, the woman said quickly, 'Sit down, here.' She dusted a chair with her sleeve and gestured towards it. 'What wouldst thou like? Tea? I think there's some fresh bread left.'

Hannah had rarely tasted either bread or tea, but she accepted them, and tried to tell herself that the woman wanted to wait on her and she must not mind. She supposed there were so few guests in this lonely place that she welcomed anyone. It was hardly surprising, if her only constant companion was the brutal man whose vibrant snores formed a continual accompaniment to their talk.

Hannah ate hungrily and sipped at the tea, while the woman wandered restlessly about the room, in the manner of one seeking occupation, any occupation, though she did now and then stoop to pick something up. Once, with her back to Hannah, she said casually, 'John Burton died lately, I heard.'

The remark caught Hannah off guard; the tears of a moment ago had not receded very far. She could trust herself only to murmur something incoherent.

'He was a good man,' said the woman next.

Hannah stared at her. 'Thou knew him then?'

Though she could not see her face clearly, she saw that the woman had coloured. Evidently she had known him in some way that caused her strong emotion, or so it appeared. Yet what could John Burton have had to do with this unattractive and slatternly woman?

'Not rightly,' the woman admitted, just a little to Hannah's relief. She sat down suddenly, facing Hannah across the table. 'He did me a kindness once. I reckon he wouldn't have remembered, but I do. At Richmond it was – oh, twenty year or more ago now. I had money stolen. I didn't know what to do for the best; I was that upset. John Burton came by just then. He gave me every penny he had on him – stayed and talked a bit too. I knew him by sight, and by what folks said of him. They were right, he was a good man, and kind. He said he did not want the money back. Maybe he knew my father would have thrashed me for losing it. Anyway, I've cause to think kindly of him.'

Hannah was moved by the little story. She thought the woman was right, and John Burton would have forgotten all about the incident. There had been many acts of kindness in his life; she had taken them very much for granted until now, looking back and remembering. Such a small thing, yet this woman's face was soft with gratitude years afterwards, because of it. It showed, Hannah supposed, how little kindness there had been in her life, for her to recall that incident so clearly.

'Thou wilt miss him,' said the woman then. 'He was thy father.'

'Aye,' said Hannah. There seemed something a little odd about the remark, but she could not think what it was.

The woman poured herself some tea and sipped at it, still in that nervous manner. Then she sat back with her eyes on Hannah's face, looking at her in a way that made the girl feel uncomfortable. She did not quite know where to look to avoid that gaze. She tried smiling, but won only a faint response, so she began to look about the room, this way and that, staring into dark corners, not seeing very much (there was only one candle alight).

'Thou art beautiful.'

The words were soft, full of wonder. Hannah turned startled eyes back to the woman's face. Her expression now had a disquieting intensity. She had spoken as if the words had sprung to her lips, not by any deliberate choice, but as an impulsive expression of a momentary emotion. Hannah felt at once both touched and embarrassed; particularly embarrassed. What did one say to such a remark, coming from a near stranger in such unlikely circumstances? It was hard to believe that her appearance at this moment, after all she had been through, was really so exceptional as to deserve such a spontaneous cry of admiration. She tried to think of some suitable reply – 'I thank thee,' for example – but could think of nothing that quite seemed to fit.

The woman did not seem to notice Hannah's silence. She took a gulp of tea and then gazed down into her cup and asked with a studied casualness that was not casual at all, 'Didst thou have a happy childhood, Hannah Burton?'

'Aye – aye, of course.' Hannah had not meant to sound chilly, for this woman merited her compassion, but her odd manner, the remarks and questions that were disconcertingly personal for so casual an acquaintance, made her feel uncomfortable. She wondered if the violent unhappiness of her life here had unhinged her mind in some way. She knew that the tone of her own reply was positively frosty, repelling further closeness.

109

Unfortunately, its effect seemed to be quite lost on her companion, who did not even look at her, but went on, 'Hast thou minded, being raised a Quaker? Were they strict with thee – thy parents, I mean?'

'I – I never thought about it,' Hannah stammered. She thought: I must say something, to stop her talking like this. She began to regret her impulse to stay downstairs. She ate quickly, so that she could finish the bread and tea and plead weariness to justify her escape.

The woman continued to stare gloomily into her cup, although fortunately she said nothing more. Hannah was on the point of thanking her and taking her leave, when her companion swore suddenly and stood up, pushing back her stool with a sharp sound. 'I need something stronger.' She went to a shelf and took down a bottle. 'Wilt thou have some? It's brandy – real French stuff.'

Hannah shook her head and rose to her feet. 'No, I thank thee. I am tired. I think I should like to go back to my bed.'

The woman stood looking at her rather blankly for a moment, almost as if she did not understand what was being said to her. Then, abruptly, she took a glass from somewhere, poured a measure of brandy and drank it in one gulp. After that, with deliberate care, she put the bottle down and the glass, and walked back to the table. She moved cups around in an absent sort of way. Hannah saw that her hands were trembling. 'Stay a while,' she said.

What *did* she want? Hannah wondered. She knew what she wanted herself. She was not tired, but she was very uneasy, and longed to be once more in the relative safety of the cold, dark room upstairs. Yet she had been taught that she must always have compassion for anyone in trouble, and that this woman was in trouble was clear. There had been a plea for help in her voice just then.

As she hesitated, she heard the woman say, 'Hast

thou ever wondered ... about thy mother?' It was said as a child might speak, putting forward some inducement in the not-very-strong hope that it might persuade an adult to do as he wished.

Hannah did not immediately take in what was said, still less the possibilities that the words implied. Never in her life had anyone put such a question to her. Until now all the questions had come from her, and others had tried only to prevent her from asking them. She said, 'Sometimes . . .' and then she fell silent.

Was it possible that this woman was asking, not as a way of keeping her here, nor yet because she was not quite right in the head, but for a purpose? Was it even possible that she knew something, more indeed than the very little that was all Hannah had ever been told? Hannah felt she could scarcely breathe; the whole dark and shabby room seemed to be holding its breath with her. She was afraid, very afraid, yet desperate to know, only she could not find words to draw out an answer. She groped for her chair and sat down again. She saw that her own hands were trembling too.

Suddenly the woman went to the fire and poked it, sending a shower of sparks erupting into the wide chimney space. 'I'll tell thee something, Hannah Burton,' she said. Her voice sounded a little muffled, but Hannah was listening so carefully that she thought she would have heard her from the head of the stairs.

'There was a lass once,' the woman went on. 'A lass called Christian.' A derisive note crept into her voice. 'A fine name that, God help us. Christian she was not. Nor were the folks she lived with.' She stood up and came slowly back to the table. 'Hast thou ever heard of a lass called Christian?'

Quite unable to speak, all her attention on her companion, Hannah shook her head. It was not quite true; it was not an unknown name, but no one she knew bore it.

'I knew her,' the woman continued. 'She wasn't all

bad. She'd not been taught right, of course, but she knew some things all the same. Only – well, there was no one who loved her much. She was lonely sometimes. One day a man came by – there's always a man, isn't there? He dazzled her. She thought he was an angel, with heaven in his hands. It felt like it, just that once. Thou canst guess the end. He went away, and she found he'd left her something to remember him by.' There was a little pause, and then the woman sat down, her hands clasped on the table before her, her eyes on Hannah's still, attentive face. She said, 'Thou hast been kindly reared. Thou hast been taught to tell right from wrong. Thou hast always been loved, hast thou not?'

Hannah nodded.

'Thou canst not know what it was like for that lass, when she knew what was coming to her. I hope to God thou never dost. If there's Hell waiting for us one day, it can't be worse than that. Thou must know, this Christian had no mother to care for her. Her mother died the day she was born. As for her father – well, all she'd ever had from him was blows.' She glanced at the drunken figure on the settle. 'Like him,' she said. 'Just like him. She knew he would kill her, if he ever found out.' There was a chill in her voice, as if she relived the lonely girl's fear, though it had not been hers. Or . . .? Hannah pressed her hand to her mouth, not daring to think, glad that the bitter little tale was still unfolding, to occupy her mind.

'She nearly went out of her mind, Hannah Burton. She lived in terror every moment of the day. She pulled her stays right tight, so she could scarcely breathe, so no one would see how her belly swelled. She prayed that something would stop it. She tried a few things too, wicked things I know, but she did not know what else to do. She daresn't tell anyone. She had no friends.

'Anyhow, nothing stopped it. It went on in the way these things do. She kept herself laced tight and wore loose clothes and kept out of her Dad's way as much as

112

she could. He wasn't the noticing kind, and he never guessed, thank God. It was winter too, so there weren't many folks about to notice her.

'Then her time came. It was early in the morning, there was no one about. She went out and found a barn – it was empty and falling down, so no one came there. It gave shelter enough. Two days she stayed there, and two nights. It was cold, bitter cold, and the pains seemed to go on for ever. When they ended, she had a little girl.' The voice, monotonous with misery, seemed to crack suddenly. There was a little silence, while the woman sat with bent head. Her hands on the table were pressed harshly together, tense with anguish. The next moment, a great sob was torn from her, and she looked straight at Hannah with tears running unchecked down her grimy face, and reached out one hand in a pathetic imploring gesture.

'It broke my heart, Hannah. But I had to do it, I had to! How could I raise thee here? I wouldn't raise a dog here. John Burton was kind. They said his wife was too. I knew they'd care for thee. Hannah, I did it for the best!'

'*I* did it . . .' Did she know she had given herself away, confirming for Hannah the realisation that bit by bit had been creeping through her like a cold seeping fog? The woman said no more now, but simply sat weeping and gazing at the slender young girl who faced her across the table. Her daughter.

'My mother.' A little voice hammered pitilessly in Hannah's brain. 'This is my mother.' The fog was all round her now, like the snow on the fell, but without its vigorous life. Cold, chilling, it shut her off from the shadowy room, the fire, the snoring man, the rattle of the storm outside, all her memories – from everything but that tear-stained face, distorted and strange in the candlelight.

She knew it was true. All the things she had imagined – the wild gipsy woman, free as the birds above the fells,

113

the mother who had passed on all she was to Hannah, her beauty, her rebellious spirit – they had dwindled now to this. And this was real: this pathetic, grimy, frightened woman, who looked nothing like Hannah, who might be old or young or middle-aged, but simply looked as if life had crushed all spirit out of her, this daughter of a drunken host of a squalid inn – *this* was the mother she had longed so desperately to know about, and to meet.

Horror swept over her. The room seemed to sway and turn about her. She wanted to run from it, up the stairs to the rough familiarity of the dog, out into the cleansing embrace of the snow and the peace it offered her. But she could not find any power in her limbs to move. She could only drop her head forward on her arms and sit there shivering and think, 'It is not real. It has not happened.' But she knew it had, and there was no escape.

'Hannah – Hannah my little girl, look at me! I did it for the best. Say thou dost forgive me!'

Hannah looked up, hoping perhaps to see something that might make her feel better about it all. She was weeping still, this woman who was her mother, while voice and eyes and that imploring hand were full of tenderness, even of love. A child of God, like Hannah herself, like John and Agnes, like Samuel and ... No one was outside God's love, she had always been taught; no one ought to be outside her love. She had always thought that an easy injunction to follow, for she loved without difficulty – and who ought one to love more effortlessly than one's own mother?

Yet she felt now only shrinking and repulsion. The very thought that she had come from this dirty, unhealthy body, that the things that made this woman what she was, the blood that came to her from her drunken brute of a father, that all these had played a part in making Hannah too – it was horrible, unendurable.

The woman came round the table and laid a hand on Hannah's shoulder. Her immediate instinct was to shake it off and pull herself well beyond its reach. Instead, with a great effort of will, she sat absolutely still.

'Hannah,' said her mother. 'Tell me thou dost forgive.'

Hannah tried to collect her thoughts. What was she being asked to forgive? Her mother's abandonment of her all those years ago? That was easy enough, the easiest thing in the world, to understand and to forgive. What was harder by far was to forgive this woman for being her mother at all.

From somewhere inside her Hannah found words, and pushed them croaking and cracked through a dry mouth. 'There is nothing to forgive,' she said. 'Thou didst what was best. I was happy.'

I *was* happy, she realised. I did not know how happy until now, when it has all come to an end.

Slowly, so as not to give any appearance of rejection, she rose to her feet. Her legs felt weak, scarcely able to support her. 'I am going to my room,' she said. 'I want to be alone. Please.'

She saw from the woman's face that – in spite of all the care she had taken – she had hurt her. What had she expected Hannah to do? To fall sobbing into her arms and tell her how happy she was to know her at last? Perhaps. But Hannah knew that it was utterly impossible for her to do such a thing, impossible even to make some affectionate gesture towards her.

The woman stood aside and let her go. In her room, with the door firmly bolted, Hannah lay on the bed with the dog clasped in her arms, and cried and cried. 'Oh Fly, Fly, why didst thou bring me here?'

At the end of a dreadful night, Hannah fell asleep briefly just before dawn, and woke to find that a deep silence lay over everything. The room was full of a clear white light, which showed up every bare and dingy corner of it. Hannah, heavy-eyed, full of a great weight of misery, had enough curiosity left to slide from the bed and go to look out of the window.

The storm had ended. The moor stretched in endless whiteness beneath a clear washed sky of a delicate and fragile blue. Only the surface of the snow showed any hint of the storm's ferocity. It swept up and down in blue-shaded peaks and troughs whose slopes and summits glittered in the sun, forming a sparkling seascape bearing no apparent relation to the contours of the land beneath. Here and there, a remnant of yesterday's fierce wind blew a spray of fine powdery snow from the crest of some frozen wave. Otherwise it was all stillness. The storm had gone, but in its passing had obliterated every trace of the familiar landscape. Somewhere out there, Hannah remembered then, were six of the High Farm sheep, lost in that frozen wilderness, as she had been last night. She must go out and continue her search for them, as soon as she could.

But not yet. There was something she must do first, something much harder. There were more questions she could ask, of course, but she was not sure that she wanted to ask them, after last night. There was also the poor, lonely, unhappy woman, who was her mother whether she liked it or not, and whom she had so abruptly abandoned last night. If that woman, or someone like her, had come to High Farm begging for help, she would have given it at once, unstintingly, without hesitation. She would not have found it difficult at all to feel compassion and to give with love. Why was it so very much harder to care for the woman who had given her life? It ought not to be. She must not allow it to be.

116

She found her clothes – they had been dried and folded and laid at the foot of the bed, perhaps while she slept yesterday. She dressed, called Fly to come with her and drew a deep breath. And then she went downstairs.

She had forgotten the man, until she reached the parlour. There was no sign of him, but if he should be about she knew it would be difficult to talk to her mother. Presumably she was still afraid that he might find out the truth.

Hannah pushed open the kitchen door. To her relief the man still lay in exactly the same place, though his breathing was a little quieter and a threadbare rug had been flung over him. The room had been tidied, after a fashion. The floor was no cleaner, but the furniture had been righted, the scattered objects returned to their places, and the fire was burning with renewed brightness. The woman was nowhere to be seen.

Hannah was wondering whether to go and look for her (and if so in which direction), when she came in from outside, carrying a bucket of coals and stamping her feet to shake the snow from her clogs. She shot a quick glance at Hannah and coloured a little; then she closed the door and carried the bucket to stand it near the fire. After that she turned back to Hannah, while she rubbed dusty hands on her apron.

'Thou must break thy fast,' she said, in a soft and tentative voice. She sounded as though she was afraid of stirring up Hannah's animosity against her.

'I'm not hungry,' said Hannah, quite truthfully, but it sounded like a rejection, so she added, 'but I'll sit down with thee, if thou art having something. And if I could have a bite for the dog —'

The look of gratitude on her mother's face was so marked that she felt ashamed. It took so little, but that little required such an effort in the giving!

Hannah stood watching while the woman busied herself bringing cheese and bread to the table and making

tea and setting out plates and cups, and putting some
kind of meat in a dish for Fly. Then she said, 'Thou
art called Christian, didst thou say?' It might have been
invented, of course, to fit the fiction that it was not her
but someone else to whom that dreadful thing had
happened.

'Christian Lambert, Tom Lambert's daughter.'

She said it as if that identified her, as if it was the only
thing of significance about her, as perhaps it was.

Hannah looked at the man: Tom Lambert, her
grandfather, her own flesh and blood, bloated and
red and breathing loudly through an open mouth full
of broken and blackened teeth. She shivered.

'He'll not wake for hours yet,' Christian assured her.
Perhaps she thought Hannah's shiver indicated fear. It
must seem a natural enough reaction to her.

Hannah sat down at the table, and because she did
not want to eat and her hands were idle she took out
her knitting and began to work at it; she had it with
her, of course, as always.

Christian stood watching her for a little while. Then
she said, 'Thou dost knit well, and fast. Did Agnes
Burton teach thee?'

'They both did.'

'If I'd learned to knit, maybe I could have thought to
keep myself, and thee. But there was no one to teach
me.'

On such small things, Hannah reflected, had her
happiness depended.

Christian sat down at the table and poured tea for
them both. Hannah, taking the cup pushed towards
her, thought how odd it was that she should eat and
drink so luxuriously in so poor a place. But that was
a trivial matter, and there was something far more
important she knew she must confront. It might lead
her further into misery, but she had come too far now
(however unwillingly) to turn her back on it.

'My father,' she said. 'Who was he?' She spoke softly,

as Christian did, in case the man was not sleeping soundly and should overhear.

'He was a drover, in a plaid.' All at once Christian's voice was dreamy, gentle with memory. But to Hannah her reply expressed more poignantly than anything she had said so far how slight had been the relationship that had given her daughter life. 'A drover, in a plaid' – he passed before her eyes, momentarily caught, and then disappearing from sight; not a man, with responsibilities, and friends, a family perhaps, a home behind him and a destination before him, with gifts and failings, beliefs and doubts and hopes.

'He came from Scotland.' That was something more, but then the plaid had told her that already. 'He'd come once before, the last year.' Christian's face was like her voice, dreamy, full of tender reminiscence. Once again Hannah had a sense of the dreariness of her life, in which an act of kindness or a single squalid moment of passion (she supposed that was what it was) could mean so much.

'I remembered him when he came back,' Christian went on. 'He was different from the rest. Young, like I was; tall . . .' Her gaze sharpened slightly and focused on Hannah. 'Thou art like him. Thou hast his eyes and his hair. His face was the same shape, and fair too. And so handsome! He could have charmed the birds from the trees. There was no one like him.

'He rested his cattle here over the Sunday, and came in for a meal or two, and a talk. He could talk, Hannah – thou hast heard nothing like it, the way he could talk. At night he lay out with the beasts, the way the drovers do, wrapped in his plaid. He lit a fire, all red and yellow and shining on the black moor, with the stars over him and the light running up and down on his face and his long body. I went out, just to be friendly. We'd talked a bit before. He spoke to me like no one else did, like a gentleman, I'd say, only no gentleman ever spoke to me like that. So when my Father was asleep I went out.

It was warm by the fire, and he talked and sang a bit, and shared his whisky flask. I only went for the comfort of it, because he was kind. But ...' She paused and closed her eyes, as if she was seeing it all, fresh in her mind. When she spoke again, it was in a whisper, full of wonder and remembered joy. 'He was like a prince – and, oh, I wanted him, like I've wanted no one else! The stars shone so bright and the fire and ... and as long as I live I shall never forget that night, never.'

She halted, and Hannah saw that she had quite forgotten where she was or who she was talking to. Even Hannah, with her little experience of love, was caught up in her mother's memory – a fragment of joy clutched to her there beneath the stars, beside the little crackling fire. Had it been worth the pain that came after, to have that moment of happiness, the only one in a long and bitter life? Perhaps even Christian would not be able to answer that. Yet she could relive that moment of rapture with an intensity that made it real for her. That must count for something.

'He went away then, thou didst say,' Hannah prompted her gently – this slatternly woman who had (momentarily) become again a dreaming girl not far removed from the daughter who listened to her story.

Christian stirred, and opened her eyes; and her face grew hard and all the lines of care and disappointment returned. 'Aye,' she said with bitter harshness. 'Next morning, first thing, him and his dog and his cattle. I never saw him again nor had word of him. The next year I looked for him every day. I thought maybe if I told him what had happened, then he'd wed me, and I could come and ask for thee back. But he never came. Most of them came back, so I thought, long afterwards, Perhaps he's dead. Hector MacDonald, they called him. That's all I ever knew.' She paused again, and swallowed hard, and rubbed her eyes with a hand that left smudges of coal dust across her bruised face. 'He wasn't just any man, Hannah. I'm not that kind of lass. He's the only man I've ever been with. And I did the best I could for thee, thou knows that, dost thou not?' Hannah nodded, but was given no time to speak. 'I knew they were kind folks at High Farm. They had no bairns of their own. I was sure they'd care for thee. I used to listen to the talk, to know how things were with thee – I still do, come to that. Sometimes I'd see thee passing. I could see that thou wert well and happy, so I didn't feel quite so bad.

'I never meant thee to know, never. There was him, of course.' She glanced at the man. 'But yesterday, when we found thee . . . I couldn't help myself, I had to tell thee. It was from love I did it, thou knows, just from love. I'm that proud, the way thou hast turned out.' She gave a faint smile, which had an odd misplaced look, as if her features were not made for so carefree a thing. 'I am glad thou art here. I am glad I have told thee. Now we can be friends, a true mother and daughter.'

Hannah looked at her with a curious and disagreeable mixture of pity and guilt and revulsion warring inside her. She did indeed feel real compassion for a woman who had been given so little and had suffered so much, and even a faint gratitude for the concern for herself which had led her to abandon her child. It seemed that it had truly been a cruel and anguished decision. As a result, she, Hannah, had indeed found a happiness beyond the wildest imaginings of this poor woman. Yet . . . she could not warm to her, could not feel for her any of the love or tenderness that she knew was so desperately wanted. Was it some failing in herself not to feel it? Should it not be a natural, instinctive thing, born in her, to love the woman who had carried her through nine terrible months, and given birth to her in agonising and friendless solitude?

And if she could not love at first, surely it was not too much to ask that she should try to love, that she should offer her friendship, in her actions, if she could not do it with her feelings? Yet the very idea of ever seeing the woman again repelled her, still more of allowing her to strengthen the links that already bound them together.

For a little while she allowed Christian to question her about her life, answering the questions as simply and briefly as she could without hurting the woman. After a time, she judged that she had done all she ought, and that now she could decently intrude her other responsibilities.

'I shall have to go,' she said. 'We've lost sheep out there. I must find them.'

Christian stared at her, appalled. 'They'll be under the snow, long since. Thou canst not go yet. There are no ways dug.'

'I'll find a way. Fly will help.' She steeled herself to reach out and take her mother's hand, and pressed gently. 'I must try. If it gets bad, I'll come back. In any case,' she added brightly, 'I will be back to pay what I owe.' She knew that promise was not enough, that she must force out the warmer reassurance. 'Besides,' she added, 'I shall want to see thee again, soon.' She did not think she had ever before deviated from the Quaker demand for complete sincerity of speech. But she knew that this time it was right to do so.

She found it easier to get away than she had feared, because the man – her grandfather – awoke, and in the explosions of ill-temper that followed there was no possibility of any more private talk between the woman and herself. It meant too that Hannah carried away with her more clearly than ever the memory of her mother's harassed and frightened face. It would help her in the struggle to think kindly of her.

But as she stepped out into the snow and the icy wind, with Fly at her side and her stick once more in her hand, her strongest sensation was one of overpowering relief. She would find a way through the snow, however deep the drifts; nothing, absolutely nothing, would induce her to go back to the inn today. Or ever, some part of her said, but she preferred not to think of that. All she wanted now was to be safe at home.

Home, with Agnes, her dear mother. 'I am thy mother,' she had said once, 'because I have cared for thee and loved thee and watched over thee from the first.' She had been right, and right too that John Burton had the same claim to be her father. Hannah knew it now as she never had before, in her bones and her heart. That other woman might have some claim on her (she would have to consider that claim one day – but not yet, oh, not yet!), but it was to Hannah and John that she truly belonged, and to whom she owed everything. If only she had known how true that was, before John died! It was too late now to tell him how much she had loved him. He had died while she still chafed at the restrictions of home, and craved for some mother of her dreams, who had never existed at all.

She did not weep now, though she thought of John with such poignant regret. There was a constriction in her throat, but she set her face to the wind and pressed her lips together and gave her attention to finding her way home. Never again would she wish herself anywhere but at Hollinthwaite, with Agnes. For her there would be no more dreams, no more impatience with the routines of her life. She might not have Robert (she thought of him suddenly, with surprise, because he had been entirely banished from her mind until now, and because the thought of him did not give her any particular pain), but she had everything else.

It was not easy to find a path around the drifts, and even there the snow was very deep. More than once, she lost a clog and had to drag it free of the snow while she balanced precariously on one leg. Her feet got very wet.

She did not care. With every step, she was putting a greater distance between herself and the inn. Besides, Fly was a great help, sensing the best way to go, with his eager canine instinct. It was time, Hannah thought, to keep her eyes open for any sign of the lost sheep. As they came to the more sheltered parts of the moor, there were sheep here and there, wandering about in search of food. She realised when she saw the brand on them that she had come on the heugh where the Low Farm sheep grazed. They were gathered together, feeding on some freshly spread hay. There were pony and dog tracks in the snow nearby. Someone had been up to them today, then. Fly became very excited, following the tracks with his nose. She called him to her and walked on. She saw then that the tracks did not return the way they had come, down the slope of the hill, but continued up again, on over the fell. Maybe Low Farm had sheep missing too.

She went that way, because it led to their own sheep heugh, and there she saw ahead of her, poised between snow and sky, the outline of a man on a pony, black against the horizon. He had halted at that high point, presumably to look about him. He must have seen her, for he turned the pony round and came as quickly as he could back towards her. She heard him call, and knew then that it was Samuel.

He came up to her, dismounted, and before she had time to speak he had caught her in his arms and was crushing her in a fierce, anguished hug. 'Oh, Hannah, Hannah! I thought thou hadst foundered!' He was kissing her too, his mouth moving with tender urgency over her face, and he was murmuring loving little words. 'Oh my darling, my love – oh, Hannah, I couldn't live without thee! Oh, I love thee so!'

She had clung to him at first, so full of relief and delight was she to see him, and to be once again with someone familiar and loved, someone from home. Now she grew alarmed. She disentangled herself as best she could (it was not easy), and held him at arm's length. He was breathing fast, with a high excited colour, and he looked a little dazed. She thought that he had not realised until then what he was doing. She was not even sure that he quite knew now.

He gave a tremulous little smile, happy enough, and took her hand. 'Thou art safe.' His voice shook a little. 'Thank God!'

Hannah felt the need to be entirely practical. 'There are sheep missing still.'

He shook his head. 'I found them, all but one. They're in with ours. The other must wait. Thy mother needs thee more. She came round last night to say thou hadst not returned. Mary stayed with her, while I came to look.'

'Thou hast been out all night?' She was moved by such heroic devotion.

He looked rather sorry that honesty compelled him to deny it. 'No, not until the storm ended.' He paused, looking at her as if he could not gaze enough; then he said briskly, 'Let's get home. Thou must ride. Come!'

She did not argue, but swung herself into the saddle. Samuel walked alongside, and the two dogs, eyeing one another with the suspicion of old rivals, trotted behind. It was so extraordinarily easy, this descent into the dale, after all the wanderings of the past twenty-four hours. Yet for Hannah, however short, it was an emotional journey. To be coming home, knowing now in full to what it was she returned; that silenced her as they went, with the silence of feelings too deep for words. She spoke now and then, to answer Samuel's questions as to where she had been. She gave him no details, of course, just the barest facts, and no hint of what she had found at the inn. She would have been relieved that he said little either, had she not recognised what it was that kept him silent.

He was relieved at finding her, after a night of agonising fear; but the fear came not from the simple brotherly friendship she had though he felt for her, but from what she had glimpsed, and experienced, in that moment of their meeting. Samuel loved her, with

125

all the force of which his quiet and gentle nature was capable. In this way, he loved her as deeply as Robert had done, perhaps even more than Robert had done.

It was deeply disturbing, yet another discovery to rock the none-too-stable foundations of her life. And she did not want any more discoveries to cope with, just at the moment. She wanted peace and order and to find everything exactly as she had left it, so that she could savour it, because for the first time she knew how rich she was in having it.

Poor Samuel. If he had felt like this for long, how he must have suffered, when she seemed promised to Robert – so much pain, which she had not even suspected. It was more of a strain on her sympathy to think of how his hopes must have grown when Robert went away, and day after day they had no word of him.

She did not want to have to think of Samuel's feelings at all. Like the woman at the inn, they were something she would have to consider sooner or later. But not now.

They were home, turning into the yard of High Farm, where the snow was already trodden and muddy; and across which, the next moment, Agnes came running, just as Hannah slid from the pony's back.

There was nothing to hold her back now, no constraints or doubts. She clung to Agnes, and Agnes clung to her, and they both wept with a joyful abandoned gratitude that they were together again. Then they went indoors with their arms about one another, and neither of them noticed when Samuel led Mary Harker silently away. Agnes brought ale and havercakes, and they sat at the table in that warm and spotless kitchen, and talked and talked as they had not done for months – no, Hannah recognised, as they had never done before, for she had never talked so freely and with such love. She talked not simply of her ordeal, and Agnes's fears, and the sheep – in fact, scarcely of them at all. They talked of many things, but most of all of John, remembering with shared tenderness how much he had meant to them both. They cried a good deal, but without bitterness.

One thing only Hannah did not say, though it was always there at the forefront of her mind. She said nothing at all about the woman at the inn. She thought perhaps she never would.

CHAPTER SEVEN

i

'Is thy father at home, Samuel?'

Samuel jumped. Absorbed in the letter he was reading, he had not heard Hannah come into the parlour behind him. Now he looked quickly round, colouring with pleasure.

'My father? No – yes – I don't know. He went out, I think. Hast thou tried the woolroom?'

'He's not there.' Sometimes she could not help but feel exasperated with Samuel's vagueness, his apparent ability to shut out absolutely everything that went on around him, except the single thing that happened to interest him at the time. Yet her exasperation was always tinged with affection. It was difficult to be truly angry with someone so consistently kind, who loved her so much, who could at times show an unexpected sensitively to what she felt, as if he had been attentive to her all along, whatever the appearances to the contrary.

Even now, she saw his gaze move from her face to the letter and back again. She knew he had heard the question that, unspoken, indeed scarcely formed, had passed briefly through her mind when she saw what he was doing. He waved the letter, saying casually, 'My old teacher from school ... we have been corresponding on the subject of sedges.' He laid the letter down on the pile of books and papers scattering the table before him.

It had not been from Robert, then; but she had not seriously considered that it might be, not for a moment. She was not sure even that she really hoped any longer that Robert would write. She rarely thought of him, and on the whole she was contented with her life. Robert did not matter to her any more. Yet sometimes, now and then, she would sense some lingering uneasiness, like a spark suddenly discovered in a fire thought dead, which showed her that not everything of what she once had felt had been extinguished. That was all it was, of course; the last remnant of something that had once been alive but was now beyond reviving, and would soon be gone for ever. She could even, sometimes, imagine herself married to Samuel. One day, perhaps, if he should ask – as she knew he never would, without much better cause than she had ever given him.

'Mary might know,' Samuel was saying now. It was a moment or two before Hannah realised what he was talking about. He said next, 'No, she went out with . . . oh!' He clapped a hand to his forehead. 'Of course! How foolish! I remember now! My father took Mary with him, so she could spend the day with her sister. They've gone to Thornside. He had to see lawyer Broderick about my Uncle Samuel's will. Something like that. He won't be back until late.'

Hannah sat down on a stool near his chair. 'What's to become of the mill, dost thou know?' She tried not to think of the lovely autumn day when she had gazed on that scene of dereliction with Robert's hand about hers.

'Who can say? It'll be sold, I suppose. It wasn't all Uncle Samuel's fault it failed. There are enough corn mills already.'

'Mills can do other things. Like fulling, say.'

'There's a fulling mill at Hawes.'

'Aye, of course there is.'

'Anyway, was it urgent, thy business with my father? Shall I give him a message from thee?'

'I don't know.' She frowned. 'I'd best see him myself . . . It's the spinning,' she added, so Samuel should not feel she thought him undeserving of an explanation. 'The last batch. I think it's what Jane Coates did. But she's never spun badly before. It's all uneven, full of lumps, and knots too. Mother says it's not fit to knit with. We always thought Jane Coates was one of the best, too. I thought maybe thy father would know what to do.'

'I know what Robert would say: "Tell her she's not working for us any more."'

Hannah was shocked. She had never heard quite that bitter note in Samuel's voice before, still less the hint of malice she could also detect in the words. It distressed her, and even angered her a little, for she could think of nothing that might possibly justify it – except perhaps some jealousy of his brother still lingering after all this time. 'How canst thou say that, Samuel! He'd do no such thing, not without knowing why it went wrong.' He might lack Samuel's gentle kindliness, but Robert was a generous man all the same, she knew that.

Whatever it was that had lain behind Samuel's sudden outburst, it vanished as quickly as it had come. Hannah almost wondered if she had imagined it. Samuel said quietly, 'Maybe he'd not. Maybe that's what thou shouldst do then – go and see Jane Coates.'

'She works for thy father.'

'He'd not mind.'

'No.' Abruptly, she ceased to think of Robert. She had been putting it off for so long, the visit she knew she must make. It was Monday today, the day of Middleham market. It was three months since she had last ridden up the drove road to spend an hour or two at the inn in her grandfather's absence. This morning she had told herself that the spinning was more important, she could not go to see her mother today. But she knew quite well, of course, that Jane Coates lived on the western edge of Arkengarthdale, just a mile from the Drovers' Inn. Anyone going from Hollinthwaite to see her would have to pass the inn. That was precisely why Hannah had not gone to see her the moment the problem arose, and had come instead to Low Farm, hoping that Joseph Gayle would take the matter out of her hands. The fact that he now and then confided just such tasks to her, even when they concerned his own business, because she was good at dealing with such things, had not prevented her from coming here today. If he asked her to go, then she would have to do so. Until then, she had a slender excuse to keep her from going that way.

Samuel had deprived her of it. There was no escape for her now. She hoped none of her disappointment showed on her face. 'I'll do that then,' she said. 'I'd best go today. I'll look in on thy father tomorrow. Tell him I came.'

Once, she would have enjoyed the solitary ride astride the stolid pony, with the summer wind in her face, the cloud patterns chasing one another rapidly over the surface of the moor, the curlews calling, and the meadow pipits and the lapwings; once she might even have sung with them. But not today, with this errand before her.

She had gone back to the inn to pay what she owed soon after that first meeting in last year's snow. It was then that her mother had told her that the best day to come was Monday, when her grandfather was absent. On that day they could talk freely, without fear of discovery; the occasional guests at the inn, coming from far afield never showed any interest in Hannah's presence. It was quite clear that Christian Lambert had no doubt that her daughter would want to come and see her as often as she could. Since Hannah could think of no acceptable reason for refusing to come, she had done so, reluctantly, whenever her conscience would not let her put it off any longer. She had never had any difficulty in finding a reason for her absence that satisfied Agnes, although she always made sure that what she told the old woman was true, if not the whole truth. The difficult part was forcing herself to go at all.

131

It did not get any easier. She took no pleasure herself in the time she spent in the unsavoury surroundings of the inn. She did not find (as she had hoped) that she came to feel any warmth towards her mother. On the contrary, that enforced intimacy, the expressions of affection, the demonstrativeness, hesitant at first and then growing in confidence, continued to repel her, though she used all the willpower at her command to hide what she felt. When she thought about it, she was surprised that it was possible to have so little in common with one's own flesh and blood. On the other hand, she wondered sometimes, uneasily, if she did have more in common with Christian than she could bear to accept, and if it was that which made it all so much harder: the thought that she was kin to a woman she could neither like nor respect, with the same impulses and failings beneath her wholly dissimilar surface.

She knew that what gave Christian the greatest pleasure was for her to arrive hungry, just as a meal was prepared. Today she reached the inn at mid-morning, too soon to eat. She was tempted to halt then, in the hope that she might be able to make her escape more easily and quickly. Instead, she rode on past the inn, to call first on Jane Coates; that way she would return over the moor just at dinner time.

The faulty spinning was easily explained. Jane Coates had been taken seriously ill, and her daughter, a child of ten, had worked day and night to finish the spinning herself. The child explained it all, out of her mother's hearing, with eyes all shadows in her thin white face, while the two younger children clung to her skirts and the baby howled for attention. Their father, a lead miner, was out at work.

Hannah could not bring herself to complain of the child's work to the mother, who looked, to her inexperienced eyes, close to death. The little girl knitted as they talked, and that, Hannah saw, she did with quick competence. Perhaps Joseph Gayle would be willing to buy some of her work on a regular basis, if her mother could no longer manage the spinning. Hannah reassured the child, looked in on a neighbour to check that the family had what help they needed, and then set out again, with sadness added to her already gloomy mood.

Two hours or so with her mother did not make her feel any happier. She was quite sure that Christian prepared dinner with special care on a Monday, just in case Hannah should call. It made her feel all the more guilty to see the tender boiled mutton, the Yorkshire pudding, golden brown and fragrant, the dish of new peas glistening with butter, the ham and cheese, set before her on the table – food such as they ate at High Farm only on festive occasions. Christian was more talkative than ever today, and more emotional, full of tears and caresses. By the time she was able to leave at last, Hannah was exhausted from the strain of responding with warmth and gentleness to her mother's ministrations. At least, she thought thankfully, it was over; she need not go back again for at least a month. She at once felt guilty that she should be so relieved, and determined that she would not leave it so long again, and that she would be more loving, more as Christian wanted her to be, next time.

Gradually the wind seemed to clear her head, to refresh her and drive out all the difficulties of the day. She did not hurry over the last miles of the road (it would have been difficult to do so anyway, on her slow pony), but savoured every moment of this little taste of freedom between the completed duties, and those that awaited her at home. Of course, the home tasks were not unpleasant or particularly burdensome: there was the evening milking to be done yet, the hens to be barred in, the pony to be stabled and fed; supper to get, and knitting to be done, by their own fireside or in a neighbouring kitchen, with songs and talk and reading; and there was Agnes to share those tasks with her, in the loving and equal companionship that had so recently been established between them. But even so, Hannah grew tired of it sometimes, and ached for some other prospect, some change or excitement of a pleasurable kind. This last hour or two of her journey, alone on the fell where she had been conceived and born, was the nearest she could hope to come to satisfying that ache.

As the depression left her and her spirits rose, she felt like singing, but she did not do so. That would be to demonstrate her likeness to the woman at the inn, whose miserable life had passed in a darkness without guidance and without hope. Hannah wanted instead to resemble Agnes and John, and those like them, who were able to control all their impulses to vanity and triviality with such apparent effortlessness. That she found it so hard might be discouraging, but to give way would be to admit to a frailty only too like that of her mother. So she did not sing, but simply gave herself up – with her eyes, her ears, her nose, all her senses – to enjoyment of the place and the day.

She was not, after all, alone. It was hardly surprising, at this time of year, on this road. It was more surprising perhaps that she had met no one until now. Even so, she felt a surge of irritation when she saw, taking shape on the brow of the hill ahead of her, the unmistakable heaving black outline of a herd of cattle.

Even on her slow pony she came up to them very soon. She guided the animal off the road some time before she reached them, and round in a wide semi-circle, so as not to startle the beasts or turn them from their course. Behind them rode the drover on his own pony, calling an occasional command to his dog. Hannah drew rein and watched him, as she often did now, since last year. She noted the plaid and the bonnet, the haversack in which he carried oatmeal for the journey and a whisky flask, and the tall broad frame of the man, as big-boned and muscled as the largest of his beasts. He was sandy-haired, with freckles on a sunburned pink skin. Not her father, then, if indeed she had his colouring. But so, once, her father had ridden, on this very road, resting his beasts (as this man might well do) at the inn across the moor.

'Good day to ye, lassie!'

She jumped, coloured, returned his greeting in some incoherent manner. What would he say if she were to ask him, 'Dost thou know Hector MacDonald?'

For a moment she was almost tempted to do so. But not quite. On the whole she thought that she would rather not discover any more about her origins. What she had learned so far had done her no good at all, except to attach her more strongly than ever to Agnes and Hollinthwaite. She dug her heels into the pony's side and went on her way, hearing the drover begin to play some kind of pipe as she left him behind, a sweet plaintive little tune, as lonely as the curlew's cry, but fainter, soon lost in the wind.

A little further, and she realised, as the road dipped into a small shallow valley, that there was another traveller coming her way, a solitary rider this time, like herself. He could not be going far; he could not be a packman, or a drover returning from the sale of his beasts, for his horse was unburdened by any kind of pack or bag. It *was* a horse too, she saw as he came nearer, not one of the sturdy galloways most riders used on these moorland roads. It was a fine, strong, big-boned brown gelding, such as a man of some means might ride. The rider's clothes told the same story: a neat brown wig beneath the bicorne hat, a good cloth coat, lace ruffles just visible at his wrists and more lace at his throat, gleaming boots and close-fitting breeches – this was a gentleman out riding not far from home. Not that 'gentleman' was a term Hannah had ever been taught to use. Men were men, and women were women, and all were equally children of God, to none of whom any special gestures of deference or servility were due. Nevertheless, this man showed all the signs of affluence all the assurance in the set of his broad shoulders, that told her he was used to having his way. Hannah wondered who he might be. There were no wealthy families resident in the immediate neighbourhood of Hollinthwaite, but he might be from a little further afield, or even a visitor from a good way off, lodging at an inn or with friends in the district.

He came nearer, not with the casual air of someone who was simply enjoying the ride, but briskly and purposefully, so that she almost had the feeling that she was the object of his journey. She studied the face beneath the wig: square-jawed, the dark eyes alert beneath emphatic brows, the nose somehow as assertive as all the other features, the face of a young man already mature, very sure of himself.

She caught her breath. Without knowing what she was doing, she drew rein, and sat there quite still, watching. How could she mistake those features for any others – the strong angles of the face, which long ago had carved their image upon her memory and her heart? She knew him even better than she knew herself, he who had first shown her what she was, and who had loved her for it. Her lips moved, silently forming a name. 'Robert.'

She released her breath, ran her eyes again over both horse and rider. She was imagining things. There was a likeness, of course, enough to set her heart beating painfully in a way she had forgotten, but that was all. Robert Gayle, son of a Quaker hosier from Hollinthwaite, would never ride such a horse, or appear all decked out in wig and lace and fancy clothes. It was ridiculous for her to be so disquieted by a stranger that her hands trembled uncontrollably, as they were doing now.

The rider halted in his turn. He put up a hand – she saw a ring gleam somewhere on the strong brown fingers – and removed his hat and bowed from the waist, with all the assurance of a man who had learned such gestures from infancy, gestures that no Quaker home would ever have taught him. Then he smiled.

She could not mistake that smile, that easy, cheerful, carefree smile, which seemed to tug irresistibly at her heart. It was . . . it must be!

He swung himself from the saddle with all the old vigorous grace she remembered so well, and came right up to her, leading his horse. She could see the full extent of his finery now, the little details of decoration on his coat and waistcoat, the signs of luxury even. Whatever had become of him in the three years since they last had news of him, one thing at least was clear: he had done well for himself, in the sense of those words that the world understood. Hannah knew he had changed, too, perhaps in ways less obvious than the un-Quakerish cut of his clothes, but for her at this moment he was the Robert she remembered.

She slid to the ground as he came near, waiting. She felt her whole body take fire with delight and joy and trepidation. He had come home, come back to her, Robert, who loved her still, whom she loved with every part of her – had never ceased to love, she realised now. It was as if he had never been away.

She longed to run into his arms, to feel him and hold him, but some little shyness kept her where she was. Perhaps he sensed it, or even shared it, for (still smiling) he reached out and took her hands in his.

The next moment, he raised them one after the other to his lips and pressed a kiss upon them. She stared at him, astonished as much by the ease of the gesture as by its unexpectedness. It was almost as if he did such things every day. Where could he have been, to learn such things in just four years, so that he could bow and kiss hands as if he had always done so?

He let her hands fall again, but retained them in his own light clasp, while his eyes searched her face. What was he seeing, she wondered? A beauty that had faded, a drabness he had forgotten in the years of absence?

For the first time in her life, she was acutely conscious of the unrelieved plainness of her clothes.

His smile subsided a little, but to something gentler and quieter, and the brightness of his eyes softened too. 'Hannah,' he said. It sounded almost like a sigh of contentment.

If she had not been sure before, she would have known now that it was Robert, hearing his voice. How could she have forgotten how deep it was, how resonant? Or was it that the years had deepened it still further? She wanted to speak – there was, after all, so much to say – but the effect of his voice upon her was so devastating that her brain seemed to have ceased to function at all.

She smiled foolishly, and blushed, and contented herself with tightening her fingers about his, and swinging his hands out and in, like a child expressing its joy in the only way it could.

'There was no one at home,' he went on, after a moment. 'I called on your mother. She said you had come this way. I took a fancy to ride to meet you.'

He sounded so matter of fact, as if he shared none of her overpowering joy in this meeting after so long away. There was something else too about what he said, something that seemed to put a distance between them. In the confusion of her emotions she could not think what it was, but the little chill it brought was enough to free her tongue to speak.

'We did not know where thou hadst gone. Thou didst not write.' A moment ago, she would not have thought of spoiling their meeting with words of reproach, and even now she regretted them almost as soon as they were out. She had spoken impulsively, and it was too late now to retract them.

He seemed unperturbed, however, and simply went on smiling. 'I told you I would come back. As you see, I am here.'

Then she knew, what it was: he said 'you', not 'thou'

or 'thee', as once he would have done. It was another sign, like the fine clothes, of how far he had moved from the simple Quaker way of life – and from the Dales way, too, for Dales speech also often retained the intimate 'thou', which in other places was fast dying out.

But she felt better, knowing that this was why his speech sounded less warm than she remembered. She was not used to such a way of talking from those close to her, that was all. It did not mean that Robert had ceased to care. On the contrary, he had remembered his promise; he had come to claim her, as he had said he would. Set against that, the unwritten letters, the long silence, the disconcerting signs of change, were nothing.

Even so, she could not quite do what would have been the natural thing to do, for a girl faced with the man who had come at last to claim her as his bride. Some little hesitancy kept her from putting her arms about him, as she longed so much to do, and he made no move that might have encouraged her.

'Where are they all, do you know? My father, Mary, Samuel – there was no one at home.'

'Samuel was there this morning. Perhaps he went out to look for one of his plants.'

'Has he still got that bee in his bonnet?' There was just the hint of a sneer in Robert's voice. Hannah, not liking it, said quickly,

'He takes it very seriously. He makes notes and sketches and corresponds a great deal with other people who know about plants. He's found things that no one else has found.' It did not, she thought, sound very impressive after all, but she did not quite know how to do any better. She turned her attention to Robert's other question. 'Thy father went to Thornside today. He took Mary with him.' She paused. 'Thou wilt not know that thy Uncle Samuel is dead.' She did not suppose he would be greatly distressed to hear of it, but she spoke gently all the same.

'I know,' he said. 'I heard of it through a man I met in Liverpool. That's why . . .' He broke off, and said instead, 'Is that what took my father to Thornside? What does he plan to do with the mill, do you know?'

'I think he will sell it,' said Hannah. 'But I don't know whether he has come to a decision yet. Samuel said he went to call on lawyer Broderick – that would be about the mill, I suppose.'

She was surprised at Robert's close interest in what she said. He stood there frowning, clearly deep in thought. One hand still held hers, but she had a feeling that for the moment at least he had forgotten she was there.

'Thy father will be home tonight, and Mary,' she put in quietly.

He glanced at her, and then grinned, and before she knew what was happening, he had put his arms about her. 'Until then, I have you, my most lovely Hannah,' he said softly, and then he drew her close and brought his mouth down on hers.

All her doubts and hesitations vanished like snow before the south west wind. *This* was where she was meant to be, where she belonged, here in Robert's arms. They were together at last, and nothing now would ever be allowed to separate them again, so far as it lay in her power. She had forgotten how right it felt, how good, to be with Robert, forgotten too the aching need in her that only he could satisfy, though he had not done it yet. Perhaps now, today, since they would so soon be man and wife, the long waiting over. . .

But it was clear that, for Robert, the waiting was still not quite over. With that impressive self-command, which once before had spared her from herself, he drew away, murmuring softly 'I had forgotten how sweet your lips are, my love.'

The sound of bells, gently tinkling, reached them.

They looked round, just as a train of packhorses appeared one by one over the brow of the hill, descending the slope like a string of beads slipping steadily down towards them. Robert grinned at Hannah. 'Let us go back. We can talk as we go.'

Hannah regretted their interrupted solitude, but she could console herself with the simpler pleasure of Robert's companionship. They mounted, and then Robert, gathering up his reins, glanced at Hannah, and laughed suddenly.

'Oh Hannah, seeing you there astride that pony – what a gipsy you look! I've always liked that about you, your wild gipsy ways.'

Hannah coloured, not quite sure whether to feel flattered or offended. 'Everyone rides this way in the Dales,' she pointed out. 'Except gentry, of course.'

'Ah, but not everyone has your beauty, Hannah. Most women simply look clumsy and vulgar.' His voice had become warm and husky with meaning, and Hannah could only hear it with delight. It was not possible to feel offended after that. They remained where they were for a moment, smiling at one another, and then Robert said, 'Let's go!' and urged his horse forward.

'Thou hast been in Liverpool then?' Hannah said as they went. By now the train of packhorses had been left well behind. 'Is that where thou didst go from London?'

'No, I went to Manchester first. I have been there a good deal of the time. But I have been in many places, Hannah, seen things you have never dreamed of, met men of all kinds.' His eyes, like his voice, were full of excitement. 'I always wanted to see the world. Maybe there's much still to see, but I've tasted well of it all the same. I've been away, and now I know what I want from life.'

'So thou hast come back.'

'Aye, because what I want is *here*. Not under my father's roof, in the kind of life he wanted me to have. But here all the same.'

He did not say, 'With you, Hannah,' but she was sure that was what he meant. Once again joy swamped her, depriving her of anything but a longing to shout aloud, to urge her pony into a gallop (which would be a near-impossible feat), to sing her ecstasy louder than the lark trilling overhead.

They rode on, saying little, though now and then Hannah glanced at Robert, and he at her, and – their eyes meeting – she saw her own happiness reflected in his face.

She was about to return to the subject of how he had lived during the past four years, when, just where the road descended into the dale, she saw a man scrambling down the bank from the hill to their right.

She knew that long gangling frame at once, the old but comfortable coat, the bag slung across his shoulder, in which he carried notebooks and sketching materials, the faint but permanent look of anxiety on the bespectacled face. She just had time to register that it was Samuel, and to brace herself for the hurt that their meeting like this must give him, before he caught sight of them.

For a moment, then, she saw him stripped of his defences, with all his emotions nakedly exposed. He stood very still, his hands fallen to his sides, his mouth a little open, his expression mingling disbelief and dismay, and behind it a raw pain that made her long to run to him and comfort him, except that it was out of her power to bring comfort, because it was she, and Robert whom she loved, who were the cause of the pain.

'Well, well – my dear brother!' Robert murmured. 'It seems you were right, Hannah.'

By the time they came up with him, Samuel had himself under control again. He was a little pale still, but his expression was calm and he even managed a thin smile. Without a sign either of surprise or pleasure, he looked up at his brother. 'Thou hast come home,' he said unnecessarily. He glanced from Robert to Hannah and back again, as if in puzzlement as to why the two of them should be riding down to Thornside together, but he asked no questions, and Robert did not enlighten him.

Hannah, uncomfortable and embarrassed, but not wanting him to develop any misconceptions, said after a moment, 'Robert found no one at home. Mother told him where I was, so he came this way.'

'And met thee; I see.' After that, Samuel fell silent again. His self control might enable him to hide his feelings (from his brother at least), but it did not go so far as to allow him to welcome Robert with any warmth. That might come later, when the first shock had faded, but for the time being it was impossible.

'Are you on your way home?' Robert asked, and on receiving an affirmative answer from Samuel, swung down from the saddle. 'We'll go together,' he said, with sudden generosity. Hannah thought only how uncomfortable it would be, for the three of them. How could she enjoy Robert's company with a third person there, and that one the man who had every reason to be hurt by the situation?

'I shall go on,' she said. 'I'm late already.' And before anyone could object, she had urged her pony into a trot and left them behind.

ii

'To my mind,' said Joseph Gayle on Tuesday evening, as he sat at supper with his sons, 'it's time thou told us why thou hast come home. A whole day thou hast been back, and thou hast said not a word.'

Robert took a drink from the tankard of ale at his elbow. He saw Samuel watching him as he did so, as if he had his own ideas as to why his older brother had returned. Since Robert had told him little as they walked home yesterday afternoon, Samuel had been driven to working it out for himself. It had not been difficult: he had made his fortune, and returned for Hannah. For Samuel it was obvious. Robert had, after all, openly sought out her company today, spending much of the morning at High Farm.

But if that was it, Robert had his own reasons for evading their questions and keeping it to himself. He smiled blandly. 'Is it not enough that I'm back? The prodigal returned – except that I have not wasted my substance, nor do I need forgiveness. Are you not pleased?'

'Thou knows I am glad to see thee,' Joseph retorted, with a frown that rather belied his words. 'But I know thee well enough to be sure thou hast some purpose in coming home. Thou wouldst not be here else. And thou hast asked questions enough thyself, if thou hast answered none. I'd say thou knows as much of my business now as I do myself.' He looked his son over with a critical eye. 'Thou hast clearly done well for thyself, as some might say. What is there for thee in Hollinthwaite now? I'll not believe thou hast set thy heart on becoming a hosier, after all this time.'

'I had in mind you might be wanting an extra pair of hands, with the mill empty.'

Joseph looked blank, 'The mill . . .?'

'Thornside mill.'

'What dost thou want with Thornside mill?' His eyes sharpened suddenly, full of suspicion. 'Thou art in trouble – is that it?'

Robert looked amused rather than offended. 'Of course not! As you say, I've done well. I could have stayed in Manchester.'

'Manchester! I thought it was Liverpool.'

'I have commercial interests in both towns – and in London too. But mostly in Manchester.'

'What kind of commercial interests? Was this with thy Uncle William's money?'

'At first, yes. "Cast thy bread upon the waters . . ." I did, and reaped an abundant harvest. Moderately abundant, anyway,' he amended quickly. 'As for the details, I won't bore you with them. Suffice it to say, I learned a great deal – which ought to please you.' His tone made it clear that any attempt at further probing would get nowhere. 'What about the mill, then?'

'What about it? I'd thought of selling. Hast thou other ideas?'

Robert shrugged, as if it was all a matter of supreme indifference to him. Yet his eyes gleamed. 'It could be built up maybe – reopened.'

'Thou knows as well as I do there's no room for another corn mill at Thornside.'

'There are other kinds of mill,' said Robert carelessly.

'Aye, there are. What hast thou in mind then?'

'Oh, I've a few thoughts. But maybe I'll keep them to myself, just for the present. Tell me, do you need the money from the sale of the mill? Is that why you plan to sell?'

'No. It's just going to waste, that's all.'

'Then you would let me take it over – give me a free hand?'

'Thou wouldst need money to do anything with it. I didn't say I'd cash to spare.'

'But *I* have.'

'Enough for that? It's not all show then, this ... finery.' There was disapproval in his tone as well as curiosity, a curiosity that Robert had no intention of satisfying.

'I have means of my own, and another source ... I won't go into that now. But I must have a free hand. No interference.'

'Thou knows I'd not let thee have it without knowing what thou hadst in mind.'

'Then I'll go and take a look, see someone I have to see; then I'll have a scheme to put to you. I can guarantee you'll see the sense of it. More than that, you'll be glad to give me what I ask.'

Joseph Gayle's expression conceded absolutely

nothing. Impassive, even a little grim, he nodded.
'We'll see. Tell me what thou hast in mind, then I'll
tell thee what I think of it.'

Robert's face was full of restrained triumph. He
leaned back comfortably in his chair, as if he was
certain now of victory. Then he said to Samuel, 'You
are very silent, brother.'

'There did not seem to be anything for me to say,'
said Samuel.

'Have you no opinion about the mill?'

'I thought it a good plan to sell it. But I haven't the
benefit of thy knowledge of the world.' There was just
a hint of malice in his tone, and for a moment Robert
looked surprised, even amused.

'Do you think I shouldn't try and make anything of
it then?'

'It's as thou wilt – as Father wishes. It's not for me
to say.'

'You live at home. You've lived at home all these
years. You must have some opinions about what is
done.'

'Not me. I leave that to those with a gift for it.'

'And stick to your plants?' The contempt in Robert's
voice was unmistakable. 'Does that keep you happy?'

Samuel, who had begun to believe that happiness
might after all be within his reach, only to see the door
shut in his face once again yesterday afternoon, tried
not to let that bitter reflection intrude. He ignored the
question of happiness, and said defensively, 'I teach a
little too.'

'Botany, I suppose?' Robert sounded close to
laughter.

'Mathematics, for the most part.'

'And there's a call for that in Hollinthwaite? Has
Friend Garnett given up schoolmastering then?'

'He has no gift for mathematics, beyond the first
elements. I take those who want more advanced
teaching.'

'Rather you than me. It sounds tedious beyond words.' He stood up suddenly, shaking his ruffles into place about his wrists with a slight yet elegant gesture. 'There's someone I must see, if you'll excuse me.' He even bowed slightly to them both, before going out into the night.

Half a dozen or so of the Burtons' neighbours had gathered this evening in the kitchen at High Farm. In the summer time, when daylight lasted so long, these 'sittings' took place infrequently. But the hay was safely cut and the nights were beginning to draw in, and so tonight they had come with their knitting, since it was more pleasant to work in company.

As it happened, the callers tonight were all Quakers, so there was no singing, and while they worked Hannah read to them from Woolman's *Considerations on the True Harmony of Mankind*, one of John Burton's favourite works, and so hers too, because in reading it she felt near to him again.

There was something good, she thought, about this ending to the first day of Robert's return. On coming home last night, and in his company this morning, she had been so overwhelmed by joy, so ecstatic, so full of a wild, restless delight, that she could not settle to anything. She had flown from one task to another as if her feet must have no time to touch the ground. Agnes, knowing the reason for her happiness, had only with difficulty refrained from expressing her exasperation with Hannah's mood.

Then, tonight, with supper over, as the sun sank below the horizon and a stillness settled over the shadowed valley, the neighbours had come quietly in the lingering summer twilight and gathered, talking slowly and softly, about the fire; and Hannah, coming to join them, had felt the tranquillity of it all steal over her, calming all her turbulence and replacing it with a serene happiness. Now, with the door standing wide and the sweet air flowing in, bringing with it the last sleepy chirping of the birds, the distant calls of sheep and lambs; with the rhythmic click of the needles forming a harmony with her own quiet clear voice; with the knitters rocking in time to their work, while all their attention was on the words she was reading, Hannah felt that this was a deeper and truer happiness than she had felt before. Robert's love, her love for him, were bound up with this moment, holy like all of life; fleeting, and yet a part of eternity; rooted firmly in all that they were and all that they were meant to be. This was not the ecstasy of falling in love; this was the deeper joy of knowing that their two lives were bound together now until the end, and that this was part of the purpose for which they had been born. She did not feel less, for having lost that restlessness. On the contrary, she felt so much, with such intensity, that now and then tears sprang to her eyes.

'. . . *in the Pursuit of Wealth, People do that to others which they know would not be acceptable to themselves, either in exercising an absolute Power over them, or otherwise laying on them unequitable Burdens . . .*'

Hannah heard steps on the track, the squeak of the gate, someone crossing the yard. She knew it was Robert, before ever his shadowy figure took shape in the doorway, outlined by the grey-blue dusk.

'. . . *Thus the Harmony of Society is broken, and from hence Commotions and Wars do frequently arise in the World.*' She finished the paragraph and laid down the book and smiled at him. He would sense the wonder of this moment, just as she did, and come quietly to sit with them, so as not to break the stillness.

Heads turned to look at him. He removed his hat (another un-Quakerly gesture, that mark of worldly respect), and bowed, and said cheerfully, 'Forgive me for interrupting, my friends. Good evening to you all.' That greeting too was one he would not once have used; as John Burton had said to Hannah, long ago:

'"Good evening" is an empty greeting. What evening is not good, since the Lord made them all?'

For a tiny fraction of time, Hannah felt disappointment pierce her serenity, but so briefly that she scarcely noticed it. The next moment, all the tumultuous joy of this afternoon came back in force. She felt herself blushing and trembling; she lost all sense of the tranquil evening, the people round her, of everything but Robert smiling and coming towards her. Him she saw with all the dazzling clarity of love, a man of such height and grace and splendour that she could only gaze at him, dumb with adoration.

She was aware, dimly, that someone was greeting him and asking questions, someone else replying to a remark of his. Then he reached her, and bent and took her hands. She saw his eyes go briefly to Agnes, and then return to her. He said, 'I have something to attend to at Thornside tomorrow, Hannah – something that concerns us both. Will you come with me?'

She too glanced at Agnes, when at last she was able to take her eyes from Robert's face. Agnes looked from one to the other of them, as if trying to read all their motives and emotions and intentions on their faces. Then she said, 'As thou wilt, Hannah.'

Hannah smiled up at Robert. 'I'll come with thee,' she said. She knew that the questions and the answer, apparently so insignificant, were both of them much more than that, because they had been put so publicly, and in such a way. Robert had asked her to trust herself to him and she had done so, not just for tomorrow's journey, but for ever.

CHAPTER EIGHT

i

They set out just after dawn the next morning, riding side by side across the still valley and up the hill, Robert on his handsome workmanlike horse, Hannah on her elderly pony. They said nothing for some time, though now and then they glanced at one another, smiling, their eyes held for a moment. They knew they had no need of words. There was the whole day before them, and in any case to try to express their happiness in words would be difficult, if not impossible. Even so, there was just a little shyness between them, part of it rooted perhaps in the intense quietness of that early hour, when any small sound would have seemed exaggeratedly loud.

Once up the hill it was different. The sun rose, and a brisk little wind brought life and sound to the fell. The restraint left them. Hannah said, 'What is it we're to do at Thornside?'

'You'll see soon enough,' Robert promised airily. Then he added, 'I've been hearing high praise of you, from my father.'

She coloured a little, with pleasure. 'Oh?'

'He didn't say so in as many words, but I can see he wishes he had you as a daughter, in place of us. We are a source of disappointment to him, I fear.' It did not sound as if the thought disturbed him very much.

'Samuel has other gifts,' Hannah pointed out. 'As for thee – now thou art home, it will be different.'

He smiled a little. 'You think so? Perhaps. I have yet to make my father see that.'

Hannah looked at him gravely. 'He does not like

thy finery, I suppose.' She hesitated, seeking the right words. What she wanted to say was important, but she did not want to anger him by putting it badly. 'There is one thing I must know, Robert. Wilt thou come to meeting still? Art thou still a Friend?'

He was not offended, nor even particularly surprised. 'Why should I not be?'

'Some would say thou hast turned thy back on the testimonies – plainness of dress and speech and the like.'

'Not all Friends are as narrow as you in Hollinthwaite,' Robert said, with a smile that took the sting from the words. 'Never fear, there will be no risk that you'll be disowned for marrying me. I shall be in my place at meeting on Sunday, without fail.'

'Thou sayst "Sunday". Why not First Day, as we all say?' She knew she sounded reproachful, but it was a measure of the unease she felt, in spite of his reassurances, and that first clear and open reference to their impending marriage.

'Because, my dear, sweet Hannah, even you are not the whole world. Out there beyond these dales most people wouldn't know what you were talking about if you were to say "First Day". At best, it would mark one out as a little quaint – not quite fit for the best society.'

'And what is the "best society", pray?' Hannah demanded, a little acidly. 'And since when hast thou cared what it thought of thee?'

He smiled, but rather as one smiles at the naïvety of a child, with a faintly patronising air. 'If you had travelled as I have, you would know that to get on in the world you must fall in with the world's ways, and that means cultivating the men who have money and power. You can't do that without some compliance with their manners. He caught the troubled look in her eyes, and went on more earnestly, 'If the world was made up of Friends, it would be different. There would be no bowing and scraping, no "Yes, my lord" here, and "As you say, honoured sir" there, and we could all look one another in the eye and "thee" and "thou" with the best of them. I dare say it would be like living in Paradise, if perhaps a trifle dull.' He said that with a faint rueful smile, as if to imply that she must not take him too seriously. 'But, as it is, Friends are only a tiny part of humanity, of no significance whatever. You'd understand, if you'd seen what I have.'

She was not in the least reassured by his words. She was too dismayed even to regret that anything should have come between them to spoil what had promised to be a perfect day. 'Thou hast changed, Robert Gayle,' she said. 'I thought perhaps it was just a little change – fine clothes, a worldly way of talking, that did not go deep. But that's not all, is it? Thou art another man altogether. I do not think I know thee any more.'

He drew rein at that, obliging her to do the same. She sat very still, while her pony happily seized the opportunity to graze on the long moorland grass, and listened gravely to what Robert had to say. It was clear from his voice and his expression that it mattered very much to him that she should understand.

'Hannah, I have not changed at all,' he said earnestly. 'All that has happened is that I have discovered what is right for me. All my life, before I left home, I felt wrong and ill at ease. Even in my Uncle William's house – it was better there, but still I did not quite fit. I did not know why. I only know I had to find my own way of living. It is not enough to go on in the same way, just because it is expected of you.'

It could have been herself speaking. Hannah had felt it too, exactly as he described it, the sense of being different, of not quite belonging, of wanting more from life than the routine that had surrounded her from childhood. She had explained her own unease and restlessness as being a natural consequence of the circumstances of her birth, but for Robert that could not be true. She had always sensed this kinship between them, the discontent they shared. It was a part – an important part perhaps – of what attracted her to him. If she had not quite recognised that before, she did so now. They were two of a kind, and that was why they belonged together. How could she ever have doubted it, even for a moment? Or been irritated by the way his independent spirit had manifested itself?

'So long,' she said, still cautious, 'as it is the way the light leads thee, and not just the way of the world – or the "best society".' She smiled faintly at those last words.

'I please myself first. And since I *like* that kind of company, then I suit my ways to it. Whatever pleases me, that I'll do.'

Hannah frowned a little. She wanted to understand precisely what he was saying, because it would help her to understand herself and her own confused feelings. Faced with her own restlessness, the wayward impulses that were so much a part of her, she had thought she saw which way she ought to go, clearly enough. Yet Robert, faced with a similar rebelliousness, seemed to be taking a very different path; and it was Robert with whom she was to share the rest of her life, not Agnes or Samuel. It was vital that she should know why Robert had made this choice. 'To please thyself,' she said, 'that is not the same as to follow the light.'

'Is it not? It seems to me they're different words for the same thing. I want to make the best of my life, the very best. I shall have to work hard for it, in all kinds of ways. Very likely I shall have to give up some passing pleasure, because it would hold me back. But in the end, I shall have what I want, and there will be no regrets for the sacrifices I have made. That sounds to me precisely the kind of thing we have had preached at us all our lives. Do you not agree?'

She was not sure. Certainly it sounded much the same, on the surface at least. Yet it all seemed a little cold. Where in all this, she thought, did other people come in, those amongst whom he must live, whatever his ultimate goal might be? She wanted very much to agree with him. But for the time being, honesty would let her say only, 'It *seems* very like.'

He did not wait for her to say more, but reached out and caressed her hand. 'I don't just want the best for me, Hannah,' he said softly, 'but for you too, of course. You are a part of my life. We shall make our way together.'

She gazed at him steadily, and felt her doubts recede before the tenderness of that reassurance. He was her Robert still, beneath the worldly surface; she had no cause at all to mistrust him, for they understood one another so well, better than ever perhaps, after today.

He raised her hand quickly to his mouth and kissed it, and then he said, 'We'd best get on. There's a good deal to do today, and an appointment to keep.' He turned his horse back on to the track.

'An appointment?' She urged her pony alongside.

He nodded, grinning at her, all the old brightness restored to his eyes. 'First we shall see our new home and I shall show you what we can make of it.'

'But shall we not live at High Farm? My mother cannot manage alone. It's hard enough as it is, just with the two of us.' She was distressed that this new difficulty had arisen so soon between them.

'There'll be no more hard times for you, Hannah. No more driving sheep or spinning or knitting. You shall be a lady of leisure – and a rich one too, soon enough, I can promise you.'

It had never occurred to her to want such a prospect as Robert offered her now, nor could she understand how he had it in his power to promise it to her. Did the fine clothes indicate riches on that scale? 'How . . .?' she faltered.

He looked triumphant, a man offering a priceless gift to his bride, certain of her pleasure. 'You remember

Uncle Samuel's mill?' She nodded. 'I've plans for it, great plans. I'll tell you about them when we're there, so you can picture how it will be. Then I've to see a gentleman who will, I hope, come in on the scheme. I want him to meet you too. It will be hard work at first – for you as well as for me. But a few months, no more, and it will be another story. I am not the only one, you know, but it will be me they'll remember and talk of.' He had halted again, his shining eyes holding her gaze. 'Changes are coming, Hannah, great changes, and all for the better, I promise you. The Dales will never be the same again. We are living in extraordinary times, believe me. It is happening everywhere, all over England. I have seen it – I know!'

She did not understand. How could she, when in fact he had explained nothing? But his voice, deep and alluring, his eyes, his whole manner, woke some answering excitement in her, which was much more than just the customary instinctive response to his physical presence. Whatever vision it was that set his eyes alight, he wanted her to share it with him, and she could not fail to be stirred by that.

She laughed, and he did too, loudly and happily, and pressed his heels into his horse's flanks, and the animal sprang forward at a canter, with Hannah following as fast as she could behind.

'Robert!' she called. 'Wait! Tell me what thou hast in mind!'

'All in good time,' he returned with airy good humour, but he did slow enough to allow her to catch up.

Thornside hummed gently beneath the sun with the ordinary sounds of a working day. From the open doorways of weavers' cottages came the clack and clatter of looms; in the street the whirr of spinning wheels rose more softly from a group of women and girls who had gathered there to work. Here, from an alleyway leading to a carpenter's yard, came the rasp of a saw; there, passing the cobbler's, the sounds of hammering emerged through the open window; and all the time, a constant sound threading the air, came the songs and talk and laughter of the knitters, gathered by the churchyard wall, on street corners, in yards and alleyways, men and women and children, enjoying the sun while their hands moved on, ceaselessly busy, and their bodies swayed to the rhythm of the work.

As they rode, Robert and Hannah looked about them. Hannah, glad to be here in Robert's company, felt in tune with the lively scene, her senses keenly awake to the comforting warmth of the sun, the busy sounds, the smells – dung, leather, wood, animals, the sharp dyeshop odours, peatsmoke, food cooking, the familiar smells of the many alehouses and inns – all the indications of humanity busy, yet happy in one another's company. There was poverty in Thornside, and drunkenness and cruelty and pain and sickness, as there was everywhere, but this morning they were not much in evidence, forgotten for the moment in the blessedness of a warm day and good humoured neighbours.

She glanced at Robert, and saw at once that in this he did not share her feelings at all. She was astonished at the extent of the disapproval evident on his face.

Catching her eye, he said impatiently, '*This* is what must change – and soon, if I have my way!'

These were passing Amos Holgate's blacksmith's shop on the southern edge of the town, the last house on their right, set a little apart from the others for fear of fire. From the dark, glowing interior, the clash of hammer on anvil reached them, and the voices of men carrying on a shouted conversation through the din; some political argument, by the sound of it. Hannah waited until they were past, and it was quieter, before she said, 'I don't understand. What dost thou want to change?'

'All that!' he declared, with a sweeping gesture towards the town straggling up the hill behind them. 'That whole idle way of life.'

'Idle! But everyone's busy all the time, all day long.'

'Not what I'd call busy. I've learned what hard work is. I've seen what can be done. Then I come home, and this is what I find. I'd forgotten until now. Here we are, mid-morning, and how many people are actually working hard, really hard? I'll wager more than half the people were out gossiping in the street. That, while it's daylight and they could see to get on with what they should be doing. How many looms were idle as we passed by? I saw three at least, for sure.'

'But they were doing something else.'

'Gossiping. Basking in the sun.'

'And knitting. Always knitting.'

'Oh, the everlasting knitting! What kind of work is that? Something to occupy the hands, that's all. It'll certainly never make them rich.'

Hannah smiled gently. 'Perhaps they don't wish to be rich.'

'That's exactly it!' Robert said with emphasis. 'That's the whole trouble. No one has any ambition. They'll do just enough work to keep themselves alive, and a bit over, and then they stop, to go drinking, or gossiping, or cockfighting – any excuse. If they knit, it's only to say they're not wholly idle. But it's idleness all the same.'

'How canst thou say that? Think how hard they work, all of them, from dawn to dusk, just to keep alive. I know, for it's the way I live too. If anything, there is too much work. Thou canst not think it right that there should be no time for rest and quiet talk or reflection, no time for the children to go to school?'

'I'm not talking about people like you, or my father or whatever. But these people here, and some we know at Hollinthwaite – what use would they make of more leisure? It's just an excuse for drunkenness, at best – at worst, they indulge in envious and troublesome talk. As for schooling, so long as a child can write its name and mind its manners, I don't see what use most of them have for school. Just so they can read corrupting books, when they'd be better working. Oh no, leave that to the better sort of people, who know how to make good use of it.' He caught her astonished and indignant expression, and smiled gently. 'Oh, I know – we are all God's children. But that does not make us equal in aptitude. There will always be some who are born to lead, others who must be led, and wisely, we hope. Look at the lives of these people around you, and see the truth of what I say. There is no order, no routine, no purpose. What is more, they have no wish to improve their lot. Think of the squalor they live in. Draw in a breath of it, the smell will tell you what I mean. You would make sure all was clean and neat before you sat idly down with your knitting. Not these people: for them it's all hand to mouth, without thought, because they are unable to think. They will survive, most of them, but they will never prosper, never be rich. They will never improve at all, if someone does not show them how.'

'But they are content, for the most part. Is that not good?'

'Is it? Pigs are content, so long as they have their mud. They can't see beyond their four walls and their bellies. People like that don't make a great nation.'

She stared at him, unable to reconcile this tirade against idleness with the Robert she knew, who liked fine clothes and the 'best' society and had turned his back on his Quaker upbringing, with its emphasis on simplicity and seriousness. Yet there was seriousness in what he said now, and a moral purpose of a kind. There was, quite clearly, more of the sober Quaker remaining in him than she had thought.

'What dost thou think is needed, to make a "great nation"?' she asked then, with genuine curiosity. It seemed an odd phrase to her, expressing an idea to which she had never given any thought. What was a 'nation'? A number of people, a vast number, living in one country? For her, what was important was the little land she knew, this land of fell and dale where she had lived all her twenty-one years, and the people, neighbours and friends, amongst whom she passed her days. The world outside mattered too, because all human beings mattered, and no one could live in isolation from his fellows. But what she had always been taught were of no importance at all were the artificial boundaries that people in one place erected against those in another – saying: 'We are Frenchmen, keep out'; 'We are Turks, keep out'; 'We are Russians, or Chinese, or Indians, or English.' If the word 'nation' meant little, what sense was there in the idea of a *great* nation'?

Yet Robert's answer came unhesitatingly, as if this was something he had considered a great deal and saw very clearly. 'Prosperity,' he said. 'Freedom for trade to grow. Energy. Ambition. Pride in oneself. Vision. The will to change, to break with the past, to make a place in the world.'

The words, however fervently expressed, made little sense to Hannah. 'But is it not better if people are content to have enough to eat, and enough to keep and educate their families – a trade, a little land, neighbours and friends to share their joys and their sorrows? All of that, but no more, because any more only makes people greedy and cruel and selfish?'

'As I said, if stagnation is a good thing, then that is fair enough.' He smiled suddenly. 'I can't expect you to understand yet. You haven't seen what I've seen. You don't know any better. But you will – and then you'll know what *could* be done, and you'll see exactly what it is that these poor stupid people are missing, and what possibilities we can offer them, you and I.'

'I thought I was to be a lady of leisure,' she reminded him lightly. 'Is that not stagnation?'

'Oh, only if you want to be. In any case, you are a

woman. The future does not depend on you – except as a mother, of course.'

The airy dismissiveness of his tone might have irritated her, had she not been diverted by the thought of bearing his children, and the tender glance accompanying those last words, which told her that he too was thinking of that prospect. Besides, they had turned into the lane leading to the mill, and memories came jostling for her attention with the extraordinary and varied impressions of this day.

The mill had seemed near to ruin when she last saw it, six years ago. She knew that nothing had been done to it since then, that old Samuel Gayle had lived on, uncaring, and died a month ago, and that inevitably everything must have grown very much worse. Yet still, as they emerged from the dappled shade of the lane to the sunlight beyond, she drew rein and stared in dismay at the scale of the dereliction before her.

By now, half the roof had fallen in, exposing rotting and broken rafters to the sky. Many of the grimy window panes had broken, or been broken by passing children, and the outbuildings had almost totally collapsed. The yard was waist-high with thistles and grass and nettles, which had already begun to overrun the sunny sheltered garden beyond. It was hard to remember how trim and lovingly-tended that garden once had been. It was that, perhaps, which shocked Hannah most; to think that all those years of careful work could be obliterated in so short a time. It brought home to her the feebleness of man, in the face of the natural world amongst which he lived.

She was about to say something of the kind to Robert, when she saw that he had already slung his horse's reins about an adjacent post and was striding towards the broken, permanently half-open door of the mill. She quickly slid to the ground, tethered her own pony and hurried after him.

Inside, coated with dust and moss and the remnants

of birds' nests, the machinery of the mill filled a large part of the high-raftered room. The roof here was apparently intact, though it was clear from the streaked walls and the lingering smell of damp that it had not been rainproof for a long time. Beneath it, the great millstones were still in place, though the wooden structures around them were worn and full of woodworm. Over them, a boarded loft, reached by wooden steps, gave access to the hopper through which, long ago, grain had been fed to the grinding stones. Robert, having glanced around below, leapt up the steps, taking all ten in four strides. Hannah followed him.

Here, in spite of the damp and the neglect, it was warm, for a window faced south and let in the sun, and the dusty homely smell of hot wood filled the air. In a corner facing the window a heap of empty sacks (nibbled here and there by mice) still lay where Uncle Samuel had left them on the day he had last ground corn. How many years ago was that? Hannah wondered.

Robert kicked with his heel at the floorboards. 'Good and sound,' he said approvingly. 'And ample space for machinery.'

Hannah glanced down at the millstones, and the mechanism that linked them to the millwheel and the hopper and the chute where the flour had once emerged. 'It'll take some moving again,' she said.

Robert looked momentarily puzzled. 'What —? Oh, that!' He came to her and laid his hands on her shoulders and turned her to face him, full of excitement. 'There'll be *new* machinery, Hannah. I shall have all that out. This isn't going to be a corn mill. It is going to be a spinning mill, and I shall have the very latest machines – spinning machines!'

She stared at him. 'Spinning!' She thought at once of summer days, out on the hillside, in the kitchen while the soft rain fell outside, with the gentle whirr of the little foot-operated machine forming a constant, soothing background to her thoughts, and the carded wool springy and oily between her fingers. For her, that was a thing of the past, but others spun still, preparing the wool for the knitters – everywhere, all over the Dales, women and girls sat long hours at their wheels, impatient to be done. She thought of poor Jane Coates, and the child who had struggled to do her mother's work.

But what could that laborious process, never quite fast enough to keep pace with the needs of knitters and weavers, have to do with this half-ruined corn mill, and the great waterwheel that had for so long stood motionless beside the beck? She supposed, now she thought about it, that she had heard talk of spinning machines, but she had never paid much attention to it.

Robert nodded. 'I've seen them at work, Hannah – in Arkwright's great mill at Cromford, around Manchester. Think of it: they work day in, day out, and never tire. They need only water to power them, and God knows we're never short of water here. Think how much they will spin.'

'The work of many women,' said Hannah thoughtfully.

'And better done, what's more. Think of the weavers that could be supplied – more than Thornside can hold, I'd guess. I shall build cottages for them, close by out there, where they can work under my supervision, so I know the work's up to standard. Imagine it, a vast enterprise, a great enterprise – and you will be a part of it!'

Hannah was beginning to imagine it, or thought she was. A mass of questions surged up in her, competing for her attention, but it was all so new and so strange that she did not know what to say. In any case, Robert did not wait for her reaction. He went on in the same eager, enthusiastic tone, 'Things are changing, Hannah, whether we like it or not. For myself, I welcome it. I see the opportunities waiting there like ripe fruit for the picking. I have never had any intention of standing by while someone else gets the benefit. That's not my way, and never has been. It will not be easy; there may be opposition. There was trouble in Lancashire, when the first mills opened there. But it was ignorance and stupidity, that's all. The machines will come, and the changes, and no one can stop them. The people who'll suffer will be the ones who turn their backs on change and refuse to have a part of it. They'll get what they deserve. They're seeing the sense of it now, in Lancashire and Derbyshire, wherever the mills have opened; prosperity's coming fast. That's why I came home. I saw what was happening there – I had a small part in it – and I realised how far behind we are here, what opportunities there are. If there's to be prosperity and progress in the Dales, then there's no time to lose. We must begin at once,'

Hannah laughed softly, and a little unsteadily. 'I think thou art going too fast for me.'

'Nonsense!' He moved closer and put his arms about her. His hands moved over her in urgent caressing gestures, as if in such a way he could make her feel the rightness of what he said. 'No, Hannah my darling, you'll learn quickly. You'll want to be a part of it, I know you will, as much as I do. You've a good practical head on your shoulders. What's more, you're like me, you can see things that other people are too blinkered to see. You know how to dream, you've the will to reach out for your dream.' The hands moved to cradle her face and his voice slid in one swift move from eager exposition to softness. 'I love you, Hannah. We're meant to be together, to do this together.' Then he bent to kiss her.

Excited, stirred by all these confusing, crowding new impressions, moved by his tenderness, everything fused now into a fiery, consuming whole. For a moment Hannah was conscious only of the sun hot on her back, the smell of warm wood; and of

163

the things that told her senses that this was Robert and no one else. The smell of him, compounded of horse-leather, tobacco, clean linen, fresh moorland air, the indefinable, unique smell of his skin; the feel of his head, when she slid her hands beneath his wig, all strong bone and bristling hair, and of his body, hard and angular against hers, its lines somehow made to form a whole with the curves and hollows of her own body.

Then she was conscious of nothing, only of being swept up in a great wild rush of feeling that led her inevitably, rightly, to the piled sacks in the sunlit corner, and his hands exploring, and strange, thrilling, shiveringly wonderful caresses; and then the exquisite agony of warm strong hands on naked skin; and then his coming, just when she could endure their separation not a moment longer; and at last a fierce ecstatic union of flesh and spirit that seemed in that instant to answer all the needs she had ever known in the long restless years of her life.

Afterwards she wanted to go on lying there, sleepy and warm and content in his arms, but he became suddenly briskly active again. He sprang to his feet (how could he? Her own limbs felt heavy and indolent with satisfied desire) and quickly tidied his clothes and straightened the wig over his cropped hair. He paused then, grinning cheerfully down at her. 'It's safe enough now. We'll be wed very soon. If there's been any little slip, no one will know.'

It was a second or two before she realised what he meant, and then she felt a momentary sense of shock. She had not even thought of consequences, in the overwhelming emotion of their union. She supposed she should be thankful that he had. Instead, she felt obscurely disappointed by the brisk reassuring practicality of his tone, even a little hurt that such a detached attitude should have any place in the torrential outpouring of their love. He had sounded almost calculating, as if he had measured up the whole situation before allowing his emotions to have their way. She had been grateful to him once, because he had done precisely that, and spared her from the shame she might have suffered. It was hardly logical of her now to wish he had been less far-sighted.

In any case, the next moment he made it clear that he had not after all been as cool about it all as she had thought. 'It might have been better to wait until it was tied up,' he said thoughtfully. 'But never mind. What's done is done, and I've no fear it'll turn out badly.' He grinned again at her puzzled and anxious expression. 'Get tidied up now. We must find ourselves a bite to eat and then put on our best society manners. We're to call on Sir George Scarr this afternoon.'

Hannah was not greatly enlightened. She knew the man by name, as one of the wealthiest landowners in Wensleydale, but that was all. Then she remembered. 'Then *he*'s the gentleman who's to come in on thy scheme, is that it?'

'That's right.'

She sat up and began, obediently if with no great speed or agility, to set her clothes to rights. 'Why should he? What has he to do with thee?'

'I met his cousin in Liverpool. We did a good deal of business together. He introduced me once, when we were in London. Sir George is one of the new breed of improving landowners – *and* he has more money than he knows what to do with. I made a good impression on him. In fact, it was he who mentioned this mill, in a letter to his cousin. He suggested I should be told it was empty, as I might see the possibilities it offered. So, naturally, I arranged to see him as soon as I could. I wanted you to be with me. After all, you are one of my assets.'

At any other time Hannah might not have cared to be so described, as if she were a mere sheep or a horse, but now, suffused still with the glow of his lovemaking, she only smiled. She ran her fingers through the tangled mass of her hair, and then began to push it under her cap. 'And if he does not want to put money into it?'

'He will,' said Robert with confidence. 'He is a man of vision. But – if the impossible should happen – then I've some capital myself. I'd have to go more slowly, of course. We might have to consider delaying our marriage a little. But I shall do it nevertheless. Only, he will see the sense of it.' He reached down to pull her to her feet and into his arms. 'Help me, Hannah. Show what a practical woman you are; the ideal wife. Let him see that with you to run the domestic side, keep accounts, act as my deputy, I can't fail.'

They ate at an inn at the village of Bainbridge, just across the river Ure. Hannah was surprised to find how hungry she was, but even so she scarcely noticed what she ate. She was brimful with happiness, and a blissful animal contentment, and she did everything Robert asked of her without thought, almost without knowing what she was doing.

After the meal they went on their way into the gentle green valley in whose depths stretched the quiet shining lake of Semerwater. On its northern slopes, commanding a view of exquisite serenity, surrounded by a luxuriant park and a neat formal garden, stood the rambling stone mansion where Sir George Scarr's family had lived for generations. Many of the landowning families in this part of Wensleydale had been staunchly Quaker since George Fox first came preaching in the dale in the turbulent years following the Civil War, but the Scarrs were not of that number. Staunchly Anglican and unswervingly loyal to the Crown, they spent a part of each year in London, enjoying what Robert called the 'best society'. But Sir George, inheriting commercial and other interests from his late wife's family, was also much interested in the improvement of his land and stock and crops, and (so Robert explained in more detail as they neared the house) was always ready to hear of a new scheme in which to invest.

At the house, they gave up their horses to a groom and were admitted by a stately butler to a dim and beautiful hall, and then to an equally sombre library, where they were asked, politely but without warmth, to wait.

It was then that Hannah suddenly felt terrified at the prospect before her. Robert had made it clear that he depended on her, that he demanded her 'best society manners' and – by implication – that if she failed him their marriage might even have to be delayed. Yet she was unused to calling on such people as this. She had scarcely even set foot in any of the more wealthy Quaker homes, but there at least her simplicity of dress and manner would have been not only acceptable but welcome. Here it would be a different matter. Should she try and suit her speech and her behaviour to the company, as Robert did? She would not know where to begin, or what to say.

She did not exactly regret the sweetness of their union in the mill, but she did find herself wishing that it had not left her in this utterly indolent state, wanting only to go over and over in her mind the joy she had known, and the continuing happiness of being loved and chosen by Robert. When so much depended upon it, she would have wished to be clear headed and alert, not like this.

There was a mirror set into the wall at one side, between two high bookcases. Hannah went to look at herself in it. The reflection did not cheer her. She looked, she thought, so plain, so severe, so much the simple country girl. She tidied a stray wisp or two of hair – and then the door opened.

Sir George Scarr was a large man, elegantly dressed in what Hannah supposed was the height of fashion, though his clothes were luxurious rather than showy, a richer version of what Robert wore. His manner was graceful but not affected, with just a trace of haughtiness. He came forward and shook Robert's hand, greeting him pleasantly, and then he paused and looked from Robert to Hannah and back again. 'Ah, I do not believe I have had the honour . . .?' He raised a questioning eyebrow.

Robert bowed deeply, enough to show respect, but without exaggeration, and then he too smiled, all charming deference. Hannah, fascinated by a side of Robert she had never seen before, could not take her eyes from him.

'I know, sir. You expected me to come alone. But I so wished you to make the acquaintance of Miss Burton, who is shortly to do me the honour of becoming my wife. She will, of course, give me every assistance in the project of which I wrote to you, as long as it should prove necessary. She is, I assure you, a young woman of rare capabilities.'

He did not, at the moment, sound like the Robert she knew at all. He had become a young man of the world, smooth, polished, assured, talking to a gentleman of superior rank as if he had moved in such circles all his life. She had an odd sense of unreality. Everything seemed strange, all that had happened since the new Robert rode into view on the fell two days ago, but especially today – the ride, the talk, the lovemaking at the mill, and now this. Strangest of all, perhaps, was to hear herself spoken of, with such formality, as 'Miss Burton'. It was as if he was not talking about her at all.

A little silence had followed Robert's explanation. Hannah, becoming conscious of it, looked at her host, and saw with alarm that, far from being disarmed by Robert's words, Sir George was even frowning a little. 'Indeed!' he said, with marked coldness. 'This must put rather a different complexion on the whole business, young man. Unless perhaps Miss Burton has money?'

Hannah found herself grinning at the very idea, but not for long. The matter was clearly too serious for that.

On the other hand, Robert looked wholly unperturbed. 'Better than that, sir. She has a good mind and capable hands. She will be no burden on my resources – on the contrary, she is skilled in the housewifely arts, writes a good hand and is able to cast accounts. If you wish to have her qualities and virtues confirmed, you have only to apply to my father.' He smiled faintly. 'He has been heard to say that she is worth two of his sons.'

'She is, nevertheless, another mouth to be fed, another body to be clothed.'

Hannah, irritated by a discussion of her qualities that seemed to ignore her presence completely, said suddenly, 'As thou seest, I am not a woman for finery. I have known hard work and plain fare all my life, and marriage will not make me think differently.' Almost at once, she wished the words unsaid. Would Sir George think her unpardonably blunt? Would he notice the Quaker speech, which made no concessions to his rank?

For the first time he turned to look at her with real attention. Yes, she thought, he had noticed; and he saw now the sober, old-fashioned clothes, and the lack of ornament. She watched him steadily, determined not to let him see how apprehensive she was.

'A Quakeress, your Miss Burton; all to the good. I know you come of Quaker stock. In some respects it is a point in your favour. I must admit that, as a Justice, I have had cause too often to come across your kind on the wrong side of the law. But you have a name for honesty and hard work, despite that unfortunate stubbornness, and those awkward principles, so subversive to good government. I am, of course, glad you have left such exaggerations behind you, whilst, I understand, retaining the more desirable principles in which you were raised. As for your wife, it can do no harm in a woman.' At last he spoke directly to Hannah. 'No, young woman, I do not doubt your aptitude for this enterprise, but there is another matter to consider.' He returned his attention to Robert. 'Marriage implies the possibility, nay, the probability, of children. They can be a considerable financial burden, as I know to my cost.'

'By the time that happens,' Robert assured him, 'the business will be firmly established.'

'But it could be within nine months of your marriage.'

'Certainly, sir,' Robert agreed calmly.

Sir George smiled and shook his head. 'You are very sure of yourself, young man. That may be a factor in your favour, or it may not. Let us look into the matter more closely. I take it you have brought the figures I asked for?'

Robert took a folded sheaf of papers from his pocket and Sir George signalled to his guests to be seated at a round walnut table set near a window. Robert spread the papers on the polished surface and began eagerly to explain, emphasising his words with lavish gestures of the hands. Sir George listened with great attention, interrupting now and then to put some probing question. Hannah, who at another time would have been anxious to miss none of the conversation, which was after all of direct concern to herself, felt her attention wandering. Her own part in the matter (which had in any case been negligible) was clearly over, the sun shining on her through the window was hot, the mood of indolent contentment was with her still. She looked out on the immaculately tended garden, all geometrical lines and clipped hedges, and only half heard the talk between the two men.

When, now and then, she returned her full attention to her companions, she thought that Robert was making a convincing case. The sums of money under consideration were astonishingly large, far beyond anything she had been used to, but the older man was clearly impressed by Robert's grasp of the subject. Hannah began to realise too how Robert had passed the years of his absence, some of them anyway. He spoke, often, of mills he had seen. He implied once that he had been employed in one in some managing capacity – 'The best way to learn,' he explained. For it was clear that he had set out to learn all he could about a subject that clearly fascinated him. His enthusiasm touched even Hannah, who was scarcely listening; and the way he used what he had learned to support his argument. Fragments of their talk penetrated her drowsy tranquillity, fixing themselves in her consciousness.

'I anticipate a local workforce, but I have here an alternative proposition, and the figures, should that not prove possible. A population used to idle, independent ways can be difficult to train for the mills, unless caught young. I aim to employ perhaps three hundred by the time I reach capacity . . .'

Three hundred! Hannah thought in astonishment. As far as the scheme had taken any shape in her mind at all, she had envisaged that only she and Robert would be involved in it, with perhaps one or two others if the mill should succeed. Even now, she could not quite take in the significance of what Robert said.

'The buildings need a good deal of repair, but the structure of the mill is sound . . .'

'And the machines themselves?' That was Sir George. 'You will build them under licence, I take it?'

'Ah, no, sir. Arkwright is asking two thousand pounds or more for a licence. The question of his patents is before the courts at the moment. But, whatever the outcome, I have an acquaintance, one Henry Birley, who had a hand in building the machines at Chorley. He has agreed to come and work for me, when I give the word . . .

'I expect to keep the machines working for thirteen hours at a time, as the light allows – it may be less in winter . . .

'There are few days in the year when the beck isn't running well. I can't remember it drying up altogether. If there are problems, they can generally be solved, by diversion of the watercourse or some such thing. I can show you the possibilities on site, if you wish.'

'And the supply of cotton?'

Robert had already begun his reply – 'Your cousin will supply us with most of what we need . . .' – before Hannah's mind had grasped the word.

Cotton? she thought. What has cotton to do with it? She began to attend to everything that was said. Robert had not corrected Sir George, had not said, as she would have done, 'Cotton, sir? You mean wool. We shall be spinning wool.' On the contrary, when Sir George went on, 'You think our local weavers can be trained to work with cotton?' Robert simply said smoothly, 'I am sure of it, when they see the advantages.'

Hannah longed to question him. But how could she, without throwing all his careful tactics into disarray? To show that she did not know of his plans would create a disastrous impression. Yet he had misled her . . . Or had he? She thought over their talk at the mill. He had spoken of spinning machines; he had said nothing of cotton. But he had said nothing of wool either, and nor, she thought now, had she. It was only that she had not considered any other possibility.

'Of course,' he was saying now, 'the linen weavers will have no difficulty. Cotton is little different in the weaving from flax. As for the rest, they will learn to adapt, both their looms and their techniques. I anticipate bringing more into the area. In that case I shall have to supply accommodation, something simple and basic. I have some sketchy figures here.'

'And once your cotton's spun and woven, what then? There are no canals within reach, and none planned, that I know of. I looked into the possibility myself, but the terrain is quite unsuitable.'

'That is not a difficulty, sir. Cotton is easy to transport – nothing to break or damage. The turnpike road through the dale provides access for waggons to and from Richmond and Lancaster. Those are the routes we are most likely to require. The fell roads are adequate, in summer at least, should we occasionally need to send goods by another way.'

'Nevertheless, the cost of transport will add to your prices. Road tolls mount up over long distances, and we're well away from the main centres of trade.'

Robert leaned back in his chair, hands stretched out on the table before him, and smiled easily. 'My manufacturing costs will be so low that I shall compete on equal terms with any Manchester mill owner.'

'You sound very sure.'

'You have the figures.' He gestured towards the papers, now piled before Sir George.

The older man looked them over once more, turning the pages, pausing now and then to study some point with closer attention. Hannah watched him, and Robert too, wondering if any anxiety or doubt lay behind that calm exterior. She could see now, more clearly than ever, what he had meant when he told her that he had found what he wanted in life. She could see it in his assurance, his fluency, his enthusiasm. He was a man at peace with himself, knowing precisely where he was going and why. Yet did she share those goals, or even understand fully what they were? She had thought she did, when he talked of them. But in fact he had told her very little. It had been his manner and his touch that had moved her, more than what he said. And she had, after all, failed to realise exactly what he was saying, even in the simple matter of the mill. She tried not to give way to the unease stirring to life again within her. After all, it was her future too that was being decided here today; it was Sir George's response that ought to hold all her attention, in these tense moments of waiting before he gave it. She caught Robert's eye, and he smiled, supremely confident even now.

Sir George made some non-committal sound, shuffled the papers into an orderly pile, straightened, and then looked steadily across the table at Robert. Hannah knew she was holding her breath, and that Robert must be too, though he gave no sign of it.

'Well, young man, I like your scheme. It is precisely the kind of thing I hoped you would come up with. I am glad my confidence in you was not misplaced. I am prepared to invest in the project – and to the extent of the proposed sum.'

How could Robert look so calm? Hannah wondered. He seemed pleased enough, but not in the least elated, though he must be, under the surface. All he said was, 'Thank you, sir.'

Sir George rose to his feet and reached across to shake Robert's hand. 'I'll have my lawyer draw up an agreement with all speed. Come and see me next week and we can get it all signed.'

'I shall look forward to it,' said Robert. 'You will have no objection, I hope, if I call in the builders, and send word to Mr Henry Birley concerning the machines?'

'None at all. Let me know if you need an advance of cash at this stage.'

'I will. Thank you.'

Hannah thought that now they would be free to go, and she would be able at last to put to Robert the many questions that were clamouring for attention, which she longed to hear him answer to her satisfaction, reassuring her about everything. But it seemed that Sir George had other ideas.

'Now that our business is concluded, a little harmless pleasure is in order, I suggest. You will, I hope, take tea with Miss Scarr and myself – you and Miss Burton both, that is.'

Robert did not even glance at Hannah. 'We should be honoured, sir,' he said.

So they went with their host to a low-ceilinged drawing room, where a young woman of about Hannah's age sat embroidering beside a hearth in which stood a great vase of summer flowers. Introductions were made.

'Harriet, let me make Miss Burton known to you; Miss Burton, my daughter, Miss Scarr, my great comfort since her brother's marriage.'

Tea was brought on a silver tray. Hannah was ushered to a chair whose upholstery and shape encouraged relaxation; it would have been almost impossible to knit successfully in such a chair, Hannah reflected.

No one had ever taught her how to make conversation, or sip tea from delicate china cups, or school her features to an expression of polite interest while talk of astonishing triviality passed to and fro about her. Miss Scarr had clearly learned those arts from her cradle, as had her father; Robert, presumably self-taught, behaved as if he had too, so effectively that Miss Scarr, a pale and insipid looking young woman, seemed captivated by him. Even her father gave every sign of enjoying the young man's company.

Hannah, silent and uncomfortable, stammering a confused reply when spoken to, feeling completely out of place, yet wanting to create a good impression for Robert's sake, was heartily relieved when, at long last, the time came for them to take their leave. At the door, the groom had their horses ready. They mounted and rode away, saying nothing until they had left the house well behind them.

Hannah glanced at Robert. His head was held high, his eyes bright. There was a glow of happiness about him, expressing itself then in the broadest of grins. 'That was perfect! Everything went magnificently. It couldn't have been better!' It was obvious that he was pleased with himself and pleased with the whole world, including, Hannah supposed, herself.

She did not want to spoil that happy mood. She did not want to do anything that might put any distance between them, or allow any of her own unease to rise to the surface. She wanted to be unreservedly happy, as he was, full of thoughts of all they had shared today, all they would share in the years to come. But then there were things he had not shared with her, whether by her fault or his, and they could not come to a complete happiness so long as she did not know all that there was to know.

After a little silence, she said, as lightly as she could, 'I thought thou meant to put wool spinning machines in Thornside mill. But thou didst not, didst thou?'

She was surprised when he laughed. 'Wool? Whatever gave you that idea? That's the past, not the future. Cotton's where the money is, I promise you that.'

'But cotton won't grow in Yorkshire.'

He laughed again, a note of amiable superiority in the ringing tones. 'Of course not, you goose! It's a crop of hot climates – India, the West Indies. It's Barbados cotton I intend to use, for the most part.'

Appalled and disbelieving, Hannah stared at him. 'Barbados? But they use slave labour in Barbados!'

'Clever girl! I see you're not quite ignorant of life outside Yorkshire. Yes, Sir George's cousin has a cotton plantation there. I've other contacts too. We've done business together for a while now. I shall take most of what he produces. Good quality stuff it is too, better than Indian cotton.'

Hannah was poised on the edge of relief. 'Then he doesn't own slaves? Like the Quaker owners who've freed their slaves – perhaps he is a Friend?'

'Of course he owns slaves. Only a fool would do anything else in that climate. White men can't work in it.'

'Nor can black men for long, from what I've heard,' Hannah retorted.

'What do you know about it, pray? Or any of those self-righteous Quaker pamphleteers, come to that.'

'John Woolman lived amongst it, in America.' She felt it all as a terrible pain, as if Robert had cast scorn on her deepest and tenderest feelings. His fine clothes and worldly speech, they were little things, superficial things, to her at least. But for him to speak so contemptuously of one of the most generous of Quaker principles, that hurt her unbearably. She wanted to find she was mistaken, that he was teasing her, that he did not really believe what he was saying; that in some obscure way she had misunderstood him.

'He was never a plantation owner, who had to live on his land. He only ever saw it from the outside. Besides, his kind only see what they want to see. Oh, they mean well; they start from the idea that negroes are like us, and want to live as we do. That's nonsense, all of it. Plantation life – it's luxury for a negro. He's known nothing like that in Africa. Regular food, no need to hunt, a roof over his head, many a comfort. All right, he has to work for it, and negroes are idle by nature. They have to be made to work. But once used to it, they couldn't ask for anything more.'

'Thou hast not asked them.'

'Nor have you, or most of the other Quakers either. At least I've talked to traders and owners, and I've seen slave ships. I made it my business to find out. I *know* what I'm talking about. Negroes haven't our mental capacities, you know. They don't feel things as we do. They're more like cattle. Think of them like that and you can see how well off they are.'

'John Woolman's concern was for the moral harm it did to owners too, by keeping slaves,' Hannah put in quietly.

Robert laughed. 'Very kind of him, I'm sure. You'd not find any owners to thank him for it.' He must have seen that his light tone only distressed her the more, for his expression and his voice quickly took on a new gravity. 'Hannah, I *do* know what I'm saying, truly I do. Surely you do not think I would have gone into this lightly, knowing the Quaker teaching? I had to be sure before I took any further steps. I *am* sure, sure enough to have put money in slave ships. I've interests in one still, and very profitable it is too. But if your conscience still troubles you, think of this – in Africa the negroes are heathens, savages; in captivity

177

they often learn Christianity. That can't be wrong, can it?'

She wanted to believe him. She wanted to share his feelings in everything, and his hopes and ambitions. Today, at the mill, sure of them both, she had given herself to him in the most unambiguous way that a woman knew. She had not doubted then that they were close enough in mind and heart for the union of their bodies to be simply an act of completion. She shrank now from the possibility that she had been wrong, and that only in their coupling had they come near to one another at all.

Could he be right, and all those people she so deeply admired, in particular John Woolman, whose teachings had been a part of her life since John and Agnes were first moved by his example; could they be wrong? Was it over-sensitivity that made men like him speak out against the sufferings of slaves, whether on the slave ships, or on the plantations of the New World, when in truth the slaves were not suffering at all? Could it be true that the negroes were indeed better off, deprived of their liberty but civilised and converted? Her whole spirit rose in protest against the very idea; yet it was Robert, whom she loved, who told her so. Could she bring herself to disbelieve him? And if she were to do so, might not the consequences be appalling, unthinkable, for herself if not for him?

Without being conscious of it, she had reined in her pony and come to a halt, and Robert did the same. For some time now they had been sitting there, immobile, gazing at one another. He, she knew, was waiting for the signs that she had accepted his argument, and was ready once more to share his plans for the future. As for Hannah herself, she did not know; she could not think what to do or say. She felt that so long as she remained in his company she would not be able to think clearly. His physical presence was so overpowering in its effect upon her, his manner so assured, that she found it difficult to think at all, still less to question anything he said.

'I don't know,' she said at last. 'I need to consider it well.'

He laughed, but softly this time. 'You do that, my sweet. You'll see the sense of what I say. If you want further convincing, think what a transformation that Barbados cotton will bring to the Dales.'

They rode on, while once again his resonantly persuasive voice urged her to share his enthusiasm for the great changes that were coming, his eagerness to be at the forefront of those changes. She let him talk, saying little, feeling herself drawn by his words and his manner, and glad of it. But the enchantment was no longer complete. Her doubts remained; in fact, as she heard him they began to grow, fed by a phrase here, a suggestion there, all indications of a way of thinking and of looking at life that seemed far removed from the Robert she had known before he went away.

She was glad when, as they began to descend the hill into Swaledale, he fell briefly silent and then changed the subject completely.

'By the by, Hannah, what happened about Jane Coates? My father expected a report from you, I believe.'

She was dismayed. 'Oh, of course! I had forgot! What with thy return and all . . .'

'You'd been to see her when I met you, Samuel told me. A matter of poor spinning, I gather.'

She told him quickly what she had found, and what proposal she intended to put to his father, ashamed that her own happiness should have driven it all from her mind.

He shook his head. 'You are too soft-hearted, my love. Sentiment has no place in business, you know.'

She stared at him. Unbidden, and most certainly unwelcome, the thought came into her mind of what Samuel had said the other day. 'I know what Robert would say: "Tell her she's not working for me any

179

more."' 'What wouldst thou have done?' she asked slowly, fearing his reply.

He shrugged. 'What do you think? The prosperity of the business must come first. Let pity rule you, and you'll soon be begging for bread as well. Why do you think my father's not a rich man?'

'Perhaps,' Hannah suggested, 'he does not think riches are important. Nor does he think his business is an end in itself.'

'Nonsense. Everyone wants to be rich, if he's honest. That's why my cotton mill will succeed.' So they were back to mills, and he had not, quite, answered her question. She could still tell herself that Samuel had misjudged his brother; but she no longer believed it. She was glad that Robert's talk allowed her no opportunity to dwell on the matter.

Outside High Farm, he dismounted and came to lift her to the ground, though they both knew quite well that she was perfectly capable of dismounting unaided. The feel of his hands at her waist, the way he drew her to him afterwards, the tenderness and passion combined in his expression as he looked down at her – they all had their old power to set her pulses racing, to fill her only with a longing to stay with him for ever.

He held her face in his hands. 'Thank you for coming with me,' he murmured softly. 'I have travelled hundreds of miles, but you are still the most beautiful woman I know.' He kissed her, lingeringly, as if he could not bear to bring the kiss to an end. 'Tomorrow we'll make all the arrangements for our marriage. I'll come early. Be ready.'

She clung to him for a moment, as if that were answer enough. And then she left him and went into the house, to Agnes's eager curiosity.

ii

That evening, as he had promised, Robert laid his plans before his father. He had no doubt that he would gain

Joseph Gayle's approval, though (just to be sure) he carefully omitted to bring to his father's attention anything concerning cotton supplies or Barbados. He had a suitably evasive answer prepared, in case his father should ask any too probing questions. He did not want to tell a lie if he could help it, but if pressed he would do so, of course. He had learned his lesson from Hannah's unexpectedly fierce reaction this afternoon.

He sat back in his chair at the parlour table and watched the candlelight glow on his father's gaunt face while the old man studied the papers. He could see not the faintest hint of what Joseph Gayle was thinking; but then he was a man who scarcely ever showed his feelings, who would not do so even when he turned, full of admiration, to give his son's scheme his blessing. It was to Samuel that Robert would have to look for open recognition of his energy and intelligence. It would be given reluctantly, but Samuel was incapable of hiding his thoughts, and Robert had often seen on his face a grudging recognition of his brother's superiority. He knew quite well that Samuel envied him and stood in awe of him, even when he disapproved of him. It was a thought that gave Robert a great deal of quiet satisfaction.

The old man finished his reading; it had taken him a long time, while the clock ticked and the candle flickered and the rain that had come with evening swished softly down outside. But at long last he restored the papers to tidiness, and straightened, and looked steadily across the table at his son. So, this afternoon, Sir George Scarr had prepared to give his approval of the scheme, but he had smiled and spoken warmly as, Robert knew, Joseph Gayle would not.

In fact his first response took the form of a sharp question. 'What does Hannah Burton think of all this?'

Robert stared at him. It seemed to him an extraordinary question, wholly irrelevant to the whole business. Why should Hannah's opinion matter to anyone but himself, who intended to marry her? 'She's with me heart and soul, of course,' he said lightly, after a moment. So she would be, very soon, when she had taken time to reflect, and he had worked on her a little more. He had no doubt about that at all. She was a spirited creature, and argumentative, and she had womanish scruples and a soft heart. But she loved him, and in the end that would be enough.

'More fool her!' growled Joseph Gayle. 'I thought better of her than that!'

Robert thought he must have misunderstood his father. The only other alternative was that his father had failed to understand the precise nature of the project before him. He was old, of course; his wits had been sharp enough once, but Robert had been away for a long time and it was possible that his father's mental powers were fading. 'I can't think what you mean, Father,' Robert said, more mildly than he felt. Silly old fool, he was thinking, as he looked at the lined and unsmiling face before him.

'Canst thou not? Didst thou really think I'd be behind thee on this? Cotton mill! What do Dalesfolk want with a cotton mill?'

Robert, finding his suspicions of his father's mental state amply confirmed, controlled his temper as best he could. He would gain nothing by saying precisely what he thought of such a reaction. Instead, quietly, forcefully, with all the eloquence at his command, he went over the whole project from the beginning, omitting nothing – not the potential of Thornside mill, the practical arguments in favour of cotton spinning, the benefits that must follow for the whole district, his own experience in that field, the excitement of being caught up in a new enterprise with a great future ahead of it. He exerted all his considerable charm, as if he were trying to win over not his own father (who ought to have every reason to think well of him), but a stranger whose support was vital to his scheme.

At the end there was a long silence, while Joseph Gayle studied his son's face with eyes that were cold and shrewd and unfriendly, as if what he had heard had driven out all kindly feeling. Then he said, 'There's only one person thou hast thought of in all this, Robert – and that's thyself.'

Robert was annoyed to feel his colour rise. He hoped his father had not noticed. 'What's wrong with that then? Don't tell me you became a hosier for the good of your neighbours. A man makes his living as suits him best – and by whatever means brings the greatest profit.'

Joseph Gayle shook his head. 'No, Robert. Thou art mistaken. A man must make enough to keep himself and his family. But I'm a hosier because my father was one, and his father before him, and because there was need of a hosier in this place. I was fitted for it, and so I did it, as best I could. I had no thought, ever, to make money from it, more than to supply my needs.'

'Then you should have!' Robert burst out, unable any longer to control his temper. 'That's just what's wrong with this place, with all of you. You'll never try anything new. If it was good enough for your father, it's good enough for you. You don't see that if everyone was like you there'd be no progress at all, ever.'

'And what's "progress" then? Change for change's sake? That's not my way and never has been.'

'No, progress is change that is good for everyone. Why can't you see the benefits I could bring? At least let me try!'

'No son of mine will have a hand in bringing cotton mills up here.'

'You know nothing about them!'

'I've been to Manchester; I've seen them. And I didn't like what I saw. Sheep is what we live by; that's what gives us our independence, and that's how it stays, as long as I have my say.'

Robert glared at him in fury, and then glanced at

Samuel, who had the faintest hint of a smile playing about his lips. Stung beyond endurance, Robert crashed his fist down on the table. 'I know what it is! It's Sam – he's your favourite! It's him you want to see at Thornside mill!'

Samuel, the smile vanishing at once, opened his mouth in astonishment. His father cast a sidelong glance at his younger son and laughed, curtly and without amusement. 'Samuel! Him! He'd starve in days – thou knows that, and so does he. He'd not be daft enough to give it a second thought. No, that's nowt to do with it. In fact, I reckon I'll sell the place. Best be shot of it as soon as I can. But, mind, I'm choosy who I sell to.'

Robert pressed his hands on the table and forced himself to his feet, pushing back his chair with a loud noise. 'You're a blind, stupid, ignorant old man! You'd rather stick fast in the nice warm safe mud of your old ways than dare to lift your head and look out. And I thought you had a head for business! I should have known better.' He swung round then and marched out of the room, slamming the door behind him.

Where he went, Samuel did not know, except that he left the house and did not return to the room they shared until his younger brother had been asleep for some time. Disturbed by the candle placed on the bedside chest, Samuel turned over and opened sleepy eyes to look up at the tall square figure lit by the uncertain flame. He could not see too well at this distance, without his spectacles, but he thought there was still a grim look about his brother's features.

'What wilt thou do now?' he asked softly. 'About the mill, I mean. Wilt thou go away again?' He hoped there was no trace in his voice of the delight such a prospect would give him. In any case, he thought it unlikely. Robert would soon be married to Hannah, who would not readily leave Agnes. More likely Robert would turn his energies to improving High Farm's land, perhaps extending its possessions.

'Good God, no!' said Robert. 'I don't give up that easily. No, Hannah will talk him round. He thinks well of her – better than he does of his own son,' he added, with a hint of bitterness. That first question of his father's still rankled, almost more than anything else that had been said between them this evening. But then if Hannah's opinion was so important to Joseph Gayle, it was up to Robert to make use of that fact.

'Maybe that's because he's seen more of her in the past years,' Samuel suggested.

Robert, undressed, pulled on his nightshirt. 'Does it not anger you, that he thinks higher of her than of you?'

'Why should it? She's got a good head for business, and I haven't. I don't see why that should trouble me.'

'No,' said Robert drily, as he climbed into bed. 'You wouldn't.' He blew out the candle and was soon asleep. Samuel, in the dark, knew that the comforting oblivion from which Robert had woken him had gone beyond his reach. Once again, as last night, he was faced with the long slow wakeful hours in which starkly before him he saw only the one simple unchanging truth: that he would never now marry Hannah. Now that it was a certainty, he wished that the forthcoming wedding was over. He even hoped that his father would give in on the matter of the mill. Surely it would be easier to bear the agony of losing what he had dreamed might be his, if Robert and Hannah were to live where he would not see them every day? It was foolish of him, of course, ever to have allowed himself to think of her as his wife. Such things did not happen to him, only to Robert, as they always had.

iii

Hannah too was wakeful that night. She did not tell Agnes much about the visit to Thornside, except to say, vaguely, that Robert had a scheme for his uncle's mill, but she did not know what would come of it.

185

After supper she took all the books and pamphlets she could find on the subject of slavery from the parlour self, John Woolman's *Journal* among them, and carried them upstairs to her room, where she lay in bed studying them all by the inadequate light of her candle. Agnes would have rebuked her for straining her eyes, but Hannah knew that she would not be able to rest until she had thought over everything that had happened today and decided what she must do. It might help her to make a decision if she looked at these familiar writings in the light of what Robert had said to her.

It took only a few minutes, hearing those beloved familiar voices in her head, to show her what she had known all along to be true; that they were right, and Robert was deeply wrong. How could she ever have thought otherwise, when she had so often heard these angry and sorrowful voices bearing witness against greed and injustice and oppression, following – as she had been taught to do – the light that each man had in his heart, if he would only see it? Robert had said that was the same as following his own will, and she had half believed him; but not any more. Away from the intoxication of his presence, in the quiet of her room, she knew that the self-interest that Robert claimed to follow was another thing altogether. And it was self-interest that had made him so eloquent on behalf of slavery. Because it suited him to make use of that vile institution, he found arguments in its favour.

She had now to decide whether in truth Robert believed what he had told her, that slavery was not an evil, or whether he had simply been using what he knew to be empty words to win her over. It might seem a small distinction, but Hannah knew that it was a fundamental one. To call evil good was a more serious thing by far than to be guilty of a temporary dishonesty, for it might be irreversible.

It was very hard to think clearly. She was tired, and so

much had happened today. She would begin to follow a train of thought, and again and again a different thought, a recollection, some remembered incident, would intrude itself on her attention, deflecting her from her purpose. Most often, it was the memory of her union with Robert in the mill that came to mind, and she wished it would not, for it brought with it now a painful stomach-churning sense of guilt.

She had not felt guilty at the time, or in the contented afterglow of the event. It had felt so right, and so inevitable, the natural end of her long love for Robert, and his for her. She knew that her sense of guilt was closely bound up with what she had learned from Robert afterwards and also (if she were honest with herself) with the unease that had intruded itself between them early in the ride to Thornside.

For a woman to give herself completely to the man she loved, whom she had pledged to marry, certain of his love for her; that was not a matter for shame at all, except that some might say they should have waited for the wedding day. But very many couples did not, and it was not this aspect of it that troubled her. It was the fear that the man to whom she had given herself, and whom she loved, was not the Robert she had known before he went away, but someone who had changed beyond recognition.

His enthusiasm had excited her. She had been exhilarated and delighted by his wish to share all his hopes with her, and his presumption that she would feel as he did. Yet when she thought more carefully of what he had said, now that she was removed from the enchantment of his eyes and his voice and his vigorous masculinity, then his vision lost all its charm. If anyone but Robert had told her of such a project, she would have been repelled by his self-interest and greed and materialism, his ruthless unconcern for anyone but himself. Only, it *was* Robert who had told her, and she loved Robert . . .

187

Did she? Was he still the Robert she had known? He had always been restless, impatient, strong willed: those qualities, close kin to something in her own nature, had been part of his attraction for her. As for the rest, how well had she known him? When they had been together, he had talked of her beauty and paid her many tender compliments, but he had rarely been serious for long about anything at all. Now, she remembered things she had scarcely noticed at the time – his disagreements with his father, for example. From what he had said today, from what Samuel had said, she wondered uneasily if it was the ruthlessness she found so disquieting that had alienated his father all those years ago. If that was so, then he had changed less than she had thought; he had simply thrown off the few things that had masked what he really was – the Quaker clothes, the plain speech. Could she really have been so blind as not to have seen what kind of man he was from the first?

She did not want to believe that. She had given herself to him; they were to be married very soon. Everyone expected it of them now. She could not turn back. Yet did she really want to share her life with the man she had glimpsed today?

Some time past midnight she reached the point of despair. In her mind Robert became a figure of nightmare, a creature of darkness and evil who had possessed her, but of whom she must free herself if she were not to perish in his grasp. I shall tell him tomorrow, she thought; we cannot be married. And then she was terrified at the consequences of such an act, of the public anger that would be heaped upon her, of Robert's fury at his humiliation.

Shame swept her, because it was her doing that had brought her to this, her impulsive giving of herself to him. It was her mother's blood, running in her veins, the same unbridled appetite that had given her life. She might long to be a part of Agnes's gentle, serene, disciplined world, she might try to tell herself that she too was modest and chaste and walking in the light. But it was all a sham, and her real home was the dark and lonely inn, with its fear and violence and misery. She hated it, shrank from it, but never, never could she hope to break free as long as she lived.

Dawn came, creeping grey and cheerless into her room. But it brought some consolation, for the fears of the night receded, and in the growing light they looked somehow foolish and hysterical. It might even be that she was wrong and Robert was right, at least as far as the cotton mill was concerned. He had seen the mills, he must know better than she what prospects they offered. Perhaps she was as set in her ways as the other Dalesfolk. Perhaps it was time for her too to break free, to risk everything. It was in her nature to do so, after all.

But if she was right, then it was surely not beyond her power to make Robert see things as she saw them? He had chosen her out of all the women in the world, he valued her opinion. He would give careful attention to anything she said, if he knew it was what, after long thought, she deeply believed. She must put her trust in his good sense and her own powers of persuasion, with the Lord's help. Robert had, after all, been brought up among Friends, born to that inheritance as she had not. That must count for something, even now.

iv

Hannah came to the door the moment she heard, through the beating of the rain, the sound of Robert hurrying across the yard. As soon as she saw him, every last trace of doubt fell away. How could she have forgotten how much she loved him? Just to look at him seemed to turn her limbs to water, like snow when the thaw came. The sensation was so intense, so overwhelming, that it hurt, piercing yet infinitely sweet, like their coming together yesterday.

He came to her, drenched, indifferent to the rain and the mud on his boots, smiling that winning, carefree, entrancing smile whose effect on her she could never have put into words. She took his hands and drew him into the passage and he bent at once to kiss her gently and lightly on the mouth.

'Now,' he said softly. 'We must talk to your mother first, must we not?'

She remembered then where her night-time reflections had led her. She had come downstairs this morning knowing precisely what she must say to him, and that she must say it before they made any arrangements for their marriage. Now she regretted that decision, and wondered fleetingly if it really mattered very much after all. It was such a small thing, and she loved Robert so much. Why risk spoiling today with the disagreements (trivial in retrospect) that had marred yesterday? But she reminded herself that the decision had been made and if she did not speak now she might regret it later. Better to get it done with now.

'Just one moment,' she said quietly, trying to make her tone light and casual. 'There's something I must say first.'

He made a wry face. 'That sounds ill-omened.' But he went with her cheerfully enough into the chill and empty parlour, where she closed the door and turned to face him.

'Robert, I have thought well about what thou hadst to say yesterday —'

'And thou dost find thou canst not bear to be my wife!' His eyes sparkled, leaving her in no doubt that he was teasing her. He would have been astounded had he known how the words made her flinch.

'If I am to be thy wife, Robert —'

'*If!*' His smile faded a little, and the light words had a sharper edge. 'There was no "if" about it yesterday.'

'Nor is there now, not in truth,' she conceded. 'But

there was much in what thou didst say to me yesterday that I had not heard before. I had need of time. Well, I have had time now. It seems to me, if I am to be thy wife and thy partner, then I have a right to a say —'

'By all means!' he agreed airily, with a wave of the hand. 'Have your say! Though I seem to recollect you were not quite silent yesterday.'

'But I had not thought it over then. Now I have.'

'Ah!' He looked pleased. 'That is gratifying. Go on.' He held her hands and smiled gently down at her.

'Tell me first – there are machines that spin wool, are there not?'

'Yes . . .' he said, with a hint of reluctance. 'But they are not so far advanced as the cotton spinning machines. Most are small and worked by hand. There are few in mills, turned by water power.'

'But those that there are, they spin faster than a woman could, and more evenly?'

'Maybe. I've not gone into it much. The wool business is too hedged about with ancient rules and regulations for my taste. Cotton's a new trade, so that leaves the manufacturer with a free hand.'

'Never mind that for now. These machines that spin wool – they would cost no more than the cotton machines, I suppose?'

'I suppose not. But —'

She tightened her grasp on his hands. 'Let me go on. This is important. Thou must know, I have thought well about it. I know from thy father, from what I've seen myself, it is the spinning that holds things back for everyone. Sometimes it is badly done, then the knitting is poor too. It is never quite done fast enough. When we had to spin all our own wool, we had too little time to knit it up afterwards. For the weavers it is worse. Now they have the looms with flying shuttles, they go too fast for the spinners, and many days they have to sit idle for want of yarn. To have machines to do that work would be a great burden lifted from us all. We could knit more stockings and caps and gloves to sell, and we'd have more time for other things. Children could go to school, because their work would not be needed so much, and there'd be a little more money, to pay for their books and teachers. Aye,' she caught his eyes and smiled, 'I know thou dost believe that wool is finished. But I cannot think thee right in that. Sheep have been a part of these dales – oh, as long as there have been sheep, I would say. They are what we've always lived by. We know about them. It is born and bred in us, from tupping and lambing, to clipping and salving. And we know about wool and all the things that can be done with it.' A smile briefly broke the gravity of her expression. 'In this cold climate we'd be foolish to wear owt else. I can't see there'll ever come a day when there'll be no call for it. If some folks want cotton, then let those who have no other trade spin and weave it for them.

'What if thou shouldst bring in thy cotton mill, what then, when there's a storm at sea and all thy cargo of cotton is lost, or the crop fails far off across the world? What can we do then, or thee, or anyone, to keep folks in work? Thy mill workers must work long hours, thou didst say. They will have no time to till their land. Perhaps they will sell it, thinking to make a living for ever from cotton, as thou wouldst have them do. Then when bad times come, how will they live? They will have forgotten how to knit, or never have learned; they won't know how to spin, or not on a spinning wheel, and besides they'll have no sheep to give them wool. Have they to starve in bad times, where once they could have been sure of work and food?'

'They can hire themselves out. There's always work to be found, by those willing to look for it.'

'Here in the Dales? There are few enough great landowners who want hired labourers.'

'Then they'll have to move away, won't they?' He released her hands, clearly losing patience with her. 'If you want it bluntly, Hannah, there's one good reason not to go in for wool-spinning – there's no money in it.'

'Not here in the Dales, where we live by wool?'

'I tell you, Hannah, handknitting is dying out. It must die out. They're already knitting with machines in Nottingham.'

'So they have for years, but it has made no difference.'

'There are new machines every day, improved ones. Besides, people want lighter clothes now – the people who pay good prices, that is – clothes that are comfortable and easy to wash. They want silk and cotton. Oh, maybe you'd get by for a few years, spinning wool. But if you want to make your fortune, then it has to be cotton.'

At that moment something cut through the links of passion and love that joined Hannah to Robert, and she saw him, coolly, stripped of that aura: a cocky, assertive young man, who could not even begin to understand how she felt or thought.

'Is that the only thing that matters to thee – to line thy pockets? she demanded accusingly.

'What else is there?' He shrugged, and then, sensing perhaps the ominous shift in her mood, he added cajolingly, 'I told you yesterday, it's not the money by itself. It's what it will buy – prosperity, all the things you've never dreamed were possible, comforts and luxuries, real improvements.'

'For thy workers? Or for thee? How do Arkwright's workers live?'

'Better than most folks round here. You should see their houses, the food they have to eat. You'd soon see I know what I'm talking about.'

'But how many hours do they have at home? Are they free to walk out on the fells? Do they have land to work, a pig for meat and a cow for milk? How long didst thou say they must work at thy mill, each day?'

'Thirteen hours, in summer at least. In an orderly manner, the same hours every day. Sunday will be for cleaning and repairing the machinery, of course, so the hours will be shorter. But the workers like it, once they grow used to it. They know where they are: fixed hours, fixed wages. They quickly become clean and happy and industrious.'

'Like slaves,' said Hannah drily.

'These are English people!' He sounded indignant at the comparison. 'It's quite different. They are free to enter into employment or not, as they choose. And they do choose, believe me.' He grasped her hands again. 'What's the difference to the workers, whether it's wool or cotton, tell me that? Would the work not be much the same?'

She had of course no means of telling whether that was true or not, but she said, 'Just a small woollen mill would make all the difference, I should think. It would not need three hundred people to run it, would it? Would not a handful be enough? It would help the knitters and the weavers, not take away all they have.'

'Maybe, for a short while. But, Hannah, like it or not, the cotton mills will come to the Dales. If I don't do it, someone else will. Why should we not be there at the start?'

She felt as if they were beginning to go round in circles. She said quietly, but with an increasing sense of hopelessness, 'Give a thought to what I say, Robert. I could be happy with a woollen mill.'

'You will be happy with a cotton mill, I promise you that. And I have no intention whatsoever of setting up a woollen mill. I do not act against my better judgement. Besides, Sir George promised the money for cotton, not wool. Make up your mind to it, Hannah. You're like my father, suspicious of change. But once see the sense of it, and you'll come round, as he will.'

She seized on that last phrase. 'Then thy father opposes thee too? He will not let thee have the mill?'

194

'He will,' said Robert easily. 'He'll see the sense of it. When you tell him you're with me, then he'll change his tune. And you'll do that, won't you, because I ask it?' He smiled cajolingly, clearly expecting her immediate capitulation.

She did not give it, but she knew all the same that in this she had to acknowledge defeat. She felt very tired and more than a little depressed, and she had no wish now to go on battering him with arguments to which he was clearly impervious. But, victorious in that matter, he might be ready to give way on another. 'There is one thing, Robert —'

Conscious of her implied acquiescence, he kissed her before prompting easily, 'Yes?'

'We must take no cotton from slave plantations.'

He shook his head firmly. 'Oh no, Hannah, not that! I take the best cotton, and that comes from Barbados. Besides, I've given my word, and I don't go back on it.'

'What a sense of honour!' she threw at him, her voice resonant with scorn. 'Thou wilt not break with some fat slave owner, but thou art content to make thy money from the most evil trade the world has ever known!'

'Did you not hear me yesterday? Do you heed nothing I say? They're all lies, the stories you've been told.'

She shook her head. 'No, Robert. I am sorry, but I cannot believe thee. What is thy authority? The word of slave traders and slave owners, men who grow fat on the suffering of our African brothers and sisters? I will not take their word against John Woolman's testimony. He had no need to speak out. It gave him pain to argue against men he liked. But he knew it was what he must do. And I know what I must do too.' She paused to draw breath, and then concluded vehemently, 'I *cannot* – I will not – have any part in an enterprise that has any truck with slavery!'

At that he made a great furious, sweeping gesture with his hand. 'Stupid, mawkish woman! This is business, not a tuppenny novel!'

Hannah, who had never in her life read a novel, ignored the remark and retorted, 'All of life is subject to the truth, Robert – in thy business as much as within thy family.'

'Don't preach at me! I can tell you, if you want to do well in business, you must put that kind of talk aside.'

She shook her head. 'Never!'

'Hannah, I shall not give in, so you can get that into your stubborn little head, like it or not. *I* make the decisions about Thornside mill, all of them.'

'What kind of partner shall I be then, with no voice?'

'You're a woman, a wife. Do what you like in the house. In the mill I decide. And I make my decisions only and always on the basis of what's best for business.'

'And for thee!'

'Very well, and for me. *Me*, mind – not for you, not for my father, not for our neighbours, nor for any whining hypocritical Friends who think they know better than we lesser mortals what's good for us. *That*'s what's going to make this country prosper – men who have the courage to break free of the past and change things, whatever the odds, whatever the obstacles in their path. And no one, not even you, will stop me now!'

'I wish for changes too, Robert.' Even to her ears, her voice sounded very small and desolate, yet with a note of passionate conviction vibrating beneath its quiet tones. 'But not riches, or great industries, or a nation of manufacturers striving to make and sell more than anyone else. That is a mean and ignoble end, not worth the seeking. What I would ask for is a world where men and women care for one another, a world without slavery and cruelty and oppression and war, where no one goes hungry or ignorant, where all live together in freedom and dignity and simplicity as brothers and sisters.'

'Hannah!' he broke in derisively. 'Men have been babbling such nonsense since time began. Where has

it ever got them? Laughed at, stoned, beaten, killed –
and the world's not a whit better for it. Martyrdom's
for fools!'

'Better that, than never to have tried!'

'Hannah, I'm not asking you to be a saint. All I want
is a wife.'

She drew a deep, steadying breath, though it was
hard, and painful. 'That is what I wish too, Robert –
to be thy wife. But I cannot wed thee while this stands
between us.'

He stared at her in half-laughing incredulity. 'Are
you threatening me?'

'No,' she replied quietly. 'I am saying only what
must be.' So soft and steady a voice, so unflinching
a gaze, when, inside, her heart was thudding in great
throbbing beats, and she felt as if she could scarcely
breathe. Let him give way! Oh Lord, let him give way!
she prayed, while she knew – and shrank from – what
she must do if he did not do so.

Robert became brisk and sensible. 'Don't be foolish,
Hannah! For God's sake, let's go and get on with
the arrangements for our marriage. This haggling is
getting us nowhere.'

'Without agreement we cannot marry.'

'You'll come round. Give it time. You'll see the right
of it soon enough.' His voice was infinitely coaxing, and
his eyes on her face were full of tenderness. She knew
he still did not quite believe that she meant what she
said.

'Robert, I am in earnest. I will not be thy wife so long
as though dost set thy face against what is right.'

After that, he was silent for a long time. She watched
him, seeing all kinds of emotions pass fleetingly or at
length over his face: wonder, anger, inquiry, bewilderment, astonishment, irritation, exasperation, amusement; and at last anger again, a sudden fierce explosion
of anger that sent his hand out to clasp her arm in a
ferocious grip.

'I see what it is! I see it all now! It's that damned brother of mine! He's been at you, hasn't he? Filling your head full of nonsense. Oh, I know that quiet, meek way of his! All the time I've been away, he's been scheming, to win you, to win my father, in everything. He's always been jealous, hasn't he? Slimy little worm that he is! That's it, isn't it?'

She cried out at the pain of his grip, but also because of the rage that exploded in her too. He was so far from the truth, so far from beginning to understand what she was saying. She tried to pull free, but she only hurt herself the more. Through the pain, she threw at him, 'No one's been scheming. Thou knows that! I have always believed this, always, and so do they all, and thou too, or why claim to be a Friend at all?'

The expression that twisted his mouth was more of a sneer than a grin. 'For you, of course. So you wouldn't be disowned for marrying me. Why else? You don't think I care for all that gibberish any more, do you?'

She stood there, his hands still on her arm, staring at him, her breath held in shock. Yet she had known it all along; something deep inside her had told her so. He had not changed. He had always been like this. It was she who had been blind. Her fierce, impulsive love, which had seemed so good, so transfiguring, had simply hidden the truth from her. She saw that love now for what it was: not love at all, but lust, an evil, squalid, dirty thing, which had possessed her, was close to overpowering her, so that if she did not act at once she would be dragged inexorably into some mire from which there would be no escape as long as she lived, some place of misery and darkness, like the hell in which her mother lived.

She forced it aside, let her breath go, released the anguish of it all in a furious retort. 'I tell thee one thing, Robert Gayle – thy brother's a better man than thou wilt ever be!'

He flung her from him with an abrupt, infuriated

gesture, which for a moment hurt her more than his grasp had done and sent her stumbling back until a chair stopped her. She put out a hand to steady herself, hearing Robert spit at her.

'Marry *him*, then! See what kind of a milksop husband he makes you!'

She threw up her head. 'Then I will! For one thing's certain – no woman could ever be happy with thee!'

She pushed past him, ran to the door, out to the passage, across the yard, down the hill and over the beck to Low Farm. She was leaving the darkness behind her, all the evil impulses of her nature, all her mother's blighted inheritance. She was going to Samuel, to light and peace and kindliness, to the way she had been taught to follow.

She found him at work in the parlour, preparing for the pupil he was to see later that morning. He had his back to her and was reading with such concentration that she had to speak his name in a furious hiss before he looked up. Then he adjusted his spectacles and examined the pale, trembling girl before him with a mixture of concern and alarm.

'Hannah! What ails thee?'

'Nowt,' she said, in a hard brisk voice. 'I'll marry thee, that's all.'

She had in all her life seen nothing to match the utter disbelieving amazement on Samuel's face. He stared at her, opening and closing his mouth without any sound emerging. The colour drained from his face and then flooded back, and spread until every inch of his skin was deeply red. He closed his mouth, and swallowed hard several times, and then he said in a tiny, silly voice, half croak, half squeak, 'What didst thou say?'

She found that she too could not breathe steadily, or speak with any ease. The stubborn, impulsive purpose that had brought her here was already losing its force. She was no longer quite sure why she was here or what she was doing. But she had begun, so she must go on. 'Marry me,' she said, without firmness.

She was not surprised that he still could not believe her. 'But thou art to wed Robert.'

She shook her head, vehemently, for of that at least she was absolutely sure. 'Never, Samuel, never! He's not what I thought . . . Since he came back . . . Before . . .' Her voice was harsh and rough, her eyes brimming with unshed tears. Soon she would weep in earnest.

'I know,' said Samuel, nodding. He had regained some degree of control. 'I've —'

'Don't!' That she should say it, that was one thing; she could not bear to hear it from him. She felt as if every part of her was hurting terribly, too much for words. She wanted to end it, quickly. She said, 'So it's thee I'll marry, if thou wilt have me.'

He gazed at her in wonder, like a man suddenly given a distant glimpse of Paradise, but not quite able to believe it was real. 'If I'll have thee . . .!' His voice was soft with awe. 'Oh, Hannah, there's nothing in all the world I want more . . . I never thought . . . If thou art certain, quite certain.'

She nodded fiercely, but it was as if something outside herself was forcing her to that affirmation, not the feelings at her heart. 'I am certain. Completely certain.'

He still could not believe that it was as simple as that. 'But, Robert – what will he say?'

She did not want to think of Robert. She did not even want to remember that Robert existed. He did not exist, not her Robert, the man she had loved. He had been an illusion, all along. When she saw what he really was, she had fled from him as if from a ghost – from darkness to light, to safety. Only it did not feel like a haven. It all felt grey and unreal. She seemed to be moving in a fog that might lift at any moment and show her the full horror of this place. She said, quickly, 'He doesn't want to wed me. We find we don't suit.'

Samuel stood up then, slowly, like a man in a dream. He studied her face with great care, searching it for the least sign of doubt or hesitation. What he saw she did not know, but eventually he said, 'Thou art not happy about it.' He sounded resigned, as if that was only to be expected.

Hannah forced a smile, exaggeratedly bright. 'I am content. I wish to be thy wife.' There was some kind of truth in it. She was in too deep now ever to turn back. Samuel was not like Robert. She could not reject him without hurting him more than he could ever deserve.

She reached out and took his hands in hers, and looked into his face, the kindly, unimpressive face of a man who all his life would seek strenuously to do what was right, who, if he ever acted from self-interest, would do so unconsciously, from a temporary confusion about his motives; the face of a man to whom she had often gone in times of trouble, but who must never know of the anguish that raged now beneath her calm exterior.

'Dost think I would say it if it were not true?' she asked, and saw the anxious lines of his face soften slowly into joy.

CHAPTER NINE

'In the presence of the Lord and of this assembly, I take this my Friend Samuel Gayle to be my husband, promising by divine assistance to be unto him a loving and faithful wife, until it shall please the Lord by death to separate us.'

It was done. She was Samuel's wife. She had given her heart and her body to Robert – but she must not think of that. She crushed the thought, as she had done time and time again during the days since she had made her choice. Robert no longer had any place in her life. She belonged now, for ever, to Samuel; as Samuel belonged to her.

Outside the meeting house there was much restrained kissing and embracing, which kept her from thinking. She glimpsed Samuel's bright, proud, happy face and, at a distance, Robert watching her with that look of sneering contempt with which, lately, he had greeted her whenever they met. It hurt her, but it angered her more. He had clearly tried to avoid her as much as was possible during the past days. She supposed he had come to the meeting house today because not to have done so would cause comment; and because he did not want anyone to have grounds for saying, 'Poor Robert – see how he suffers!' She was quite sure he did not suffer.

They all went up to High Farm for the simple abundance of the wedding feast, which she and Agnes and Mary Harker had spent several days preparing. She ate little. She sat at Samuel's side amongst the guests and felt as if she was not really there, as if it was all a dream.

There was no dancing afterwards, of course, as this was a Quaker wedding, and no singing, but the guests lingered long after they had satisfied their hunger, talking happily about past weddings and other family events, glad of the rare opportunity to rejoice at an unequivocally Quaker marriage. Some time before dark all but the immediate members of the family took their leave. Soon only Samuel and Hannah and Agnes would be left, to begin their new life together. Because Agnes was a widow and needed Hannah's help on the farm, Samuel was to move in with them, and so this first night of their marriage, like every night to come, would be spent in the bed where John and Agnes had slept each night that they were together. Agnes, at her own insistence, would have Hannah's little room, high under the roof. But it was not quite time for that yet. There were the last – and closest – guests to be seen on their way.

Robert had been present at the meal, but had kept well out of Hannah's way, amongst the guests seated furthest from the newly married couple. She had been conscious of him, of course, and of the hateful expression of his eyes when, from time to time, she found herself looking his way. But to her relief he appeared to have left early, for she had not seen him for several hours.

Joseph Gayle still sat at the table, talking in a desultory way, as if he could not bear to go home to a house which no longer contained his younger son. But at last he rose to his feet and said, 'I'd best be going now.' He laid a hand on Hannah's shoulder. 'I'll say one thing, Hannah. Samuel's mother would have been proud to see this day. I'm that glad myself I hardly know how to tell thee.' The emotional roughness of his voice gave emphasis to what he said.

Hannah kissed him, but could find no suitable reply. Her predominant feeling was one of guilt, because she knew how unworthy she was of the old man's approval.

Samuel went to the door with his father, and Agnes and Hannah began to tidy up and gather together the dishes. Hannah took a pile of plates to the kitchen for washing.

She had expected to find the room empty, but in the doorway, suddenly conscious that someone was there before her, she drew in a sharp breath, from surprise. Facing her across the littered table, just as if he had been waiting for her, was Robert.

'I thought thou hadst gone,' Hannah said. She knew that her breathing had quickened, though whether from apprehension or the old attraction still tugging at her she could not be sure.

'I was taking the air, that's all. You surely don't think I'd go without seizing a last moment alone with you, do you?' He had his back to the window and she could not see his face, but the unpleasantness of his tone told her quite enough. 'I hope you're satisfied, now you've lost me the mill.'

For a moment the cold anger of that accusation stopped her breath. Then she began, with difficulty, to resume breathing, her eyes on the dark unseen face. 'What dost thou mean?'

'Don't play the innocent with me! You knew full well that if you weren't a part of my plans, then my father would never agree to them.'

She had not once given a thought to that aspect of the matter. It was in a kind of panic that she had run to Samuel, and since that day she had made strenuous efforts not to think of Robert at all. Now, just for an instant, she found herself feeling sorry for his lost hopes. Then she realised more clearly what his words implied. She drew a deep breath, to try and keep some steadiness in her voice.

'Thy father would never have agreed with thee. He was set against it from the start. Besides, thou knows I think him right in that.' She paused, just long enough to close the door behind her, and then she continued in an undertone, 'Dost thou forget it was thou didst urge me to marry Samuel?'

He waved a hand airily. 'Oh, never fear, he's welcome to you! You don't think I'd have had you after all that preaching, do you? I've always thought Friends gave too much freedom to their womenfolk. When I marry, my wife will second my wishes, not oppose them.' The look in her eyes told him how much she still opposed them, and how his contempt for her opinion stirred up all her anger against him. 'You'll turn it into a woollen mill, I suppose?' he demanded.

The anger subsided, to be replaced by bewilderment. 'What . . .?'

'Thornside mill – you and Samuel. You'll set up your precious woollen mill. He'll do exactly what you want, of course.'

'But we're not going to Thornside. We're to live here.'

'Really?' His tone was sharp with disbelief.

'Thou hast no cause to think otherwise.'

Behind her the door clattered open. She looked round as Samuel himself came in. For an instant she saw his face, tender and happy, as his eyes came to rest on her. He closed the door and stepped nearer. Then he realised Robert was there, and a little of the warmth went, to be replaced by the faintly defensive look he always had in his brother's company; even now, Hannah thought, just a little irritably, when he had every reason to be able to look Robert confidently in the eye.

'I did not know thou wast still here,' he said uncertainly.

'Disappointed, dear brother?' Samuel seemed unsurprised by the sneering unpleasantness of his tone. Hannah found herself wondering if Robert often spoke to him like that, at least when no one else was by. She had, after all, only lately begun to discover Robert's real nature.

'But,' Robert went on in the same mocking tone, 'I had to be sure all was well with you before I left. It must be such a burden for your poor befuddled brain, to have such a prospect before you. Oh, in case you don't follow my drift: I was telling Hannah – I gather you are to have Thornside mill.'

'Me? That's the first I've heard of it. As far as I know, it's to be sold.' Hannah stared at him. How could he speak so casually, faced with his brother's crushing contempt? She would have wanted to fight him; she would have done so now, on Samuel's behalf, except that she had the feeling that she would be intruding into something that had its roots far in the past, in experiences of which she knew nothing. She did not, after all, know what Samuel thought of such treatment, and, besides, for her to leap to his defence might only emphasise his weakness in his brother's eyes. But she wished she did not find herself sharing some of Robert's contempt for Samuel's spinelessness.

Robert shrugged. 'Ah well, what does it matter? I'll be looking for other premises, that's all I know.'

So her precipitate action had gone for nothing after all! 'Then thou hast still set thy heart on a cotton mill?'

He turned cold eyes on her. She had not thought those brown eyes could look cold. 'Of course. Even my father can't halt progress.' He looked from Hannah to Samuel and back again. There was something speculative in his gaze. A faint smile, scarcely perceptible, touched his lips. 'Well, I'll take my leave of you both. You must be panting to be left alone to taste the delights of your wedding night to the full.'

The chill in his eyes seemed to reach Hannah at last, for she felt frozen, bracing herself against something that she sensed was hovering unspoken between them – something that must remain unspoken, at all costs. Only all power had left her, to do anything to ensure that end. She could neither move nor speak.

In the dimness near the door, Samuel had coloured a little. Robert's smile grew. It was a thoroughly unpleasant smile by now.

'Of course,' he went on, brightly, his voice very clear in the silence, though it was not raised in any way, 'it's more of a pleasure when one of you has a little experience. You are fortunate in that, you two. The first time can be such a fumbling affair.'

Hannah saw how shocked Samuel was, and how deeply embarrassed. 'Robert! That's not true! Thou knows —'

'Not you, brother dear. I do not doubt that you are the purest of virgins, unsullied and untouched. No, I was referring to your lovely bride, the so virtuous and high-minded Hannah. Speaking for myself, I wouldn't care to wed a whore, but it's as well someone will have her. She'll be able to teach you a thing or two, I'm sure. I enjoyed her greatly at Thornside mill, three weeks ago. When you go there, note the sacks in the loft — you'll maybe see the impression of her body still, where I pressed it to them.' He looked again from one to another of the two still figures, with their white, appalled faces. He smiled more than ever, and then made two neat little bows, one to each of them. 'I must be on my way, brother and . . . sister: does that make it incest, I wonder? I give you goodnight.' And then he swung round and walked briskly but calmly out of the room. Into the silence there came, after a moment, the sound of an outer door closing, and of steps crossing the yard, accompanied by a cheerful whistle.

Hannah could not move. She felt dazed, caught still in the frozen immobility that had struck her when she had first sensed what Robert had meant to do. Why had she not stopped him, somehow, anyhow, before it was too late? But then he had deliberately planned it all, from the chance meeting in the kitchen to its appalling end; Hannah had no doubt at all of that.

And once Robert had made up his mind to a course of action, then nothing and no one would be allowed to thwart him. He would have had his way eventually whatever she might have done.

Samuel was standing equally still, equally silent. He looked at her with eyes that were at once horrified and questioning and imploring. 'It was a lie,' he croaked at last.

Hannah shook her head. 'No, it is true.' There was despair behind the quiet expressionless words.

At that moment, Agnes, cheerful and full of affectionate chatter, came into the kitchen, and somehow, automatically, not quite knowing what they were doing, they moved to help her, finding her presence both an intrusion and a relief. For the moment at least they did not have to face each other, or the terrible revelation that had been Robert's wedding gift to them.

But at last everything that could possibly be done was done, food and dishes cleared away, washed and stored, chairs and stools returned to their places, the hens barred in, the peats in the hearth smothered for the night. Agnes turned smiling to them both and said, 'That's enough for today. You'd best get to bed.' She came to kiss them both, while they forced some kind of smile for her benefit. 'God keep you both.'

They went upstairs in silence, Hannah just ahead, Samuel carrying the candle, neither looking at one another nor touching. Hannah pushed open the bedroom door and he followed her in, closing it behind him. She did not look round, but went to the window and stood gazing out into the dusk without seeing anything of the familiar view – familiar, yet just a little unfamiliar from the angle of this window, from which she had rarely looked. She knew Samuel had come to a halt just inside the door, and that he was looking at her, but she dared not turn round to meet what was in his eyes. Even without looking at him, she could sense the confusion of hurt and bewilderment that filled him. If it had been anger now, that would have been easier to face.

'Hannah, look at me, please!'

She did turn then, because she owed him that at least, the courage to face him. But she had known that, confronted with all the evidence of his pain, it would be harder, much harder, to retain her courage. She was right. His expression held all the anguish that she had expected, together with a kind of silent plea that she might somehow be able to tell him he was mistaken, that it was all a silly misunderstanding. He looked so pale, so drawn and exhausted, his common-place features cruelly unattractive under the stress of painful emotion, with no trace now of the proud and happy young man who had walked to High Farm at her side a few short hours ago. Was this how he would look when he was old? It was hard at the moment to remember that he was, like her, only twenty-one.

'He did not really mean it. He is jealous. I cannot blame him for that. But I think thou dost not know what he accused thee of.' He sounded as if he was trying to convince himself, not her.

She swallowed, and forced herself to stay calm, her eyes steady on his face. 'I do know,' she said. 'I wish I did not.' She swallowed again, trying to let the words flow freely through the constriction in her throat. 'I thought . . .' Why was it so hard to say, when the thing was so simple? 'I did not know how he had changed. I thought he was Robert, the Robert I used to know. No, I never knew him, I think. I thought I did, and it was him I loved.' She was terrified that if she said any more she would cry, so she fell silent. She knew that now, to Samuel, her eyes must look imploring, begging him to understand.

Little changed in his expression. After a moment he slowly shook his head, as if at some dismaying reflection that he could not bear to put into words. At last – it seemed like hours later – he asked drily, 'Art thou with child?'

Somehow in all the feelings of guilt, the chaotic emotions of the past days, she had not even considered that possibility. Now, it added a new dimension to her present anguish. 'I don't know. I don't think so.' She was trying to convince herself as much as him.

He watched her for some time longer. There was no pleading in his eyes now, nor any bewilderment. He simply looked gloomily pensive, as if trying from the depths of his shock to understand how the woman he loved could ever have behaved like this. For she knew it was appalling, what she had been forced to confess to him tonight. It was not just the betrayal, her coming to him already soiled (as he must see it), having given her body to another man. It was also the fact that she had admitted to loving that other man, not simply years ago, but only three weeks ago, deeply and surely enough to surrender herself to him. Being Samuel, he would be left with some eternally gnawing doubt that the love lingered still, in spite of what she said.

Worst of all perhaps was the deceit. She had asked him to marry her, knowing what had happened between herself and Robert, and prepared, apparently, to keep the truth hidden from Samuel for ever. She had not thought Robert would want to speak of it, but that did not excuse her in any way, she who had preached morality with such fervour to Robert. What words could ever be adequate to express her remorse, or ask Samuel's forgiveness? What indeed could she do to put things right? She doubted if a lifetime would be long enough for what ought to be done.

Eventually he stirred, as if about to take a step forward, though for the moment he did not do so. 'We'd best go to bed,' he said.

She had wondered what it would be like, lying in bed with Samuel, held in his arms, with his hands caressing her, his thin body pressed to hers. She supposed he had never been with a woman; certainly he would not have his brother's experience. He might be shy and awkward. She had thought that he might need her help and her encouragement. She had thought how she would tenderly woo him to passion and its consummation, guided by the knowledge she had gained with Robert, and by her affection for Samuel, her real desire to make him happy. She had wondered, though she had tried not to dwell on it, for it hurt too much, if she would be able to respond to him as she had to Robert, and if she would find herself all the time comparing him, to his disadvantage, with his brother.

It was nothing like that at all. On opposite sides of the room, not looking at one another, they undressed and put on their night clothes. Then they climbed into bed. Samuel blew out the candle and lay down with his back to Hannah, as far from her as possible and very still. He said nothing at all.

For a long time, hoping that he might move or speak or do something to break the hateful tension of that silence, Hannah lay on her back with her head turned just enough so that she could make out his outline in the darkness, a blur against the faint pallor of the pillow. She longed to reach out and touch him, to seek comfort and offer it too, but she did not dare to do so. At last she said, 'Samuel, I am sorry. I am truly sorry.'

He did not move. His only response, scarcely heard, was a faint grunt, which told her nothing of what he felt. She did not dare to try any other means of attracting his attention. She had, after all, done him harm enough already.

The night seemed endless. If she slept at all, it was only briefly and lightly, without any sense of repose. She supposed Samuel slept, because even when she moved restlessly from side to side he did not stir. He might almost have been dead, for all the indication of life he gave. Only the faint sound of his breathing in the dark, and the warmth that reached her across the distance that separated them, told her that the shape in the bed was that of a living man. She thought, 'I loved Robert, and then I found he was a stranger. So I married Samuel, and now he is a stranger too.' She felt like weeping, but she would not allow herself to do so. After all, she had only herself to blame for this misery.

Next morning, as soon as the dawn light had grown strong enough for there to be no need of a candle, Hannah slid out of bed, and Samuel did the same. As they dressed she watched him, darting furtive glances at his face. He looked as pale and drawn as she knew she must, worse even than he had last night, in the first shock of her revelation. She realised that he had slept no more than she had. She was astonished at the self control that had kept him unmoving in the same position all night long. Self control – or was it rather the immobility of despair? It occurred to her, as something rather trivial and unimportant, that anyone seeing them would conclude (rightly enough) that something had gone disastrously wrong with their wedding night. She hoped they need not meet anyone today.

They could not avoid Agnes, of course. They came down to the kitchen in silence – they had neither of them said one word to the other since last night – and Agnes turned to smile at them, with some surprise in her expression. 'I thought you'd be lying late this morning.'

As they came where the light from the kitchen window fell on their faces, she broke off, clearly shocked by what she saw. Hannah knew that she was on the point of asking what was wrong, but she checked herself. Perhaps she did not want to do so while Samuel was there. Hannah determined that, as far as lay in her power, Agnes would have no opportunity to question her alone, at least until the worst was over; if it was ever to be over.

She was not hungry, and she shrank from the company of others, however few. What she wanted more than anything was to escape on to the fell, where she could be alone, and no one would scan her expression or wonder what was wrong, and where she might have time to understand her own feelings and think what must be done. There must be some way of escape for herself and for Samuel from the horror that had engulfed them, though whether together or apart she did not know. She did not even know what she would choose for them both, if any choice remained to them; except the impossible, that all this might never have happened. In any case, how far back would she go, in wishing things undone? To Robert's disclosure last night? The marriage ceremony? The break with Robert? The lovemaking at the mill? Or – further back than all, a long way back, the root of everything perhaps – to the day of the sheep clipping, when he had first shown her the face of the woman he loved?

It was Samuel who, as soon as their desultory breakfast was over, made his escape on to the fell. Hannah, conscious that in the flurry of wedding preparations many routine tasks had been neglected, tried to give her attention to some of them. She knew it would be impossible to avoid being alone with Agnes, but to put off the inevitable, she took a batch of stockings out to the beck for the washing that was necessary to shrink them to the right size and firmness for selling. Agnes, not so easily put off, found a few pairs she had overlooked, and came out to her.

'Thou hast missed these.' She laid them on the grass beside Hannah, who did not look round. Agnes stood for a little while in silence, and then said, 'All's not well, Hannah lass. What is it?'

Hannah, head bent, continued to rub hard with the soap at the harsh oily wool – dark charcoal brown, from one of the black sheep. 'It's a good colour, this wool. We've enough left for a dozen more pairs of stockings.'

'Hannah —'

'What wouldst think to a pair of gloves in the pattern I worked last winter? That would look well. I could knit them for thee.'

It was like two separate, unconnected conversations, heard simultaneously and entwined together purely by accident. Agnes made no comment on what Hannah said, but at the same time acknowledged defeat herself. She said only, 'When a woman's wed, there are things she must keep to herself. But thou knows, I think, if ever thou shouldst want to talk, I'll hear thee, and gladly.' Then, when no sign came from Hannah that she had even taken in what was said, Agnes returned slowly to the house.

The two women were knitting by the fire when Samuel returned. It was growing dark, at the end of what had seemed an interminable day. Hannah had dreaded Samuel's return, yet now she was glad to see him, sensing the immediate release of tension brought by this intervention of a third person, before whom any intimate talk was no longer possible. Agnes at once put her knitting aside and became smiling and animated. 'Hast eaten, my lad? I'll get thee something.'

'I am not hungry, I thank thee,' Samuel said quietly, without smiling. Hannah shot a furtive look at him. There was more colour to his face than there had been this morning, but that might simply be the result of a day in the fresh air. In every other respect he looked as drawn and weary as ever. No, Hannah amended, more weary, with the look of a man who had been battered by so many emotions for so long that he had emerged at last drained of all energy, reduced to the empty calmness of exhaustion, in which he had ceased to feel pain because he was simply too weary to feel anything.

Hannah, unable to look any longer, bent her head. She heard Samuel say, 'I shall go to bed.' She knew he was watching her, willing her to go with him, but she shrank from doing so. There was a little pause, and then she heard him leave the room. The sound of the stairs creaking beneath his tread seemed painfully loud in the stillness.

'Thou hadst best go up too,' said Agnes.

Hannah could think of no excuse to stay, and so she gave in. She knitted carefully to the centre of a row, folded her knitting and put it in her pocket. Then she kissed Agnes and made her way up the stairs.

Samuel seemed to be waiting for her, unless he was simply too troubled by his thoughts to make any move to get into bed. He stood near the window, quite still. Hannah could see, even in the unlit dusk, that he was frowning. As she closed the door, he turned to face her.

'I have struggled to clear my mind today, Hannah, to know what must be done,' he said quietly, his tone without expression. 'I forgive thee. But . . .' He paused, and then went on, with a sudden quivering of the voice, 'Thou must not ask me to put it from my mind, not yet. I do not know if I can learn to love thee again, as I did once. I love thee still,' – he did not sound very sure about that, Hannah thought – 'but it cannot be as it was. I must have more time.'

Hannah stood looking at him, biting her lip as she did so. She was not quite sure how she felt, except that a sense of misery was uppermost, because their deep and happy friendship had been destroyed so quickly and so effortlessly, as if it had never been. But then friendship required trust and openness, and she had failed him in both those things.

Samuel had already turned away and begun to undress. Hannah now did the same. She knew that once again a great emptiness would lie between them in bed, symbolic of the gulf that now divided them

– tonight, and for many, many nights to come. She wondered, even, if their marriage would ever become a marriage in anything but name, or whether what she had done would always keep Samuel from being able to consummate it. Bleakly, she contemplated a future in which this separation became a permanent thing, so that they would be unable ever to share or to confide in one another, as once they might have done. They would have to accept too the impossibility of confiding so painful and private a matter in anyone else, and the knowledge that there could never be children born to them, unless by any chance she were to find herself carrying Robert's child; which was an appalling prospect, certain only to make everything much worse. She lay in the dark, filled with dread, unable to find any comfort anywhere, in anything.

Joseph Gayle came round at supper time next day. Hannah and Samuel – independently, for they discussed nothing together – made a strenuous effort to behave as if nothing was wrong. If they were more silent than usual, Joseph Gayle noticed nothing. He was in any case too full of his own news to allow the silence to last for long.

'Robert's found himself a mill,' he said, as he accepted Agnes's warm invitation to take a bowl of porridge with them.

Hannah felt as if her heart was turning right over. She wanted to question Joseph at once, but she knew how much her colour had risen, and she did not dare to risk lifting her head or speaking. Samuel clearly had himself under greater control, for Hannah heard him say, in a tone of polite interest, 'Has he? Where?'

'Well, by rights it's not a mill yet, just the land. A mile out of Thornside, south west of thy uncle's mill. Maybe thou knows Newgill farm?'

'Aye.'

'Just there. The house is a ruin, past repair. He'll pull

216

it down and build his mill there. Sir George Scarr's come up with the cash, it seems.'

So that was that. The cotton mills would come to Thornside after all, as Robert had promised they would. Hannah felt that she did not greatly care any more.

But on making her way up to bed that night, pleading a genuine tiredness to escape from the company, she had one fear set at rest: she knew she was not carrying Robert's child. For a little time, she felt a real lifting of the spirits. The tiredness left her, though she went to bed all the same. She lay there with the candle burning, feeling as if in some way the blood that poured from her body was taking her sin away with it, promising a new beginning. When Samuel came up, much later, she greeted him with a warm smile.

'Samuel, I am not with child.'

He stood looking at her from the doorway. She could not tell from his expression what he was thinking. After a moment or two, he said, 'I see. I am glad.' But he did not sound particularly glad, or sorry either. She realised with a chill that nothing had changed.

CHAPTER TEN

i

For some weeks now the Hollinthwaite cows had been grazing on the fog, the after-grass that greened the meadows after the hay had been cut, providing additional feed for the beasts before Martinmas, when they would be brought in for the winter. It was to the hay meadow then that Hannah went to milk the two High Farm cows. On her way, walking briskly in the crisp hazy air, she came up with another young woman, bound on the same errand: Jane Alderson, who was now Jane Dinsdale, and heavily pregnant.

Hannah smiled at her, and saw how, automatically, her eyes went at once to Hannah's waist. They all did that, all the village women, looking for the first signs of swelling. Hannah knew what they were thinking, and bore the looks and the occasional spoken hints as patiently as she was able. She could hardly say, 'Do not look to us for anything. There will be no child born to me and Samuel.'

The backcans, empty now before milking, were light on the women's backs, and left their hands free. But there were the milking stools to carry, and Jane had hooked her arms through the legs of hers so that – a little awkwardly – she could knit as she went.

'There's that many things I want for the bairn,' she said. 'I cannot spare a moment from the knitting.'

'I suppose thou must be spinning all the time, at home.' Jane was married to Mark Dinsdale, Hollinthwaite's only weaver. Like most weavers whose looms were equipped with the new flying shuttle, he found that the supply of spun yarn never quite kept pace with his needs.

Jane smiled knowingly. 'Ah, now there thou art mistaken. Not any more, I don't. We have all the yarn we need now, and to spare.' Her smile broadened. 'We've got one of those jennies. Sixteen bobbins at once, it spins – and in half the time, I'd say. It's easy enough to work too, much easier than a spinning wheel.'

'It's worked by hand then?' Hannah felt a genuine curiosity about the new machine.

'Aye,' said Jane. 'Of course, it won't do the carding. I tell thee, carding used to be the easy part, fast done. Now it seems to take hours. Mark says there's a good carding machine made now, but it needs water to power it.'

'It's a small machine then, the jenny?'

'Aye. There are bigger ones, but what we've got is enough for us. We haven't that much space. He heard of it from Kit Dinsdale – thou knows, his cousin from Thornside. He's right envious, Kit is. He hasn't even room for a small machine.' Hannah knew how crowded and cramped many of the houses at Thornside were, so that a loom alone would already take more space than many a family could comfortably spare.

'Wouldst mind if I were to call on thee to see it?'

Jane seemed to find such interest surprising, but she said amiably enough, 'Of course not. Come whenever thou wilt. Once milking's done, I'll be at home all day.'

Hannah sat with her head pressed against the flank of the first cow, drowsily watching the jets of milk sing into the can as her hands rhythmically squeezed and pulled at the teats. The creamy liquid frothed slowly up the sides of the receptacle, warm and sweet smelling, but she scarcely saw it. Her thoughts were on the little conversation with Jane: a trivial enough exchange of talk between neighbours, on the surface at least, but it had set all kinds of reflections rippling out in her mind. It was a long time since her brain had been so busy, almost as if Jane's chance remarks had pierced through the long sleep of her misery and jolted her suddenly awake.

They had been terrible, these first months of married life, the more so because there was no one in whom she felt able to confide. Samuel was almost always polite to her, even considerate, in a detached sort of way, as he would be to a stranger. But there was no warmth in his manner, still less any encouragement to intimacy. Sometimes Hannah longed to try and reach him, by pleading, or a touch or a caress, but she was held back not just by the near-certainty of rejection, but also by a sense that such treatment of her was, after all, no more than she deserved.

If Samuel had not been by nature so quiet and self effacing, his manner to her might have caused comment from their neighbours. Agnes, of course, knew things were badly wrong, but she hid her anxieties in public with the same determination that Hannah used to give the appearance of calm happiness.

But hiding her misery did not make it go away. On the contrary, it seemed only to fester there, like a neglected sore, poisoning every part of a life that once had offered her a measure of satisfaction and contentment. Every day seemed grey and featureless, its routines without joy, without even any sense of purpose. She passed her life continually in the company of other people, yet she felt desperately alone.

What made it worse was that Robert was clearly prospering. He was rarely at home and (mercifully) they never met, but reports reached High Farm of the progress of his mill. The land had been cleared, the new building had already reached first floor level, advertisements had been placed in local papers for workers to build and operate the machines. Her rejection of him had made not the slightest difference to his progress that she could see. The cotton mills were coming to the Dales, exactly as he had planned, and certainly he would be using cotton contaminated by the barbarity of slavery. She could not have married him and allowed herself to become a part of that; but what good otherwise had her rejection of him done?

Except that it left her free, free of all he stood for, free, in spite of everything, to continue to oppose him, if the chance should arise. It had not occurred to her before that she might do so. People did not oppose Robert, not if they were sensible, level-headed people; but had not John Burton often said to Hannah, 'What the world calls foolishness, lass, be sure that's nearly always the right way to go'? And what better way to oppose Robert's grandiose plans, than by doing what lay in her power to help the weavers and knitters of the Dales in their age-old industry, now so greatly threatened? In the houses of Thornside there was little space for the jennies that could spin yarn so quickly, for knitting as well as weaving. But Thornside mill had space enough, and water too, fit to power a machine that could card the wool for the jennies to work. It began to take shape in her mind. She saw the rooms restored, rearranged, not crowded as Robert's mill would be with an unimaginable mass of people who scarcely saw the light of day. No, Thornside mill would be equipped with perhaps three or four machines, worked by herself and a few men who had no other work to do. It would be a place to which farmers would bring their fleeces after clipping, or weavers the wool they had bought in, to be carded and spun at whatever cost was necessary to keep the machines in repair and provide a simple living for herself and Samuel – like a corn mill, useful, necessary, part of the life of the dale and its people.

She finished the milking, swung the full can onto her back and made her way home, walking as fast as was possible without spilling the milk. She left the can in the dairy – she would return later to separate the milk and churn the butter – and ran, through a sudden squally shower of rain, to the Dinsdales' cottage in the main street.

Jane welcomed her, putting aside her own dairy work, and led her to the main room of the house, lit by long windows, where Mark, working at his loom, nodded to her.

At the far side of the room stood a machine, smaller and lower than the loom, but, like it, made of wood. At one end of it was set a row of sixteen spindles, matched by a row of bobbins part way along, beneath the frame of the machine. Across its width rested a wooden clamp to which the woollen threads were connected from bobbin to spindle. At the side a wheel with a handle stood at rest.

'See – it works like this,' said Jane. She placed her right hand on the handle, her left on the clamp. 'Pull the clamp back, like this. See how the wool's drawn off the bobbins. Thou hast need of a steady hand. Now, a turn of the wheel – that moves the spindles, to give a twist to the yarn. Wait here, to get it right. Now, pull back as far as it goes. See how the spindles turn the other way. Back now, and they change again. There, see now, the yarn's winding on the bobbins. And they're ready to use, just like that.'

Hannah watched with great attention and asked many questions, and then at Jane's suggestion operated the machine herself for a time. 'It's a good even yarn,' she said, examining the woollen thread that emerged at the end. 'What wool dost thou use?'

'Any short staple does well. It's not so good with long staple wool. But then Dales' wool's mostly short.'

The loom halted abruptly, and the noisy clatter ceased. 'For worsted, Arkwright's machines are best,' Mark said. 'But they need water power. Anyhow, I only weave rough cloth.'

'Wouldst thou like to weave fine cloth?'

'Not me. But if I did, I'd have to buy in the yarn. There are some do that, of course.'

'At Thornside?'

'Aye. But here too – Joseph Gayle buys worsted, for his best stockings, doesn't he?'

'Aye, so he does.'

Mark looked at her curiously. 'What's it to thee, all this? Is Joseph Gayle going to set himself up with a jenny? Or . . .' He studied her face with close attention. 'Thornside mill, is that it? There's a good head of water there.'

Hannah coloured. She did not want to talk of this to anyone, before she had seen Samuel and Joseph Gayle. 'I don't know,' she said. 'I had a mind to see thy machine, that's all.'

'Aye well, if that's where thy thoughts lead thee, they could do worse.' He began to resume his weaving.

At home again, Hannah set to work on the churning, all the while straining her ears for the sounds that would tell her Samuel had finished with his pupils for the morning. Then, the moment their clogs sounded in the yard, she ran to the parlour.

He was just emerging from the room as she reached it, his arms full of books. He paused for a moment, looking at her without any significant change of expression, and then made a move to go on his way. Just for an instant, Hannah was tempted to give up before she had even begun. But then she thought how unbearable their life was, and how this might even be a way of escape for them from it, and knew she had to try. She reached out and caught his arm, trying not to see the way he flinched at her touch.

'Samuel, I must talk with thee.'

He stayed where he was, looking at her with a faintly questioning expression. 'In there,' she added. 'In private.'

Without a word, he turned and went back into the parlour, and she followed him, closing the door behind her. 'Tell me – thy father has not yet sold Thornside mill, has he?'

'To my knowledge, no,' he said, without interest. Then he added, 'Will this take long? I have other things to do before dinner.'

She *would* not allow herself to be discouraged by his coldness. 'I will be quick,' she said. 'It is about the mill. Thou knows the difficulties thy father has had with the spinning. It is the same for the weavers — '

'Hannah, I don't see . . .'

She raised a hand. 'Thou wilt see, soon enough. There are machines that can spin wool — '

'Robert told thee of them, I suppose?'

She coloured, but did not falter. 'If we were to go to Thornside mill and set up machines there . . . What dost thou think?'

His features scarcely moved, yet in a tiny fraction of time his expression changed from blank indifference to utter astonishment. '*We*! To Thornside mill!' The next instant Hannah saw hurt revealed there, to be quickly masked by a faint echo of Robert's most derisive expression. She had never seen Samuel look like Robert before. 'I had forgot. It has sweet memories for thee. So that's it! Thou wilt be able to live it over again in thy mind.'

She drew in a sharp, painful breath. She had not even thought of that until now. Yet how could she have failed to take it into account? How indeed could she bear to contemplate going again to the place where the thing had happened that – momentarily so wonderful – had been so appalling in its consequences? Yet it ought to make no difference, *must* make no difference, if what she had decided to do was right. Once she had seen the place again, once the mill was rebuilt, there would be no trace left of that day. She would take possession, with Samuel, and drive out every thought of Robert.

She forced herself to be calm, and ignored Samuel's taunt. She said, 'Listen! Listen to what I have in mind.' She began to explain it all to him, quietly, and then with increasing eagerness. She wanted this mill, she wanted to leave Hollinthwaite and its dreary unhappiness, she wanted to fill her life with purposeful activity, something new, which she had all the necessary skills to undertake, something that would demand all the powers she would never use in the bearing and raising of children. She wanted to break through the barrier of Samuel's indifference and draw him near to her again, by means of this shared enterprise. What she wanted above all was to show Robert that he was wrong, that wool was not a thing of the past, that it was wool and not cotton that offered a future to the Dales.

Samuel heard her in silence, his face registering no more than a slightly bored patience. At the end he said only, 'What of Agnes? Hast thou thought of her?'

She had known she would have to face that question, but she had not wanted to do so yet. 'She could come with us.'

'Dost thou really believe she would wish to leave High Farm?'

If Hannah had married Robert, the same problem would have arisen. It had not seemed insurmountable to her then. But it would not help her present cause to point that out to Samuel. 'We'll talk to thy father first,' she said. 'Without his agreement, we can do nothing. We shall have to make enquiries about machines — '

'We? No, Hannah, not "we". Thou mayst do as thou wilt. I shall not hinder thee. But I have my own work, and I shall do it, whether I live here or at Thornside. I am not suited to business. My father has told thee that often enough.'

'Thou hast not tried this business!'

'Nor do I wish to.' He gathered the books, which he had not troubled to put down, more firmly into his arms. 'I have things to do, if thou hast not.'

She watched him go, trying to console herself with the reflection that at the least he had not actually opposed her.

*

Joseph Gayle was in one of the outbuildings at Low Farm, packing stockings into a crate. He glanced round at her and nodded. 'Stockings for Stockton – or London, I should say.' He began to grumble a little, as he often did. 'It's not the sea trip I mind, it's getting them there. Now if we could send a waggon load, that would be another matter. But thou canst not get more than a thimbleful at once on a pony's back.'

'Maybe they'll build us a turnpike road,' Hannah suggested.

'Pigs might fly.' He looked at her with closer attention, 'Wert thou wanting aught, lass?'

'There's something I should like to put to thee.'

'In that case thou'd best come in by the fire. No sense in getting cold.' He closed the crate and they moved towards the house. 'Thou knows Robert's gone?'

Why did her heart seem to turn right over, as if the news mattered to her? 'Gone?' . . . Never to see him again!

'Aye. To his mill. There's enough of it done for a roof over his head. So he's gone.'

Just a few miles away, but far enough. She need no longer feel apprehension clutch at her whenever she approached Low Farm, for fear they might meet. But if she and Samuel were to move to Thornside mill . . . She must not think of that.

'It is a mill I want to talk about,' she said, as she sat down on a stool at the kitchen table, Joseph having first made sure that Mary Harker was busy elsewhere. 'Thornside mill.'

'Oh aye?' Sitting opposite her, hands linked on the scrubbed wood, he studied her face. He said no more, but waited for her to enlarge on the subject.

'Wouldst thou let it to me and Samuel?'

'To you? For what purpose? You have a house – or does High Farm not suit?' His gaze sharpened. 'Is owt wrong? Thou hast never quarrelled with Agnes!' Perhaps then, in spite of all their efforts to hide it from him, he had noticed that something was wrong at High Farm. Hannah said quickly,

'It's not that. I – we – thought to set up a wool carding and spinning mill.'

'*Wool* spinning?' His brows formed an abrupt line above his eyes. 'Is this Samuel's idea?' His tone was thoroughly sceptical.

She shook her head. 'No, it is mine.'

'So thou dost see Samuel as a business man, dost thou?'

'No. Nor does he. I would manage it.'

He gave a silent whistle through pursed lips. 'All by thyself? Well now, what dost thou know of wool spinning, my lass – aside from what thou does with thy spinning wheel, that is?'

She was annoyed to find herself colouring beneath the shrewd scrutiny. 'I have seen a spinning jenny, and worked it, a little. I know there are machines to card and spin, which can be powered by water. What I do not know yet, I can learn.'

'Hm. Maybe thou canst. But thou art just wed. Is Samuel to mind thy bairns for thee when they come, so thou canst manage thy mill?' He smiled faintly at so ludicrous an idea.

'I can do both,' she said firmly. It was easy enough to promise, since she knew there was no likelihood that it would arise. 'I know I can, and well too.'

He studied her face carefully in silence for a moment; then he said, 'I believe thee, lass. Now, thou hadst best tell me why thou dost think we need a woollen mill at Thornside.'

Hannah was glad that he assumed she was not simply concerned, as Robert was, with making money. She explained how Robert's plans had first made her think of the needs of the knitters and weavers, and how her talk with Jane Dinsdale had suggested a way to meet those needs. She put her case with fluency and conviction, unhampered now by the awkwardness that had constrained her when talking to Samuel. She was beginning to be fired with enthusiasm for her scheme. She believed in it, she was eager to see it take shape before her, she longed to create before the eyes of all those who knew her this work which would proclaim to them all that Hannah Gayle, failed wife, inadequate Quaker, bastard child of a contemptible mother, could yet be a force for good in the Dales, to which she belonged yet did not belong. She knew that Joseph heard her with attention. She knew too that he was impressed by what she said; she could see it in the way his eyes gleamed in his still face.

When she had finished speaking, he considered her words carefully for a short time, and then he said, 'Well, lass, it's fine scheme, as far as it goes. Thou hast convinced me we need a wool mill at Thornside. But there's more to it than that, isn't there now? Tell me: thou didst ask if I would *let* the mill to thee. Thou hast in mind to pay rent then?'

'Well . . .' She hesitated, smiling at him a little wryly. 'I thought maybe thou wouldst give us a year or two for nothing, just at first.'

'Thou knows I'd give thee the mill straight off, if I thought it right. I'd be glad enough to keep it in the family. I've no wish to sell land or property, if there's no call for it. But that mill's a ruin, near enough. Hast thou thought what it will cost thee to build it up again? Then thou wilt have thy machines to pay for, and the men to work them, and that's all before thou canst hope to make a penny on it. Wilt thou go begging to George Scarr, like Robert did? He'd not back you both, I'd guess.'

'No – no, I would not go to him. I thought . . .'

He nodded, smiling a little. 'Aye. Thou didst think maybe I'd dig into my pockets, didst thou not? Well, maybe I would have, if there was owt in them to spare. But there's not. A little maybe, but not the kind of money thou hast need of. No, Hannah. If thou art to have thy mill, thou must needs find a partner with a good bit of cash to throw around.' He leaned across the table towards her. 'Here's my advice. Find out all thou canst about the machines thou wouldst use – how they are made, how they work, what they cost. Go to Dick Alderson, or some other builder if thou canst find a better. Tell him what thou hast in mind for the mill, ask him what it would cost thee. Then write it all down plain for me to see, find thyself a partner, and thou shalt have Thornside mill with my blessing. I give thee my word I'll not think of selling, so long as thou hast need of it.'

Hannah thanked Joseph politely and then set out again for High Farm, but as she went she knew she was both disappointed and angry. It was not just Samuel who had failed her, which was understandable after all, but Joseph too, even though he was clearly impressed by her plans. He knew her capabilities, he could surely trust her to do what she set out to do? He might even have been able, had he really wished, to find her the necessary money from somewhere. But even if he could not do so (and that she was prepared to accept), there must have been something more he could have done than simply send her away empty handed. He must have friends or acquaintances with money to spare. He could at the least have put in a word for her with them, or suggested to whom she might take her scheme. He must know as well as she did that a woman alone, with no real experience of the new machines, had no chance of persuading a near stranger to finance her, however thoroughly she might prepare herself for her project, however sure she might be of her own abilities. Did he think Samuel would give her the help he had refused, or even that Samuel was competent to do so?

The rain was falling more heavily than ever, and with its coldness her anger congealed to a bitter sense of hopelessness. She had thought she glimpsed a way of escape from the misery of her present existence. It was as if, through a suddenly opening door, she had seen for a moment some place of hope and freedom, only to have the door slammed firmly again in her face with a cruel finality, shutting out the light and the air. In a moment she would in truth be shut in again, by the walls of High Farm; she had reached the farmyard gate.

There she paused and, on a sudden impulse, turned away and walked on up the hill, ignoring the rain and the cold. Thou art foolish, she told herself severely; it is only a mill. If this is not the way, there will be others. But at the moment she could not believe it. She only knew that she had thought she saw what she ought to do, and now that path was closed to her.

She walked for a long time, without really knowing where she was going, until she came to a halt at last and looked about her and realised she was only about half a mile from the Drover's Inn. It was Second Day – Monday – so her grandfather would be at Middleham. After a moment's thought she made her way towards the gaunt, rain-washed building.

She had never in all the two years since they had first met felt so in sympathy with the slatternly woman at the inn as she did today. The circumstances of her marriage had changed everything, but she had not been prepared to see it before. Now she knew that her own position, beneath the orderly and acceptable surface, was not after all very different from that of her mother. For each of them that one single mistake – the same mistake – of loving and giving too much, too readily and impulsively, without considering the consequences, had brought them to disaster in their different ways. Each, now, had to live with those consequences, for the rest of their lives.

'Something's up, my lass,' Christian said, once Hannah had settled herself near the fire. 'Only just wed, yet thou art not happy. I thought things weren't right last time thou wast here. Now I'm sure of it.'

Hannah looked up at her and forced a faint smile. Shall I tell her the truth? she wondered; that truth I could never tell Agnes. Christian at least would understand what had tempted her daughter to give herself to Robert, as none of her devout friends at home would understand. But would she also be able to see why Hannah had turned her back on Robert, why she had married Samuel, why she felt such guilt for what she had done to them both? That was another matter altogether – and it was *that* aspect of it which Agnes would have understood completely, had Hannah felt able to confide in her.

It was there her difficulty lay, for neither of these two women who claimed to be her mother could begin to comprehend the whole of it, for each had in herself only a part of the nature that formed the complicated and contradictory person who was Hannah.

So she said nothing, only murmured, 'I am well enough, I thank thee,' and tried very hard to appear cheerful and even happy. Then Christian, who had apparently accepted her assurance, brought the usual small feast to the table and, while they ate, gave Hannah a long account of all the miseries she had endured at her father's hands since their last meeting.

For once, Samuel's sure escape from all his troubles seemed to be failing him. No matter how hard he attempted to concentrate on what he was doing, he could not rediscover that blissful state of forgetfulness of everything but his beloved plants. Three times he tried to begin a short paragraph on the characteristics of the mouse ear hawkweed (*Pilosella officinarum* in the new Linnean classification), to accompany the water-colour sketch made three days ago. But somehow the lines of communication between his brain and his pen seemed to have become irrevocably severed, so that, though he dipped the pen in the ink and put it to the paper, nothing happened at all. After the third attempt, he gave up and laid the implement down. He pulled off his spectacles and rubbed his eyes, and then, abruptly, bent his head and thrust his fingers despairingly into his hair, acutely aware now of the rattling of the rain on the window, the hissing of moisture as it fell down the chimney onto the glowing peats of the parlour fire, the thick surrounding silence, which seemed to press in on him, like a kind of stifling pervasive wool, invading his limbs and his brain, bringing not comfort and warmth but a sense of hopelessness.

It was not so very long – just three short months – since he had thought he had gained his heart's desire. It had taken him some time to grasp that it was true, that, incredibly, wonderfully, Hannah wanted to marry not Robert, not any other man, but him. Night after night before his marriage he had lain awake while Robert breathed heavily beside him, and gazed through the window at the stars and thanked God with every ounce of his being for this gift that had been offered to him, and asked only for guidance that he should not betray so great a trust. Sometimes he had found himself fighting a tiny niggle of doubt, in the form of a small voice that whispered, 'It cannot be true. Something will go wrong. Such things do not happen to you.' But somehow that had only intensified his joy, because it had made him conscious of its fragility. The sense of wonder, like a great golden glow illuminating everything he did, had stayed with him right up to the moment when he had stood in the kitchen and seen Hannah's face as Robert told him what had happened between them, and known, though he did not want to know, that what he heard was completely and horribly true in every respect.

He could not remember now precisely what he had felt at that moment. It had all been a kind of nightmare, a time of torturing, anguished darkness from which he had struggled in vain to wake. Through it all, only Hannah had been clear to his eyes – beautiful, beloved, his Hannah, his friend, his adored wife, turned to some kind of monster before him. It was as if the lovely shining façade had cracked to reveal the crawling rottenness underneath. In the end, out on the fells, walking like a man possessed, in furious, aimless wanderings, trying to lay his mind open to some kind of quietness, he had in part come to his senses.

But waking from the nightmare had brought no relief. He had been accustomed to disappointment all his life. In that at least there was nothing new. Except that it *was* new, to find that the girl who for so long had been at the heart of his whole existence, to a far greater extent than he had ever realised until now, was tainted, and not only fallible, but fallen, in the most appalling sense of the word. He did not even consider blaming Robert for what had happened. Robert was like that, it was only to be expected of him. But Hannah – no, he had never dreamed that she could do such a thing. It seemed a bitter irony to remember now how Hannah had told him that she had turned from Robert because she had found that he was no longer the man she had loved. Samuel, too, had found himself similarly misled. He found he had not really known Hannah at all. But he could not turn from her, for he had bound himself to her for ever.

Out there on the fell he had seen clearly enough what he must do. He must forgive her, and behave towards her as a loving husband ought to his wife, however greatly she had erred. So, in resignation and misery, he had returned home to do precisely that, and to face a future that seemed to hold no hope of happiness ever again. His work had been the only thing that gave him comfort, by allowing him for a little time to shut out all thought of his mutilated happiness and of this mockery of a marriage. But today even that had failed.

Now, to torment him, came thoughts of what he had hoped for from marriage – the loving companionship between two people were both friends and lovers, sharing everything with mutual contentment. The reality mocked the dream, just as the quiet public surface hid a dark and agonising loneliness that must last to the end of his life. There would not even be children to bring him comfort. He could not imagine himself playing his part in their conception, not with Hannah, not ever. He had no wish to go where Robert had gone before. The very thought was torture to him. He had never been with a woman; he supposed now he never would.

Abruptly, fighting these unbidden and unwanted thoughts, he rubbed his eyes again, put on his spectacles, reached for his pen. Then he realised that he could scarcely see the paper, so dark had it become. It must be later than he had thought. He was surprised that no one had called him to supper. At that moment the door opened behind him and he looked round to see Agnes standing there.

'Hast thou seen aught of Hannah?' she asked. Her voice had an anxious note.

'No. Is she in our room?' 'Our' room: it was a mockery of union, that phrase and that room, and the bed where they lay so painfully apart.

'She went out after dinner – to see thy father, she said. But he says she left him hours ago.'

Samuel pulled out his watch and peered at it. 'Six o'clock. She's very late.' He glanced towards the rain-lashed window.

'We'd best eat,' said Agnes. 'We've waited long enough. She'll have called on Jane Dinsdale maybe, and forgotten the time in talk.' It did not sound much like Hannah, but they neither of them broke the pretence by pointing that out. Samuel, guessing why she had gone to see his father, wondered if perhaps she had gone on afterwards to Thornside. But he did not want to think of that, so he did not suggest they look in the stable to see if her pony was missing.

Samuel and Agnes had finished eating when Hannah returned home at last, her cloak heavy and dripping with the rain and splashed with mud. Agnes gave a cry and ran to help her out of it.

'Thou art soaked, lass. Thou must be famished too. Come and eat, here by the fire.'

'No, I thank thee,' said Hannah quietly. 'I have eaten already.' Then she slipped from the room and made her way quickly upstairs.

Samuel stared for a moment at the closed door. She had eaten already – at Thornside? If so, where, and in whose company? Seized by a raw and helpless anger, he pushed back his stool and rose to his feet and without a word to Agnes ran up the stairs after his wife.

She had not troubled to light a candle, so that he could only just make her out. He thought she was sitting on the edge of the bed. She wanted the dark then, to hide her shame.

He had brought no light with him, so he fumbled his way to the bedside chest and with trembling hands lit the candle. Its soft flame showed him the grave stillness of her face and her eyes, very dark, watching him. He came and stood over her.

'Where didst thou eat, Hannah?'

The note of angry accusation brought a faint hint of surprise to her expression. 'What is that to thee?'

Enraged, he grasped her shoulder and gave it a little shake. 'Thou wast with Robert – that's it, isn't it? At Thornside, with thy lover?'

She pulled herself free, easily enough. For all his anger he could not hurt her. 'Oh, don't be so stupid, Samuel! How canst thou think such a thing?'

'How do I know what to think? I trusted thee once. I never doubted thee. I knew thee as I knew myself, so I thought. Then . . .' Unable to go on, he finished the sentence with a silent and helpless gesture of the hands. After a moment he said wearily, 'Where wert thou then? I have a right to know, I think.'

She considered the matter, and then she said, 'Maybe

235

thou hast. I went to the Drovers' Inn, up on Hollinthwaite moor. That's all.'

He stared at her in bewilderment. 'The Drovers' Inn?
Where thou wast snowed in that time?' She nodded.
'But why?'

'I went to call on my mother.' She spoke very quietly,
although he heard well enough. Yet the words made no
sense to him.

'What art thou saying?'

'My mother – she lives there.'

'But Agnes is thy mother.'

'She did not give birth to me.'

'No ...' He stared at her, the words faltering out
uncertainly, following his thoughts. 'Thy mother ... at
the ... There was a woman ...' He watched Hannah's
expression. 'Thou knew then, when thou wast stuck fast
there. That's right, isn't it?' He saw her nod. After a
moment he asked, 'Dost see her much?'

'Sometimes. Now and then. It's only right.'

'Aye ... Does Agnes know?'

'No. No one but her and me. Until now.'

He studied the face of the woman who had kept so
many secrets hidden from him. Were there others, like
this, which she had never told him of? What was she
thinking and feeling behind that quiet expression? He
wondered indeed if she had ever borne any resemblance to the childhood friend he had thought he knew
so well. He felt now as if each day drove them further
apart, showing some new aspect of her character that
was wholly alien to the Hannah he knew. Yet she was
bound to him by the closest ties that could bind a
man and a woman. He thought: My closest tie is
with a stranger. It was as if he were stranded alone
in some desert place with only an unrecognised and
thus unpredictable wild animal for company.

'Has she told thee how – the circumstances – of thy
birth ...?'

She nodded, and then, simply and briefly, she told

236

him. He listened carefully. He saw for himself the drover, far from home, filling an idle moment with a willing woman, the way men often did; the frightened girl, faced with the consequences of her sin, desperate for some way out; the helpless infant abandoned on a day cold enough to kill a strong man. He remembered, with some difficulty, the woman at the inn. She had been nothing like Hannah in appearance, that much he could recollect. But in other ways? The passionate nature so hungry for satisfaction that it was beyond control, in spite of all the demands of prudence and morality, the ability to keep a secret for days, weeks, years if necessary, the streak of ruthlessness under pressure, which had made Christian Lambert abandon her baby, and Hannah leave Robert and take his brother, without any apparent scruple? For the first time he felt he was beginning to know the real Hannah. He saw quite clearly now why she had chosen him.

'That's why thou asked me to wed thee then – for fear thou wast with child, to save thyself? Robert would not have thee, but thou must have someone, to spare thyself shame.'

He wondered why she looked so hurt. Could the truth hurt?

'So I am like my mother, just the same. Is that what thou hast in mind?'

'What else can I think?'

Hannah, with a look of sudden crushing weariness, slumped there on the bed. 'I did not think of that when I wed thee. I never gave a thought to a child.'

'Why then? Why wed me?'

She bent her head so that he could not see her face, but he could see how her hands twisted together in her lap. 'Because . . . because I loved thee, I think. If I could not have Robert, there was no one else.'

'The last resort of a desperate woman!' said Samuel bitterly. He did not really believe her explanation. If she believed it, she was deceiving herself.

She looked up. 'No! That's not what I meant! Thou knows how close we've been, always . . .' She broke off, as if she realised how hollow that sounded.

'I thought so once. I know better now.'

'Samuel . . .' She reached up and tried to take his hands in hers, but he pulled them away and stepped back. 'We can be again, if only . . .'

'If only what? If only I could forget what kind of woman I've found thee to be? A bastard born of a slut, fast growing like thy mother?'

'Don't! It's not true!'

'Is it not?'

'We are all children of the same Father.'

'Don't preach at me – thou of all people! Dost thou know what is worst for me in all of this? The deceit, that thou couldst wed me, *ask* me to wed thee, knowing thou hadst given thyself to Robert. That, I . . . Oh, I forgive thee. I said I did. But . . .'

'Thou hast not forgiven.' She was silent for a moment, and then she said, 'Nor have I forgiven myself, if that is any consolation. I did wrong, and there is no excuse – except that I acted without thought, and then it was too late. I thought thou need never know, and it would not matter. But it did matter, and it does. I wish I had not done it. I wish I had never come to thee that day.'

The sincerity of feeling in those words was unmistakable. Samuel stood looking down at her for some time longer and then, abruptly, he dropped on the bed near her. His strongest sensation now was not of anger or bitterness, though he felt both, but of a great sadness. 'We both have cause to wish that,' he said at last. 'But what's done is done. I suppose we must make the best of it somehow, though at the moment I cannot see the way clear.'

Hannah made a move to lay her hand over his, but he realised that the note of sympathy in his voice had gone further than he intended, so he stood up again and walked to the window, where he propped himself on the sill, facing her. 'My father – what did he have to say about the mill?'

He could see that the question surprised her, so far was it from what they had been discussing with such gravity. She looked as if, at first, she could not think what he was talking about. Then she said, 'He liked the plan. But he will not pay for it.'

He wanted to sound as if he were interested, and to behave towards her with the loving concern that he ought to feel. But at the same time he did not want to encourage her to take advantage of that concern by any demonstration of affection. He said carefully, 'What wilt thou do then?'

She shrugged, as if she no longer cared very much. 'What can I do? He told me to find a partner. But I am a woman alone. No one will give money to me.'

Was she asking him to play his part, by adding his masculine weight to her scheme? He was not sure. On the whole he thought not, for he was not after all likely to be much of an asset to her. 'Thou must try to find someone.'

She shook her head. 'I see no point. That would be to waste my time. No, if it is not to be, then I must make the best of it.'

'It is not like thee to give up so easily.'

She looked surprised. 'Thou dost not want me to give up.'

'No. It seemed to me it would give thee an interest. It is likely we shall have many years to live together. We cannot pass them all in misery.'

She said nothing to that. He thought, gloomily, that she was looking, as he was, at the bleak prospect of their lives stretching ahead in this desolation of separateness, and finding no possible hope of happiness for them.

'Perhaps thou wilt find a way,' he said at last. He could not see how, but she had a more stubborn will than he had. Besides, he could think of nothing else to say, and he did not want them to go to bed in a mood of total despair. It was not, of course, as easy as that to rekindle hope between them.

ii

Hannah was digging up the last of the potatoes in the little plot behind the farm when Agnes returned from taking their latest batch of stockings to Joseph Gayle. She did not, as Hannah would have expected, go at once to the kitchen to see to the dinner, but instead came in search of Hannah.

Hannah rubbed the earth from a couple of potatoes and placed them in the basket to be carried to the outhouse for storage, and then she straightened and smiled at Agnes. She was surprised that Agnes, far from returning the smile, even looked a little grim. She felt a tremor of apprehension. Was some new disaster about to fall on her? Could it be, even, that Agnes had discovered the truth about her and Robert? She waited, saying nothing, while Agnes came up to her.

'I am grieved to learn thou hast kept something from me,' Agnes said. Hannah felt her colour rise, but allowed the old woman to continue. 'Thou hast a right to keep things to thyself, if thou wilt, but when all Swaledale knows I think it hard that I'm the last to hear.'

It could not be her and Robert then; at least, she hoped it could not. 'What hast thou heard?' she asked, trying to sound casual.

'Thy scheme for Thornside mill. It seems Friend Joseph knows of it – but not him alone. Thou hast even spoken of it to Mark Dinsdale.'

Hannah was so relieved that her other secret was safe still, that she smiled warmly and clasped Agnes's hands in her own earthy grasp. 'I said nowt to Mark Dinsdale. He guessed what was in my mind, that's all.' Then she thought perhaps Agnes did have cause for complaint after all. It was not as if there had been any reason to keep it from her; once, they had shared everything, or

240

almost everything. 'I suppose I did not tell thee because it had come to nothing.'

Agnes subjected her to a thoughtful scrutiny. 'I should like to hear of thy scheme all the same, from thee. I will help thee with the potatoes, and thou shalt tell me as we work.' She bent at once to gather a handful that Hannah had already unearthed.

As she continued to do so, Hannah gave Agnes a brief account of her project. There seemed little point in going into much detail about something that was already doomed. Besides which, she had few details to put forward, of a scheme that had never been more than an idea.

When she had finished, Agnes said, 'Hast thou thoughts of the women who spin now – how they would feel, if thy machines took their work?' It was the kind of question that had faced her throughout her life, from John even more than from Agnes, forcing her to confront the full implications of all she did, and take responsibility for it. Sometimes the rigour of their attitude had irritated her, but it had become a part of her too. It was that above all which had torn her from Robert.

'I have thought of it,' she replied quietly. 'My machines would only have been there for those who wished to make use of them. That would have been the bigger men, I think – the weavers with many orders to meet, even hosiers like Samuel's father. But the women who spin and knit the wool from their own sheep, or buy just a little wool to work – I think they would have gone on as they always have. It would be cheaper for them to do it themselves, and they can spare the time. On the other hand, if they had wished to knit more, they could have bought their yarn ready-spun. I think, truthfully, that no one would have been hurt.'

Agnes, pausing in her work, gave a little nod. 'I think thou art right. But I had to know that thou hadst considered it well.'

'Does it matter, since it is not to be?'

'Thou knows it always matters, that thou shouldst have these things in thy mind. Thy father would have told thee so. But,' and her face softened a little, 'thou art wrong, I think, to say nothing will come of it. Thou hast need of a partner, thou sayst? Well then, I shall be thy partner.'

Hannah came to a sudden halt, and stared at her, astonished and utterly uncomprehending. 'Thou? But how?'

'I shall sell High Farm. That will meet all thy needs, I think.'

There was a long silence. Hannah looked at the low honey-coloured buildings over which the autumn sun slanted, the sheltering trees, the little garden, the view of the dale beyond; and then she returned her gaze to Agnes's quiet, lined face, and her grey eyes, serene, and yet at this moment bright with something close to amusement, as if she was enjoying the effect her words had upon Hannah.

'Thou canst not do that!' said Hannah at last. 'This is thy home.' And mine, she thought suddenly. She had looked forward so coolly to leaving it, without a trace of regret, even with eagerness. Now the whole prospect seemed painful in the extreme.

Agnes smiled gently. 'It is a house, that is all, a building. Property does not matter. It is not a living thing. It is folks who matter. Thou, and Samuel.'

'And thou too,' said Hannah, through the lump that had developed in her throat. 'And the mill is just a building too. It does not matter either.'

'Perhaps it would be a means to bring healing.'

Hannah bent her head. She thought, with shame, that this was where her sin had brought her, to the point where Agnes was ready to make this appalling sacrifice, if it might mend the rift between herself and Samuel; for she knew that was what Agnes implied. 'I could never ask that of thee, never!' she said in a fierce undertone. 'But I thank thee from the bottom of my heart for thinking of it.' She reached out to embrace the old woman, and found herself held firmly, so that Agnes could look into her face.

'Hannah, hear me! This is not an idle thought, nor one I have not considered well. I have not had long to think of it, I know, but I am convinced that this is what we must do.'

'But to leave here – it would break thy heart!'

Agnes shook her head. 'No, my lass, I'm made of stronger stuff than that. I shall carry my memories with me. As for the rest – if there is a little hurt in it, then it will soon pass. There will be a new life to build. I shall look to that.'

Hannah hugged her, because there were no adequate words to express the depth of her emotion at what Agnes offered. In the end, she neither accepted nor refused, but said only, 'It is too soon. Thou must think further, and so must I. We'll talk of it again in a few days.'

But she did tell Samuel of Agnes's offer, when she found herself briefly alone with him at supper time. She could see that he was as moved and astonished as she had been. 'Thou canst not accept, of course,' he said. 'But for her to offer so much – she is generous beyond words.'

'I thought I knew her so well,' said Hannah, 'but this . . . I never thought!'

'It is hard to know another person. Harder than I ever dreamed once.'

'It can be as hard to know thyself. Thou canst be deceived about that too.'

He was silent for a moment, while they looked at one another, taking in all the implications of that thought. 'Aye,' Samuel said slowly at last. 'That is true.'

Then Agnes came in and they began to talk of something else.

CHAPTER ELEVEN

It was nearly the end of November, the eleventh month, when Hannah rode to Thornside to meet Dick Alderson at the mill.

The formalities of selling High Farm were almost complete. It had been easy enough to find a buyer, for the land was good by Swaledale standards, if a little neglected since John Burton's death. Soon Agnes and Hannah and Samuel would move into Low Farm until Thornside mill was ready for occupation. The most urgent task now was to set the building work in motion. Dick Alderson, already engaged in building a barn and walls for a farm on the edge of Thornside common, had arranged to meet Hannah today to discuss what she had in mind.

It was good to be occupied with plans and other practical yet absorbing matters. Now that the farm was sold, Hannah was able for the first time to look ahead. She had never quite believed it would happen, right up to the last moment, if only because it had all depended on Agnes. She was not absolutely sure even now that Agnes was really so enthusiastically in favour of the project as she maintained. It was not just that she wanted to help Hannah, she had insisted. She thought the scheme was a good one in itself, and wanted very much to be a part of it. She could surely find no surer way of convincing them all of her sincerity than by selling her home. But even so Hannah was not sure. When the moment came to leave, would Agnes not find herself bitterly regretting the decision she had made? Would Hannah not find she regretted it herself?

But she had no intention of allowing such considerations to trouble her today. Time enough to face them when they confronted her unavoidably. Today, as she took the drove road onto the moor, she set herself to think of Thornside mill. Room by room she went through it in her mind, as far as she remembered it, that is, for it was several months since she had been there. They would need living quarters, of course, large enough for herself and Samuel and Agnes, and perhaps ... no, that would be sufficient; there would never be more than the three of them. Samuel must have a study, where he could read and write and teach his pupils; for herself an office would be necessary. But it was the mill that was the most important. The millwheel, restored to use, fed by the improved mill-race, could probably remain where it was. The carding machine (she had sent for plans) must be installed so that the wheel could power it; where the millstones were at present, she thought. The jennies, hand turned, could be installed on the upper floor, and that could be extended to cover the whole area, with access by crane for the wool, so that it could be stored until needed in the driest part of the building ... But then it would be more logical to install the carding machine upstairs, since carding was the first process the wool must undergo. The jennies, then, could be built downstairs, with access through an opening from above for the carded wool. At some times of year – especially just after clipping – they would need considerable storage space for the unprocessed fleeces. There should be room on the upper floor for that, in the far corner ...

She saw, not fleeces, wrapped and tied in bales, but sacks, old and empty, piled in the sunlight. A brief wistful vision of Robert coming to her in tenderness gave way in a moment to the look in his eyes as she had seen them last, in the kitchen at High Farm, cold and hard and merciless as he told Samuel precisely what had happened on that sun-warmed pile of sacks.

She pushed the thought away as best she could. It was a new life that was to begin at Thornside. All that – Robert, the day at the mill, his betrayal of their secret – was behind her now, in the past. Very soon no trace would remain to remind her of what had happened there. It was her future, with Samuel, that mattered now.

But she could not push it away. She reached Thornside and found that wherever she looked amongst its noise and bustle she expected her eyes to come to rest on Robert – there, in the archway leading to Weaver's Yard, where many of the Thornside weavers lived; amongst the men gathered to talk in an alehouse doorway; in a group arguing by the churchyard wall. His mill was, after all, only two miles away, south west of his Uncle Samuel's mill, on the beck that ran to the west of Thornside, parallel with Thornside beck. He must come often to the town, to see the weavers perhaps, to buy food, or seek some craftsman to carry out a task at his mill. They said it was almost ready for use.

By the time she reached the mill lane, Hannah was limp with agitation. She felt relieved as she turned beneath the leafless trees. She had not seen him, and now she was safe. She would not find him here.

But in spirit there was no escape from him. He might have been riding beside her for all the difference it made. She could think of nothing but him, and the sunlit loft with the sacks, which waited for her at the end of the lane. Did he remember too, with the same painful clarity? Would Hannah find he had ridden this way, by chance, drawn by curiosity about the place where something so devastatingly important had happened to him, by a longing to try and recapture something of the unclouded joy of that time? She doubted it. She did not think now that he had ever felt as she did about their union. It was likely that she had not been the first woman he had lain with. Perhaps, she tried to tell herself, it had all been without significance, a momentary pleasure soon ended. Yet she could not rid herself of a growing conviction that at the end of the lane she would find Robert standing in the yard, waiting with the sure instinct of a lover for the arrival he could have no possible reason to expect.

She emerged into the full cold light of the winter sun, slanting low over the treetops . . . He was there, with his back to her, gazing intently at the ruinous buildings, one hand holding his horse's bridle . . . She was conscious only of him, seeing nothing else —

Then he turned, and Dick Alderson's square mundane figure came towards her. She felt relieved, disappointed and very foolish, all at once. She hoped fervently that he would not see anything out of the ordinary in her face.

'Now then, Hannah Gayle – it's in a poor way. Let's be hearing what thou hast in mind for it.'

Thankful for his brusque directness, Hannah dismounted, showed him where the horses could be left, and then went with him into the mill. Where first? she thought; and then she knew. She would face the loft first of all, and then perhaps she could put it behind her.

It was odd. She did not know if it was because it was winter now, and the sun was lower, or because it all smelled much more strongly of damp and decay, or because, quite simply, Robert was not with her; but she found it hard now she was here again to believe that in this place just four months ago something so hugely important had happened to her. She climbed the steps with an ever-faster beating heart, and then found that it did not even look as she remembered it, though the sacks were still there in the corner and the sun slanted onto them through the window. It was simply a loft, badly in need of repair, which must somehow be incorporated into her woollen mill. She began, without emotion, to put various possibilities before the builder and invite his opinion on them, and all thought of Robert left her.

Dick Alderson the builder was helpful, practical, and had the ability to see at once how a problem might be solved, a wall added here or pulled down there, a new window inserted, a door widened. He seemed to understand at once exactly what she wanted from the building, however inexpertly she explained her requirements. Dick Alderson the man was another matter. She had known him all her life, and he had always been a man of few but forthright words, but she had never known him to be so curt and unfriendly as he was today. At first she was thankful for it, as a relief from the excess of emotion she had felt on coming here. After a time it began to disconcert her. His manner told her quite clearly that if she gave him a job to do he would do it to the best of his ability, but that she could not expect his friendship as well. Or his approval: that was it, she decided. For some reason he did not approve of her.

It puzzled her, and it was disturbing, but she could think of no possible explanation for it. When there was a little pause, most of the business having been discussed, she tried to introduce a personal and friendly note to their talk.

'I saw thy little grandson yesterday,' she said. 'Jane says he is to be named Richard, for thee.'

There was, briefly, a noticeable softening of her companion's expression. 'Aye. He's a fine little lad. A good lass, our Jane,' he added, in a tone that conveyed something more than approval of his daughter. 'A good wife, a grand little housewife. Mark wants for nothing, with our Jane to care for him. And now they've a family. She's the makings of a wonderful mother too. Of course, she'll not have so much time to give Mark a hand with his work, but then he'll not mind. Any man wants his wife to put her family first. Why wed, if he wants no more than a business partner?'

Hannah, beginning to realise why Dick Alderson disapproved of her, said defensively, 'It's different when there are no bairns.'

He shot a glance at her. 'Aye,' he said drily. 'But a new-wed woman's like to have bairns, unless there's owt wrong with her. If she's wise she doesn't take on more work, not that she can't get out of in a hurry. It's the man has to bear the brunt of it if she falls with child.' He made a sweeping gesture towards the surrounding building. 'A grand place for a carding mill here, I grant you that. But I said to Mr Gayle – I don't mind telling you straight – it's a man should be running this, not a woman, not a young woman anyway. A widow maybe could run it, well enough. There were plenty who were ready to take it on too, if he'd been willing to sell. But he wouldn't make up his mind to it, and here we are.'

'Thou wilt see – it will be none the worse for being in my charge,' Hannah said, trying hard to control her indignation. He was, after all, only putting into words what many in Hollinthwaite must be saying behind her back, and for that she ought to be grateful to him. It was not his fault that he did not know all the circumstances that had led to her decision. 'And if it's a man thou wants to see here, there will be Samuel.'

'Aye, so there will.' His expression told her plainly enough what he thought of that. 'You know as well as I do how much difference that'll make.' Then he shrugged. 'However, it's nowt to do with me what kind of mess other folks make of their lives. I get on with my job and let them get on with theirs. When do you want me to make a start?'

When he had gone – to return to his present work – Hannah made her way back to Thornside. As she rode, she tried firmly to put a slight sense of depression behind her. After all, what did it matter what other people thought of her, so long as her conscience

249

was clear and she knew that she could undertake successfully the task that lay before her? She had Agnes's approval, and Joseph Gayle's; and Samuel, despite all their difficulties, was behind her. She had no need of anything more.

In Thornside she made her way to the house of the town's wheelwright, Thomas Bell. She found him in his workshop, standing over his apprentice and watching with a critical eye as the lad shaped the newly fitted spokes of a cartwheel. Hannah, not wanting to interrupt a difficult task, came to a halt some distance from them, waiting quietly until the wheelwright noticed her presence. He gave a little nod, said something to the lad, and came towards her.

'You have business with me, Mrs Gayle?' His tone was pleasant enough, but not very warm, and he did not smile. Hannah, who knew this was not necessarily a matter of any significance, pulled a number of papers from her pocket and unfolded them.

'I have some drawings here. They show a carding engine. And here, this is a spinning jenny. I know thou art skilled in the construction of such things. I heard it was thou made the machines for the cotton mill at Newgill. I am in need of someone to build these machines for Thornside mill.'

'Oh aye?' He took the papers and studied them in silence for a moment or two. Then he looked up and shook his head. 'These plans are no good to me, Mrs Gayle. Not enough detail. See here — ' He indicated one of the more complicated areas of one of the drawings. 'That's done too small. You can't see what connects to what. You'll have to get some better plans if you want anyone to build them for you.'

Hannah was dismayed. 'But how will I do that?'

'Same as everyone else does, who wants to have his own machines. Go and take a look at a mill, see how the machines work. I'd guess you've never seen a carding engine?'

She shook her head. 'But . . . hast thou not made one for the cotton mill? It would be much the same.'

'Aye, that's as maybe. But that was a job I did for Mr Gayle. That's between him and me. He paid me over the odds to keep it to myself. Besides, for all I know wool carding's quite another matter from cotton. You'd best go and take a look at a machine. Then come back and I'll see what I can do.'

Hannah felt exasperated, and further depressed by this new obstacle in her path. What would Samuel say if she were to announce that she must go in person to the mill near Leeds which had sent her these plans? Had they in fact deliberately sent inaccurate drawings, to prevent any possible future rivalry? If that was so, then they might even refuse to allow her to see the machines for herself. 'The jennies at least – *those* plans are right, I know. Thou must have made jennies enough.'

'Maybe I have, maybe I haven't.' He looked the plan of the jenny over again, shaking his head. 'Poor, this drawing, very poor. You did it yourself, I suppose?'

'Yes,' she said, colouring under his criticism. She had not thought it was so bad. To her it looked clear and detailed; as did the plans of the carding machine, but of course she had not seen the original of that.

'Should have got a craftsman to do it for a you, that's clear.'

'But wilt thou make one for me – a large one, with forty spindles?

'Well now, I don't see as I can, not from this plan.'

'From thy knowledge of what to do, then.'

'I can see what would happen then. I'd finish your machine, and you'd turn round and say, "No, that's not what I wanted, that won't do." And where would I be then, with all my work gone for nothing? No, I must have plans, good plans. Find yourself someone with a quick eye, who can draw.'

Samuel, though Hannah. But the skill that enabled him to draw a flower or a leaf in all its delicacy of detail

251

might not be what was needed for the starker lines of a machine. Besides, she had already asked him, before she drew the plans herself, and he had said, 'It's thy scheme. Thou must be the one to do it.'

She hesitated, looking from the wheelwright to the plan and back again.

After a moment, the man went on suddenly, 'Better still, get back to Hollinthwaite and leave the mill to someone who knows what he's doing.'

That again; the same disapproval she had met in Dick Alderson. Though this was worse, for Dick Alderson had not actually cast doubts on her competence. Hannah swept the wheelwright with a cold glance. 'I shall return in due course, with new plans,' she said, and then she turned and walked out of the shop.

Out in the street again, she found she was trembling with anger. 'I must not be angry, I must not lose my temper,' she told herself, but it was no use. She tried to make herself look coolly at what had happened. Perhaps indeed she had done the drawings badly. Perhaps what had seemed to her to be careful planning had not been that at all. She was certainly inexperienced. Was it true, as the wheelwright had seemed to imply in his final advice, that she was simply incapable of understanding what was needed to run the mill? It had never occurred to her that a woman might lack the necessary mental powers for the work. All her life she had believed that the only factors that prevented a woman from tackling any task open to a man were a lack of physical strength, and the demands of childbearing and the raising of children. Nothing else had ever prevented the women she knew from taking an equal, or at the very least complementary, part in the work of farm or craft. It was only now that she began to doubt. Anger gave way to a renewed state of depression, even a sense of inadequacy.

She had intended to call next on Kit Dinsdale, Mark's cousin. She had heard from Mark that he and his fellow weavers were much interested in her scheme and, as she hoped they would be her chief customers, she wanted to let them know how the plans were progressing. But now she felt discouraged. What point was there in going to see him, if she had little progress to report and only delays and difficulties to lay before him?

'That is foolish. I shall *not* be defeated,' she told herself firmly, and turned her steps towards Weavers' Yard.

Kit Dinsdale's cottage was tiny, its single ground floor room lit by a long window against which the loom stood, with the result that what little space remained was in near darkness. Here his pale wife sat spinning, while their little girl, seated on the floor at her feet, carded the wool. It was too cold today for them to work outside. Since there was no room for anyone else indoors, Hannah came to a halt in the doorway.

'Kit Dinsdale,' she said, raising her voice so that it would carry above the clattering of the loom. The weaver looked round, nodded, and squeezed his way towards her.

They went into the yard, in search of space and privacy – not easy, for the yard was shared with the five other cramped cottages that opened onto it. But they found a sunlit corner, and then Kit said, 'It's settled then?' His eyes, deeply set in a face blanched, like those of his wife and child, by too long indoors, were bright with expectation.

Hannah wished she could still answer him as cheerfully as she would have done if she had been faced with this same question some hours ago. Instead, she could only say as convincingly as she was able, 'Not all of it. But it will be soon, I hope.'

He frowned a little. 'I heard High Farm was sold.'

'So it is, all but a few details. I have been with the builder this morning.'

'That's all right then!' He looked relieved. 'How

253

long until the mill's ready, do you think?' He glanced towards the shadowed cottage doorway. 'I want to see my little lass playing out with the other bairns, and my Sarah with time to go to market and gossip a bit with her neighbours. It's no life this, all work, day in, day out. I've been that envious of Mark, with his jenny to take the burden off their shoulders. It won't be long, will it? A few weeks maybe – next spring, say? You'd best be quick,' he added, lowering his voice a little. 'Mr Gayle's advertising for weavers. Some are going over to cotton, to be sure of work. So long as we know the woollen mill's coming, most of us will stay with wool. It's what we do best. But we must be sure.'

'Thou canst be sure,' Hannah told him, as firmly as she was able.

'But when, that's what we want to know?'

'I can't tell,' Hannah admitted. 'There is a difficulty with the plans. For the machines, that is. Tom Bell tells me they are not clear enough.'

'He must know how to build a jenny, even without plans. He's made a good few. Maybe you want a larger one, but the principle's the same. I tell you who else has made jennies – one that I know of, anyway – James Taylor. You know, the joiner in Church Lane. He makes clock cases for Tobias Wheeler too, so maybe they'd work together on a machine. Wheeler could make the small working parts.'

'For the carding machine? Aye, that is a possibility. But if the plans aren't right, they'll not be able to do them either.'

'Have you the plans there? May I see?'

She handed them to him and he looked them over with great attention. Then he said quietly, 'There's nowt wrong with these, that I can see. Mind, I'm not a wheelwright. But they look good clear plans to me.'

Hannah stared at him in bewilderment. 'But . . . if thou art right, why did Tom Bell say he could not do it, that they were no good?'

Kit shook his head. 'I can't rightly say. Only — '

'Only what?'

'He's done work for Mr Gayle. He'll still have a good bit to do for him, before he's done. Maybe Mr Gayle's put him on his guard, not to do owt for you.'

'But . . .' She fell silent. What could she say to that? That it was an outrageous suggestion? That Robert could have no possible reason to do this to her? That there was nothing in what Tom Bell had said to lead her to believe that it could be true? Yet . . .

'Take your plans to James Taylor,' Kit advised. 'I'll wager he'll make no difficulty about it.'

So she did, and Kit was quite right. James Taylor, ankle deep in woodshavings, pronounced the plans perfectly clear and well drawn, and was happy to build her machines, calling on his neighbour, the clockmaker, for the more intricate parts of the carding engine. Hannah left the workshop with feelings that mingled satisfaction and anger.

Everything was going well after all. The building would begin in a week or two, work could start on the machines as soon as there was a roof to cover them. Yet she had suffered that quite unnecessary, and inexcusable, hindrance to her plans, which might have been far more serious than it had in fact proved to be. She was furious that Robert (if it was he) should so have tried to thwart her.

Her first impulse was to ride at once to Newgill and tell him precisely what she thought of such behaviour, but common sense held her back. Her suspicions might in any case be unfounded, but even if they were not she was unlikely to achieve anything by seeking him out. Nor did she want to see him, not at all.

She decided instead to take one last look at Thornside mill before riding home. That would calm her, and cheer her, to imagine it as it soon would be, restored, rebuilt, lived in, with the great wheel working again under the sparkling rush of water.

Now, of course, it was quiet, but for the constant sound of water and the gentle sighing of the wind in the trees. In the cold autumn sunlight it had a tranquil look, even in its present ruined state. Hannah drew rein and thought suddenly, 'I *like* this place!' Odd, when so much that hurt her had happened here, yet she knew that what she felt had nothing to do with past experiences. It was simply that she felt right here, that without knowing it until now she had loved this place from the start.

She dismounted and led her pony to where she could tether him near some not too weedy grass; and then came to a sudden halt. There, on the far side of the yard, in the exact spot where she had intended to tether her pony, another horse already grazed, a big brown handsome animal, with a fine saddle, almost new, on his back.

She did not know, she could not be sure, but she thought she had seen the horse before. But whether she had or no, he had no right to be here, on her property, hers and Samuel's.

She tethered her pony some distance from the intruding horse, in case it should be ill-humoured, and then, angry and yet afraid of what she might find, she went in search of his rider.

She had been right. It was Robert who strode casually out from the ruinous houseplace of the mill, and saw her, and then stood absolutely still.

Hannah was surprised at the extent of the shock that she saw on his face. She had not thought that Robert, always so assured, so utterly in control of himself and those around him, could ever be so much at the mercy of an unforeseen emotion. It did not last long. One moment, his eyes looked very dark, unusually sombre in his white face, his lips parted in a silent cry of astonishment, and dismay, and some other more complicated emotion.

The next moment she wondered if she had imagined

it all, for the smoothly smiling countenance that she knew so well had slid imperceptibly yet surely into place again, masking whatever it was she had glimpsed before. Robert strolled towards her with a casualness that looked natural enough, the easy smile, just touched with malevolence, there on his face as if it had always been there. *Had* she imagined that moment of naked emotion?

He came right up to her and bowed, not quite respectfully. When he raised his eyes to her face she was alarmed at the way her body responded to him. 'He is not my Robert,' she told herself warningly. 'Not the man I loved.'

She did not return his smile. She knew her expression was severe, and hoped it showed no sign of weakness or softness at all, nothing that might give him reason to believe that he still had any power over her – as he had not, of course, not since the day she had deliberately turned her back on him.

Except that he had tried to interfere to thwart her plans for the mill. She reminded herself of that, and opened her mouth to challenge him with it. But he had already forestalled her by speaking first.

'I heard you met Dick Alderson here today,' he said smoothly. 'You are not very good at taking advice, my dear sister. It quite astonished me to hear what you planned to do. Though, of course, I always knew my father had his eye on this mill for Samuel.'

Hannah wondered if he was remembering, as she was, that this was the first time they had come face to face since that terrible confrontation on her wedding day, when he had set out deliberately to destroy her hope of happiness with Samuel, and so cruelly succeeded.

Now he went on lightly, 'I suppose you must have something to do with your time. Other women have children . . .' His eyes strayed to her trim waist and the scarcely perceptible curve of hips and stomach.

Hannah coloured, and was angry with herself for doing so. 'It's early yet. There's more than time for children.' Her tone, she thought, sounded snappish and irritable rather than indignant.

The bright derisive gaze did not waver. 'Ah, but if you thought there was any immediate likelihood of children, you'd not have taken this on, would you?' He gestured towards the mill. 'You know you're going to have to do it all alone. Samuel's worse than useless.'

The outright contempt in his tone stung her to burst out, 'Thou art unjust, and thou knows it! He's got a quick mind, and he puts his best, his very best, into everything he does!'

'Oh, when it comes to anything to do with plants, there's no equalling him, I'll grant you that. But anything practical — '

'No one can carve wood like he does.'

Robert gave a shout of laughter. 'Now I see your mill cannot fail! With my brother to carve knitting sheaths for your knitters . . .' Then his tone changed, though there was still contempt beneath the gravity. 'Don't fool yourself, Hannah, my dear — '

'I am not thy dear!'

He bowed his head. 'That is clearly my misfortune.' It was obvious that he meant precisely the opposite. 'It's also beside the point. Why did you not give heed to what I told you? Cotton mills are the future. That's where any wise man puts his money.'

'So thou told me,' she put in, but he ignored her and swept on,

'The mill at Aysgarth's already thriving. I've heard there are plans for one at Hawes, and two or three other places. You know Miles Pickering, from Carperby way? He's looking for a site for one. So you see, even Quakers aren't above looking to the future, when they see where it leads. The days of wool are over. If you've any sense you'll get out of this before it's too late. Believe me, your puny little woollen mill has no hope of success.'

'And thou hast done thy best to make sure of that,' she put in tartly.

He looked genuinely surprised. 'You have lost me there, sweet one.' The endearment was venomous with malice; there was no tenderness in it at all.

'Then Tom Bell spoke for himself when he would not build my machines?'

He made no attempt to deny what she implied. 'Oh, that! That was good business practice, that's all. The wise manufacturer protects his secrets. If Tom Bell works for me, then he does not work for my rivals, it's as simple as that.'

'How can I be thy rival? This will be just a paltry woollen mill!' Her eyes were bright with triumph, at having caught him out in an inconsistency.

'It is a matter of general principle, that's all,' he said, with a dismissive gesture. 'If you like, take it as a kindly attempt on my part to save you from bankruptcy. A pity I did not succeed. For, believe me, your ruin is as certain as anything can be. And what will you do then? The mill garth isn't enough to give you a living, and Samuel's got no skills that will fill your bellies. You should never have thought of selling High Farm, of course. But it's not too late to get yourself another piece of land.'

'I never thought I'd hear that argument from thee! I thought that in thy wonderful new world no one would have any need to till the land.'

'Not the small men who just scrape a living, of course not. That way's as dead as hand knitting, or soon will be. All over England the great landowners are enclosing commons and consolidating holdings. We're just behindhand here, as usual. But it will come. The big men will buy up the little plots, enclose and improve. Then we'll see the land made truly productive. There'll be an abundance of crops and livestock: cattle, corn, enough to feed everyone, and more.'

'In *this* climate, at this height?' Hannah demanded in disbelief.

'With the new methods a landowner can do anything, I assure you. I know. I've seen it done and talked to the best improvers.'

'When I see corn growing on the fells, then I'll believe thee,' Hannah retorted, unimpressed.

'It will come, it will come. And fat lowland sheep good for their meat too, not our scrawny, half-wild animals.'

'Oh, we shall still be allowed sheep, shall we? So long as we don't clip them for wool, I suppose?'

'You can do as you please, Hannah, my dear,' Robert said, in the tone of one bored by his companion's persistent stupidity. 'You won't find a market for it, that's all. The best knitted goods come from the towns, Nottingham and so forth, where the frame knitters don't waste their energies in the fields. But what's the use of talking to you? You're obviously set on self destruction.' He paused, then added in the tone of one struck by a new thought, 'There's maybe one thing you haven't considered.' He waited for her to ask him what it was, but when she failed to do so, went on, 'You take it for granted your mill will be welcomed, don't you?'

'It has already been welcomed,' she retorted.

'By the spinners you'll put out of work? Odd that you of all people should not have thought of that.'

'No one will be put out of work who does not want to be.'

'I don't doubt they said that when they set up the first jennies, in Lancashire. They caused a deal of trouble too – riots, and machine smashing.'

'There are already jennies in the Dales.'

'Not in mills, not with carding engines too, under the same roof.' He smiled faintly. 'A warning, that's all. For your own good. Backward people don't like change, however good for them it may be.'

'Perhaps thou hadst best have a care then!' she retorted.

'Oh, I have, right from the start. The moment the first machines were in, I had men watching them, with guns and dogs. *And* I made sure everyone knew it. I am glad to say I have had no trouble, none at all. But then I suppose that solution would not be agreeable to you.'

'Thou knows it would not. Nor am I afraid.'

'Then you should be, Hannah, you should be.'

There was so much menace in his tone that Hannah could not avoid a shiver of apprehension. And then she was angry that he should so try to upset her. She drew herself up to her full height and looked him in the eye and said coldly, 'I have no guns, but I have right on my side. This is private property and thou art neither invited nor welcome. I must ask thee to leave.'

She saw with satisfaction that her haughty dismissal had stung him. 'It is my father's land, Hannah. I have as much right to it as you, remember that! But I shall go, dear sister, never fear! Only, believe me, I look forward more than I can say to the day when you and Samuel come crawling to me for help, and I have the immense satisfaction of hearing you admit I was in the right of it all the time.'

'That thou wilt never hear, never!' she flung back at him, but he had already turned away and was untying his horse. She did not even know if her words had reached him.

CHAPTER TWELVE

i

On the fell there was still little sign of spring. Only Samuel, Hannah thought, would have been able to see the hints of new growth in the varied browns of the landscape. But once below the brow of the hill, amongst pastures and trees, it was another matter. Here the air was soft, and willows and sycamores were hazed with green; celandines opened brilliantly yellow on the banks, tentative primroses unfolded pale petals, the river shone blue beneath a far blue sky.

For Hannah the loveliness of new growth brought with it, always, a sense of the fragility of things; of this beauty, so easily battered by storm or blight, so easily scarred by man's greedy search for wealth; of human happiness, that fleeting and uncertain thing. It had, after all, been at just this time of year that she had first found herself brought face to face with insecurity and doubt. Since then, a sense of poignancy had been, for her, inseparable from spring. This year, the first spring since her marriage to Samuel, could only reinforce that sense.

As she crossed the river and made her way towards Meeting House Lane, she ceased to notice the signs of spring. Instead, a strong sense of reluctance took shape and swelled and grew inside her. She did not want to go home, because home meant Samuel, that polite stranger who shared her bed, and because, for the past three months, she no longer had a home at all. It was to Low Farm she was returning now, where she and Samuel and Agnes had been living since the new owner moved into High Farm. Thornside mill was progressing well, but it was not yet quite ready. After all, the builder had begun his work in the worst months of the year. It had not been too bad a winter, but progress must inevitably be held up from time to time. Now that spring was here, perhaps things would move more quickly. Hannah fervently hoped they would. She had been surprised to find how much she had minded leaving High Farm. It made it worse to live so near, and be able to see the changes the new owner made: the trees cut down, the new barn built, the different way he cared for the animals. The sooner they could all move right away, to their new life at Thornside, the better it would be.

She tried not to allow her eyes to stray across the beck as she reached Low Farm. She concentrated instead on the prosperous-looking buildings of Samuel's home. Samuel, taking advantage of the fine day and the drying wind of the past week, was digging in the small kitchen garden in front of the house. Agnes was at the beck, washing – clothes or stockings, Hannah could not see which.

Except that she was not washing. She was kneeling motionless on the bank and gazing across at the house where she and John had lived all their married life, where almost all the happiness she had ever known, as well as the sorrow, had come to her. Hannah was not alone in finding the leaving hard.

Of course, she had known it would be worse for Agnes. That had been obvious from the first, and only natural, after all. But Agnes had seemed cheerful enough, determinedly making herself useful at Low Farm, as far as was possible in an establishment already running smoothly under Mary Harker's care. Now, seeing her, Hannah was struck by the utter dejection of her bearing. It was hard to tell, of course; but for Agnes to be so inactive, drooping yet not bent to her task, so impervious to everything but what she gazed at – that implied some unhappiness deeper than Hannah had suspected.

She stabled the pony and went to Agnes, who did not even appear to have heard her coming. She did not look round. 'Mother — '

Agnes gave a little jump. She rubbed one hand across her eyes before looking round, though it was only too clear to Hannah that she had been weeping. What Hannah saw too, with shame that she had not noticed it before, was how much thinner Agnes had become since they left High Farm, and how tired she looked, as if she was not sleeping well.

Agnes forced a smile. 'Didst thou find all well at Thornside?' Her voice sounded husky and uncertain, as if she spoke with difficulty.

'Yes.' What could she say or do to comfort Agnes? She had nothing to offer. The farm was irrevocably lost, and they could not go to Thornside yet. She knelt down on the bank beside the other woman. 'May I help thee?'

Agnes began to rub vigorously at Samuel's shirt, as if only Hannah's arrival had interrupted her. 'I can manage well enough, lass, I thank thee.' Without looking round again, she asked, 'Didst thou find thyself a man to work thy machines?'

'George Holgate's going to give it a try.'

'Amos Holgate's lad? The crippled one?'

'Oh, he's got a weakness in the legs, that's all. He'll never make a blacksmith like his father – the work's too heavy. But the mill may suit him well enough. He's to come on a month's trial – each way, that is. But he'll come in first as soon as they start building the machines, to give a hand when he can.'

'Does he know about the machines, how they work?'

'Not yet. But this way he'll learn as he goes. He'll know what to do to keep them in good trim too.'

'Aye, well, that sounds like good sense. A pleasant enough lad, he seems.'

'Aye.'

'I'll just get done here, then it will be supper time. Mary was all but ready.'

It sounded like the gentlest of dismissals. Hannah said, 'I'll see if she wants a hand.' She waited a moment, looking down at Agnes's bent head for any sign that the old woman wanted her to stay; but none came, so she made her way back to the farm.

She crossed the garden just as Samuel was returning to the house. He stood aside to let her go first. 'She's had enough of living here,' he said gravely, in an undertone. Hannah knew from the direction of his gaze who he meant. 'How long before we can move? She'll be ill if she has to go on living so near High Farm.'

'I know,' said Hannah, conscious again of a twinge of shame, that she should not have noticed before what was clearly obvious to Samuel, who did not know Agnes as well as she did. 'They've the roof on. They start on the plastering tomorrow.'

'It could still be weeks yet.'

'They're doing their best.' She had encouraged the builders to complete the mill area first, so that work could begin as soon as possible on the machinery; next week, she hoped. But that meant, of course, that the house end must wait. Now she wondered if she ought to have ordered it to be done the other way round. But she said nothing of that to Samuel. The decisions were hers, and the responsibility for their outcome. It was what they both wanted.

At supper time – choosing a moment when she had gone to bring a pot from the fire, and had her back to them all – Hannah said casually, 'Kit Dinsdale tells me Robert can't find workers for his mill.' Her colour rose, as she had known it would, but it had faded a little by the time she returned to the table, and the others might simply attribute it to the heat of the fire.

'I thought it was supposed to be working by now,' Joseph Gayle said.

'So it was. Some of the machines are spinning, Kit says. But not many want to work there.'

'What did he expect?' Robert's father commented. 'Shut up in one place thirteen hours a day. That's no work for a man or woman used to their own independence. I'd sooner starve — and I'd not be alone in that, I'd say.' He glanced at Hannah. 'What of thy mill? Hast thou found workers? Or was Dick Alderson right, and not a one would beg work from an ignorant woman?' There was the faintest hint of a smile on his face, though the talk had been no smiling matter to Hannah; nor had Dick Alderson been the only one involved.

'Five came, though there were three left when they realised they'd be working for me. I took on George Holgate. He wanted the job most, and I liked him.'

'He doesn't mind thy long hours, then?'

'He won't have to work thirteen hours a day. He'll have to give me a hand, and the work will be varied. In the cotton mill it's the same work, the same machine all the time. He'd been to ask about work there, but he said it wasn't for him. He said a man would need to be strong and well to last long in the mill, but that it's not work for a healthy man.'

'Canst thou be sure he'll not have to work as long or as hard for thee,' Samuel demanded; 'if thy mill does well, and thou findest thyself with more orders than there's time for?'

'If it gets too much, I'll hire more hands. No one at my mill is going to say he's worked too hard.'

ii

'So I said to her — '

Hannah, glancing longingly towards the window, broke in on Mary Harker's flow of talk. 'Rain!' she said, and ran.

The household linen, washed and carried out to dry in the bright hot early morning sun, was spread over the currant bushes to dry. Hannah and Mary, joined soon by Agnes, gathered up sheets in armfuls and ran through the brisk cold rain to the kitchen, where they hung the washing over a clothes horse and every available stool and chair near the fire.

Hannah went to the door to check that everything was in; and saw a horseman emerging from the lane. She stayed where she was, watching him. He had his head bent against the rain, and his hat hid his face. His coat, darkened with the wet, clothed a thin body, not very tall. It was only as he came up to the farm and dismounted, awkwardly, dropping on to uneven legs, that she recognised George Holgate, second son of Thornside's blacksmith, whom she had hired two weeks ago.

She went out to meet him. 'Is owt wrong?' she asked anxiously, her first apprehension strengthened by the gravity of his pale face. Then she reminded herself that the rain was cold and he was wet and tired from his journey and that the pony would be in need of food and shelter. 'Go in,' she said. 'Warm thyself by the fire. I'll see to the pony.'

When she came in from the stable, the young man was seated in the corner of the settle closest to the fire, with his coat hung on a chair to dry and a tankard of mulled ale in his hands, but the troubled expression still on his face. He stood up as Hannah came in, though she protested. Perhaps he felt better able to deliver bad news on his feet, looking her in the eye.

'Thou knows they started on the gearing for the carding engine last week?'

'Aye.'

'They'd done a good bit by Saturday night. Yesterday it was all shut up of course, being Sunday. I went to the mill first thing today, to open up, like you said. The lock was broken, smashed, and half the door. Someone's got at the machinery.'

Hannah had a brief mental picture of Robert's faintly

smiling face as he warned her that precisely this might happen. It was for that reason she had insisted that a good lock was fitted to the mill door, before work began on the machinery. 'Is there much damage?'

'Mr Taylor says they'll have to start again, him and Mr Wheeler. There's nowt left in one piece, nowt at all.'

All that work, all her planning and waiting – for this! 'Who could have done such a thing?' she demanded.

'I don't know, Mrs Gayle. All I know is there was talk, back end of last week.'

'What kind of talk?'

'Alehouse talk. In Widow Wilson's alehouse, so I heard. About how the mill would put spinners out of work and bring in weavers from the south, to take work from our weavers.'

'That's not true. Thou knows it's not.'

'I weren't there. Nor anyone else that knew better, seemingly; all but our Simon. He put them right, but they'd not listen. It got to hot words, then to blows. He got the best of it. He's Thornside's champion wrestler, thou knows. But whether he stopped the talk for good, I don't know. Looks as though he didn't, I'd say.'

'But why should anyone say such a thing? How could they think it?'

'Maybe someone told them wrong. They're a rough crowd at Widow Wilson's. If there's trouble anywhere, it's bound to start there. Simon said there were strangers there, too, not just the usual crowd. He thought one of them might be Mr Birley.'

'Who's Mr Birley?'

'Mr Gayle's manager at the cotton mill. But Simon wasn't sure. He's only seen him once before. He lives at the mill.'

Hannah stared at George in silence. If that was right, if his brother had not been mistaken, then Robert's manager had been drinking in an alehouse on the night there was talk about her woollen mill; and some time during the following forty-eight hours, angry men (she supposed) had broken into her mill to smash the new machinery before it was even completed. Was it fanciful to suppose there must be a connection? Or to make a further connection, right back to Robert himself, who had warned her – only it had sounded like a threat – that just this thing might happen?

Perhaps it was fanciful. Perhaps there was no connection at all. Robert had been quite right when he had said machines had been smashed before. Yet . . .

'What dost think happened?' she asked abruptly.

'I don't know. But if someone wanted to make trouble, if there was grudge . . . They do say Robert Gayle wanted Thornside mill, and his father wouldn't let him have it. It must have cost him a fair bit more, to buy land and build from scratch. But thou'lt know more about that than me.'

'Yes,' Hannah agreed grimly. She was thinking quickly, planning what to do. 'Get a bite to eat and rest a while. Then I'll ride back with thee and see for myself.'

He nodded. 'I thought maybe thou'd wouldst want me to move in – to the mill, I mean. Keep a watch on things.'

'Maybe,' she said. 'For a short time. And thou'd get paid for it. But thou hast thine own life to lead. I'd not ask so much for long. I'll find some other way.'

She had made her decision even before she set out for Thornside, in an interval of sunshine that seemed unlikely to last. In fact, the answer was obvious: they must move to Thornside, herself and Samuel and Agnes, as soon as was humanly possible, even before work on the living quarters was finished, if necessary. Not only would it allow her to keep an eye on the machines, but it would be best for Agnes too, for them all.

At Thornside, having inspected the damage and conferred with James Taylor, she left him to resume

269

work on the machine and went in search of Dick Alderson. He agreed to have two rooms ready to accommodate them by the end of the week; and then Hannah rode home, to tell Agnes and Samuel what she intended.

iii

The move went smoothly enough. The day was dry and the road not too muddy. The few items of furniture they were to take with them were piled awkwardly on Agnes's two-wheeled cart, the smaller items – clothing, books, kitchen utensils – stowed on the backs of four ponies. They started loading up before dawn, and an hour later were ready to leave. Joseph went with them, to help with the unpacking at the other end. Mary Harker, a little tearful and full of advice, came to see them on their way, but no one else wept. They set out in silence, Agnes with an expression of rigid self control, resolutely refusing to look behind her, Hannah with head bent, telling herself she ought to be happy, for she was embarking at last on her great adventure, Samuel lost in some gloomy thoughts of his own. Joseph alone seemed much as he always was, but then he had never been a naturally talkative or cheerful man.

'This is no longer my home,' Hannah thought, as they passed the last house before they came to the river. 'I shall come back to Hollinthwaite, but I shall not belong.' She had thought often enough that she had never belonged. Yet now, turning her back on the village, she knew that she was more firmly rooted in this place than she had thought, enough for the leaving of it to be painful.

It was strange, too, when, later, the cart and the ponies turned into the lane towards Thornside mill. Hannah found her heart beating fast, uncomfortably so, not simply with excitement but also with apprehension. She was coming back yet again to the place in which her love for Robert, short lived as it had proved

270

to be, had been sealed. Would that experience mark this place for ever? It had already marked her marriage. Living here, would she ever be able to erase that mark, or blot it out with new experiences, new joys, of a fuller and more lasting kind?

The mill came in sight, then the house, with its handsome door lintel, on which, as if with heavy irony, letters had been carved: S.G.H., and the date, 1786. Hannah had not asked for it to be done, but Dick Alderson, a traditionalist, had set their seal upon it.

He had done his best to make most of the ground floor habitable: the kitchen, and the parlour facing it across the hallway. It would be cramped accommodation, affording little privacy for any of them, but Hannah hoped they would not have to endure it for long. Just a week or two, Dick Alderson had said, a little vaguely.

It was as well they had few goods with them, for by the time they had finished unloading, the two rooms were crammed with furniture and smaller objects, piled up in corners because there was no room for them to be put out for use. In the parlour, Hannah and Samuel's bed stood almost inaccessible amongst mounds of books, stacked chairs and tables, the linen chest, boxes and bags containing a jumble of belongings. In the kitchen, space was left for a table, three stools, and Agnes's small bed, half hidden behind yet more temporarily homeless items. When the last piece of furniture had been carried in, Hannah stood in the kitchen doorway and looked at it all and tried not to feel depressed. It was, she reflected, hardly an ideal beginning to life in their new home.

'Let's get a fire lit,' Joseph said briskly, and set to work at once to find kindling and bring in peats from the small decaying store found in one of the outbuildings. Hannah had arranged for a load of coal to be delivered, to keep them going until it was time to cut peats from the place on Thornside common where the mill traditionally had rights to seek fuel, but the coal would not come until tomorrow. Pushing aside her depression as best she could, Hannah went to help Agnes, who was unearthing the necessary utensils and food to provide some kind of meal for them all. Samuel, still silent and gloomy, gave his father a hand.

Well into the afternoon the fire was burning brightly, they had eaten, and the two rooms had been made as habitable as was possible in the circumstances. 'I'll be off then,' said Joseph, and they saw him on his way, riding the leader of his string of ponies.

It was an awkward moment, the one that followed. For Agnes there must have been a grim finality about it, reminding her forcibly that this, now, was where she was likely to live out her remaining years; even Hannah felt something of that sensation. To counter it, she decided that she would take Agnes and Samuel to look at the mill, to show them how the machines were progressing and explain how they would work. She looked round to where she had last seen Samuel, standing just behind her to say goodbye to his father; but there was no one there.

'Where's Samuel gone?' she asked.

'I don't know,' said Agnes. They looked in the house, but here was no sign of him. 'Maybe he's in the garden,' Agnes suggested.

It seemed likely. The house was noisy with the hammering and banging of the builders upstairs. From the mill came the persistent if less obtrusive noise of the men at work on the machines. If Samuel had gone in search of a little tranquillity, that was hardly surprising.

'I'll get the beds made up,' Agnes said, to fill the time. Hannah made her way out to the garden.

It lay undisturbed in the grey stillness of the day, a tangled mass of decaying weeds touched here and there with signs of new growth. Samuel was not there.

She tried the outbuildings, of which only a small

stable area had yet been repaired, but Samuel was not there either. Could he have gone further afield, for a walk perhaps? Surely then he would have told them of his intentions? The only other possibility was the mill.

Hannah felt irritated, even a little hurt, that he should have gone to look at it alone. She had wanted to show him round herself, in the hope that she might somehow touch him with some of her enthusiasm for what she was to do here. Now, without doubt, she would find him listening to James Taylor's careful explanation of the carding engine, or being shown round by George Holgate.

She pushed open the mill door, delighting (as she always did) in the smoothness with which it opened, the way it was perfectly balanced upon its hinges. One day, she supposed, she would take it for granted, when all recollection of the old broken door had left her.

Inside, the three men were gathered about the half made gearing of the water wheel, talking quietly as they worked. But there was no sign of Samuel.

'Looking for Mr Gayle?' Tobias Wheeler asked, glancing round at her. Then he gestured towards the stairs. 'Thou'lt find him up there.'

She did not know why she felt a twinge of apprehension as she mounted the stairs to the floor above; it covered the whole area now, creating a second storey – where the carding engine was to be installed – with storage areas close by for the fleeces and the spun yarn.

Now it was empty, the floor smooth and swept clean. Overlooking the yard, double doors opened, so that fleeces could be swung up from the carts and pack-horses that delivered them, for sorting and carding. There was a window too, and near it a stack of wood and other materials waiting for work to begin on the carding engine, when the machinery to turn it was fully in place.

Samuel was there, but it was not at any of these

things that he was looking. On the contrary, he did not seem to be looking at anything at all. He simply stood to one side, gazing sombrely into the far corner, although there was nothing there at all.

Hannah was puzzled, but eager to make the most of this unexpected sign of spontaneous interest in the mill. 'Sam, what . . .?' she began. Then some quality in his extreme stillness, given emphasis by the grim line of his mouth, the bleakness of his eyes, silenced her and brought her to a halt. This was not a man held motionless by curiosity or interest, nor one ready to welcome her approach. When, the next moment, he turned to look at her, his expression chilled her.

Samuel had found the place without difficulty. He had asked Dick Alderson, when they met briefly this morning, where it was that a heap of old sacks had lain, forgotten since Uncle Samuel's day. Now he was here, he did not think he had needed to ask. Some instinct would have led him to this place, just as, now, he knew precisely where the sacks had been, in that corner which, on a brighter day, would catch all the sun. The little scene had been with him ever since Robert's disclosure had exploded in the midst of his new happiness and scattered it to the winds. Now he was in the very place where it had happened, and it might have been happening still, there before his eyes. He saw the pile of empty sacks, the sun shining on the two people . . . No, he did not want to see, it was an agony beyond words; yet he stayed and saw, possessed and tormented by the horror of it. Why had he come, why had he let her bring them to live here? He did not know. It had been some kind of madness, to think there could be any healing here. On the contrary, it was all much worse, unbearably so, as if some kind of demon was driving them both to destruction. He did not believe in demons, yet that was how it felt.

And now she was here beside him, the woman he had loved for so long, who had been lost to him even before he had thought she was his. He looked at the lovely, false face, with the bewitching blue eyes that had so effectively concealed her treachery. He saw bewilderment give way, abruptly, to recognition. She knew then why he had come here. 'This was the place, wasn't it?' he asked harshly, but in a low voice, so that the men downstairs should not hear.

He saw her colour. 'How didst thou know?' she whispered.

He ignored her question. 'Dost think of him much?'

She coloured still more, and he was pleased, though a part of him regretted the hurt that he saw in her eyes. It seemed to hurt him too, in some way he could not explain.

She answered him coolly enough, with what sounded to him almost like defiance. 'Why should I? It was over long ago.'

He did not believe her. He *could* not believe her. If he had been the one to lie with her here (the most tormenting thought of all), he would have remembered it all his life, treasured the thought, clutched it to him. They said that for a woman it meant more than for a man. Whatever she might say, something must have stayed with her, perhaps everything.

She took a step towards him, holding out her hand. 'Samuel, please! He is nothing to me now. Canst thou not — ?'

He did not wait to discover what she meant to ask. He burst out, 'Well, thou'lt be able to make it up with him now, wilt thou not? When I'm at my work, maybe. Or hast thou done it already, while the mill was a-building? All those rides over here . . .'

'Hast thou forgotten? He tried to destroy this place.'

'So thou sayest. What proof hast thou? Only hearsay. Come to that, I've only thy word damage was done at all.'

'Go and ask them downstairs then!' she retorted.

'It gave thee what thou wanted, then – to come here sooner, to be near thy lover.'

She stared at him, and he could see quite well how deeply he had hurt her. 'Samuel . . .' she murmured.

'It is no use, Hannah. I am not a fool, not any more. I've learned my lesson. But I wish to goodness I had never come here, never!' And with that he pushed brusquely past her and ran down the stairs, leaving her staring into the sudden emptiness, stunned with shock.

Samuel returned to the house and took some of his books and papers, and carried them up to the little room that was to be his study, which Dick Alderson would not be working on for some days yet. The walls were still unplastered, but the floor was clean enough, so he spread his things out there, and began to work on them.

Except at supper time, Hannah did not see him again that day, and when she woke next morning from an exhausted sleep it was obvious that he had not lain beside her all night. By the time she reached the kitchen, he was already there, looking pale and exhausted, but talking to Agnes as he always did, quietly and companionably, though he fell silent the moment he saw Hannah. She did not dare to ask him where he had slept, or indeed if he had slept at all. Agnes did not seem to have guessed that anything was wrong, more than usual.

Hannah sat down with the others to eat, telling herself that she must live her life only on the surface, dealing with the simple and practical demands it brought her, ignoring what lay underneath. It was all she could do, in the hope that one day, somehow, things would get better again. She tried to talk casually and cheerfully about the mill, offering to give Agnes the tour she had missed yesterday, and trying not to see how Samuel looked at her all the time she was talking.

Samuel excused himself first, and rose to leave the breakfast table, and then, having taken one step away from it, came to a halt at the sound of a horse approaching the mill, clattering into the yard. 'That will be George,' said Hannah. 'I didn't know he rode to work.' She was about to go to him, when she saw Samuel's face – from where he stood he could see into the yard.

She turned to follow his gaze; and froze, as he had.

It was Robert, as elegant as ever, briskly dismounting from his gleaming brown horse. The next moment he came quickly towards the kitchen door.

'What can he want so early?' Agnes asked mildly, having seen him herself. Since neither Samuel nor Hannah had moved, she went to let him in.

The sunlight framed his tall strong figure, giving emphasis somehow to its strength and assertiveness. His shadow fell across the clean new flags of the floor. It reached nowhere near Hannah and Samuel, but even so Hannah felt as if it had. It seemed to shut out the light, bringing a little chill.

Then Robert stepped inside and Agnes shut the door and reality returned, the reality of the man Hannah had once loved, and who had already done her so much hurt, standing in the kitchen of their new home on their first morning here.

He bowed, his glance taking in all three of them. 'I come to bring hearty good wishes for the success of your enterprise,' he declared. 'I was told you planned to move in yesterday.'

'That's kind,' said Agnes warmly. If she was aware of the frigidity of the young couple near the table, she gave no sign of it. 'Wilt thou not — ?' At that point something must have impressed itself upon her after all, for she fell abruptly silent, and glanced at Hannah to indicate that it was up to her to say what was necessary. There was a hint of puzzlement in her eyes, as if, suddenly becoming aware of it, she could make no sense of whatever tension it was that linked her three companions.

No one broke the silence to ask Robert to sit down with them or to eat or drink. No one went to take his hand. After watching them all for a moment or two, quite at his ease, even amused, he stepped across to Hannah, took a box from his pocket, and handed it to her.

'A small gift, to mark the occasion,' he said. She took it, and then simply stood there, holding it in her hands as if she scarcely knew she had it, and staring at him with unmistakable hostility. 'Go on – open it!' he urged her. When she continued to stare at him, a faint questioning coming to life in her eyes, he added, 'To show there are no ill feelings.' He saw her flinch, and smiled easily. 'Rivals we may be, you with your wool, me with my cotton. But that is no cause for us to be enemies.'

'Is it not?' she returned. 'I rather thought thou didst believe it was.'

'Indeed? What gave you that idea? A friendly warning, before it was too late, given for the best motives; there is no harm in that. But now that you are embarked, I can only wish you well.'

Was he referring simply to their last meeting – or to the smashing of the machinery? Was it possible she had been wrong about that? It was easy to believe now that she had misjudged him. Then she saw how he glanced at Samuel, and how Samuel was looking at her, and remembered that she had said nothing to her husband of the meeting here last autumn, and realised how Robert's words would sound to his brother. Confused and distressed (for it could only make matters worse), she gave her attention to the box and opened it, fumbling a little. Inside, it was lined with silk; and nestling in the rich blue folds was a silver watch, from which silver chains hung. Hannah gave a little cry, but not from any kind of pleasure. Robert, smiling as blandly as if she had shown unalloyed delight, leaned over and lifted the watch out of the box. He held it there, just before her eyes, gently, with both hands. It swung to and fro, and she could not take her eyes from it.

'See here, the chains attach it to your belt, so it will hang there.' His hand lightly touched her waist, and she recoiled quickly. 'And see too,' he went on, unconcerned, 'I had it engraved.' He turned it over to show her the back. 'Hannah Gayle, Thornside mill, 1786,' he read aloud.

Samuel gave a strangled, inarticulate cry, and the next moment he had left the room, slamming the door behind him. Robert smiled faintly, but his eyes never left Hannah's face. She was scarcely aware of Samuel's departure. She continued to gaze at the innocuous inscription in numb horror, and wondered how it was that Robert did not appear to see how appalled she was, or how much she was trembling. She did not know what to say. How did one thank someone for a poisoned gift, which was certain only to do harm? Was it possible that he had brought it in all innocence, not realising what effect it would have? She doubted it, yet she could not be sure.

But whatever his motives, there was only one course open to her. She took the watch from him (trying not to see how pleased he was that she had taken it), laid it in the box, snapped the lid shut, and thrust it into his hands. 'Take it!' she commanded in a harsh undertone. 'I do not want it. Please go now, at once.'

He stared at her in apparent disbelief. She watched his expression change from sardonic good humour to cold anger. Then he said, 'As you wish, Hannah Gayle. Enemies then – not rivals. It is your choice.' He swung round and marched out of the house.

To the sound of his horse clattering away across the yard, Agnes came, full of concern, and put her arms about Hannah, who had sunk trembling on to a stool.

'Oh my lass, what has happened? I did not know there was such anger between the two of you. What has he done, to make thee so angry – and Samuel too?'

Hannah made an effort to pull herself together. 'Nothing . . .' Then she caught Agnes's eye and corrected herself. 'Nothing I can speak of, or I would, I promise thee.' She freed herself gently from the loving embrace and rose to her feet. 'I must go to Samuel,' she said.

She thought she had heard him go upstairs, so that was where she went. She found him in his unfinished study, not – as she had expected – lost in some gloomy meditation, but busily packing the bag he took with him on his plant-hunting walks, with sketching materials and notebooks. He looked up as soon as she reached the doorway and said swiftly, 'That was a pretty little gift from thy lover. It must make thee happy.'

'Samuel, don't! I — '

He had scarcely let her begin before he went on, 'I want no excuses, Hannah, none of thy explanations. To tell the truth I'm sick of them. I've eyes and ears, and that's enough for me. Thou canst enjoy him in peace for all I care. I'm going away.'

'Away?' she echoed stupidly. She felt as if all the blood had drained from her body, right to her lips and fingertips.

'Aye.' He straightened, and became all at once very matter of fact, with a hardness in his tone that warned her against any further appeal to his sympathy. 'I've long wanted to gather more material for my book. This seems a good time. I shall be walking, so I'll not deprive thee of any of the ponies. I don't know how long I shall be away.' He might almost have added, 'Or whether I shall come back at all.' She seemed to hear the hint of it in his words.

'But where wilt thou go?' What he was saying to her had still not fully sunk in.

'West, I think. Dentdale, maybe Kendal way. Or

further. I shall please myself.' He said that as if the prospect gave him no pleasure at all.

Hannah took a step towards him, though she dared not reach out to touch him. 'Samuel,' she said urgently, 'thou art mistaken, about me and Robert. This morning — '

'It has nothing to do with this morning,' he retorted. 'I made my decision last night. But it has been in my mind a good while.' His gaze sharpened. 'I've a deal to do, Hannah. Will George Holgate not have come by now?'

It was a clear dismissal, and she knew there was no appeal against it. But in a last attempt to soften his mood, she said, 'I did not take the watch.'

Samuel looked at her coldly. She wondered even, for a moment, if he disbelieved her. 'Really? That must have caused thee pain.' Then he returned his attention to his packing.

After a moment, realising that there was no more she could usefully say, Hannah made her way slowly back down the stairs. In the hall she met Dick Alderson and his journeyman, and had to force herself to greet them as if nothing was wrong.

In the mill, George Holgate had indeed arrived, and the other two men. She spent the next two hours in their company, discussing some difficulty about the positioning of the carding engine, which absorbed most of her attention, but did nothing to lift the weight of misery from her spirits.

The problem solved, she was about to go back to the house, in the hope that she might find Samuel more ready to listen to her, when she turned to find that he had come into the mill. She saw that he was dressed for his journey, in his stoutest and most sober clothes, his hat on his head, his satchel, bulging more than usual, slung over his shoulder. 'I am ready,' he said quietly. 'I am going now.'

She took a step towards him, but already he had

turned away. She ran to him and caught his arm, but he showed no sign that he had even felt her touch. He simply walked quickly on, leaving her behind, not even looking round. She knew there was nothing more she could do. She halted, and watched him until he had disappeared into the lane.

CHAPTER THIRTEEN

i

It should have been a triumphant day. The last cogs and wheels had been fitted into place, the machinery tested, and today for the first time carding engine and jenny were to be set to work. By sheep clipping, only a few weeks away now, the mill would be thoroughly ready to start on full production. Before then, Hannah hoped to receive visits from the farmers and weavers and hosiers who were anxious to see what her mill had to offer, so that they could make use of it when the time came.

But as she dressed that morning in the spotless and rather austere bedroom that Samuel had never shared with her, Hannah felt no jubilation. There was of course a certain quiet satisfaction that at last her hard work had come to fruition, but it was an arid and joyless thing. When everything was so wrong with the rest of her life, the mill could offer no adequate consolation. It was indeed something to occupy her mind, but no more than that and for much of the time it did not even do that very effectively.

There had been no word from Samuel since he had walked away from the mill four weeks ago – no message, no letter, no report that anyone had seen him passing. With dread, Hannah wondered if he had gone from her life for ever.

She was not sure why she minded that possibility so much. There had been a kind of relief in his going, because his bitterness and anger had placed a terrible strain on them both. Yet she could not bear the thought that she might never see him again. Perhaps a part of her had hoped still, one day, to recapture their gentle and loving friendship. Perhaps she simply could not bear the sense of failure that his going had left her with. Perhaps it was because, if things did not get better between them, then Agnes's generous sacrifice of her farm would have gone for nothing. All she knew was that it took the happiness from this day, as from every day.

Hannah pushed her hair under her cap, smoothed the folds of her apron, and made her way on to the landing, her clogs loud on the new boards. Here it was still dark, for the sun had not risen yet, though outside the birds were noisily greeting the dawn. She could hear the distant cry of a curlew, with its reminders of so many other springs, happier by far than this, at least in retrospect. It was as if her life had darkened steadily as the years passed, until all she had to look forward to now was a greater desolation, which in the end would be complete.

She tried to shake off her sombre mood. In the kitchen, Agnes was already stirring the fire to life, but not too much, for they had to be sparing still of fuel, though the peats were cut and stacked to dry on Thornside common; that laborious task had occupied much of the two women's time during the past weeks. Agnes looked round and smiled, and Hannah forced a smile in return.

'A great day for thee, this,' Agnes said, rising to her feet. She looked tired, behind the cheerfully matter of fact manner.

'Yes,' said Hannah, trying herself to sound cheerful. They sat down together at the table, which seemed too large for just the two of them, in that vast kitchen. On the morning of Samuel's departure, Hannah had braced herself to explain to Agnes where he had gone and why, only to find that he had already told her everything before he left – everything, that is, except the real reason for his going. It was obvious enough to Hannah that Agnes had not been deceived. After all, it was an odd time for Samuel to go plant-hunting, when it might be supposed his presence would be needed at home. But Agnes had asked no questions and Hannah, though she had been tempted more than once to do so, had not told her the truth. That would have meant explaining what had happened between herself and Robert, and she did not think even Agnes's love for her would be proof against such a disclosure. Would she not see, as did Hannah herself, that, after all, the child so carefully raised had gone to the bad, like the unknown mother who had given her birth?

Hannah supposed Samuel's going must have set a few tongues wagging in the neighbourhood, but she had heard nothing of it. Her greatest fear was that Joseph Gayle might realise something was wrong, as apparently he had not done up to now. He would have to know soon; tomorrow he was coming to Thornside market, and he had promised to call at the mill. But Hannah thought he would accept Samuel's absence readily enough, so long as he did not realise how long his son had been away.

'There's the men now,' Agnes said suddenly. Hannah went to the window. George Holgate was there, of course, limping his way towards the mill door. The two men who had built the machines were here too, come to share in the day that their work had made possible. Hannah checked that her keys were on her belt; not for her now the knitting sheath tucked permanently in, ready for use. 'Let's go,' she said to Agnes, and they went out to greet the men and unlock the mill doors.

On the ground floor, where a hearth would provide heating in winter, the jenny stood, all gleaming wood, with the rows of beautifully made bobbins and spindles, forty of each, empty and waiting for the first carded wool. At one side of the room, great metal cogs and wheels and rods connected the millwheel to the machinery on the floor above. Up there, in that room where Samuel had turned on her with such bitterness, the carding engine stood ready, its wheels linked to the broad belt turned by the mechanism of the millwheel. Near it, carefully sorted according to quality, the finest here, the middling there, the dirty tangled tail wool separate again, the few fleeces Hannah had kept for this first day were waiting to be fed into the machine.

Together she and Agnes spread the wool – teased out a little by hand – on the cloth that would pass over rollers to the turning wire hooks that would card it, exactly as the old hand-held cards had done, when as a small child Hannah used to work them, seated beside Agnes as she set the spinning wheel humming. Hannah nodded to George and his face lit in a sudden grin, and he took hold of the lever that opened the sluices to release the water along the millrace and on to the wheel.

Moments later, the sound of water grew from a rush to a roar, and with a creaking and groaning and clanking all the cogs and wheels and belts and rods began to move, and the wool-spread cloth edged forward between the turning hooks.

Suddenly Hannah forgot all her troubles. She stood and watched in fascination the whole extraordinary process, that complicated, intricate mechanism working alone without the intrusion of any human agency, except to set it going and bring it to a halt. All the operator had to do was to take the wool from the first carding – the scribbling, which teased out and blended the fibres at once – and feed it into the next stage. Then they watched as the long lengths of carded wool emerged to pass at last under a final fluted roller, coming out as long thin sausages of wool ready to be wound on the bobbins of the jenny.

'I've seen nowt like it in all my life!' Agnes exclaimed, echoing Hannah's own sense of wonder.

George set to work to fill the bobbins, and they went

to help him, while James Taylor and Tobias Wheeler, as excited as everyone else, continued to feed the wool into the machine they had made. It seemed to take no time at all for the forty bobbins to be filled. A little reluctantly, George closed the sluices, and with a last groan and rattle the machinery came to a halt. Quietness flooded into the mill, the tiny gentle sound of the beck competing with their suddenly hushed voices. Then they all went downstairs.

Hannah watched as George, well taught during the past days, skilfully filled and threaded the jenny and set it working. No magical machinery now, but for all that the speed with which the spinning progressed seemed astonishing.

'When I think how many days it would take me to fill forty bobbins!' Agnes exclaimed, as she watched the backward and forward movement of the bar on the jenny, which resulted so soon in forty bobbins neatly filled with yarn just right for knitting or weaving.

'Someone's coming!' George said suddenly, his voice breaking sharply into the excited talk. They all fell silent, listening to the fast beat of hooves in the lane. Hannah, thinking 'Samuel!', and then remembering he had gone on foot, went to the door, just as a gangling boy, whom she knew very well, rode into the yard and brought his pony to an abrupt and trembling half before her. It was young John Thwaite, son of one of the Hollinthwaite elders.

'Samuel!' he gasped. 'I've come for Samuel Gayle.' He slid from the pony's back. 'It's his father – had a fall. He's right poorly.'

Oh, what shall I do? Hannah thought in dismay; but at the same time she took the boy's elbow and said gently, 'Take thy beast to the stable, see him fed and watered. Then come to the house. I'll come to thee quickly.' Then she went to call Agnes.

In the kitchen they sat the boy at the table and

brought him ale and havercakes, and he told them the whole story, between mouthfuls. 'It was that young horse of his – thou knows, the one he broke last year. He'd just set out for Reeth when, seemingly, something startled it. They found him by the roadside, hurt bad. His back, the doctor says. He says you should come quick, and Samuel.'

'He's not here,' put in Hannah. 'He's away. I don't know where.' She felt shame at having to admit that painful fact, and distress. She wondered urgently how she could get word to Samuel. Dentdale, he had said, perhaps Kendal. Surely someone must have seen him pass? Surely in these dales where families had been linked for generations by kinship and friendship, someone knew where he was, or how to find him? The rift between them seemed suddenly to shrink to next to nothing, a trivial thing, of no account against the need to bring him home.

'Stephen Wood,' said Agnes suddenly. He was one of the Thornside carriers, with a string of packhorses available to carry goods in all directions. 'He's through Dentdale once a week at least. If he won't go himself, he'll likely know who to send.'

'I'll see to it.' Hannah moved towards the door, and then halted. 'Best call on him on our way. If we ride we'll be quicker.'

They gathered together the few things they might need, saddled the galloways, and Hannah left word with George Holgate in case Samuel should return in their absence; he would stay at the mill, he promised, until she came home again. They were almost ready to leave, when she asked suddenly, 'Robert – has anyone told Robert?' In spite of the overriding practical needs of the moment, her heart beat uncomfortably fast at the thought of him. Just as the crisis had diminished the rift with Samuel, so it seemed in the same way to dissolve her anger against Robert. She found herself longing to run to him, to take him the news and to comfort him afterwards. Then she felt resentful that the thought of him should have to intrude at all at such a time. It was Samuel who would need her most. Robert needed no one.

'They said nowt about Robert,' said John. 'He'd fallen out with the old man, hadn't he?'

'He must be told, even so,' Agnes decided. 'He will want to make his peace, if . . .'

'Aye.' The boy nodded. 'You ride on then. I'll go to Newgill.'

Hannah felt both relief and disappointment, but they faded quickly. There was no time now for such feelings. The boy rode away, and soon afterwards she and Agnes set out up the hill towards Thornside, and Hollinthwaite.

ii

Robert, frowning, unfolded the letter and spread it on the table before him; but, as he read, the gloom slowly left his face. By the time he had reached the end, he was smiling broadly.

'*Sir*,' it said, in a careful, rather awkward hand, '*with regard to your enquiry concerning the supply of apprentices for your cotton mill. We can readily furnish you with twelve of the above, eight girls and four boys, from seven to twelve years of age, on the terms set down in your letter. The parish will undertake to pay two guineas for each child placed, and sufficient clothing. The apprentices to work thirteen hours of each of the six working days, for which they shall each receive one penny per week, lodging, and all things necessary to their keep.*'

Robert read the letter through twice and then began to make a few notes in his notebook. He had already calculated long since the precise numbers needed to work the existing machines. If his workers were to be children, then he might need a few in addition, to allow for extra wastage, or simple incompetence. He had made a further list of potential suppliers, some –

like this one – marked as already contacted, although this was the first reply he had received.

Faintly, through the wall that separated his office from the mill itself, came the sound of the machinery – of two machines only, for he had still not attracted more than a tiny handful of workers: two weavers' wives from Thornside, and three men whose previously workless state was easily explained, he felt, by their ineptitude. It was not really worth the effort and expense of opening the mill for the tiny amount of cotton that could be spun, except that not to open at all would be to convince everyone that his enterprise was doomed, even before it had begun. Now at last it seemed that his troubles might be over.

There was a cautious tap on the door, and then a tousled head appeared. 'Mr Gayle, sir —' Robert looked round. 'Sir George Scarr is below, and wishes to speak with you.'

Robert suppressed his customary faint sense of irritation, allowing no trace of it to show on his face. He did not like the feeling that he must always be ready to obey the least command of his partner. Partner: he was hardly that, when he supplied only the cash (and a certain amount of muted enthusiasm). Yet not once did he allow Robert to forget who was, socially speaking, the superior, and who the inferior. Robert acknowledged that, most probably, this was something ingrained in him, of which he was quite unconscious. Sir George was, after all, friendly and pleasant enough in his manner towards Robert, more so than he was even to some of his equals. But always there were those small reminders of the difference in station between them; as now, when, visiting the mill, he assumed that Robert would come down to him, sparing him the unnecessary fatigue of climbing the stairs to the office.

But Robert knew it was part of the price he paid for achieving his ambition, and so, as always, he swallowed his pride and made his way downstairs – not too quickly, not before he had made a final note and tidied his papers.

Sir George greeted him affably enough. 'Ah, Gayle! Thought I'd drop by and take a look round. A good few weeks since I saw how things were going.'

'Indeed, sir,' said Robert smoothly. 'I shall be happy to show you round. Though I fear you will find little change since your last visit.' If only he could have put off his visit for a week or two, Robert reflected, as he opened a door and released a sudden blast of noise from the two machines.

Sir George frowned slightly. 'Then you have taken on no more hands?' He had to raise his voice to be heard above the clatter; the working spinning machines were set very close to the door.

'One more,' said Robert. 'But I am glad to say that our little difficulty is about to be resolved.' The 'our' was deliberate, reminding his partner that he shared in the responsibility and the problems as much as the eventual (and certain) profits. He gestured to Sir George to precede him into the mill.

'Then you have found a means to attract workers? Not by raising wages, I trust? You said yourself that would be an unnecessary increase in costs.'

'On the contrary, sir, I shall be reducing wages considerably. That will be balanced by additional expenses elsewhere. But they will be fully justified by the results, I am convinced. My solution is children: charity children, workhouse orphans.' He smiled at his companion's startled expression. 'The parish authorities are obliged to bind them apprentice to some useful trade, as of course you know. What better trade than cotton spinning? There will be no idle hands in my mill, to be doing the devil's work.'

'Indeed no,' Sir George agreed. 'But where will you find pauper children in such numbers? There are few enough in this district, I should have thought.'

'Certainly, and they are for the most part already

taught handspinning and knitting; that, it seems, satis-
fies those responsible. But so long as I can accommodate them it doesn't matter where my apprentices come
from. I have heard this very morning from Hackney,
near London. A similar number from a poorhouse
here, another there, and the problem is solved. What's
more, they won't come with set ideas and bad habits.
Pliable, biddable, prepared to work hard on my terms
– what could be better, for the mill and for the children?
It is an act of philanthropy which yet makes sound
business sense. I have to pay an adult male perhaps as
much as ten shillings a week. The children need board
and lodgings, but a penny a week is a king's ransom
to them.'

Sir George nodded approvingly. 'It sounds an excellent scheme to me. Do you intend that these apprentices
will make up your entire workforce?'

'Very probably, if all goes well; unless there is a
sudden demand for work from local people, as there
may be, once they see the mill in full production.
Steady work of this kind must have its attractions,
even for a naturally idle population. But if I can bring
in an initial one hundred children, each bound for five
to eight years, depending on age on arrival – well,
even allowing for natural wastage, that's an assured
workforce thoroughly trained in my ways for many
years to come.'

'Indeed. I can see that. But how will you accommodate them?'

'There'll be room here in the mill for the first arrivals.
Meanwhile, I shall build a suitable lodging house close
at hand.'

Sir George smiled faintly, 'For which you will doubt-
less require further finance?'

'A certain amount, yes,' Robert said.

'You'd best give me the figures before I go. I'll see
what I can do. It seems a sound scheme to me. You'll
need adult supervision of the children, I suppose?'

'Yes, sir – but my manager has had previous experience in that respect. I can depend upon him to oversee that side of things . . . Here he is now.' As Henry Birley joined them, Robert quickly told him of this morning's letter, and the three men discussed the proposed plans at some length.

Much later, when the tour was over and the financial matters amicably settled, Robert accompanied his guest to his waiting horse, where Sir George said suddenly, 'You'll sup with us tonight, Gayle, I hope? And sit down to a rubber or two of whist with us afterwards? In fact, stay if you like. I am expecting two old friends to dine with me tomorrow. One of them is something of an authority on agricultural improvements. You might find the talk interesting. I'm sure the mill can do without you for once.'

Robert tried not to appear too delighted. In truth, he did not much want to give up a day at the mill when there were so many plans to be made. But it pleased him to think that Sir George should regard him as fit company for his 'old friends'. More than that, any opportunity to gain a stronger foothold in the landowning society of the dale was welcome; and an extended visit would allow him to further a related but slightly different object.

'I shall come with pleasure, sir,' he said, with just the right degree of warmth, gratified but not fawning.

He whistled to himself as he returned to his office to give his attention once more to the mill's business. But instead of sitting down at once at his desk, he went to the window and looked out. It faced east, and from it he could just see the wood that sheltered Thornside mill, and the tree-lined lane leading to it. For the first time in weeks he could look at the view with some kind of pleasure, instead of humiliation and anger.

He did not want to see Hannah Gayle running a successful enterprise at the mill that should have been his. But his attempts to dissuade her (overt and otherwise) had failed completely, and some instinct told him that now she was established there she would succeed – so long as no untoward accident occurred, and so long as she did not lose heart for the work. He had even (briefly) found himself wishing her well, when she first arrived. Since she was to live so near, they might well become friends again, he had thought. So he had gone with the kindest motives to take his gift to her.

He had expected to see her face light up with delight, as it used often to do for him, and to read unmistakably in her eyes the truth that she loved him still. It had after all been no more than a sudden impulse, a feminine whim, that had driven her from him. In the cold reality of her marriage she must long since have realised the enormity of her mistake. There had been a further motive, too, of course, in taking his gift: to remind Samuel yet again that he had no right to Hannah and could never hope to be happy with her.

In the event, Robert had been doubly disappointed. Samuel had left the room without giving any indication of his feelings. Hannah, far from betraying an abiding love, had returned the gift with scorn. His only consolation had come later, when he had heard that Samuel had left her with inexplicable suddenness. That departure was the direct result of his own visit, Robert did not doubt.

But that satisfaction apart, the whole business had continued to rankle. Hannah had rejected him yet again, and her mill was (so he had also heard) making good progress. 'Who would have thought she had it in her?' men said in the alehouses. 'No wonder Samuel Gayle walked out – you can see who's the man in that house.' It pleased Robert to hear Samuel spoken of so disparagingly, but everything else about the situation moved him to helpless rage.

Now things would change. His own mill, after its uncertain beginnings, was about to prosper; and in the gracious mansion with its view of Semerwater, there waited Miss Harriet Scarr, in whose company he would dine tonight, who quite openly worshipped him. She bored him too, a little, he had to admit. She was so stiflingly good-mannered, so endlessly ingratiating towards the gentlemen who surrounded her, full of small affectations that grated on his nerves . . . She was also rich and well born, a woman – a *lady* – at present quite beyond his reach. But before long he would be in a position to buy land, and build his own mansion, and establish himself as her father's equal, so that he could go to him and ask for her hand. Then at last Hannah would know what she had missed. She would see that he had no need of her, that she no longer mattered to him in the least, and that there was absolutely nothing she could do about it. The prospect gave him immense satisfaction.

There was a sudden knock on the office door. 'Mr Gayle, there's a man from Hollinthwaite asking for you. An accident, he says – to your father. Shall I show him up?'

iii

Samuel stood on the edge of the world, and was swept again by an exhilarating sense of liberation. Below him – far below – Dentdale lay all shimmering green and gold in the afternoon sun, its villages and farmhouses dwindled to toys, its busy bustling people no more than insects scuttling about almost beyond sight and sound in the hazy depths. Their troubles and pains, their loves and hates, all the messiness of human emotions, seemed far away and unimportant. Remote from them all, remote from himself, from the tormented man he had fled at Thornside, Samuel felt free and happy as never before.

He looked back on those dark days as on a time of insanity, ended by the final mad impulse that had made him walk away from Hannah five weeks ago. Only it had not been mad; it had been the sanest thing he had ever done. He could breathe freely at last, as he was doing now, drawing in great gulps of the pure moorland air. He was free of the unbearable hurt, of the constant gnawing at his nerves and his emotions; of Hannah, and the cruel mingling of love and passion and hate and disgust she aroused in him; of his father, who despised him; of neighbours, who knew him too well; and Robert, who . . . was simply Robert.

He did not know if he would ever return to them. On the whole he thought not. The freedom, which at first had seemed only to be the physical expression of his own desperate isolation of spirit, had become something positive and good, to be welcomed and embraced. Love had seemed once to be the focal point of his life. Now he saw it as a gnawing cancer at its heart, which at last he had cut away. There was no longer anything to hold him or bind him, no one to please but himself.

As the days passed, taking him always further from Thornside, he had walked alone along the wildest paths, stopping whenever he wished, to examine a plant, sketch it, make notes; to talk to a drover or a shepherd or a lead miner – lonely men like himself, who had no interest in detaining him; to eat at an inn that took his fancy. He had slept where he pleased, in cottage or inn or, more often as the nights grew warmer, out under the stars with the soft sounds of the night around him. It was a wandering gipsy existence, except that he had just enough money for his needs. He had never imagined that solitude so complete could be so delightful, or that the demands of family and friends could, in retrospect, seem so constricting.

He had walked as far as the region of lakes and mountains beyond Kendal. He thought he might choose to settle there, in some remote cottage where he could fend for himself. If he ran short of money, he could always knit something to sell. He would have shelter from winter storms, yet still be free to walk out on the fells whenever he chose. His studies would provide interest and consolation in his solitude. In fact, now that he had gathered so much material, he was thinking very seriously of taking that very step, as soon as possible. He was eager to give his full attention to the book that was to show the results of all his studies.

But first there was a plant he had seen growing from a rocky outcrop on the edge of the fell above Dentdale, as he came this way three weeks ago. It was some kind of sandwort, he knew that, but not one with which he was familiar. He had not picked any of it, partly because he was always reluctant to damage any living thing, partly because it was not then in flower. By now he thought the buds might be open, and he would be able to draw and describe – and perhaps identify – it. So he had steadily retraced his steps and was now searching what he hoped was the right area for the place where he had seen it. Once that was done, he would make his way west again and find his cottage and write his book.

He found the place at last, remembering at just the right moment that it had looked directly across the dale to a small windblown knot of scots pines. Sure enough, the tiny plant was covered now with starry white flowers, at whose centre grew minute pink anthers. He examined them carefully for a little while, and then sat down to make his drawing.

He did not know what it was precisely that triggered it off – perhaps something as simple as the way the grass grew about the rock, or the lichen on the grey surface of the stone. But whatever it was, it suddenly brought to mind another rock, on another expanse of moorland, on another day long years ago; and of himself, a boy of twelve, sitting there alone, but waiting, listening for the sound that had come to him next: his name called out. He had looked up, and there had been Hannah running across the sheepheugh towards him. And he had given her the gift he had made for her, the knitting sheath, carved so carefully, with all the love that even then had been a part of him. She had the sheath still; it had been tucked in her belt as usual on the morning he left.

But he did not want to think of Hannah. His love for her was over now, extinguished, never to be revived. Better the chill cold certainty of this new life he had embarked upon, than the tormenting flame that had for so long, and so hopelessly, consumed him.

Something moved near him. He glanced quickly round. A sheep stood there, watching him with its black and yellow eyes, more curious than apprehensive. He had sat here so long that he must seem like some essential part of the moorland, rooted in the peaty ground. So he was; so he would become. As far as he was able, he would live the rest of his life out on the open fell, walking the tracks and drove roads, with the wind in his face and all the lonely loveliness before him. He would avoid the places where men in their greed, their avid quest for luxury, had marred it: quarries, lead mines, coal pits, towns and mills. He would learn to know the plants and insects and birds and beasts of these high places better than he knew any man or woman. He would sleep under the stars and one day he would draw his last breath beneath the windswept sky, to become at last in truth a part of the dark earth. It was a thought that pleased him profoundly.

He had a last crust of bread, bought two days ago in Kendal, which he threw to the sheep. It started in fright, and then, when it saw he did not move again, came cautiously forward to eat the bread, before wandering away in search of juicier food. Samuel sat on there for a long time, in an agreeable half-dreaming state, gazing across at the hills on the far side of the dale, until he began to feel a little chilled and more than a little hungry. With some sense of reluctance, he packed his things in his bag and set off down the hill towards the little town of Dent. He could not avoid other people altogether, however much he might wish to do so: he had to buy food for the next stage of his journey. There were a few hours of the day still left, and he wanted to cover as much ground as possible before dark.

The houses of Dent crowded close about a narrow network of streets, fronted by galleries where the town's many knitters and spinners sat at work. Their songs reached him, songs he had heard himself from childhood, at the nightly sittings, in the kitchen at Low Farm, where Mary Harker sang as she worked. They were familiar, with what might once have been a soothing familiarity, but was now too shot through with hurt. He felt again the agitated beating of his heart, the pain at his temples, like an iron band clamped too tight, the anxious lurch of his stomach. He wanted only to be away from here, as soon as ever he could. He found a baker and bought bread, and at a farm bought cheese and havercakes. He had water to drink as he walked, from a flask he refilled when necessary at any handy spring – water was never short in these hills.

On his way out of the town again, his spirits seemed to lighten with every step. His heartbeat slowed and steadied to an easy rhythm, his head cleared, his limbs moved more freely. As soon as he could, he left the road that led alongside the river Dee and turned again up on to the fell, on the south side of the dale this time.

He was a little disappointed to find he was not alone. A string of packhorses was making its way towards him, carrying stone from a quarry, the first led by a small lined man. Samuel nodded at him as he passed (he was not in a mood for talk), and wondered a little at the odd look he received in return. He had taken only a few steps more when the man called after him: 'Do they call thee Samuel Gayle?'

He had an almost overwhelming urge to feign deafness and walk on, or to deny the name. He felt uneasy, even threatened. But he halted and turned round and said, warily, 'Aye.'

'Saw Stephen Wood from Thornside. He said to look out for thee.'

Samuel thought he had been right to feel threatened. He said nothing, bracing himself for what might come.

'Thy dad's poorly. Hurt in a fall. He sent for thee.'

All the enchantment of the past weeks fled from him. He saw his father stretched on his bed, in pain – dying perhaps – calling for his son; who had fled from all such ties and could not be found.

It was not possible to break free, just by running away; the ties were too strong for that. They tugged at him now, harshly and painfully. The past flooded in again, submerging him utterly. He knew he was deeply afraid.

'How poorly? When was this?'

The man shook his head. 'He's bad, that's all I know. I heard – when was it now? – Tuesday, I'd say.'

Samuel did a rapid calculation. Tuesday, Third Day; he thought it must be Fifth Day today – no, Sixth, Friday. Then the message was already four days old.

'He said thy wife came to him, to find thee,' the man was saying now.

The fire was not dead, for it hurt, agonisingly, as it flared up in him. Hannah. His father. There was no escape, no breaking free.

'I thank thee,' he said, his voice drily courteous. 'I'll go back at once.' Then he turned and retraced his steps until he came to the road that led east, to take him home.

iv

Samuel came down to Low Farm well after dark, finding his way by the hesitant light of a half moon.

There was no sign of life, nothing but the hooting of an owl from the trees behind the house, the rustle of small animals (rats perhaps) scampering away at his coming. He made his way to the house door. He had never come to it in the dark before, without any kind of light to guide him; and here, shadowed by the bulk of the house, it was very dark. He felt astonishingly afraid, now he was here. He did not want to knock, though he was not sure why. He would creep in softly, he decided, and see for himself, before letting them know of his return. 'Them' – whoever they might be, here in this house where only his father and Mary Harker lived.

He groped around for the latch and found it at last, praying that the door would not be barred on the inside. It was not. The latch clicked and the door swung open quietly. He left it open, for the faint lessening it brought to the intense darkness beyond, while he felt around for the candle and tinder box that always stood on the chest in the passage.

The sharp sound of the flint sounded appallingly loud in the stillness, the flame that leapt up was bright beyond expectation. Once the candle was alight, burning with a steady flame – it was a windless night – he closed the door as softly as he could, and then stood for some time wondering what to do next.

Could he possibly be alone in the house? There was no sound but the weird insubstantial noises of a building settling for the night. If he was not alone, then who else was here? His father, he supposed, and Mary Harker. Would there be others too? Agnes? Hannah – ? Where should he go now, to announce his return and learn how his father was? He dared not go to his father's room, fearful as he was of the consequences of coming on a sick man, suddenly, in the dark.

He had scarcely heard any warning sound when a step on the stair, a sudden glimmer of light, made him look sharply up. A voice – low, drawling, unmistakable – said, 'I might have guessed! Trust you to come back in time for the reading of the will!'

Even disturbed as he must have been in the middle of the night, it seemed that Robert had not lost his self-possession. Samuel looked up into the mocking face of his brother, and felt a little dazed. He had

301

grown unused to dealing with people, except in the most casual way. Not that he had ever been much good at it, least of all with Robert. It was some little time before he realised what precisely it was that Robert had said; and what his words implied.

'The will . . .' he whispered, faltering. Then: 'No! Father —'

Robert came on down the stairs. 'Dead,' he said, with appalling casualness. 'We buried him today – yesterday, rather. It *is* after midnight, I take it? Lawyer Broderick's coming to read the will in the morning.'

Samuel groped around behind him – the darkness seemed somehow to have become complete again – and found his way to the chest and sat heavily down. 'I only heard today.' Was that right? Or was it yesterday? It did not matter anyway.

There was a great harsh pain in his throat, so that he could hardly breathe or speak. He wanted Robert to go away and leave him alone, to take that horrible mocking face out of his sight. He felt a desperate need for time in which to understand what had happened and to learn what he felt about it.

But Robert stayed exactly where he was, looking down on his brother from his position leaning against the closed door of the parlour. 'He asked for you, you know,' he said. 'Not for me, for you.'

Samuel made an odd choking sound, quickly stifled. He desperately did not want to weep before Robert, but he knew he could not much longer hold back the sobs that were rising to swell the constriction in his throat. He bent his head and pressed his hand to his forehead, shielding his face from Robert's sharp, malicious gaze.

'He hung on longer than was expected, the doctor said, waiting for you.'

'Robert, is that thee?' The urgent whisper broke suddenly on them from above. 'Who's there, with thee?' The voice moved abruptly then from anxiety to a tender overflow of feeling, impulsive and uncalculated, forgetful of fear and sorrow and the need for guilt. There was a rush of bare feet on the stairs. 'Sam! Oh, Sam, thank God thou hast come!'

He felt her arms round him, drawing him near. She had fallen on her knees beside him, crying softly as she talked on, like a mother to her child. He turned his face to her and let the tears come at last, freely, without restraint, there against her breast. He thought of nothing, only the relief of it, to have someone near, who cared.

'Very affecting!' said Robert harshly. He ignored the furious glance which Hannah directed at him over Samuel's head. 'Would you do the same for me, if I were to indulge myself with a few tears? I have a greater claim to be consoled by you than Samuel has. I trust you have not forgotten that fact, Samuel?' When his brother did not stir, he enlarged, 'It was me she wanted, always. She only married you by chance.'

'Thou knows nowt of my feelings!' Hannah retorted. 'And if thou hast no tears to shed for thy own father, thou shouldst be ashamed, not proud.'

'Why? He let me down when I most needed him.' He saw that he had already lost Hannah's attention. He moved past them, touching Samuel briefly on the shoulder as he did so. 'When you're ready, you know where our bedroom is. We shall be like boys again – delightful, don't you think?' Then he went on up the stairs.

Samuel had heard little of what his brother said, though enough of it had reached him to bring freshly back to him all the unhappiness of his marriage to Hannah. But though the awareness of it stayed in his mind, his body and all his instincts made him cling to her still, seeking the comfort that only she could give, from the sympathy that had linked them from their earliest years.

With great tenderness, she said, 'Don't mind Robert,

303

love. He feels bad because he came too late, just as thou did.'

Samuel looked questioningly up into her face. She kissed him lightly and stroked his hair. 'There was some dinner party, more important to him than his father,' she explained, with a suddenly acid note in her voice. 'All that about his hanging on waiting for thee – he knew nowt about it, for he was not here.'

'Wert thou with him, at the end?'

She nodded. 'Me and my mother and Mary. He spoke of thee. He'd have liked to have thee with him, but we said thou wert coming, and he did not fret himself about it.'

'Was there . . .? Did he say anything . . .? A message, for me . . .?'

Even in the dimness he saw her colour. She hesitated a moment before saying, 'He said he was pleased with thee. That thou hadst done well . . . ' She broke off, but he had the clear impression that she had left something unsaid.

'What else?' When his whisper drew no response, he pursued, 'That wasn't all, was it?'

With obvious reluctance, she shook her head. 'He said it was the best thing thou hadst ever done, to wed me.'

He bent his head then, not wanting her to see in his face the confused feelings that followed. He sensed that, even now, some days afterwards, she herself found it difficult to think calmly of that so greatly misplaced approval.

The instinct that had drawn them together so impulsively had gone now. The difficulties and hurts of the past returned in force, pushing themselves to the front of their minds. Samuel felt some instinctive shrinking from the possibility of further hurt if he should give way any longer to his hunger for the consolation and understanding she had offered him. She must have felt something of the same herself, for though she had scarcely moved at all, her hands were very still on his upper arms, steadying him but no longer caressing, and there was more of gravity than of tenderness in her expression. It all only served to intensify his sense of loss at his father's death. He thought now that he had been closer to his father than to anyone, without knowing it. After all, his closeness to Hannah had proved to be an illusion. As for Robert, what linked him to his brother was something that Samuel had every reason to fear, powerful though it was.

'Thou art tired,' said Hannah softly. 'Go to bed and try to sleep. We can talk more tomorrow.' She put that forward rather as a suggestion, to be rejected if he chose, than as a promise. 'Thou wilt have to go in with Robert. I'm in with mother; and Mary . . .' She did not complete the sentence, which told him that Mary, being practical, had moved into his father's vacant room.

He was not sure whether or not he was relieved that he could not share a bed with Hannah, except that the thought of sharing with Robert was unbearable. 'I'll sleep in the kitchen,' he said.

'Thou canst not sleep properly there!'

'I'll get by.' Calmer now (the hardness was returning, covering the hurt) he rose to his feet. 'Sleep well.'

He saw the hesitation in her face. He knew she was wondering whether to protest and stay with him, their past affection – could it be still, for her, a present reality? – competing with the painful estrangement that had driven it away. In the end, for whatever reason, it was the present that won. She stayed where she was, looking at him, and said only, 'Thee too,' in a voice so low he scarcely heard it.

After that, neither of them made any move at all, as if they both felt the awkwardness of two married people turning away from one another at such a time, and neither wanted to be the one to take the first step. In the end it was Samuel who swung round and walked away from Hannah, into the kitchen, where he groped his way to the settle, his cheerless resting place for the night.

He knew he would not sleep. But then he would not have slept anywhere tonight, with the happenings of the past hours whirling about in his mind without sense or order. He heard the stairs creak beneath Hannah's feet, and a door close softly upstairs, and tried not to think what it would be like to have her arms about him still and her breast on which to lay his head.

v

'Your father's will was a short one, of recent date,' said Lawyer Broderick, clearing his throat. 'It needs no comment, so I will simply read it to you.

'*I, Joseph Gayle, of Low Farm, Hollinthwaite in Swaledale in the North Riding of Yorkshire, being of sound mind . . .*' The formal opening words droned on, scarcely heard, perhaps, for they were only what everyone expected to hear. Before moving on to the bequests, the lawyer cast a glance over the company assembled in the parlour; the two sons, the daughter-in-law, and old Mary Harker who had devoted her life to the family. Then he resumed his reading.

'*I do give and bequeath to my dear Friend Mary Harker fifty pounds per annum, so long as she shall live. The residue of my real and personal estate I leave to my son Samuel Gayle, on the sole condition that he allows to his wife Hannah, née Burton, the use and enjoyment of the property known as Thornside mill, together with whatever capital is required for the installation of a machine for the spinning of worsted yarn at the said mill. Dated this Second Day of the Ninth Month 1785.*'

The lawyer looked up into the tense astonished silence that had followed his reading. He saw that Robert Gayle had the look of a man trying to make sense of what he had heard, and to hide the anger that was growing in him the more he thought of it. Samuel simply looked stunned. Hannah suddenly

306

drew a handkerchief from her pocket and began softly to weep. Mary Harker had been sobbing loudly from the moment her name was mentioned.

Robert stood up suddenly, with a harsh grating of his chair on the floor. 'Let me see that!'

In silence the lawyer handed him the will, and watched as he read it through, disbelief and hope giving way to naked fury. He read it three times, and then said brusquely, 'I shall contest it.'

The lawyer shook his head. 'I would not recommend such a course, Mr Gayle. It is as you wish, naturally. But the will was correctly drawn. There is no possible cause to doubt that it exactly expresses your father's wishes. He made his reasons very clear to me too. He assured me you would understand.'

'Understand! I understand right enough!' He swung accusingly round on Hannah. 'You can weep! Fawning, wheedling little hypocrite! You wormed your way into his favour —'

She stopped crying at once, indignation replacing whatever had set the tears flowing. 'That's not true, Robert! I did nothing —'

'Then how did he come to leave it all to Samuel – the farm, the business, everything? You've heard him say often enough what he thought of Samuel's competence. He despised him, you know that!'

'To have a good head for business is not the only virtue in life, nor the chief one. Nor did thy father think it was. Thou knows that.'

Robert swept on, ignoring her. 'If only he'd known! I wish to God I'd told him the truth about you! I never thought; I was a fool. If only he'd known what a little whore —'

'Be quiet!' Samuel came suddenly to life and strode over to his brother, watched by a startled (and fascinated) Mary Harker, her grief forgotten. 'One more word from thee, and I'll . . . I'll . . .'

Robert smiled with mocking ill-humour at the return

of Samuel's customary hesitancy. 'You'll what, dear brother? Oh, never fear, you don't need to do anything. Hannah's done it all for you. A clever woman, I'll grant her that. But, by God, you'll regret it, both of you, I swear it. I should have been his heir, if there was any justice —'

'Thou'st said enough, more than enough!' Mary broke in sharply. 'That thou canst talk so with thy father not cold in his grave! Thou hast only thyself to blame that he did not trust thee with his things, and thou knows it. If thou didst ever love him at all, it was for what he could give thee, nowt else.'

'Be quiet, woman – this has nothing to do with you!' He turned sharply away from her shocked face, to confront his brother and Hannah once more. 'I shall try what the courts can do, I promise you. But if that doesn't work, I'll find another way. I'll see you both ruined yet.' He looked from one to the other, and his eyes took on a triumphant expression. 'One thing, you've me to thank already that you'll never be happy together. Remember that, if you're ever tempted to think I shan't get my own way with the rest of it.' He swung round then to face the lawyer. 'As for you, Broderick, you'll hear from my lawyer as soon as I've put matters in his hands. No one – dead or living – is going to slight me and get away with it.' He bowed curtly to the assembled company. 'I give you good day.' Then he marched from the room.

There was a moment of complete silence, broken only by the sobs of Mary Harker, who had begun to weep again after Robert turned on her. Then Hannah and Samuel, trembling openly, resumed their seats. Not long afterwards they heard Robert ride away.

Mary Harker, with a sudden renewal of energy, blew her nose and hurried to the kitchen to give an account of the morning's events to Agnes, who was busy preparing dinner for them all. Samuel saw the lawyer on his way and then returned to the parlour. He

closed the door behind him and stood leaning against
it, looking at Hannah in silence. She returned his gaze
steadily, trying to read in his strained and weary face
what he was thinking and feeling. She could see there
only exhaustion. He looked as if very little, a touch
perhaps, would send him sliding to the floor. Hannah
could think of nothing to say that would help him. After
what seemed a long time she said, more to break the
silence than anything, 'I did not expect this.'

'Nor I.' With an obvious effort he pulled himself fully
upright and walked to the nearest chair and sank onto
it. Then he gave way, sitting slumped, with his elbows
on his knees and his head in his hands, his fingers
pushed into his hair. 'I didn't want it either,' he added
after a moment, tonelessly.

Hannah said nothing. She looked round the room,
out of the window at the rain-washed landscape. No,
she had not wanted the farm or the business. It had
not even occurred to her that she or Samuel might
have any claim to them, as much as anything because
she had not thought of Joseph dying, or of anyone but
him living here and directing matters as he always had.
But if she had been asked she would have agreed with
Robert that, whatever his differences with his father, he
was the heir and must one day inherit.

Now that it all belonged to Samuel she could not say,
as Samuel had, that she would have had it otherwise.
She was even glad that Robert would not have the
power to hurt with his ruthless methods those who
depended on the hosiery business. She only wished
the old man was still alive, because she had been fond
of him, and even more because of the pain his death
must cause Samuel.

As for Thornside mill, she was not surprised that
their own possession of it should have been made
secure, but that the old man should have ensured
that its management remained in her hands, that was
another matter. He could not by law leave it to her,

for she was simply Samuel's wife, and could own no property herself; but he had done the next best thing. The action implied so deep an affection for her, so complete a trust in her abilities, that she could only be deeply moved by it. She would show her gratitude by making of it the success that Joseph Gayle would have wanted to see, had he lived.

Samuel spoke again, his voice sounding very loud in the stillness, though he spoke quietly, even rather dejectedly. 'Robert was right. It should have been his.' After a pause, he added, 'I was a bad son too. I was not even here. I did not love him as I ought. I blamed him for favouring Robert.' His voice had become increasingly harsh, more full of agitation.

Hannah came and knelt beside him and gently drew his hands away from his face, so that she could look into it. 'Don't, Samuel! I understand thee. I felt it too. When my father died, it was just the same. I was so ashamed, I saw so much that I had done, or had not done. We are all guilty, one way or another. But that does not mean we are beyond forgiveness. And we can still be thankful, for what is good.'

His fingers closed about hers, as if he was desperately trying to reach out for the consolation she was offering to him – consolation, and a means to reconciliation and healing, if only, somehow, they could find one another across the barrier. But Samuel was simply too tired to do more than cling to her in silence. After a while she said, 'Thou shouldst go to bed.'

In the end he took her advice and went up to the room now cleared of all traces of his brother, and slid into bed, where, almost at once, he fell deeply asleep.

He had not emerged several hours later, when at last Agnes and Hannah took their candles and went upstairs to the room they had shared since they came to the farm. Outside its door, Agnes halted and said softly, 'There's no call to keep me company. Go to Samuel, if thou wilt.'

What do I want? Hannah asked herself. 'I would not wish to wake him,' she said aloud; and then, after a moment, 'Perhaps I'll just look in to see all's well. It's cold tonight.'

The candlelight showed Samuel's thin form hunched beneath the bedclothes at the far side of the bed, as if even after the weeks of absence the habits of their brief marriage were impossible to break. Hannah went to the bedside and set the candle down on the table and stood looking at his quiet untroubled face. It was not, and never would be, a handsome face. In sleep the features were more characterless than ever, all expression smoothed out of them. But it was a face that had softened, often, with kindness for her, and the unimpressive mouth had once been ready with smiles and words of friendship. Now it was he who, in his grief and loneliness and guilt, needed a friend; and who better than one who understood so well what he was feeling now, because she had felt it too?

She reached out a hand and gently caressed his cheek. He stirred momentarily and murmured something incoherent, but did not wake. On impulse, she crept round the bed and slid in beside him, not lying apart from him this time, but moving close to him and putting her arms about him. After a moment he murmured again and turned over and put his arms about her too, and laid his head on her breast.

For a time they lay quietly together, Hannah resting her mouth on Samuel's hair, and stroking it. She thought he was asleep, that even in turning to her he had not really woken. But the next instant he moved his head, just enough so that she could look into his face, and she saw that his eyes were open. For a moment they simply lay there, looking at one another with thoughtful gravity, each trying to understand both what the other was thinking and feeling, and also the nature of their own thoughts and feelings.

Then, slowly, almost tentatively, he leaned forward

311

and kissed her, just lightly, touching her lips with his. A pause, as if to gauge its effect on her, and then he brought his mouth again to hers, and she felt his hold tighten about her and his body move closer, pressing into her. All the long lonely months of separation and estrangement seemed suddenly to melt into nothing, and a great warm flow of feeling drew them together. Gently, tenderly, a little clumsily, because Hannah had only that one fleeting experience of love to guide her, and Samuel none at all, they ended their estrangement and at last completed the promises exchanged on their wedding day.

Afterwards, as they lay smiling at one another with the happy contentment of two people who know they have done well, and in so doing put an end to a nightmare, Hannah whispered, 'No Robert between us now, nor ever again.'

'No,' Samuel agreed. Then he added, the smile leaving his face, so that he looked all at once very solemn, 'I know now, Hannah – we all have things that need forgiveness; and who's to say who has the greater guilt?'

She hugged him. 'We don't have to weigh it in the scales, only to go on loving and forgiving, for ever if we have to.'

He kissed her again, very gently. It was quite a long time after that before he blew out the candle and they fell asleep at last, held in one another's arms.

CHAPTER FOURTEEN

i

Hannah lay with her eyes closed, conscious that the first clamour of the awakening birds had subsided and the sun was already up. Before very long it would have reached the front of the house, to shine directly in through the bedroom window. She felt Samuel stir beside her; he was awake too then. He moved closer and slid an arm about her.

'Thou art still in bed, at this late hour?'

She opened her eyes and smiled, though it required a considerable effort to do so. Nothing seemed to ease the sickness, neither lying still nor moving. 'I'm just getting up,' she said. She kissed him lightly and dragged herself reluctantly to the edge of the bed.

'Is owt wrong?' he asked anxiously.

'Of course not,' she lied. Sitting up, she felt even worse, very tired and very sick indeed. But it was evident that none of this showed on her face, for Samuel studied it carefully for a moment or two and seemed reassured. He said only,

'Thou hast too much to do.'

'That's how it must be,' she returned. 'It will get easier.'

'Give thyself a rest today.'

She shook her head. 'Thou knows I cannot. I promised to got to Bainbridge this morning, about the wool.'

'Is that the long staple wool, for thy new machine?'

'Aye. If I can find a good supplier near at hand, that will be very pleasing. But I shall have to see.' She began, slowly, to dress.

'Thou art happy, looking after the mill,' Samuel

313

observed. 'I wish thou didst not have all the hosiery business too. I have wondered . . .' He hesitated, then went on, 'Dost thou mind, that I do not help thee?'

'Thou art ready enough to help if I ask it of thee. What more do I need? Besides, thou hast thy book to do.'

'Oh, that's only a pastime,' he said dismissively.

'What wilt thou do with it, when it's finished?'

'See if anyone will print it, I suppose,' he said.'But that's a long way off. It's hardly begun.' He slid to the floor and pulled off his nightshirt. 'Hannah,' he said, his voice briefly muffled in the folds, 'I have thought, more than once – would it not be just, to let Robert have what should have been his?'

Hannah stared at him. 'The business? Is that what thou means?'

After considering the matter, Samuel conceded, 'Perhaps not. Thou wert right, I think, that he would misuse it. But I cannot think my father meant that he should have nothing at all.'

'He has not got nothing. He has the cotton mill. If he hadn't, then I suppose thy father might have left him something. But he knew what he was doing, and why. Thou knows that.'

'Yes, but —'

She went to him and put her arms loosely about his neck. 'Samuel, listen to me! Even the lawyers said there was no case – he would not have dropped it else, thou knows that.'

'It was not that kind of justice I meant, not the world's justice.'

'Then by any other kind of justice, everything is as it ought to be. The things thy father left – the farm, the business – they were not gifts, nor rewards. Robert would have used them for his own ends, to make riches for himself. We shall not do that, for it is not what thy father meant us to do.'

'No. I know that.'

'Well then, spare thy compassion. Thou canst be

quite sure Robert would have none for thee, if things were different.'

'That does not make it right, if —'

Hannah kissed him again. 'Samuel, thou hast too soft a heart. Give it a little thought; thou wilt see I am right. And now I must hurry, or I shall not have time to look in on the mill before I go out.'

ii

It had gone well. The farmer near Bainbridge, a Friend like themselves, whom they saw each week at meeting, had been right to suggest that the fleeces of his much-prized flock of sheep might be precisely what Hannah needed to supply her worsted spinning machine. She liked dealing with her fellow Quakers: no haggling, no possibility of deceit, everything straightforward and in the open. She saw the wool, handled it, examined the all-important length of the staple and, having approved it, asked what price the farmer had in mind. 'Thirteen shillings the stone,' he said quietly. It was a high price, but then so was the quality. 'That's fair,' she said. 'I shall send someone for it next week.' And that was that.

Now she was walking home, uneasily conscious of clouds gathering at the head of the dale, but glad that the nausea had eased a little in the fresh air. She wished it would go altogether. For days now it had been with her, and the intense lassitude that made her so ready to lie late in bed, so disinclined to occupy herself with all the many tasks that lay before her at the moment. She was afraid too, because she was sure that something was wrong, quite seriously wrong; so afraid that she dared not speak of it to anyone, in case they should send for a doctor, who would then confirm her worst fears. But if it went on she would have to do something, for it was making life intolerable.

She tried to return her thoughts to the satisfactorily completed transactions, but it was not that in the end which banished the anxiety from her mind. She crossed

315

the bridge over the river, slipped through the wicket for pedestrians at the tollgate, and walked on. And was immediately conscious – overwhelmingly so – that she had almost reached the cotton mill. She came this way often enough, once a week at least, yet she could never pass it casually or thoughtlessly, as she would any other building.

She could not see its starkly businesslike outline yet, though she could see the trees that from this angle mercifully screened it, and already she could hear the rush of water in the beck that fed the millstream. She tried to ignore the quickening beat of her heart, and the sensations that mingled dread and excitement. Why should she feel like this? If she were to hear now that Robert had gone away for ever she could only be relieved beyond words . . .

She swallowed hard, drew a deep breath and walked on with her eyes firmly set on the more distant view of Thornside, and her own mill glimpsed away to the right, its modest buildings merging into the countryside around as Robert's never would, even when time had weathered the stones and lichened the slates. As assertive as his own personality, it rose from the greenness of the dale – it was just coming into sight there now – proclaiming to every passer-by his intention to make his mark upon their lives.

No, she *would* not look. But not looking did not ensure that her thoughts were directed, as were her eyes, to her home, where Samuel, her friend again, her husband at last, would be working at his delicate, painstaking drawings, or teaching his pupils, or thinning out seedlings in the garden for which he had developed such an enthusiasm; and Agnes would be busy in the house, or with the animals, or dealing as best she could with some question that had arisen at the mill; and the men – George, or the lad Abraham Wood who had been brought in to help him – would be sorting the first fleeces to come since the clipping, and setting the machines to card and spin, while the two craftsmen from Thornside shaped wood and fitted cogs and wheels and spindles for the new worsted spinning machine . . . Where were all the children they said were working for Robert now? There was no sign of them at all from the outside, though it was said that the second building almost completed was to provide them with lodging. At the moment they were housed in the mill itself, so Hannah had been told. But no one ever heard the sounds of children at play, or shouts or laughter, or anything but the endless rush of the water and the clatter of machinery – loud even here on the road, so there must be many machines. Could they really all be worked by children?

They *was* a child there, after all: one small boy, running round the new dormitory building (if such it was), where he halted – to crouch by the wall, as far as Hannah could see from here. A little after, a man came round the corner and spoke to him and then they walked back together the way they had come, soon disappearing from sight. Hannah had the impression, faint enough at this distance, that the child had been reluctant to go with the man, even protesting a little at first. But she could have been mistaken.

Without realising it she had come to a halt, so she could watch them more intently. It was not until the horse was almost upon her that she realised someone had come riding up from the bridge behind her. She turned swiftly; and then could not find the will to step aside or walk on or do anything but remain stupidly where she was.

Robert had no smile for her today, not even the bright mocking one she had come to expect. He did not bow his head in that characteristic way of his, which had no hint of deference or humility about it. He simply drew rein and stared coldly back at her, though she was conscious that there was something speculative in his eyes, and even, after a moment, a hint of surprise.

'I do not need to enquire after your health,' he said curtly. 'You look astonishingly well.'

The unmistakable note of disappointment in his voice amused her, and she smiled suddenly. At the same time she wondered how she could look so well when she felt so ill. It was clear from his tone that Robert saw some startling change in her since he had threatened her and Samuel with misery and ruin at their last meeting six weeks before. Could it all be her imagination, the sickness and the tiredness? Surely not, for she was conscious of them still, beneath the agitation that Robert's presence never ceased to awake in her. She retorted as cheerfully as she could, 'I see it is a grave disappointment to thee. Thou wilt be the more cast down to hear that Samuel too is well.'

Robert frowned. 'I don't care a fig how he is. It won't last, I can promise you. Anxiety is a sure route to ill health . . . They tell me he's let Low Farm.'

'Yes. To a cousin of John Hird's.'

'Father did not leave the business to Samuel so he could merely shrug it off on to someone else.'

'He has not done so. We manage the business from the mill. I think that is what thy father would have wanted. We have no time to farm the land, of course, but it is only let on a short lease, in case we should want to make use of it some day.'

'To provide a living for one of your numerous and growing offspring, I suppose?' The mocking look had returned after all, with a sharper edge of malice to it.

But its harshness was lost on Hannah. Suddenly, with all the force of the obvious, she saw, not Robert, but Samuel – herself and Samuel, lying together with their arms about one another, as they had done many times since that first night of sweet if unexciting consummation; and for the first time she made a connection between that and her present condition. The constant sickness, the tiredness – could it be . . .? Could there be an entirely simple and natural explanation of it all?

That possibility had not occurred to her until now. With all the overwhelming passion of Robert's lovemaking, she had not conceived. She had never dreamed that Samuel's hesitant tenderness (for he still approached her as if he was by no means sure of a happy outcome, as if all kinds of things might still spoil it for them) could succeed in creating new life within her, when Robert's vitality had failed. Yet . . .

Conscious of heightened colour and a sudden complete lack of interest in Robert and his concerns, she raised her eyes to his face and said, 'Thou must excuse me. I am wanted at home.' Then she turned and hurried away from him, up the hill towards Thornside.

CHAPTER FIFTEEN

i

Miss Scarr laughed, in the way that never failed to irritate Robert. It was such a silly laugh, a high-pitched giggle that was curiously mirthless. He wondered if she ever laughed naturally, from genuine amusement, or if she only laughed when it was expected of her.

But his expression betrayed nothing of what he felt. He responded to her laughter by grinning charmingly and raising her hand to his mouth to place a kiss upon its pale smooth surface. She blushed (blushing did not suit her, Robert had decided long ago, for it merely made her look blotchy and unattractive) and her laughter subsided to a shy half-smile. That at least he knew to be entirely natural; he had enough experience of such things to be able to recognise the signs that a woman was besotted with him. He had known a long time ago that he had successfully captivated Miss Harriet Scarr. It was, after all, what he had deliberately set out to do, and he was accustomed to achieving his ambitions, whatever they were.

'Oh Mr Gayle, you flatter me!' Her coy rejoinder irritated him as much as did her laugh. Hannah never spoke with such artificiality; her manner was all naturalness and simplicity . . .

But smooth, bland he showed no sign of irritation and simply continued to pay her the effusive and insincere compliments he would never have thought to make to Hannah. But then with Hannah they would not have been insincere: she *was* beautiful, charming, accomplished in the true sense of the word, and intelligent and sensitive . . . He was angry at the way his thoughts

320

kept returning to her, and to the disturbing piece of gossip that had come his way yesterday, as he discussed repairs to one of his machines with Thomas Bell. Even today's hunting had failed to drive it out of his head, as it ought to have done. He loved hunting; it had all the appeal of the forbidden, since field sports were firmly frowned upon by the Society of Friends, and even after several enjoyable seasons it had still not lost that particular charm for him. And, after all, there could not possibly be any truth in the talk – wishful thinking amongst the old women of Thornside, that was all it was.

Across the room, Sir George Scarr, who had been discussing stock-breeding with two of his more enlightened landowning neighbours, excused himself and went to give his attention to the vicar of Thornside, a scholarly man recently arrived in the parish (the previous incumbent, much given to hunting, had been more congenial company by far). When Sir George had gone, his neighbours were silent for a time, before one of them said, 'Do you think Scarr intends to apply his improving principles to his family as well as to his cattle?'

The other man looked puzzled. 'I don't follow . . .'

'There —' said his companion, nodding towards the little group about their host's daughter, amongst whom Robert Gayle was clearly the most favoured. 'Our young mill owner there – good healthy stock, you might say; give a bit of vigour to the old line. New blood —'

'Oh, surely not!' The second man was clearly startled. 'I've nothing against the young man, but —'

'He's personable – can't fault his manners; could be taken for a gentlemen, if you didn't know better – ambitious, sure to succeed, I'd say.'

'If it was me, I'd want to see a good many more signs of success than that before I'd let him within miles of my daughter. But, I grant you, Scarr seems to have no such qualms. If you're right, there'll be a good few noses put out of joint. I can think of at least three fellows within fifty miles of here who have hopes of seeing the knot tied with their own sons.'

The first man nodded, and then lowered his voice. 'I have heard things are not as secure as Scarr would like. He's dug deep a few times lately. It wouldn't take much to overset things.'

'He's taken risks before – they've always paid off. He's a shrewd eye when it comes to an investment. If I had a son I'd have my eye on the girl too.'

'As well you haven't then. You mark my words, he'll go for the experimental match there.'

'From the look of the girl, it's what she'd choose.'

'Wouldn't you? Just take a look at the alternatives. Anyway, he can afford to let her have her way – young Frederick made a good match, so the heir's taken care of. Though I wouldn't mind betting that financially speaking Gayle proves the better bargain in the end.'

'Fifty guineas that Scarr gets cold feet and weds her to some more eligible youth!'

'Done! It'll be Gayle, you'll see.'

Robert left the Hall that evening in a mood which curiously combined self satisfaction and discontent, and made him decline, for no good reason that he could think of, a pressing invitation to stay the night. On the surface it had been an entirely successful day – hunting, good food, the company of men whose society he valued, a courtship progressing well. Yet he could not shake off a sense of being at odds with the world, as if everything had lost its savour and become flat and insipid. Until recently, even his courtship of Miss Scarr had been spiced with a certain excitement, as of a difficult campaign carefully planned and put into effect. Tonight it had taken a massive effort of will to use his skills to charm and woo her. And the ultimate victory must still be a long way off. The mill was in full production now, all the major expenses in the past, but it would be some time before he had amassed enough to be able to presume to ask for the hand of Miss Harriet Scarr.

As he rode home he imagined how it would be, one day. A coach would carry him then, and 'home' would be a fine mansion, built in accordance with his wishes on a good piece of land. It still rankled that Low Farm had gone to Samuel. There would have been just enough land to provide a pleasant park, and he could have pulled down the old house and built on its foundations . . . But there was no point in dwelling on what was past and gone and could not be changed; he must look to the future. He set himself to imagine the house he would have, and the life he would lead there with Harriet, his wife. He let his mind slide quickly over the intimate details of that, to dwell instead on other aspects of it – the luxuries and comforts unknown to his father and brother, servants (many of them), good horses, several carriages, paintings and ornaments, above all the exhilarating freedoms that only money could buy.

Yet still he felt restless and bored and depressed. He urged his horse into a canter and then a gallop, trying to calm the tension of his nerves with speed. It made no real difference and, besides, he was conscious that the moonlight, though bright, was not enough to make riding fast on a rutted road a very wise activity. Bored he might be, but he was certainly not suicidal.

It was very late, after midnight, and the farms and villages were silent and in darkness, except where, here and there, a lantern in an outbuilding or a glow of light through a window suggested a sick animal or child. The night was unusually still, and very clear. The frost was already forming on the dead grass at the roadside, and hardening the ruts beneath the horse's hooves. There had been no snow yet, but it would come; it was early January now, and the first three months of the year were always the worst. Robert hated the snow: impassable roads, bitter cold, people and goods unable to get out or in without difficulty, long nights with nothing to do but drink and play cards and court a woman who did not attract him at all . . .

A little further on to his left were the buildings of his cotton mill, deeply shadowed behind the trees. There, round the far side, leading from the office on the first floor, were the two rooms where he lived at present – two rooms, damp from the proximity of the water and the little use they had, sparsely furnished, utterly cheerless. The only companionship available to him there was that of Henry Birley, whose modest house adjoined the new dormitory building where the mill's workforce was securely housed, at right angles to the mill itself. At times, the man's blunt and sombre personality suited Robert's mood; but not tonight, not when his own spirits were so low. Besides, by now the overseer would have been in bed for hours, and no considerate employer would think of waking him without good reason.

Robert did not turn into the lane. Instead, he found himself riding on up the slope towards Thornside, where many lights and scattered outbursts of singing and shouting testified to the liveliness of the town's alehouses and inns. It was not the kind of company he willingly sought out these days (it was after all hardly appropriate for a man with aspirations towards the hand of Miss Harriet Scarr), but it might supply him with a temporary distraction to lighten his thoughts.

Then he came to the turning that led to Thornside mill, and an impulse too strong to resist, of which he was scarcely aware until it had done its work, drew him aside and into the tree-lined shadows, sharply broken where the moonlight speared through bare branches, patterning the stony ground with angular shapes.

The mill came into sight, in full moonlight beyond the arch of the trees, mysterious and yet mundane, a kind of domesticated fairytale region. Robert was not in any sense a fanciful man, yet the moonlight and the lateness of the hour, perhaps too the wine he had drunk earlier, gave him the odd conviction that some invisible barrier of enchantment cut him off from

324

the tranquil buildings beyond the trees. He reined in his horse and sat gazing at them, rather stupidly, not quite knowing what he was doing or why; or perhaps not wanting to probe too deeply into his reasons for being here.

Then all at once it was quiet no longer. Sharp in the night came the sound of bolts being drawn back, a door opening; and then, out of the blackness of the house a figure, pale and ghostlike, emerged into the yard. It – she – came to a halt about a yard from the door and stood gazing up at the moon with a look of rapture on her face, all ethereal in the cold light, her heavy black hair tumbling in a cascade down her back, as dark as the shadows except where the moonlight set it glinting. She carried neither lamp nor candle, but the moon fell unrestricted on her tall figure; and the proud curve of her belly beneath the long woollen shift.

Robert stared, and felt a great silent despairing howl of anguish take shape inside him. The gossip had not lied then. It was all horribly, inescapably true. There could be no doubt at all. She was pregnant. Hannah was pregnant; and by Samuel, for it could be no one else. He knew that the only other man who could ever have tempted her was himself.

He thought of that long ago afternoon with her, here in this place, and found it still had power to move him, even after so long, in spite of all the many different women he had lain with before and since. There was something about Hannah, deny it as he would, something inescapable. And now Samuel – Samuel! – had found that truth for himself. The very thought of him enjoying her in that way made him feel sick; he could not keep himself from imagining them together. His thin, awkward, clumsy brother, mauling her lovely body, entering it – being the cause of the look of rapture that transformed her face out there tonight. He could not bear it.

Yet he could not tear himself away, not even when,

after some time (he had no idea how long), Samuel himself appeared in the doorway carrying a candle, its inadequate light showing up all the soft anxious lines of his face.

Robert heard him clearly. 'Hannah – what ails thee, love?' A world of tender concern in his voice; and the smile that she turned on him, reassuring, happy, full of love – oh, how it hurt!

'Nothing, nothing at all. The moon woke me, that's all. It's so bright. I wanted to see it better.'

The candle had blown out, but Samuel did not seem to have noticed. He put his arm about his wife – his *wife*! – holding her near. 'Thou wilt catch cold.' Then he stood beside her sharing her delight in the moonlight: two people united in tenderness and joy.

Robert wanted desperately to ride quickly away, but they would have heard him at once. Besides, something kept him there, prolonging the agony of watching them, until at last, still with their arms round one another, they turned back into the house. As they did so, Samuel kissed Hannah, and she laughed softly. The door closed, the bolts shot into place.

The silence flowed in again, more intense than ever, the country night-time silence that was compounded of the small constant sounds of water and rustling animals, a falling twig, a hooting owl, and was somehow the deeper and more complete for them. Slowly, trying instinctively to make as little noise as possible, Robert turned his horse and made his way back along the path.

What had gone wrong? He had thought that his intervention on their wedding day had succeeded better even than he had hoped. He had seen Samuel's happiness and new-found confidence crumble before his eyes. He had glimpsed as time went by the infallible signs that their marriage was an empty mockery. He had been absolutely sure that it had never been consummated, and equally certain that it never would. He had been able to console himself for Hannah's rejection of him with the thought that she and Samuel would live separate and very likely progressively more unhappy lives under the roof of their new home.

Not, he had told himself, that he had been hurt by Hannah's behaviour. No woman, indeed no other person, would ever mean so much to him that her loss could do more than inconvenience him. But it was his right, and his alone, to decide which individual should have a place in his life, according to whether or not they were of use to him. It was for him to accept or discard, not Hannah, nor anyone else. And Hannah would have been very useful to him, once he had disabused her of those unfortunate Quakerish scruples; he had only to look at the quiet efficiency with which her little mill had been restored and set running to see that. But unfortunately she had not given him time to work on her scruples. The occasional impulsiveness that was a part of her attraction for him had sent her running to Samuel, though they both knew it could only end in disaster. So he had been forced to teach her a lesson. One day perhaps, he had told himself, when unhappiness reached the point of desperation, then she would return to him, and he would take her back, on his own terms. By then she would have realised her mistake and might even be useful to him again.

Yet here tonight, lit by the moon, he had seen not only the incontrovertible evidence that the marriage was consummated, but even that – to all appearances – it was happy too. How could it have happened? He thought back to the night of Samuel's return, before that dreadful day when he had learned of his own disinheritance. He remembered how Hannah had held Samuel, how he had clung to her. Yet they had slept apart that night, he was sure of that. On the other hand, he thought he could see now the certain seeds of reconciliation. It was, he thought, yet another blow his father had dealt him in death, more surely than in life.

He reached the road, dug in his heels, urged his horse into a trot, the brisk clop of hooves on the hard ground as purposeful as his mood. He would show them! – his father if he could see him still, all those who thought like him, all those who had put their blind, stupid faith in Hannah and Samuel, a woman and a weakling. They would see that long-built-up business crumble to nothing under the mismanagement of two such ineffectual people, especially once there was a child to distract Hannah from her work. And with it, Robert promised himself, all their new found happiness would vanish too. He did not know how he would do it, not yet. But he had done it before; he could do it again.

He returned to Newgill with his depression sparked to anger, but as far from wanting sleep as ever. Perhaps his angry mood made him less careful than usual to be quiet, as he stabled his horse and made his way to the mill door that led to his rooms. But whatever the cause, just as he laid his hand on the latch, Henry Birley shot open the door of his house and stood there, hastily dressed, with a lantern in one hand and a cudgel in the other.

'Who's there!'

Robert, without a light but visible enough (he supposed) in the moonlight, turned towards his overseer. 'Forgive me if I disturbed you, Birley.'

The man relaxed. 'Oh, it's you, Mr Gayle. I heard a noise —'

'Your vigilance is appreciated,' said Robert. 'But do not let . . . ' He paused, then said on a sudden impulse, 'Now you are wakeful, why not come and take a drink with me? A few minutes, no more. You'll sleep the better for it afterwards.'

He thought for a moment the man would refuse him, but perhaps the overseer felt that such a refusal would be lacking in tact, for at last, with no great enthusiasm, he closed his door and followed Robert up the stairs.

They sat by the nearly-extinguished fire and Robert poured some of his small store of brandy for them both. Still alert, still tense with anger, he stood looking down at the square figure of his manager, who looked as if at any moment he might fall asleep. An enviable state perhaps, but Robert was glad enough that for the time being he did not share it, and that all his senses were keenly awake.

'The woollen mill, up the road – tell me, what do the townsfolk think of it; do you know?' When the man turned weary questioning eyes upon him, he prompted, 'You drink with them sometimes. You must hear talk.'

Birley shrugged. 'Little enough.'

'You've done your bit to sow a few doubts.'

'Aye, true enough, I have. But after the first there were not many heard me – not once the mill got going. Even the folks who doubted a woman so young could ever manage it have shut up now. No, I'd say it's accepted, part of the place.'

'Like us here.'

The man hesitated.

'Not like us then? Come, how is it different?' He began to feel impatient with Birley's drowsy slowness.

'I can't rightly say. Maybe it's like the other trades in Thornside – the blacksmith's, the wheelwright's – a place they can use at their convenience, those that want to that is, or have need of it. Useful, but no threat to them or their livelihoods. It's us they resent, I'd say, if they think about it.'

'But there's a rival hosiery business on their doorsteps now. The hosiers in Thornside can't like that.'

'Maybe not. I don't know. But old Mr Gayle always did business over this way anyway. It's no great change. Not that I've had words with any of the Thornside hosiers.'

'Maybe you should,' Robert said, not quite casually.

Birley shot a glance at him. He looked as if he was beginning to wake up.

'Maybe I will. But I can't promise they'll have anything to say on the matter, still less any more than that.'

'Someone must. Thornside's a big enough place. There are always malcontents to be found somewhere.'

'Aye, there are. But you'll not find them among the weavers and hosiers, I'd guess. You know yourself how the weavers are glad to be able to stick with wool. If it wasn't for the spinning mill we'd not have had the trouble we did finding weavers to work for us. No, it's us they resent, and it'll be worse once we bring in the first of the men from down south. It's we should be anxious what folks think, I'd say.'

'If they don't want outsiders to come and work for me, then they should have taken the work offered themselves,' said Robert impatiently. 'In any case, if there are difficulties, we shall be prepared – and better than they ever could be at the woollen mill too.' He brushed that rather awkward subject aside and returned to his first concern. 'The spinners then, what of them? There must be discontent there?'

Birley shook his head. 'Not that I've heard. Oh, you might find one or two, I suppose. But most of them have never done spinning alone, and they're glad enough to have more time for knitting. No, the only malcontents in Thornside are a few men without work or land, the feckless kind who look to trouble for amusement – and could be bought, of course . . . '

'For the price of a drink or two . . . ' Robert prompted gently.

'A little more than that, if they're to do much more than shout a bit.'

'A little more then, whatever it takes. But be discreet, Birley – I rely on you.'

'You know you can always do that, Mr Gayle,' the man promised.

Hannah paused to watch Eli Johnson at work, not because he needed supervision, for he was a skilled worker who took a pride in everything he did, but simply because to watch him gave her pleasure.

He stood by a post attached vertically to the wall on the first floor of the mill, to which a comb (warmed beforehand at the adjacent stove) was attached, its graduated rows of long teeth parallel to the floor. On these teeth the wool had been pulled, and Eli Johnson was now drawing it out with a second comb. In his hands it looked a simple enough process, but Hannah, who had tried it once under his guidance, knew how much strength and skill it required. She had made sure he knew how impressed she was, of course, because, being new to the mill, he had been a little unsure of her still, not quite convinced that a young and inexperienced woman could run a business efficiently, a little wary of being ordered about by one. Like her other workers, he had come to her only because he needed employment; like them, he had quickly learned to appreciate the distinctive atmosphere of Thornside mill, where the success of the enterprise was built on trust and mutual respect.

Once all the wool had been combed and recombed, to remove the short fibres and draw out the long ones so that they lay side by side, not tangled together as was the short staple wool after carding, then the spinning could begin. The worsted spinning machine, worked, unlike the jenny, by the mill's water-wheel, had been in use for some time now, supplying high quality yarn for the best knitters and the finer weavers. Hannah's interest in the process was heightened by her sense of pride that she had been the first to bring worsted spinning to the dale. No more expensive yarn brought in from outside, but their own supply here on their doorstep – she knew that the knitters and weavers were grateful to her for it, just as she was grateful to Joseph Gayle, who had made it all possible by his legacy.

Even so – for all her interest, all her pleasure in the skill of the men who worked for her – lately some of the edge of excitement had gone from her work in the mill. Very often these days it took an enormous effort of will to carry her out of the house in the morning to the duties that awaited her here. She would have preferred to spend her time indoors, watching Samuel put the final touches to the exquisitely carved cradle he was making, or sewing seams in the fine linen that was to clothe the baby, or simply sitting and dreaming of the moment when the vigorous moving creature that lay unseen inside her swollen belly, unknown yet a part of her, would lie in her arms. Less than a month now, and it would be time . . .

Sometimes she was afraid, with a sudden brief onrush of panic, because she knew how often childbirth ended in death. She knew that awareness was behind much of Samuel's protective concern for her: the fear that she would suffer the fate of his mother, who had survived his birth too short a time for him to have any memory of her.

'Does Robert remember her?' Hannah had asked him one day, when, in what he clearly realised the next instant was an unguarded moment, Samuel had spoken of his mother.

'I don't know,' said Samuel; and then he added, 'He was only three, but maybe he does. Only he's never spoken of it.'

Hannah wondered how Robert had felt then, a bewildered child suddenly deprived of his mother. But she could not really imagine him suffering any deep or painful emotion. As for Samuel – was a baby conscious enough of what went on around it to know its mother had gone? Could a scar remain, even when there was no memory of a wound?

She was not afraid of dying, though she feared

pain and sickness. But she did not want her life to end so soon, just as it had begun to offer her such richness. Most of the time she did not even consider the possibility.

She watched until Eli Johnson took the long soft filaments of combed wool from the combs and handed them to young Abraham Wood, who filled the bobbins that fed the rollers of the worsted spinning machine. Downstairs, she paused to see how Sarah Dinsdale – Kit's wife, newly employed at the mill – was progressing at the jenny, which she was working under George's supervision. Then she nodded and smiled at them all and went out into the crisp cold evening air of the yard.

Soon the workers would pack up and go home, George Holgate last of all, for he had lately taken on the responsibility of seeing that everything was locked up for the night, to spare her. There was scarcely an hour of daylight left now, though the winter days were already noticeably lengthening, hinting at spring to come.

Hannah closed the door on the clatter of the machinery and stood still, gazing up over the darkening trees to the pale winter sky. There was already a star gleaming against the green tinted rim of the horizon. She glanced towards the lane; and at that moment Samuel emerged from its shadows, driving the cart full of the knitted goods collected today. 'I'll not have thee jolted about in a cart, so near thy time,' he had told Hannah, and undertaken to make the deliveries and collections himself.

There had been another errand too, and he told Hannah about it while he unloaded the cart and stabled the pony. 'She's well, thy mother,' he said. 'But I couldn't stay long, of course.' Then he added, 'Hannah, my love, hast thou not thought sometimes how much better it would be if thou hadst . . . We could talk then, freely . . . If Agnes knew . . . '

She looked into his earnest troubled face. 'Thou knows I cannot tell her. It would hurt her so.'

'I am not sure. I wonder sometimes —' He broke off, and then resumed, 'But thou knows her best of course.'

She knew herself too, enough to recognise that it was not, principally, a fear of hurting Agnes that kept her from telling the truth about Christian Lambert, not any more. She did not really believe that Agnes would be hurt by it, beyond recall. It was rather that she did not want Agnes to know what kind of woman had given her birth, as if it would inevitably be one step on the road to the full knowledge of what Hannah was and what she once had done, in case she might then see an inevitable pattern in it all. One day perhaps when, if ever, all this was so far behind her that it could not matter any more, then she might tell; but not yet.

They began to walk together across the yard. 'She asked that thou wouldst come with the baby,' said Samuel, 'as soon as thou wert fit again.'

Hannah shrank from the thought of taking so precious a creature to that place, of having it too contaminated by such an association. She owed something to Christian, or she supposed she did, but her child — no, she wanted the child to be free of all that. But she only smiled and said evasively, 'Not before the warm weather comes. Then we shall see.'

In bed that night she could not sleep. The weight inside her lay awkwardly, so that she could not make herself comfortable. She heard the house sink into quietness, leaving only odd creakings and rustlings and the gentle sound of Samuel's breathing as he slept, a foreground to the outdoor sounds. A wind had risen at dusk, not a boisterous roaring storm wind but a thin whining bitter wind from the north east, which might have promised snow if it was not so cold. There was no moon tonight, so it was very dark, though beyond the closed, uncurtained window she could see the stars.

She could feel the wind too, finding a way somehow through a little crevice or cranny about the panes.

Somewhere a door banged. The sound reached her, making little impression at first. Then she thought: There should not be a door left open to bang like that. Had George Holgate, usually so reliable, let her down? More likely it was some door in the outhouses, across the yard. But it had seemed to come from further off.

There was another sound too, one she could not quite place. The wind, certainly, and no more than that, but in her uncomfortable sleepless state it was enough to drag her from her bed across the cold floorboards to the window. It was at least something to do, to help time pass.

She could see little below the star scattered sky; only a darkness that became a little less dense where the flagstones of the yard lay open to the sky, deeper in the shelter of buildings and trees. Now there was no sound but the wind and the beck.

No – there it came again, a banging, like a door slammed by the wind, but rhythmical now, and constant. A door banging and banging, back and forth? She did not think so. It did not sound right. There was no doubt now either that it came from somewhere to her right, round the corner of the mill.

There was probably some simple and sensible explanation, something obvious that, in the unreality of the night, had not for the moment occurred to her. But she felt just a little uneasy all the same. She found herself wishing that they still had Fly, who would have barked if a flea jumped at the end of the lane. But Fly was a good sheepdog, wasted on a household with only a cow, a pig and a few poultry in the way of livestock, and very likely miserable as well, so he had gone to the new owner of High Farm. There was nothing to tell her whether the noise she heard was one to worry about or not.

Convinced, apart from that irrational sense of unease, that there was some simple explanation of it all,
she pulled a cloak about her and crept in the dark down
the stairs and took a lantern from the kitchen to light
her way. She had her hand on the outside door when
she thought: Machine breakers, what if it is machine
breakers? Should I wake Samuel?

But there was no resentment of her mill any longer.
Everyone could see its benefits and knew it posed no
threat. She knew that herself, from her own observation, as well as from what others told her. No, there
was no one with any reason to damage her machines.
Without doubt it was something much more ordinary.

Out in the yard the noise sounded very loud, only
faintly muffled by walls – for unmistakably it came
from the mill.

Heart beating furiously, she began to run. She
thought, through the banging, that she heard a shout,
sharp, quickly ended. Then the noise stopped. It was
very quiet, but for the rush of the water. But she sensed
with a prickling of the skin that she was not alone there
in the yard. She held the lantern high to look around;
and turned sharply, just as someone stepped out of the
shadow near the mill door.

iii

Robert felt cold, so cold that it was almost as if he did
not feel at all, yet he was consumed by an anger like
nothing he had ever known before. He tethered his
horse to the ring by the door and marched into the
mill.

He found Henry Birley at once, though the man
was out of sight beyond the deafening ranks of the
machines, directing a nervous little girl as she crawled
beneath the fast moving rollers and bobbins and belts
and spindles of the furthest machine.

'Birley!' Robert shouted, above the din.

The man turned, his frown transforming itself almost

at once to a smile, which then faded a little at the stern pallor of his employer's face.

'My office! Now!' Robert swung round, not even looking to see if the overseer followed him. But then he knew Birley would not dare do otherwise.

He followed, searching his mind for some reason to justify the anxious sense of guilt that stirred there, but could find none. On the contrary, Mr Gayle had told him how pleased he was, only yesterday.

'Shut the door!' The snapped order made him jump. He obeyed it at once, and then turned, trying to force his manner into one of calm unconcern, to face Robert, who was standing in the middle of the room glaring at him with a look that was at once, in some odd way, both icy and blazing.

'The other night —' said Robert. 'You did not tell me there were injuries.' His voice was hard with a scarcely restrained fury, but Birley merely looked puzzled.

'They all came back safe, Mr Gayle, every one of them, I'm sure of that.'

'God, I don't mean your hired rogues!'

Birley frowned a little. 'What then?'

Robert reached out suddenly, grasped Birley by the lapels of the coat. 'Hannah Gayle is sick and like to die – that's what!' He shook the man back and forth to give emphasis to the furious words. Birley, his teeth rattling together, his hat jolted to the floor, knew that Robert was very close indeed to losing all control of himself.

'But . . . but what is that to do with me?' His voice had become whining and plaintive.

'From a blow on the head, the cold, a labour brought on too soon, from shock! They have the whole tale in town. My brother found her that night, laid out in the yard, near dead.'

Birley felt the colour leave his face. 'No one saw,' they'd assured him. 'No trouble, not a bit of it.' Then he wondered why Robert cared so much, when he had wanted harm done to them. He must have known there was a risk. Maybe he was afraid, now, that every step would be taken to find the culprits, that the trail might lead to him, in spite of all his caution. 'They can't know we had owt to do with it,' he pointed out, glad that the shaking had stopped, but with a wary eye on Robert's grim face. The hands still held his coat in a ferocious grip.

'We? You, Birley, you! You who had no right to lay a finger on her!'

So it's me now, is it? thought Birley resentfully; as if it wasn't his orders sent me, his money paid the men. 'The machines were smashed, like you said. What were they to do, if the woman came? Let her see them, so she'd know who to set the law on?'

'So you *did* know about it!' Robert's grasp tightened still further, and he pulled the man towards him, as if he wanted to tear him to pieces with his teeth.

'No – no! I'm just saying what must have happened, that's all. I regret it. I'm sorry, of course I am. But . . .' How to calm his employer, what to say for the best? 'If she dies, it'll be from the childbirth like as not, won't it? That's nature, not murder.'

For a moment then he was quite certain that it was Robert who would commit murder, with him the victim. The next moment he felt himself flung furiously aside. 'Damn you! Damn you to hell!'

He fell back against the wall, banging his head. There was an interval during which, sick, dazed, he saw nothing. Then Robert's face came dimly into focus, the white rage still burning away all the easy, careless politeness, the calm, the irony. It was the face of quite another man, swept up in a storm of emotion beyond his control; and one that Henry Birley, having known nothing like it before, found incomprehensible and utterly terrifying.

'Get out of here!'

He scrambled to his feet, reached for his hat, tottered from the room, closing the door behind him with an enormous and trembling sense of relief. Yet as he groped his way, swaying, down the stairs, he felt afraid still, because he knew that what he had seen on Robert's face would not easily pass, and might always come again.

As the sound of Birley's steps on the stairs receded, Robert, who had remained standing exactly where he was, staring grimly at the closed door, seemed to come slowly awake. He stirred, gave himself a little shake, and moved at last. It did not seem as if the awakening was a pleasant experience, for the frown on his face only deepened, and the angry light in his eyes gave way to pain.

He went slowly to the window and stared out at the cold bright afternoon, at the winter landscape frozen under the hard light; at the mill across the road, a little way up the hill.

He had gone there today, in an agony of fear, the moment he had heard the news in Thornside. All thought of the differences between them had left him, of anything but of Hannah. He had scarcely known what he was doing, or what he hoped to find waiting for him at the mill – some reassurance perhaps that the rumours were wrong, that it all had nothing to do with him.

It had been true, all of it, and both Agnes and Samuel were at Hannah's bedside, where the doctor was too, waiting for whatever was to come, giving her comfort, assuring her of their love. As he longed to do, so much, he who had loved her first and longest.

But George Holgate, coming to meet him with the news, had been cool, more than a little distant, and had given him no opportunity to do more than send a message of good wishes to them all – which would very likely arrive divested even of the little feeling he had allowed himself to show.

Had Holgate known, somehow, that he was responsible for what had happened? How could he? It was impossible. No one knew, nor ever would. He had made sure that there would be nothing that could be traced to him.

But somehow that did not make him feel any better, for it was not fear of discovery that haunted him.

It is my doing – *mine*! It was that thought which circled endlessly in his mind; it was himself he hated. When he had raged at Birley it was Robert Gayle he had held in his grasp and cursed.

What had made him do this to the woman he loved, the only woman he had ever loved? Spite, hurt pride, jealousy, resentment – all of them perhaps. And now, now that he knew how blind, how stupid, how *wrong* he had been, it was too late. 'She's right poorly,' Holgate had said. 'There's no telling how it will go, but the doctor said not to hope too much.'

Not to hope – for a world in which Hannah's blue eyes would turn to him, bright with anger or scorn perhaps, but no less alluring for that; in which he could feel her nearness, the warmth of her, smell the sweet clean scent of her. He did not ask now for her to love him, or even to look kindly on him; only that she should live.

And that it should not be his fault, this thing that had happened. Oh, to go back, to last week, last year; to that day when she had come to him and pleaded for him to change his plans, for her sake. What did it matter where his cotton came from, whether he had a cotton mill at all, set against the terrible wrenching anguish of the one simple fact that Hannah was dying and he might never see her again?

And if she were to die, how could he live, knowing that he had killed her, as surely as if he had aimed the blow that felled her?

There was nothing he could do or say that would ease his agony. He sank to the floor and brought his head down and steadily, rhythmically, banged it on the window sill, as if somehow by punishing himself he could make it all come right.

The baby – a girl – was born that evening, after a long
and agonising labour. Samuel, temporarily banished
from the room, was allowed in again to see the tiny
fragile creature held in Agnes's arms; and Hannah, so
pale and still, as if life had almost left her. No pain now,
no writhing and groaning, but nothing else either, only
a faint uneven breathing and eyes that fluttered open
as he came to her, and then closed again.

He could not bear it. Better to have no child, to be
estranged for ever, than this! He wanted to hold her
in his arms, caress her and kiss her to life again, to
restore to her somehow, from his weak and ineffectual
self, the vigour and vitality that had always seemed so
much stronger than his own.

Instead he went and held out his arms to Agnes. 'May
I?' he whispered. He saw her hesitate momentarily,
holding the little quiet creature closer. Then she sighed
and carefully, very carefully, laid the child in his arms.

She felt so light and insubstantial, his daughter, like
a baby rabbit he had held once, warm and soft, for she
was well wrapped in washed lambswool. Her features
were tiny and pink and wrinkled, beneath a fuzz of
brown hair; an odd, ugly little thing to come from so
lovely a mother.

He was terrified that he might fall and drop her, or
hold her too tightly and crush her, but he carried her to
the bed and knelt there, holding the child so that she lay
on the pillow beside Hannah. 'Our little girl, my love,'
he murmured. 'See.'

She turned her head very slightly, and slowly, as if
such a small movement took an immense effort. Her
eyes were open, very blue in her white face, and
exhausted, and their gaze settled at last on the child. She
did not smile, but Samuel knew she would have done
so if she had not been so tired. Then after a moment,
with equal slowness, she moved a hand, without raising

341

it from the bed, and laid it by the baby's head, so that her fingers touched the soft cheek and stirred there, caressingly, against it. Samuel wanted to weep, from love and fear and grief, but he forced himself for her sake to calmness.

'Rachel,' he whispered, harshly, through the painful obstruction in his throat. 'Our little Rachel.'

It was the name they had chosen together, in the happy weeks of planning for this day. Then, he had tried to tell himself that all would be well, that she would give birth without difficulty. But always he had been haunted by the fear that his present happiness was too good to last, that for him a few short weeks of joy were the most he could hope for. He knew, now that it had happened, that he ought to be resigned, for it was God's will and he must bow before it, thankful at least that he had been prepared for it. But he felt no resignation, only a wild protesting anguish, a sense of injustice, that after all they had endured a lasting happiness should still be denied them. He bent his head, because his view of Hannah had become suddenly misted with tears, and he did not want to trouble her with his grief in the little time that was left.

Hannah had no intention of dying, though she knew from their faces that this was what they all expected. She was tired beyond words, with a weariness greater than anything she had ever felt before. It would be so easy to close her eyes and give herself up to the peace that had succeeded the pain, the sense that it was all over, her work done.

But it was not done. There was her child, who needed a mother – a young mother, not Agnes who was already old; and Samuel, who needed her almost as much. She had no intention of leaving them. And besides she wanted to see this child grow, to know her and love her.

She knew that somehow she would fight the deadly

languor that was tightening its grasp upon her, and
live.

v

'They say,' said Henry Birley carefully, with a furtive
glance at his employer's grim face, 'that Mrs Gayle's
doing fine now.' He had gone to immense trouble to
gather the information, wanting very much to be the
bearer of good news to Mr Gayle, who had become so
withdrawn and ill-humoured since he had heard of his
sister-in-law's illness.

Robert, clearly not allowing himself to be easily
cheered, said with a marked note of scepticism, 'Oh?
Where did you hear that?'

'In town. They'd hired Sim Lawson's wife as wet
nurse, just for the first few days. But it seems Mrs
Gayle's nursing the child herself now. Your brother
has been seen in town, so she must be better – well
enough to be left anyway.'

Robert's face gave little away. There might have been
some lightening of his expression, or there might not;
Henry Birley could not be sure. He felt disappointed,
even a little annoyed, that his efforts should have no
significant effect. Had he misjudged the situation, and
was Robert not, after all, concerned for the well being
of his brother's wife?

'They say they're already repairing the machines.
There was enough left from your father's money to
pay for it, I'm told, but only just, so folks say. They
say too that your brother was making enquiries about
a good watch dog.' Still Robert showed little interest,
beyond a faintly sneering look about the mouth.

'A bit late for that, I'd say.'

Had he seen Robert's face when at last he retreated to
his office and closed his door behind him, Henry Birley
would have been satisfied. But Robert, ashamed of the
unaccustomed flow of emotion which he had allowed
to wash over him when he first heard of the injury to

Hannah, had no intention of allowing such a thing to happen again. Never, never must anyone else have the power to move or disturb him beyond his own control. If he was pleased now to know that Hannah was going to live after all, it was because he would be able to put the whole disquieting episode behind him. He need no longer fear a sense of guilt (quite unreasonable, for it had all been an accident, no more, and he had not really had any part in it), nor be troubled by a most unwelcome concern for a woman who could no longer mean anything to him.

If he had learned anything from the whole sorry business it was that it was beneath him, a waste of his time and energy, to seek revenge on Hannah for her slighting of him. True, it was not in his interests that the woollen mill should flourish, but the best way to fight it was to ensure the overwhelming success of his own mill. In future, he resolved now, he would not even allow Hannah to intrude upon his thoughts.

He felt his eyes move towards the window, and the glimpse of the mill, but he forced them away, back to the pile of papers – too long neglected – awaiting his attention upon his desk.

vi

It was six weeks before Hannah was well enough to travel to Hollinthwaite moor to take Rachel to see her grandmother, and by then it was March and a fine spell of warm weather marked the coming of spring.

Samuel went with her, of course. He had scarcely let her out of his sight since the terrible night when, woken by some unattributable sound, he had risen from his bed to find her lying bleeding and unconscious near the mill door. She was well again, he knew, quite well; but he could not reason himself into his old ease of mind. Besides, there was joy too, as well as reassurance, in being constantly in the company of Hannah and the baby.

They rode on the cart, and combined the journey with the collecting of the month's work from the knitters: it supplied a reason for the journey, to satisfy Agnes.

All the hesitations that Hannah had felt before the baby's birth about making this journey had left her now. The agony of that labour, made endurable only by the loving concern of those around her; the rush of tenderness that had swamped her when she first touched her little daughter, the overwhelming love she had felt ever since – all these things stirred in her a new understanding of her mother, and a sympathy she had never quite been able to feel before. They had both been through the extraordinary, momentous experience of childbirth, as Agnes had not; but for Christian it had been endured in a terrifying isolation, and the love for her child that had come with its birth had faced her only with a further anguish. It was in Hannah's power to recompense her for some of that anguish. How could she refuse to do it?

As for her fear that her daughter would be contaminated by contact with her grandmother, Hannah knew that was an unworthy scruple. A child raised in a loving home, taught by the best example (as Hannah and Samuel had every intention that she should be) would take no harm from an occasional visit to such a place. More than that, a day might come – would surely come – when Rachel would want to know something of her origins. What better preparation for that day than to see how her mother treated Christian with courtesy and love? Rachel's birth showed Hannah how to do it, because she herself was the link that would draw them closer.

That was the other thing she had felt, with Rachel's coming: a resurgence of the longing, dormant now for many years, to know more of the shadowy man who had been her father. If nothing else, he had given her the slender body and long limbs that Rachel too seemed to have inherited. Somehow, now that she was a mother, part of a new family, belonging as she had never quite belonged before, it mattered more than ever that she should know all there was to know of her origins.

The sad thing was to think that perhaps she *did* know all there was to know, that she had no hope ever of learning anything further about the man Christian had loved so disastrously.

'What was it George Holgate said to thee yesterday?' Samuel's question broke in on her thoughts. It was so far from the subject of them that for a moment she looked puzzled, and he enlarged, 'He was talking of that night, is that not so? Hast thou convinced him it was not Robert who did it?'

She hesitated a moment before replying. 'He would not be convinced, whatever I said. He knows it was Robert before, and there was no one else with any cause to wish us ill. It seems plain to him.'

'And to thee? Thou canst not think he is right?' He sounded distressed at the very idea.

'I don't know,' she said, quite truthfully, though she did not go on to admit that on the whole she shared George's suspicions.

'But he came to ask after thee, when thou wert ill. Why should he do that, if thy illness was his doing?' Some instinct told her that he was not so much arguing a case in which he believed as trying desperately to convince himself that the suspicions about his brother were wrong, while knowing instinctively that they were not.

'Even if he was behind the machine breaking, I do not suppose he meant me any harm – not actual, bodily harm, that is.'

'Then he came because he was troubled at what had happened, and ashamed perhaps? If indeed it was his doing.'

'Very likely,' Hannah agreed. She did not tell him of George Holgate's strongly expressed opinion that

Robert had come only to make sure that his hired men had done their work properly, and to gloat over her fate. She thought it unlikely herself, but how could she be sure? Robert had openly and willingly done her harm enough already.

Samuel shook his head sadly. 'He is my brother, I cannot bear to think he should nurse such malice against us. But ... If he had come to ask after thee again, then I would have been sure he could not have had a hand in it. But he did not come. Perhaps it was from guilt —'

'Or he came from guilt, and later thought better of it,' Hannah suggested. 'He is not a man who would feel guilty long I think.' Then, because she could see how this dwelling on his brother's shortcomings distressed Samuel, she began quietly to talk of something else.

The Drovers' Inn, when they came within sight of it, had lost its customary look of isolation. It was early in the year for cattle to be driven south. Usually it was not until May, when the roads had dried out and hardened after the winter snow and rain, that the droves began again. But already today a herd of cattle, dun and black and red, a moving, seething mass against the quiet neutral colours of the moorland, was grazing on the grass beyond the inn. Hannah – thinking: She will be busy with guests, she will have no time for us – was surprised at how disappointed she felt. And then she saw that the drover was out there with the herd, directing his dog, and thought perhaps it would be all right after all. And then she thought of her father, and how he must once have looked just as this man did, dark against the sky, a lonely figure far from home, with a dangerous appeal for a young girl starved of love.

When they came nearer there was less to make her think of her father. The man, large and sandy haired, had something familiar about him; she had seen him before, she supposed. But then most of the drovers came again and again, year after year. It was her father who had never returned. Hannah looked down at the infant deeply asleep in her arms: Hector MacDonald's granddaughter, with an inheritance in her veins about which perhaps she would know nothing, ever. But surely she would want to know what it was that had gone to make her the person she was, as much as his daughter had wished to know.

Christian, alone at the inn, was enchanted to see them. 'I'm that glad you didn't come sooner – I'd company then. But he's just off now.' She turned to look at the child and – when Hannah forced herself to surrender Rachel to her grandmother – to hold her in her arms. She wept a little, smiling all the time through her tears; and Hannah kissed her and for the first time felt no shrinking and no reluctance. She was a mother too.

On the way home Samuel and Hannah came upon the drove of cattle, the beasts straddling the road, blocking their path.

'Agnes'll have a long wait for supper,' Samuel said, in the resigned tones of a habitually patient man.

After a moment Hannah said suddenly, 'Stop! Wait a moment.' She laid the baby very carefully on the cart behind her, moving the piles of stockings so that they hemmed her protectively in. And then she jumped down.

Samuel assumed she meant to ask the drover to move his beasts aside, as he might have done himself if the waiting went on too long. The drover too thought that was why she had come, for he nodded and smiled and said, 'In a hurry, lassie? I'll let ye by – just wait a wee moment.'

But Hannah, after a hurried 'I thank thee,' said, 'Not yet – wait!' Then, as he looked at her questioningly, she added, 'Dost thou know of a Hector MacDonald – a drover, like thyself?'

The man frowned, shook his head doubtfully.

'He used to come this way – oh, twenty years or more

ago.' It astonished her suddenly to think how long it was. 'Maybe it was before thy time.' She had never thought until now that her father could be anything but the young man he had always been in Christian's imaginings. Yet she herself was twenty-three; this man who faced her now was very likely much younger than her father, if he still lived.

The drover shook his head again. 'A wee bit, maybe. But there are some they talk of still. Where was he from, do ye know? What kind of man was he?'

If I knew that all my questions would be over, Hannah thought ruefully. Aloud, she said, 'I know only his name, and that he was young and dark and a drover.' And he looked like me; but she could not say that.

'I could ask maybe. There are those who've been droving longer than me. Is that what ye'd like?'

Was it? She did not know, but after a moment she nodded. 'I thank thee, yes.'

'And where can I find ye, if I have word?'

'Thornside mill. But, please, it would be for my ears only, no one else. Ask for Hannah Gayle.'

'I'll do that, if I hear. But it's not a name I remember at all. I've known a MacDonald or two, but no Hector, not that I recall. But . . . well, ye never know.'

He called to the dog and drove the cattle off the road, enough for the cart to pass. As they left him behind, Samuel said, 'Thou had much to say to him. Did he not wish to let us by?'

Hannah shook her head. 'It wasn't that.' She was reluctant, but in the end she said, 'I asked if he knew a Hector MacDonald.' As he looked puzzled, she added, 'My father. He said he would make enquiries.'

Samuel looked at her thoughtfully for some time. Then he said, 'I see,' and urged the pony on a little faster.

CHAPTER SIXTEEN

i

They came out of Bainbridge meeting house into the bright midday sunlight, Rachel running ahead on her sturdy little legs, her soft brown hair tumbling from the confines of her cap. Her parents followed more soberly, Hannah carrying the infant Joseph (asleep as usual) in her arms, Samuel exchanging a word with Agnes, who walked just behind him. At the gate they paused, like many others, to talk to neighbours and those from further afield whom they generally met only at meeting. Samuel reached for Rachel's hand, in case she should take it into her head to run out on the road. There was little traffic on First Day, but the turnpike road passed the meeting house, and it was as well to be careful. The child laughed and swung on her father's arm, impatient with the adult talk, but enjoying the affectionate caresses that came her way.

Two hours ago, as they had walked down from Thornside, the air had been full of the distant sound of church bells. Now it was quiet, with a Sunday stillness, except where a blackbird sang from the ash tree that overhung the meeting house wall, and the horses of those who lived furthest afield, tethered near the gate, stamped restlessly, ready for home. Hannah always enjoyed this moment of companionable talk at the end of meeting. It had been strange, when they first came to Thornside, to find herself in a place where she knew so few of those around her. At Hollinthwaite she had known everyone, and they her, and if she had not liked them all, at least each had the appeal of long familiarity; and many of them had been Quakers, or

350

had some remaining links with that sect. At Thornside there were few Friends and no meeting house. It had taken a long time before she had begun to feel a part of Bainbridge meeting, still longer before she felt that Thornside accepted her. Rachel's coming had made a difference, she thought, and the attack on the mill that had precipitated the child's arrival and aroused sympathy and indignation amongst their neighbours. But Hannah knew that some of it was her own doing too, because her mill quietly and modestly supplied a need in Thornside, and had quickly become an essential part of the place. It was good to move amongst these people here, or through the market at Thornside, and know that she was looked upon as Hannah Gayle of Thornside mill, a person of consequence in her own right. She allowed herself a little swell of pride at the thought, whilst acknowledging what she owed to others too – to Agnes, and Joseph Gayle, and the mill workers; and to Samuel, her dear husband, and father of her children.

The sound of a carriage bowling along the road from the Thornside direction reached them, very loud and clear in the stillness; they heard it long before it came into view. It was a fine new well sprung carriage, pulled by four powerful bays, and it passed the quiet little gathering of Quakers at considerable speed, as if it spurned all possible obstacles in its path. They had a brief glimpse of three passengers inside, two men and a woman, all powdered and dressed in silks; and then the coach was gone, making for the toll gate and the steep hill beyond the village. Hannah turned too late to see them at all.

'George Scarr,' someone said. 'Been to morning service at Thornside.'

'With his new son-in-law for company,' someone else added.

'Not quite,' said the first speaker. 'Thou'lt know when they're to wed, I suppose, Friend Samuel?'

Hannah, conscious that there was more behind the words than she had as yet grasped, saw Samuel colour and then glance at her before replying. She was surprised to see that he looked almost furtive. 'I know it's to be soon,' he said carefully. 'But how soon I cannot be sure.'

Their neighbour shook her head. 'He'll cut himself off from the Society for good, by that marriage. But then perhaps there was no hope of his return.'

'There is always hope,' said Samuel quietly. At the same time something began to fall ominously into place in Hannah's mind. Robert – could it be Robert they meant?

'A good match, in worldly terms, for those who care for such vanities,' she heard someone say, rather primly. 'The son of a hosier to wed a baronet's daughter – who would have thought it!'

'As thou says, it is only worthy of remark if thou hast a care for such vanities,' said Samuel, with an unaccustomed note of impatience. Hannah felt his hand close about her elbow. 'We must be on our way. Come Rachel, thy waiting is at an end.'

Hannah supposed she went with him, but she was conscious of nothing around her. There was one thought only in her head: Robert is to be married.

Why should it hurt so much, like a knife stabbing into her flesh and twisting there, prolonging the agony? He was nothing to her now, nothing at all. They scarcely saw him these days. He moved in quite different circles, dining and hunting with the gentry, attending the parish church at Thornside, busying himself with his mill which, they gathered, was prospering. Prospering enough for Robert Gayle, hosier's son, to be accepted as a suitor for the hand of Miss Harriet Scarr, that pale and refined young lady she had met years ago, on the day . . .

In any case, what memories she had of Robert were all painful, or most of them: of wrongs he had done her, anger and pain. She ought to rejoice that he now loved another woman, and so had quite another focus for his attention, and his arrogance, and his jealousy.

Could he love Miss Scarr?

What did it matter if he did or not? It was none of her business, of no possible interest – or consequence – to Hannah Gayle.

She was aware of Agnes, behind them, talking with a neighbour, though about what she had no idea. Rachel must be holding Agnes's hand now, for her high piping voice broke in now and then on their talk. Hannah became conscious that the others had fallen behind a little, and then still more, until they were out of earshot. Or had Samuel simply walked faster, guiding her with him, that unusually commanding hand still at her elbow?

She turned to look at him, and found he was looking at her. 'Thou didst not tell me – about Robert.'

He had no need to ask her what she meant, but it was a moment or two before he replied, as if he found it difficult to know what to say. 'I was not sure,' he said uncomfortably. 'Not until lately. Then I did not know . . . I thought . . . I was afraid thou wouldst think —'

She broke in on his hesitancy. 'What should I think? It is his affair who he marries.' Her tone was brisk, but she had coloured deeply. She wondered if Samuel was deceived by what was meant to be a note of indifference.

'So I think too,' was his response, and she thought she saw relief in his expression. 'We can only hope that he may be happy.' He broke off, but she knew that there was something further he wished to say, for his face became graver, with a look of concentration, as if he was gathering his resources for some not entirely easy undertaking. 'Hannah . . .' She watched him, waiting. 'The thought came to me this morning . . . No, not just this morning, for it has been with me for some time now, but today more than ever. He has cut himself off from Friends – that is a sadness, but it is his own choice, and he will only ever return by his own choice. But he is still my brother. I have never felt easy at our estrangement. I could wish that . . .'

That we should be friends again, as brothers should: he did not need to finish the sentence. She had already seen it in his face. She thought, angrily, How can he think of it, after all that has happened? Can he not see how I feel?

But how could he be expected to see? And did she really want him to see, when she knew herself how confused and disquieting her feelings were, even after all this time. She was sure of one thing only: that she did not want to be close to Robert ever again. She did not want to visit his house and receive him into hers, she did not want to have to be polite to his wife. Yet . . .

She knew she was being unreasonable, as well as foolish. Samuel was quite right: they were brothers, and it was wrong that no attempt should be made to heal the rift between them. In any case, Samuel was sure to fail. Robert did not easily forgive, and besides he was unlikely to welcome any intrusion by his family into the elevated circles in which he now moved. Hannah was quite sure he had thrown off the Quaker disregard for rank and class with all the other trappings of his childhood.

Gravely, trying to be calm, she said, 'Of course, thou must do all in thy power to heal the breach between thee and Robert.' Then she forced a smile, and saw him smile warmly back at her, delighted by her approval.

ii

Robert did not even consider letting his brother know of his impending marriage, still less sending him an invitation to attend the ceremony. As far as he was concerned there were no ties remaining between the two of them. The Scarrs provided all the family he needed (so long as they were of use to him); for the rest, what mattered first and foremost was that no one should have any hold upon him, until such time as he had sons of his own growing up under his own roof.

That roof at least he had at last. It was a fine new slate roof, covering the large and comfortable house he had built for himself on the far bank of Semerwater, looking across from its hundred acres of parkland (not completely laid out yet), meadow and pasture to the draughty and extensive mansion of his wife's birth, whose only merit, in his eyes, was its antiquity. He enjoyed the sensation that filled him whenever he came within sight of Gayle House, a sense of pride in his own achievement. He had not after all needed his father's support or encouragement, still less the inheritance that should have been his. Alone, he had established his mill and struggled through early setbacks to make it prosper, until now at last he was a landowner in his own right, with a fine house in which the bride of his choice waited for his return. All this, in five short years. It was an astonishing and gratifying rise, and one that gave him constant pleasure. Admittedly, his father-in-law had contributed something, that could not be denied, but what was such a negligible sum of money to a man of such wealth, especially when he knew he could only profit from it? And everything else – the initial scheme, the hard work, the ambition – had been supplied by Robert Gayle.

He followed the road that led from the turnpike south to Semerwater and the point, soon reached, where he could draw rein and gaze with satisfaction at Gayle House. Satisfaction, yes; but this evening he was conscious also of what could only be called discontent, as if a small voice said to him, 'Is this all? You are there, you have arrived – is this to be the end of it, nothing more to strive for, to hope for, as long as you live?'

That was foolish. Of course it was not all. The mill would expand – he was already taking on more apprentices and extending the hours that were worked; he now had land to farm, where he could try out all the new methods so often discussed at Sir George Scarr's dinner table; and then, before long, he would have sons, to teach and guide to manhood in the way he thought best, which would most certainly not be his father's way.

There was no sign yet of an heir on the way, to inherit Gayle House and its lands and the mill, and all the other enterprises that he would undertake in a long life. But he had only been married a month, and these things did not always happen overnight. Odd to think that in the past he had always been relieved at that thought . . .

Any day now, though, he would come home and Harriet would be waiting for the sound of his return, eager to hurry to him with her news, so full of it that she could not bear to keep it back a moment longer. For once that high-pitched note of excitement, the blushing, the rapid nervous laugh, would not irritate, because he would share her delight. It might even be today.

He had certainly done his part. It had not in fact been as straightforward as he had anticipated. He had known she loved him. He was well used to women throwing themselves at him, eager for his attentions. He had expected her to be no different. It had been a shock then to come to her in their bedroom on their wedding night and find her trembling and pale and tearful, not simply nervous but terrified. What does she think I shall do to her? he had thought with exasperation. When she had shrunk and sobbed at his approach he had, for a moment, been tempted to force her. And then he had thought that she might (obliquely at least) complain to her father; and besides, for good or ill they had to make some kind of life together. So he had schooled himself to patience and set out to woo her and had in some measure succeeded. But he knew she had not really found it a pleasant experience – bearable, yes, less frightening than imagination had led

356

her to believe, but that was all. And repetition had not greatly improved things. There were even times when he had found it hard to perform, seeing the way she set her teeth and closed her eyes, ready to endure what was to come. Lately, he had set himself to think of Hannah before he went to her, and then imagined all the time that it was Hannah he lay with; that had worked better, for him at least. To get a son on Hannah – that would have been the fulfilment of a dream. Sometimes he toyed with the thought that it might still be possible. It amused him, to think of Samuel unknowingly raising his brother's child. But the only children Hannah had borne had been Samuel's, legitimately gotten on his lawful wife.

'Damn Samuel!' he said aloud, and dug his heels savagely into his horse's flanks. The animal sprang forward, cantering down the slope towards the lake.

From the outside, his pleasure in his new house was almost inexhaustible. Inside, it was another matter. In here, with the exception of the purely masculine areas of gunroom and study, he had given Harriet a free hand. He had not thought he minded in the least how his house was furnished; the subject did not interest him at all. And she had impeccable taste, he knew. All he wanted was a style that proclaimed to every caller his wealth and success and newly acquired rank. Or so he had thought. Now he found that everything about the house, indoors, grated on his nerves. Everything about that restrained decor – pale paintwork, spindly chairs, delicately patterned papers, musical instruments of inlaid wood, beautifully woven carpets, fine paintings, innumerable fragile china ornaments, gilded clocks – seemed to breath her spirit, so that there was no escape from it anywhere in the house. It was as if she were always there, even in her absence. Outside, he loved the house. Inside he feared he was already beginning to hate it.

He gave his horse up to the groom – *his* groom – and

handed his hat and gloves to the servant who opened the door to him (another source of satisfaction). Harriet did not come running to meet him, so he strode across the beautifully polished boards of the hall, making for his study. At the foot of the stairs he became aware of voices reaching him from the drawing room (no parlour for him). Harriet was talking to someone. She must have a visitor then, someone who had either called without warning, an infrequent occurrence in this isolated place, or whose expected arrival had not been disclosed to him. He changed direction and went to open the drawing room door, a question on his lips.

It remained unspoken. Robert stood astonished on the threshold, staring in disbelief at the man who sat, looking uncomfortable, in one of their comfortable armchairs, trying strenuously to make conversation – with little success it would seem, from the hint of strain on Harriet's face.

Robert found his voice, and the words, uncompromising and far from welcoming, 'What the devil are you doing here?'

Samuel, looking flustered (he was a man now: why could he still not behave with a man's dignity? thought Robert irritably), rose to his feet and came forward, holding out his hand. 'I came ... I wanted very much to give thee good wishes on thy marriage. I would have come before ... I did once, but thou wert not at home. Today at the mill they said I would find thee here ...'

Robert stayed exactly where he was, his expression stony. 'I am not in need of your good will, brother. I have lived quite well without it until now.'

'But thou hast had it, always,' Samuel persevered earnestly. 'Thou art my brother.'

'A pity then that you did not remember that years ago, when it would have made a difference. It was not the most devotedly fraternal of acts, to steal my inheritance.'

Samuel opened his mouth to speak and then closed

it again. He glanced uncomfortably towards his sister-in-law's appalled and embarrassed face, and then back at his brother, trying to convey by his expression his feeling that it would be better if they were to talk alone, in private. He thought at first that Robert was going to suggest just that, for he stood to one side and gestured towards the still open door, beyond which the interested servant listened in fascination. Then he said,

'May I speed you on your way? We can have nothing to say to one another, I assure you.'

Samuel stayed where he was. 'But . . .' He gulped and began again. 'Robert, please – I wish so much that this was not between us . . . To be able to welcome thee, and thy wife, to my house, as a brother should – I want it so much. Hannah does too. I bring her good wishes with mine, and her sisterly love.'

For a moment Robert's lips twisted with something that was not quite amusement. There was a long silence. Samuel, watching him, desperately searched his face for the signs of a desire for reconciliation. He thought: He is moved, just a little; if only he will give way to his better feelings. He had them still, Samuel was sure of it.

He had told Hannah so today, in the tone of one trying to convince himself. 'He must long to be a part of his family again,' he had assured her. 'I know I do. It is only natural. There is no one else left of our family.' He had thought for a moment that there was a hint of scepticism in Hannah's expression, but then she had kissed him and said, 'I know that. And yes, take him whatever message thou would wish to give from me.' For he had begged her to send some word with him that might add weight to what he said himself.

It was not long-suppressed family sentiment that was stirring to life in Robert now, pushing aside the anger and resentment he felt for this contemptible younger brother who had so wronged him. He had no wish at all to renew the ties he had so thankfully cut – and would have cut even had there been no quarrel. Even the thought of eating at his brother's table bored him beyond words; he wanted no more of that stifling Quaker respectability, not to mention the relentlessly plain food. Except – Hannah had sent her 'sisterly love'. Had those been her very words? Did Samuel indeed have her blessing, even her encouragement, to come here today? Was it perhaps her oblique way – the only way open to her – of letting him know that she was still his for the asking, even after all this time, if he were only to make it possible for them to meet again? What could be more natural, after all, than that she should have been driven to distraction by the tedium of marriage to Samuel? She was a woman of spirit; he knew only too well what fire burned beneath her demure exterior. She needed a man like himself, who could meet her needs in full, excite her and enrich her life. And it would add an agreeable spice to his own existence, and surely drive out every trace of that incipient discontent he had felt today. Harriet would be more bearable to him for no longer being the only woman in his life.

Was that enough to tempt him to put pride aside and accept Samuel's proffered friendship? He studied the eager longing of his brother's expression. His eyes were like a spaniel's, soft and imploring in the way that had never failed in the past to sting Robert to some further unkindness. He glanced at his wife. How damned plain she is! he thought. Pale, but without Hannah's creamy loveliness of complexion, which contrasted so exquisitely with the midnight darkness of her hair ... He remembered how it had tumbled down her back that day in the loft ... No, Harriet's pallor was the unhealthy pastiness of a complexion kept too much indoors, whose sallowness an occasional touch of rouge only served to accentuate. Against the nondescript mousiness of her hair, crimped with difficulty into unnatural looking curls, and the indeterminate colour of her light eyes, her pallor was simply part of the general drabness of her appearance, which no fine clothes and affected gestures could alleviate.

There was, Robert thought now with a tiny sense of shock, something about her appearance which reminded him suddenly of Samuel. He looked from one to another of them, the gloom lifting a little from his face. Yes, that was it: two people who could pass through life unheeded by anyone, and leave it without being missed in the least. They could have been made for one another. A pity it was too late now for that obvious and rational coupling. He had a momentary, diverting vision of these two unutterably dull people swept up in an illicit love affair. But there was too much bitterness in the course of his thoughts for him to laugh out loud. It was a joke that needed to be shared with a congenial partner; and he suspected that Hannah would not have found it amusing ... Unless she had changed very much, of course; it would be good to know.

Why should he not find out, after all? An opportunity had come his way, unexpectedly, which might offer the chance of a diversion, at the very least. What point was there in life, if one failed to seize the chances it offered? He smiled at his brother, so suddenly that Samuel had no time to hide his astonishment, still less his relief and delight.

'You are quite right, my dear Samuel. Let the past be buried. We shall be friends again.' And he stepped forward and clasped his brother's hands.

iii

Hannah knew how it had gone the moment she saw Samuel's face. He came to her at once and hugged her warmly, without any of his usual restraint.

'Hannah, my love, all is well – we are to dine there tomorrow!'

361

She bent her head to his shoulder so he could not see her face, while she forced her voice to a note of delight. 'I am glad,' she lied. She thought how ironic it was that she, who had been taught above all things to be open and honest in all she did and said, had told so many lies in her short life.

Or was it a lie? The following evening as she put on her best meeting house clothes and combed her hair, she could feel the excitement bubbling through her. Her hands trembled, so that she dropped things and fumbled as she picked them up, and could not tie the lacings of her bodice. She knew it was not fear, or not wholly that; but it was not a pleasurable sensation all the same. She wished tonight was over, that it was morning again and that all this was behind her. She wished that they did not have to meet Robert at all, that none of this had happened, that Samuel had been content with things as they were or Robert had proved deaf to his pleas. Yet how would she feel if Samuel were to come into the room now and say, 'We are not going. Robert will not see us'?

She knew the answer quite well. She would be relieved, certainly; but disappointed too. Everything would become a little flat as a result; flat as her daily existence had been for a long time now – orderly, secure, even contented, but lacking in excitement.

She paused in her dressing and sat down on the edge of the bed and considered the matter. It was true. She supposed she was happy, in a way. Samuel was the most kind and attentive of husbands, the most loving of fathers. If, sometimes, she felt a longing to escape from his quiet predictability, that was her failure, not his. She loved the children, delighted in their growing, enjoyed their company. The mill was running smoothly and providing them with a comfortable livelihood. She did not want anything to disrupt the order of her life, to stir her to discontent.

But the discontent was already there. She had not

wanted to admit it, but she saw it clearly now. And – whatever the effect on her emotions, however disturbing – she wanted to see Robert again.

She wanted to see him, yet, vehemently, angrily, she did not. She knew that a part of her was annoyed with Samuel for understanding so little and forcing this upon her.

But they were going and there was no escape. Robert even sent a carriage to fetch them, so that they could travel in comfort. It was amazingly comfortable too; Hannah had never experienced such luxury. Her most comfortable journeys before now had been made on horseback, or perched on a wooden seat on the cart. Now they sat on velvet-covered seats that were upholstered in a way that she would have thought extravagant on a parlour chair, and looked out through a window at the rain from the wind and weather proof shelter of that sumptuous interior.

'Well I never!' Agnes had exclaimed as she saw them off. 'He *has* gone up in the world!'

Hannah herself had not realised how true that was until today. Samuel had said little after his visit, except that it was a fine big house, with servants. The carriage was the first clue Hannah had as to what to expect.

Even so, the scale of the house was a surprise. It was not a mansion perhaps, but compared with Low Farm it was vast and elegant. Inside, the luxury, the evidence of wealth, astonished her. Had he gained so much in five short years? He had been right when he had told her it would not take long.

Hannah felt a little daunted by the servant, who looked as if he thought two such lowly guests were a little beneath his dignity, or that of the house. She and Samuel found themselves ushered coldly into a drawing room extravagantly ablaze with candles, where Harriet Scarr – no, Harriet *Gayle* – sat near a superfluous fire, wearing white frilled muslin, with a broad sash of blue satin, in a self consciously girlish style unlike anything that Hannah remembered having seen before. She supposed it must be the height of fashion, something of which she knew nothing. The cut of her own clothes had changed not at all since she was a child, and nor had those of Samuel or Agnes. She could see Harriet's eyes scan the unbleached linen of her simple bodice and skirt, the cap that concealed her hair, even while her lips formed a welcoming smile. Her hair, Hannah noticed, was elaborately curled and piled high on her head, though a few ringlets had been allowed to fall casually to her shoulders. On top of the whole edifice a blue satin turban was perched.

'Mr Gayle will join us soon,' said Robert's wife. 'Please, do sit down.' She gestured towards the many chairs arranged about the room, but did not rise to her feet. Hannah thought her welcome a little lacking in warmth, but then she must know, of course, that Robert had once planned to marry Hannah. The fact that she was now his wife was something Hannah could still not quite believe.

The waiting was not over yet. Hannah sat down, conscious of little but a fast beating heart and the knowledge that at any moment Robert would walk into the room.

'Samuel – Hannah – forgive me. I was detained later at the mill than I intended.'

He came towards them, holding out a hand to each, and he was smiling with what looked like real affection. His voice had not changed, but the warmth and courtesy of the words startled her, and disturbed her more than she would have thought possible. She felt tears rush to her eyes. She had an almost irresistible impulse to rush forward and embrace him. As it was, when he came to her and rested his hands momentarily on her shoulders and kissed her cheek, she felt as if the earth trembled at the touch; certainly she was trembling.

Why did she always forget how his presence affected

her? In her memory he was never so disturbingly hand-some as he was in the flesh. She was dimly conscious of the splendour of his clothes: a plum coloured coat of fine broadcloth, an embroidered waistcoat, close fitting saffron breeches; the small decorative items of a lace and muslin cravat, jewelled buckles at the knee and on his low, light shoes, the gleam of a watch at his waistcoat pocket that made her think of the gift he had brought to Thornside on the first day at the mill. She wondered fleetingly what had become of it. Had he perhaps had the engraving removed, and given the watch to his wife?

He was talking to Samuel, asking after the children. She thought: He wears his own hair now. It was tied back and powdered, but its more natural shape suited him better than the wig had done. His skin was as tanned as ever, his eyes bright, the look of supreme vitality that she remembered so well hung about him still. Facing him, Samuel looked insipid, his hair lank, his whole manner uncertain.

'And you – you are well?' He was talking to her now, his eyes on her face, with none of the chill mockery she had come to hate. It was the old Robert who looked at her now, with warmth and laughter and charm and . . . But too much had changed since then; there was no going back. And she must be misreading what was in his eyes, for their love was a thing of the past.

The courtesies over, they went in to dinner. Hannah felt as if there was no one there but herself and Robert. He did not talk exclusively to her, but she did not think it was in her imagination only that his attention was always centred on her, as hers on him.

She did notice other things, though: the silver cut-lery and crystal glasses, the porcelain service on which the food was served; above all, the food itself. She had not thought that something so basic and so ordi-nary as food could make such an assault upon the senses. What had the cook (she supposed there was a cook) done to the sauce in which the mutton was served, to make something so mundane taste and smell so delicate and yet so exotic? And the fish with which the meal began – it was like no other fish that she had ever tasted, though she supposed it had come from river or lake, like most fish in the Dales. And there was such an extraordinary abundance of food, enough in this one meal to feed a large family for a month, she thought. She was conscious of a faint sense of disapproval, but it wilted before the wonderful sensations assaulting her taste buds. She had not known food could be like this. After a time, she said, 'Who has the cooking of thy food, Robert? It tastes so good.'

She wondered, seeing the startled expressions of Robert and his wife, if she had committed some breach of good manners, if perhaps commenting on the food was frowned upon. But Robert merely smiled. 'Ah, this is nothing. You should eat at my father-in-law's table. He has a new chef, Nicolas, a Frenchman – cook to a noble family once, but they fled the country last year, at the first sign of trouble, bringing Nicolas with them. My father-in-law lured him north with a king's ransom of a salary. Now *his* handiwork is indeed out of this world. Is that not so, Harriet?'

'Yes, my dear.' A meek, sweet voice, accompanied by a gentle smile. 'But Papa fears he may not stay long. He is most dreadfully homesick.'

Hannah watched with interest to see how Robert behaved towards his wife; until then he had scarcely even looked her way. Now he was attentive, polite, smiling, but the face he turned on his wife was one Hannah did not know, the face of a cool stranger. What did he feel for Harriet? He did not look like a man in love, but then had she ever known what he looked like when he was in love, or had she only imagined that she had?

'He may be tempted to return to France, I suppose – things are much calmer there now.' He turned to

366

Samuel. 'What do you think, brother? Do you suppose we have seen the end of unrest in France? Are we at the beginning of a new age?' He was smiling faintly, Hannah saw, and there was in his voice something of the old, ironic, patronising quality she had come to expect when he spoke to Samuel.

Samuel laid down his knife and fork and coloured, and then he stammered, 'I . . . I don't know . . . I have not thought . . .'

'Of course, ask you how the lesser spotted hawk-weed will do this year and we may expect a learned dissertation! But trivial matters like the overturning of governments, revolution and the like – well, who would trouble his head with such things, if he could avoid it?'

Samuel looked more embarrassed than ever. 'It is not trivial, of course. I am glad the French have their liberty. I hope we have seen the end of both tyranny and bloodshed in that country. But I cannot give an opinion on something of which I know little.' It was a dignified answer, if rather clumsily given. Perhaps Robert felt the force of it, for he said coldly, 'Then perhaps you should inform yourself better, brother,' and then returned his attention to Hannah.

'We mill owners will find ourselves with formidable competition, it there is indeed to be full liberty of trade and commerce in France,' he said, with a great deal more warmth than he had shown towards Samuel. More than the words, his manner told Hannah: We are alike, you and I; we understand one another. Against all reason, she felt herself moved by it, yet at the same time resented it.

'Shall we?' she said, a little sharply. 'I am not afraid. I cannot imagine there is any threat to my little enterprise.' She caught sight of Harriet's expression and saw both boredom and distaste in it. Perhaps, like Samuel, she had no interest at all in spinning mills. Hannah, trying to stop herself from always watching Robert, always thinking of him, tried to draw Harriet into their talk. 'Thou hast a brother, I believe – does he live far away?'

Robert seemed at once to take his cue from her and the talk became more general. She had forgotten how irresistibly charming he could be, and how amusing. She began to feel intoxicated by it all – indeed, perhaps she was intoxicated, for she was unused to drinking wine, and as the meal progressed Robert filled and refilled her glass with the glowing claret that tasted so good. After a time she knew her colour had risen and that she was talking too much. Afraid that she might say something she would later regret, she wished there was some means of escape from this too-pleasant place.

Help came unexpectedly. A cherry tart with cream and a selection of fruit had been largely eaten and Robert leaned indolently back in his chair with the look of a man who had eaten his fill (as indeed he must have done), and cast a tiny glance at his wife; and Harriet said suddenly, 'We will leave the gentlemen to their talk.' Not knowing what was happening, Hannah saw Robert rise to his feet and come to move his wife's chair back as she stood up. After a moment, catching his brother's eye, Samuel did the same for her. It was a dismissal of a kind, she supposed. A little unsure, she followed her sister-in-law from the room. By the time they reached the drawing room, where Harriet signalled her to a chair and rang for tea, Hannah understood.

'It was kind of thee to think of it,' she said. 'It is good that they should have time to talk alone. Now they can truly make friends again.'

Harriet looked a little puzzled, but smiled and said nothing. After a moment, the tea came and Harriet poured and then at last broke the silence. 'Tell me,' she said, with rather more hesitancy than usual. 'I have often wondered – do you not feel strange, a female, to be managing a mill?'

Hannah looked at her in surprise. 'Strange? No, I

do not think so. Dost thou think I should? I am used to hard work – it is a different kind of work from farming, that is all.'

'Yes.' Harriet gazed at her thoughtfully. 'I suppose it seems strange to me, because the idea of a female engaged in such things, working for her living, is something I have never come across. I know it happens of course, but I have only been acquainted with ladies before now, amongst my family and friends, that is – and they do not work for a living, unless in distressed circumstances —' She must have become aware of the look of indignation on Hannah's face, for she broke off and said quickly, 'Oh, I have offended you! Forgive me – I meant nothing by it.' She laughed uncomfortably. 'My Papa is thought eccentric, because he has an interest in trade. Yet now I am wed to a mill owner. It was by my own choice, as I am sure you know . . . And to tell you the truth, I envy you, a little.'

'Me! But why?' Married to Robert, the man she loved, yet she envied the woman he had spurned: it seemed an inexplicable attitude.

'It is a little lonely here sometimes. There is not a great deal to do. I have seen where you live – we go past on the road sometimes. To live and work in the same place, to have your family always about you and yet always be occupied – that must be an agreeable way of life.'

Hannah, seeing how her colour came and went, hearing the wistful note in her voice, found herself pitying this young woman who could express such reservations after only a few weeks of marriage. 'When thou hast children of thine own, then time will not hang heavy,' she said.

Harriet blushed again, but seemed a little consoled by the thought. On impulse, Hannah added, 'Thou art welcome at Thornside mill, whenever thou hast a mind to come.'

Harriet thanked her warmly, but Hannah sensed a

369

certain reserve, and knew she would never call without a formal invitation.

After a time the men joined them. Robert said, 'Now for some music. Hannah, you must sing for us!'

Hannah stared at him. 'Thou knows I do not sing.'

'I know you let a fine voice go to waste. Harriet, convince my sister-in-law that she must sing! She would soon pick up the tunes, if you would play for her.'

'If Hannah does not wish to sing, then I shall not press her,' said Harriet quietly.

Hannah saw the angry frown Robert directed at his wife, but all he said was, 'You sing for us then.' It did not sound a very pressing invitation, but Harriet moved to the brand new pianoforte and began to play.

It was, for Hannah, the crown of the evening. It almost made her forget Robert's presence. She sat, enthralled, listening to the notes tumbling over one another into the room, then slowing, rich and deep, then faint and plaintive. When Harriet began to sing her voice was clear and true, if unimpressive, and Hannah heard with delight how piano and voice ran together, weaving a wonderful pattern of sound. If she could only cast her scruples aside and sing, as she longed to do ... But she could not do it. She knew how Robert would gloat, and for all the reviving tumult of her feelings for him she still did not trust him. He wanted her to sing, for his own reasons; perhaps because it would, in a small way, win her back to his side. She would not give him that satisfaction, not least because she knew how much to do so would hurt Samuel.

Going home in the splendid carriage, Hannah and Samuel were silent for a long time, as if they were both too caught up in the varied impressions of the evening, and the new experiences it had offered, to know where to begin. They were perhaps about half way home when Samuel said,

'I am glad we are friends again, Robert and I.' Then: 'But it is another world.'

'Aye, so it seemed to me too.'

Another world, the one that might have been hers, if she had only married Robert . . .

She felt for Samuel's hand in the dark, and he folded his fingers about hers. She heard him sigh contentedly; she knew he was grateful for the gesture. But then he could not see her face, or guess that it was Robert who occupied her tired, over-excited mind, and the memory of how it had felt to lie in his arms and know how passionately he loved her.

CHAPTER SEVENTEEN

i

Hannah left Samuel to read a bedtime story to Rachel, and looked in on Joseph, to make sure that he was indeed sleeping peacefully in the carved cradle, contented after his recent feed. Then she went downstairs and out into the twilit yard to check that the mill doors were secure. She knew quite well that they would be: she trusted George Holgate; there was a dog now, permanently watchful, in his kennel by the back door; and she was absolutely certain that never again would Robert wish to do her harm. Yet ever since that horrible night three years ago she had carried out this daily ritual, just to be sure. On the few occasions when she had omitted to carry it out, she had found herself unable to sleep soundly from anxiety.

All was well. Hannah paused beside the millstream before returning to the house. There was a brisk little wind, not cold, but carrying with it a faint prickle of rain, sweet with the scent of peat and moorland grasses. It was going to be dark early tonight, intensely dark, for there would be no moon and already the days were shortening, warning of autumn. But for now a soft grey light still hung about the trees and the buildings. The water rushed incessantly on its way, the branches creaked in the wind, somewhere an owl hooted, but it was tranquil all the same, with no human sound to disturb her: no childish chatter, no incessant questions, no demands of any kind. For the moment, briefly, she had complete peace.

It was an outward peace only. She could not silence her thoughts so easily, or crush her feelings. They were to dine with Robert again tomorrow. The thought had filled her all day; tomorrow she would be restless with excitement. And she had thought life had become flat! No more, not since that momentous evening when they had first gone to Robert's house, and all their differences had been put behind them as if they had never been. Samuel was happy, of course, because he had made his peace with Robert; if perhaps not as happy as Hannah might have expected. As for her, the repeated visits to Gayle House had become something to be longed for, savoured, dwelt on in anticipation beforehand and, afterwards, in recollection. The wonderful food, the comfort and luxury of the surroundings, entranced and delighted her. She had not thought she cared at all about such things, but she had found in herself an unexpected depth of response to what they had to offer. Simplicity and plainness no longer seemed so wholly and unarguably desirable. She knew that it was all vanity. She thought sometimes, uneasily, that John Burton would have rebuked her for her worldliness, and she was glad that Agnes did not know how she felt.

And of course it was not just the more obvious material comforts that so entranced her. There was the music. Once Samuel had suggested, as the carriage took them to Robert's house, that they ought to ask Robert not to insist on the music, because it was not what they ought to allow themselves to enjoy; but he had spoken hesitantly, and Hannah had said quietly that it was more important that they were at peace with Robert, and if that was part of the price, so be it. Her conscience had pricked her, because she knew she was deluding herself – or Samuel, at least. She did not want the music stopped, simply because the pleasure she found in it was so intense that she could not bear to be without it. She longed desperately to join in, to sing, even to ask Harriet to show her how to play; but she had steadfastly resisted the temptation. It must be enough to hear the songs that sometimes she found herself singing as she rode, or drove the cart over the fell on some business errand.

Then there was Robert – no, *above all* there was Robert. She knew the truth now. Her feelings for him were not dead, nor ever had been; and neither, she acknowledged, were his for her. But she was married and so was he and they had to accept that things could never be again as they had once been between them. She had thought that was something she could accept with serenity. But serenity had become a thing of the past. In fact she wondered if she had ever known it. Certainly she could not remember now what it was like to be at peace.

But then what was peace? Stillness and tranquillity might be held up to her as the most desirable of states, but she wanted none of them. To be still and tranquil was to be dead. Better to be alive, vital, shivering with a sense of dangerous excitement. Life had an edge to it now that it had never had before. She knew where the limits were of course; she would not cross them. But she wanted to go on standing at the edge and looking over, and feeling her head spin at the possibilities before her. She had been conceived on the edge, born on the edge; danger and risk were a part of her heritage, in her blood. She could no more turn her back on them than she could change the colour of her eyes. If life had given her little satisfaction before now, that had been because she had tried to fight her own true nature and let herself be guided by the constraints of her foster parents' faith. Now, without rejecting everything they had given her, she had broken free and she could breathe at last.

This is happiness, she thought. She drew several long deep slow breaths, looking about her as she did so, at the moving shadows beneath the wind-tossed trees, where night had already come, the faint gleam of the water, touched with white where it foamed over the rocks just before it reached the mill.

There was some kind of animal moving through the trees beyond the stream; quite a large one, for she could just hear the sound of it above the noise of the water and the sudden alarmed barking of the dog. It was moving clumsily, with a rustling and crackling of leaves and twigs. She peered into the shadow and at last made out a dark shape lumbering across the slope towards the point where the mill buildings would soon hide it from view. A sheep probably, strayed down from the moor. She ought to go and drive it back to its grazing ground, before it injured itself or became irrevocably lost – or was stolen by someone less scrupulous than herself. She would need help, but not until later; first she would drive it into a corner of the mill garth and check the brand that would tell her whose sheep it was. At least it was going in the right direction. She made her way to the place where a narrow plank bridge crossed the stream just behind the mill.

Her coming – though she moved as softly as she could – frightened the creature, for with an increased crashing it fled on through the trees. She began to fear it would blunder its way over the wall at the top of the wood before she could come within reach of it.

She stood still, listening. The animal must have come to a halt too, for she heard nothing now, though the dog was still barking frantically from his kennel. She thought wistfully of Fly, who would have had the sheep rounded up in no time, but the new dog, set loose, would only have made matters worse. Beyond the wood she could just make out the cow, with her week-old calf, watching anxiously from a corner of the mill garth; after a little time, evidently reassured, she began quietly to graze again. An owl hooted just overhead, making Hannah jump. She took a cautious step forward, watchful for any movement. Nothing.

She wondered if perhaps the poor terrified animal

had lost its footing in its fright and fallen into the mill-stream. She could see no sign of any unusual disturbance in the water, and she had heard no bleating, but then it was too dark here under the trees to see anything very much, and the sound of the water – and the dog – masked most other sounds. She walked as far as the wall of the mill garth, seeing and hearing nothing out of the ordinary. Then she turned and made her way back along the bank of the stream, watchful for any sign of movement, any unusual sound. Nothing.

There was no point at all in going on. Whatever had become of the animal she was unlikely to find it again now. It must either have got clear away from the mill, or fatally injured itself. That was not a happy thought, but there was nothing much she could do about it now. She would come back in daylight, when she might hope to see something. Still looking about her, she returned to the house. The dog, his duty done, gave a last subdued bark and fell silent.

Samuel had just reached the bottom of the stairs as she came through the door. Something about his expression drove out all thought of stray sheep. It was more than just the tender softness that always lingered there when he had spent time with the children; this was a more obvious and positive thing, a glow of real happiness. She looked at him questioningly, but did not need to say anything, for he spoke almost at once.

'I had no time to tell thee before – this came by the post today.' He held out a book, his hand trembling a little.

'Oh!' She understood then. No wonder he had that look! She took the book, fingering the soft new leather of its binding, turning it so that she could see the title. *An Account of the Botany of the North Riding of Yorkshire, with Numerous Illustrations, by Samuel Gayle*. Then she opened it and began slowly to turn the exquisitely decorated pages.

'So it's come at last!' She smiled her delight at him.

Happiness was not just something she knew then; Samuel knew it too, and she was glad. 'It is beautiful, just what it ought to be.' She knew, almost as well as he did, how much work had gone into this book; five years at least, but also a lifetime of meticulous and painstaking observation and recording, which had found its reward at last. She closed the book and went to him and hugged him.

'I am glad for thee, my dear – and I hope everyone will buy it and read it and that thou wilt be valued as thou dost truly deserve.' And as I have never learned to do, said an uneasy little voice in her head.

Samuel smiled at her, and she realised then what it was that marked out his present happiness from any other he had experienced: it was pride, a wholly justifiable pride in his own achievement. For the first time in his life he had done something entirely alone, worked at it and seen it through to the end; something that might bring him credit in the eyes of those whose good opinion he valued. It was, Hannah realised, very much like her own pride in the mill, though she had to acknowledge that she had been forced to depend much more on others for her success than had Samuel.

Hannah had to be up early the next morning, so for once she was glad that Joseph's hungry crying woke her well before dawn. Odd, she thought wryly, as she groped her way to his cradle and lifted him and put him to her breast, how Samuel, not on the whole the heaviest of sleepers, was never disturbed by the baby crying at night, as if some little part of his mind recognised that it was not his responsibility.

Once the child was fed and settled to sleep again, Hannah dressed (she had put her clothes ready the night before) and made her way softly downstairs, running through the things that had to be done today. First, there was the cart to load with the spun yarn she had promised to deliver to Mark Dinsdale. She had to go to Hollinthwaite to collect some of the stockings for the consignment to be sent on its way tomorrow on the first stage of the journey to London. There would be no time today to call afterwards on her mother; she had to make an early start so she could be back in time to see to the packing of the stockings. She must remember too that she must call on Peter Routh, one of the Thornside dyers. Most of the yarn spun at the mill was sold and distributed undyed, but there had been a large order from a draper in Newcastle upon Tyne for best quality blue stockings. She hoped the dyer could have them ready for her by next week.

Then, of course, she must finish early at the mill, so they would not be late for dinner at Gayle House. She wanted to look her best for Robert. Was it wrong, she asked herself for the hundredth time lately, to look forward so much to a few hours in Robert's company, to feel her heart sing at the attention he paid her, to close her eyes to the hurt in Harriet's eyes? It could not be helped. For Samuel's sake, for the reconciliation he had wanted, they were forced to spend so much time together. And Robert loved her; he had always loved her, as she loved him. And it was only a question of feelings, after all. Agnes might have thought it wrong, and John Burton, and many others who thought as they did; as she once did herself. All those scruples she had felt, that had kept her from marrying Robert! They had been good in their way, but short sighted and narrow. They had made no difference at all to Robert and his mill; very likely it would have made more difference if she had married him. It was too late for that, of course, but not for them to find a lesser kind of happiness together. She was a woman now, as free as anyone to make her own choices, based on what she felt to be right. No one was truly hurt by it: Harriet would have been hurt anyway, even if Hannah had never existed, for Robert was incapable of loving her as she clearly wished to be loved.

Outside, the darkness had lifted just enough for the shapes of the buildings to have become visible, and the gleam of water on the flagstones. It was a cold wet morning, following a night of wind and rain, more like winter than the end of summer. Hannah bent her head against the weather, held the lantern high and made her way towards the stables.

The pony snorted in greeting, and she patted him and then turned to the corner where the bridle hung on a nail on the wall. She did not know quite what it was that made her swing the lantern round to illuminate the far corner of the empty stall beside her; a small sound perhaps. The next moment she caught her breath and stood there, frozen, disbelieving, her heart thudding painfully, staring at what the light had caught.

Two eyes watched her, dark eyes in a white face; a small thin frightened face, with great bruised rings about the eyes, beneath close cropped hair of some indeterminate colour. It was an old face, with the parchment skin of a very old man, yet she realised after the first shocked moment that it belonged to a child, who lay huddled in the corner as if he had just woken from sleep.

She realised that the pool of light was quivering uncertainly. Her hands, unsteady, could not hold the lantern still. But it was only a child . . .

She drew a deep breath and took a step forward. The next moment the child jumped up, pushed past her and ran into the dark towards the door. She had shut it behind her, and it had always been difficult to open from the inside, for anyone who did not know how. She heard him fumbling with the latch, his breath coming in quick, frightened gasps. She hung the lantern on a hook where it would give the best light and ran to the child and took him by the shoulders.

'Don't run! I'll not hurt thee. Tell me why thou art afraid.'

He whimpered and rattled the latch more than ever.

She could feel his agitation through the coarse shirt that covered his shoulders, and how thin he was too, the bones sharp beneath her hands. He was coughing intermittently, as if the agitation had set him off.

'Come now, love.' She spoke very softly and gently, as she might to a frightened animal. 'Sit down again and let us talk.'

He glanced over his shoulder at her, wary, suspicious, but off his guard just long enough for her to be able to slip round and press her back against the door, holding it shut. He gave a cry of fury and clutched at her, scratching and tearing. She seized his hands, clasping them firmly, but as gently as she could.

'Give over now, lad. I said I'd not harm thee. Nor will I. Who art thou, and where art thou from?'

She risked releasing his hands and he drew back a little, but his eyes never left her, watchful for his chance to escape.

'It was thee in the wood last night,' she said then, still not raising her voice above an undertone. 'That's right isn't it?' He said nothing, but she thought she saw a faint acknowledgement in his eyes. 'Thou crept in here while I was looking for thee. Thou wilt have been afraid, all alone here in the dark.' She thought she must be right in that too. 'At least it is warm and dry. I expect thou art hungry now.' She ventured a smile. 'I thought thou wert a sheep.' His expression did not change.

She looked him up and down. He was small, very small, and painfully thin, his legs and arms as frail as reeds, but with that old face he could have been any age from seven to seventy. His clothes were rough but in reasonable condition and relatively clean. Yet that could not detract from the look that hung about him, as of an ill-used dog, wary, frightened of its own shadow, mistrustful of everyone and everything, and probably half-starved as well. Yet he had spirit still; she could feel the sore places on her arms, where he had scratched her. 'Thou hast run away, I can see that,' she said after a moment, 'Did thy master treat thee badly?' It was the obvious explanation, that he was an apprentice on the run.

He nodded vigorously.

'I give thee my word,' she said then, 'that no one shall ill-use thee again. I shall not give thee up unless I can be sure of that.' She had every intention of keeping the promise, but she was under no illusions as to what it might mean. It was against the law for an apprentice to leave his master while still bound to him, and she would be aiding and abetting a criminal if she were to encourage the child to run away. On the other hand, if the apprentice could prove that the master had used him badly, then he might be released from his bonds. Hannah was quite sure that any master who could bring such a look of terror to the face of a child was not fit to have charge of an animal, still less a human being.

The boy neither moved nor spoke, nor took his wary eyes from her for a moment.

'Come in the house and have a bite to eat. Then we'll see what's to be done.' She held out her hands and repeated, 'I promise thee – I'll not give thee away. Thou art safe here. No one shall use thee ill again – no one.' She scanned his face and his tense, alert little body for some sign that it was safe to open the door, that he would not instantly run away at the first opportunity. After a time, still seeing no real sign that he trusted her, she asked, 'Where wast thou going? Hast thou folks to take thee in?' If his home was not far away and he knew his parents would be sympathetic to his plight, then everything would be so much easier. But many parents, anxious to avoid trouble, would simply return a runaway apprentice to his master. If he knew that was likely to be his fate, then he was probably running wildly, thinking only of evading capture, and he might well end his life very soon, starving and frozen on the fells; even in summer that was a very real danger.

After a short hesitation the boy nodded, but so quickly and furtively that Hannah almost wondered if she had imagined it.

'Come and eat, then we'll see how best to get thee home,' she said gently. 'Hast thou far to go? I'm driving to Swaledale myself this morning.'

The boy murmured something, one word, which sounded like 'London'; but since that made no sense to Hannah she asked him to repeat it.

'London,' he said again. 'My ma's in London.'

She stared at him, noting that he spoke with a sharply unfamiliar accent. Was that how Londoners spoke? Yet it made no sense at all. 'How canst thou be from London, if thou art apprenticed here? Or hast thou run from London —? No, that cannot be it.' A doubt struck her. He had not, after all, admitted to being a runaway apprentice. He might simply have accepted the suggestion, as a convenient answer to an awkward question. 'Art thou bound apprentice?' He nodded. 'Where then?'

This time he did not hesitate; perhaps she had at last convinced him that she could be trusted.

'The mill.'

The mill? she thought blankly; but this is the mill. Then she remembered: 'Of course, how stupid of me.' But it was not stupid, for how could a child from London be apprenticed to Newgill cotton mill, three hundred miles from the capital? 'How dost thou come to be bound apprentice so far from home?'

He shrugged his bony shoulders, and then coughed before replying. 'There's a good few of us. The guardians sent us, for work. Most of them's orphans. My ma was poor, see – she couldn't keep me. So she sent me with the others.'

Hannah was still trying to understand. 'Are you all from London – all of you at the cotton mill?'

He shook his head. 'There's some from Manchester way, and other places. I don't know all of them.'

Once again she looked up and down the small figure, her face grave. 'How old art thou?'

'Thirteen.'

'Are there many so young?'

'Most's younger. I'm one of the eldest.' A faintly boastful note had crept into his voice. 'That's how I got away. The little ones couldn't have done it. Mr Birley keeps a close eye on us. But I could tell when he wasn't looking. I knew it was the best time, when we went back after shift. It was nearly dark, see, so he wouldn't have found me if he'd looked. I'm good at hiding.' He shook his head with fierce emphasis. 'I'll not go back, not ever.'

The inescapable truth was reaching her; she could no longer refuse to admit it to her understanding. The child's cruel master was Robert, Robert whom she loved, and who loved her; who had sat at her table last week, and with whom she would dine tonight; Robert who had done so well for himself – so well, on the toil of little children torn from all that was familiar and loved, little children such as she might once have been herself, had she not been so fortunate in the place of her abandonment. She had thought she had lost all her illusions about Robert long ago. And she had known he employed children at the mill. There was no excuse for her ignorance of what this child had told her today. Yet somehow she had never allowed herself to ask the questions that she ought surely to have asked. She found she was trembling.

The boy had taken a step backwards. She thought for a moment that his fear had returned and he had shrunk away from her, and then she saw how he groped for the support of the nearest stall. His small face was whiter than ever. She ran quickly and put an arm about him. 'Come, lad – thou must eat. I'll keep my word. No harm will come to thee. When thou hast eaten, then thou shalt tell us all about it.' She was relieved that he allowed her to steer him out of the stable and across the yard to the house, where Agnes was coaxing the fire to life, watched by Rachel who sat at the table, needle tucked into the little sheath Samuel had carved for her, laboriously knitting.

Agnes did not waste more than a moment in asking questions. Before long the boy was seated at the table, with porridge in a bowl before him, which – after a moment's initial hesitation – he soon began to eat as if he had forgotten when he had last seen food. Rachel, her hands temporarily still, watched him in fascination.

'I must go and finish loading the cart,' Hannah murmured to Agnes, when she had explained the situation.

Agnes nodded. 'I'll see to him.'

But Hannah had taken no more than a step towards the door when the boy looked round and laid down his spoon and gave a little cry. All his reviving assurance crumbled away, and he looked as terrified as when she had first seen him.

'I'll go and do the loading,' Agnes said. 'Thou hadst best stay with him.'

When Samuel came down soon afterwards Hannah told him the story too.

'Then he's Robert's apprentice,' he said gravely, when she had finished. They had spoken softly, out of earshot of the boy, but he watched them suspiciously, clearly mistrustful of Samuel.

So, for a moment, was Hannah. 'I gave my word he'd come to no harm,' she said warningly.

'Nor shall he,' Samuel reassured her. 'But thou hast said nothing off ill-usage.'

'I've eyes in my head,' she retorted.

He glanced towards the boy. 'Aye. And so have I. But we'll need more than that, if it's to come to fighting Robert.'

Fighting Robert . . . The thought was a dreary one, and depressing. She had thought that was all behind her, even that it had been unnecessary. Yet was it all to start again? The indignation she had felt when she found the child faded a little. Samuel was right; they had no facts to guide them, no more than an instinct, which might be wrong. The boy's thinness and pallor, and the painful-sounding cough that shook him so frequently, might have some quite reasonable explanation, and his fear of the mill might be a fear of justifiable punishment. She did not believe it, yet a part of her wanted to.

She returned to the table and sat down facing the boy, who had abandoned the spoon altogether and was licking round the bowl, like a cat lapping up the last drops of cream. 'Now, lad.' He put down the bowl. 'I think thou hadst best tell us thy name.'

'Jack,' he said. 'Jack West.'

'So, Jack, thou took against thy work at the mill. Maybe thou canst tell us thy reasons.'

'I want to see my ma,' he replied promptly.

Hannah glanced at Samuel. It was, they would both have agreed, an entirely natural wish, but as a reason for defying Robert it was hardly sufficient. They might pity the child for being placed in work so far from his home, but that hardly amounted to ill usage. 'But thou likes the work?' Hannah pursued. She was not sure whether she was relieved or not. If there was no good reason to protect the child from discovery, things might be very awkward, especially as she had given her word not to give him up.

Jack, clearly surprised by the question, shook his head briskly. 'Nobody *likes* it,' he said emphatically.

'Why not?'

He shrugged again, as if the answer was so obvious as not to need putting into words. But evidently he realised that words were required of him. 'There's the dust – the noise. All day long, all night, if you're on night shift.'

'Night!' She remembered now; coming back from

Gayle House once they had noticed lights at Newgill, well after midnight. But they had thought only that Henry Birley must have been making a late inspection of the machinery, or perhaps carrying out some necessary repairs before the day's work began.

The boy nodded. 'One lot works days, the other nights. I'm on days. But I did nights twice, when there were a good few sick.'

'How many of you are there then?'

'About two hundred, I heard. The night workers sleep in the day. We have their beds at night.'

'How long do you all work then?'

'Thirteen hours each shift. That's to give us time to eat – we have breakfast and dinner in the mill. We can sit down to our supper – we get that in the apprentice house.'

A cold, appalled horror was crawling through Hannah. 'Thou dost not sit down otherwise?'

He shook his head. 'The machines don't stop, and they have to be watched, so we must stand. The little ones get down on their hands and knees sometimes – they have to get under the machines, when the thread gets caught up.'

'While the machines are working?' He nodded. 'But that's dangerous – truly dangerous!' Hannah could not even bear to think of it. In her mill she would have allowed no one to do such a thing until the machines were stationary.

The boy nodded. 'They get hurt sometimes. Two of them died that I know of. Mr Birley has to beat them to get them to go under. I got hurt once too.' He held up a hand to show one finger broken off above the first joint. 'I got my hand caught. I was new then. I didn't know to be careful. The stupid ones don't learn.' He shrugged again. 'Or the little ones, neither. They cry a lot, especially the girls.' On the surface his tone was full of the contempt of the mature male for the weakness of the very young, and especially the female young.

If he had developed a protective shell of bravado to cover his own fears, that was only to be expected. In the stable, cold and hungry and alone, he had lost it. But it was firmly back in place now, so that voice and manner were cheerful and matter of fact. Only the fact of his having run away, to return to a mother who had been willing to send him to such a place, showed how real his fears were.

Hannah looked at Samuel, and saw in his expression a reflection of what she was thinking. She had no need to try and convince him further. She turned back to the child. 'We'll have to think what's to be done. But first I expect thou wouldst wish to sleep.'

For some reason her words seemed to revive all his suspicion of her. He jumped to his feet, visibly shaking. 'I'll go now. I'll be on my way.'

'But London is more than two hundred miles away. Thou canst not get there without help.'

'I'll go,' he repeated stubbornly, and took a step towards the door.

There were voices in the yard, one a man's, speaking quietly, the other, Agnes's, raised almost to a shout. Hannah, puzzled at such unusual behaviour on the old woman's part, went to the window to look; and in passing caught sight of the boy's face. It was drained of colour, and he stood absolutely still, like a rabbit faced by a stoat, as if all power to move had left him.

'I tell thee, there's no one here but ourselves!' Agnes was shouting, her voice carrying clearly across the yard. Hannah swung round and took the boy by the shoulders. 'Quick! Upstairs with thee. Samuel, take him to Rachel's room. He can sleep there. Rachel, go with thy father. I'll see to them —' She gestured towards the yard.

She walked casually across to where Agnes stood by the half-laden cart, facing the three men with sticks and cudgels in their hands, her face full of innocent indignation. Agnes can tell lies too, when she sees the need, Hannah thought suddenly, with a fleeting sense of amusement.

'What is all this?' she demanded.

The man she thought was Henry Birley, Robert's overseer, stepped towards her. 'We're seeking a boy, Mrs Gayle – a real young villain, run away from Newgill last night.'

'I'll be getting in,' said Agnes, and left them.

Hannah gazed coolly at Birley. 'What has that to do with us?' she said.

'He was seen coming this way last night – that Thomas Bell saw him, though why the hell he didn't stop him, God knows, old fool that he is!'

Hannah, like Agnes, carefully suppressed all she had ever been taught about truthfulness and sincerity. 'I know nothing of it. If he was here last night he'll be miles away by now I would suppose.'

The man looked at her with stony contempt. 'You'll have no objection if we take a look around.' It was not in any sense a question or a request. He was already turning away from her, his two companions with him, to put his words into effect.

'Wait! I have every possible objection. Thou mayest look where thou wilt, outside my premises. But I will not have three men I scarcely know pushing their noses into my mill and my house. If there is searching to be done, I shall do it.'

The man tapped his thigh impatiently with the stick he carried. 'Then you'd best get on with it. I haven't got all day.'

'I shall do it in my own time, not thine. And not while thou art on my premises.'

'I'm not going till I've made sure he's not here.'

'Then thou'lt have a long wait.'

'Mrs Gayle' – he was clearly trying very hard not to lose his temper – 'I'm here on Mr Gayle's orders. The boy's broke his bond. He must be found and brought back. He is a cunning villain, Mrs Gayle, a right bad lot. And lazy with it. Why else would he run away?'

'Why else, Henry Birley?' Hannah returned, unmoved. 'Now, I have a great deal of work to do and no time to stand gossiping. I will cast an eye about the buildings when I have time. If I find anything, then maybe I will send word to Mr Gayle.'

She thought the man would make some further protest, but rather to her surprise he glowered at her for a moment and then turned and walked away. She watched until he had disappeared into the lane, and then went to check that all was well in the house.

'I don't trust that man,' she said to Agnes and Samuel; they told her the boy was already asleep. 'Keep an eye open in case they come back. And tell the others when they come for work.'

She was nearly two hours late by the time she set out at last for Hollinthwaite; and after that the whole day passed in a rush as she tried to make up for the lost time. The boy Jack slept for most of the day and then woke and ate a large meal before retreating again to his hiding place upstairs. Rachel took him a pile of her books, and even read to him for a little while (she was proud of that newly acquired skill of hers, the more so as Jack, who could not read, was clearly awed by it); and then he fell asleep again – long months of exhausting toil taking their toll at last, Hannah concluded.

They were only a little late leaving for Robert's house. As they went, Samuel said, 'We shall have to think what to do with him.'

'Aye,' agreed Hannah. 'But we must say nothing to Robert.'

'I would not think of it! After what we have heard ...' He frowned a little, anxiously. 'We must get him to London, I suppose. That will be no easy matter. We could take him to Richmond, and see him on to the coach. But who's to say what will become of him then?

He may come to all manner of harm on the journey. And what if his mother will not take him in, when he reaches home?'

'We cannot guard against every possibility,' said Hannah gently. 'But if we put him on the coach in the charge of some kindly seeming person, that will be a good deal. I think even if they set the law on him, no one will think to seek him on the public stage coach.'

'No,' said Samuel, but he was clearly still uneasy about the whole thing. 'It would have been so much better if we could have brought a case for maltreatment. It would not be comfortable, against my own brother, but the course would have been clear. As it is . . .' He sighed.

'As it is, there is no maltreatment in working a child for thirteen hours, without rest, with little food, in constant fear! Oh, Samuel, how *can* that be right?'

Samuel, of course, had no answer to give, beyond a sad shake of the head.

Hannah had expected to be excited, going to Robert's house tonight; and so she was, in a way. But it was a nervous, unhappy excitement, in which shame played a large part. It was not, after all, so easy to put her conscience aside. Now, it seemed to her astonishing that she should not have given more thought to how Robert had made his money. She had no excuse, after all; no reason to think he might be innocent of any wrong. She ought not to be able to detach her feelings from her conscience, as she had lately done. That was not freedom, to be able to put such a thing aside; or not any kind of freedom she wished to enjoy.

She realised as the butler ushered them across the hall that she had not considered what she would say to Robert this evening. Nothing, of course – nothing that would betray the child hidden in their house. Yet how could she behave as if everything was unchanged, with that knowledge constantly in her thoughts?

Samuel too had looked forward to this evening,

before the day's events had turned it all sour. Reconciliation with Robert had not made for wholly warm and brotherly relations between them. But then Robert's open contempt for him had always been there, for as long as he could remember. He had told himself he must be content to have normality restored, and not expect the miracle of a truly equal and affectionate relationship. Then, yesterday, the book had come, tangible proof that Samuel was capable of achievement, even of success, in terms that Robert might recognise. Samuel had looked forward with real pleasure to pressing a copy of his book into his brother's hand and seeing contempt change to respect and even admiration.

Now, he was not sure that this was, any longer, what he really wanted. How should he behave towards a man who had so ill-used a child? Should he even be trying to win that man's respect and affection?

He had brought the book with him all the same, because he did not know what else to do. Was it not possible that any oddity in his behaviour would betray the child? Time enough for showing his disapproval when the boy was safely away from Thornside. So, as he stepped into the drawing room, Samuel had the book clutched in his hand, the smile ready to accompany the announcement.

As usual, it was Hannah who drew Robert's gaze as he greeted them. Samuel always tried to tell himself that he imagined it, or at least that he imagined Hannah's response to Robert, the shining eyes and heightened colour, the warm and excited manner. This evening at least there was nothing of that as she returned his greeting – no smile, no warmth, the briefest and coolest of replies. Samuel saw surprise on Robert's face (quickly hidden) and then a speculative light in his eyes. Before speculation could lead to any kind of conclusion, Samuel stepped forward, holding out the book.

'I have this for thee, Robert. I should like thee to be the first to see it, after Hannah.'

Robert's surprise was gratifying. He took the book, opened it, turned a few pages. Then he looked at his brother. 'Well, well – your life's work, I see. A little dry and scholarly for my taste, but I thank you all the same.' Then he closed the book and laid it on a nearby table and turned back to Hannah. 'What are your views on steam power?' he asked. 'Do you think it likely to supersede water power?'

His manner and his words told Samuel with biting clarity that his book was of no importance, the trivial outcome of a minor pastime. It was in manufacturing that the future lay, and it was Robert, not Samuel, who would be at the very heart of that future. Samuel said nothing – what could he say, after all? In fact he was astonished now that he could ever have hoped for any other reaction. He glanced towards Harriet, and saw how she was watching her husband and Hannah, as she so often did. Samuel had realised long ago that she too saw cause for jealousy in the way they behaved towards one another. Surely she could not be imagining it too?

'I have not given it any thought,' said Hannah, with unusual crispness.

'You should, believe me,' said Robert. 'There are cotton mills already going over to steam power, in preference to water. That way the machines are no longer at the mercy of the weather, you see.'

Harriet broke in with a little laugh and a gesture towards the windows against which the rain was lashing. 'I hardly think lack of water is likely to affect your mill, my dear husband,' she said lightly. 'My father says what we need is some artificial form of sunlight, for the crops.'

They began to move towards the dining room, but rather to Samuel's surprise, Hannah did not follow Harriet's lead away from the dangerous topic of mills. On the contrary, she said suddenly,

'I had thy overseer at the mill today.'

Samuel caught his breath, wondering what was coming next. Hannah's face was grave enough, but calm, with no hint of anxiety, still less of condemnation.

He saw Robert turn towards her, his eyebrows raised, as if he too was surprised that she should bring up the subject of her own free will. 'Yes, and you treated him with rather less than the courtesy I would have expected, in the circumstances,' he said drily.

The sparkle in Hannah's eyes now had nothing to do with revived passion. 'What courtesy dost thou think fitting, for a man who frightens children so much they run away?'

'"They" do not run away; "one" has done so, and that a boy who has caused us nothing but trouble since he came to us. Lazy, foul mouthed, disobedient, a liar and a thief – what more do you require to convince you he is not worthy of your sympathy?'

Samuel could see the hesitation on Hannah's face. He knew what she felt, because he felt it too: uncertainty, doubt about the child they had left at home. Had they been deceived? Could he have gone out of his way to play on their compassion, inventing his misery and fear for his own ends? It had not even occurred to them that he might be lying, but now it seemed only too possible.

Robert said suddenly, with a new sharp note in his voice, 'Have you seen him then? You're hiding him – is that it? If that's so, then I advise you to give him up at once, before he does real harm to you or your children. He's not to be trusted for a moment, believe me.' He spoke so earnestly that Samuel found himself almost convinced. He was sure that Hannah must feel the same.

'I told Henry Birley that I would search for him and send word to thee if I found anything,' Hannah reminded Robert quietly.

'But no word came. *Did* you find anything?'

'Did I send word?' Hannah returned quietly, her

eyes steady on Robert's face. Samuel was struck with admiration. He would not have thought of a way so to tell the truth while yet giving nothing away. 'Tell me, Robert,' Hannah went on, 'if he is so bad a boy, why dost thou want him back? Better to let him go, surely?'

'He has broken his bond. It is a legal matter. Besides, if he can be tamed he will soon be old enough to be of real use to me.'

'Tamed, so that he will not want to play and run and breathe good air, as thou didst as a child?'

'Then you *have* got him! Be advised, Hannah – let me send word to Birley to go for him at once. You will regret it else.'

'It was thee told me thy workers would work thirteen hours in thy mill. Do they not work nights too now? What time does that leave for playing?'

'What time does it leave for mischief? Come now, Hannah, have you got him or no? I am within my rights to demand his return, you know that.'

'I am within my rights to say I will not have Henry Birley hanging about my mill. And the law has something to say about ill treatment of apprentices.'

'My apprentices are not ill treated. Many mills demand longer hours than I do. They are fed and clothed and warmly lodged – and taught to earn their keep. You could ask for no more.'

By now they had reached the dining room, but remained standing beside the table while Robert and Hannah argued together. Harriet broke in tentatively, 'Pray be seated, all of you . . .'

They did so, but Hannah, unwilling to be distracted, glanced round at the lavish table setting and then at the whole room, with all its marks of comfort and luxury. 'Canst thou be easy, to live like this on the money thy workers have earned for thee, in such conditions?'

'Of course I can be easy. Without my enterprise and hard work they would have nothing – nothing, Hannah! They would be out in the streets begging for bread – or stealing it, and ending up on the gallows. It is right that I should be rewarded for all I have done. And one thing more, I will not have condemnation of conditions at my mill from someone who knows nothing of them. They are as good as any cotton mill in the land. Go and call on Miles Pickering's mill – a good Quaker; is he not a member of Bainbridge Meeting?'

'No. Carperby, I believe.'

'A Friend though, for all that. His conscience does not quail at employing child apprentices, exactly as I do – go and see his mill, and then tell me you blame me. Or better still, come and look round Newgill, and see for yourself. Then perhaps you'll stop talking of things you know nothing about.'

'Very well,' said Hannah firmly. 'I shall do so. And Samuel too.' She glanced at Samuel, who stammered,

'No – no, not me. I know nothing of mills. I trust thy judgement, Hannah.'

Robert smiled unpleasantly. 'I like a man who knows his mind and holds firm opinions,' he said. And only then, leaving that remark to linger in Samuel's mind, did he allow Harriet to turn the conversation into more amicable channels.

Hannah was relieved that he said no more about his missing apprentice, but he had succeeded in making her thoroughly uneasy, partly because she feared that he might contrive to send Birley or someone else to Thornside mill to search for the boy, perhaps even this evening, in her absence; partly because, if Robert should after all be proved right about the boy (and that was not impossible), then they might return home to find he had done all kinds of unimaginable harm.

In fact, the moment they stepped out of the coach in the mill yard, Hannah thought her worst fears were about to be realised, for Agnes came hurrying to meet them with an expression of great distress.

'Hannah – Samuel – oh I am so sorry! I do not know how it happened . . .!'

Hannah stood quite still; beside her, Samuel, sharing her fear, did the same. Agnes glanced anxiously up at the coachman, who was busy turning his vehicle, and then lowered her voice.

'He's gone – the lad. Disappeared!'

They walked into the house. 'When? How?'

'I don't know, that's the worst of it. I went up about supper time, just as it was getting dark. And he was gone. The window was open, and I'd not left it open – he must have gone that way. But a good while before, I think – the rain had come in, all over the floor in a great puddle. I went out and had a look – there were a few prints in the earth under the window, going towards the beck, but that's all.'

'He didn't trust us then,' said Hannah sadly. 'He must have thought we would give him up.' Yet a part of her was a little relieved, because they need no longer worry about the rightness of what they were doing. He was beyond their reach – out in the wild wind and rain of the night, finding his way through unknown countryside.

Relieved or not, she did not sleep well that night. It did not help that the last thing Samuel said to her, in the tone of one trying hard to convince himself, was, 'Robert would not have invited thee to see his mill, if he had anything to hide. I think perhaps the lad *may* have deceived us.'

ii

Robert was waiting for Hannah when she arrived – punctually at ten in the morning, as had been arranged – to look round the cotton mill at Newgill. She had not intended to pay more attention than usual to her appearance this morning, but in spite of herself she had done so; it seemed to her that Robert had done the same. His appearance was at once elegant and jaunty, as if her visit gave him immense pleasure.

He ushered her in by the main door of the mill, and

then turned to smile at her, with all the easy charm of the old days. The acrimony of the other night seemed to be forgotten, even though it was what had brought her here today. 'You will take a glass of wine with me before we begin our tour?' he asked, in the tone of one who did not dream that she might refuse. He crooked his arm towards her, and in sudden confusion she realised he expected her to take it before going with him to wherever the wine had been put ready. She was on the point of slipping her hand through his arm, as once she used to do when she was just Robert Gayle's girl at Hollinthwaite. She felt her heart beat fast, and all the old excitement rose in her. She wanted achingly to go with him, to be alone with him as she had not been for – oh, she could not remember how long. It would be dangerous, infinitely dangerous, but the temptation was almost beyond resisting. Yet —

She had not come here to fan her reviving love for Robert into further life. She had come, in all serious-ness, to inform herself of conditions at his mill; and she must not allow her feelings to deflect her from her purpose. Time enough for that if all was well, if she found she could in all honesty say to Robert: 'I misjudged you; I am sorry.'

She forced herself to take a long steadying breath, and then she said quietly, 'I thank thee, but no, not yet. Perhaps later. May we see the mill now?'

He gave a little bow. 'I am at your service, my dear Hannah.' There was a tiny pause, while he studied her face in a way that made her colour uncomfortably. Then he said, 'It is difficult to talk in the mill, without shouting. I suggest you come up to my office first. We can be comfortable there, while I explain what you are about to see.'

She hesitated. He sounded matter of fact enough, as if he were simply being practical. But could she trust him? Or, more to the point, could she trust herself?

Then she told herself she was being foolish, and said,

'Very well,' and went with him, not touching him, but uncomfortably conscious of his closeness all the way up the stairs.

As he closed the door behind them she knew it had been a mistake to come. He stood still for a moment, his back pressed to the door, gazing at her. Then, softly, he said, 'Hannah!' and held out his hands.

She was trembling, but she stayed where she was, struggling to resist the temptation to go to him. It was so long since she had been alone with him, without fear of interruption. She had forgotten what effect the removal of that constraint could have upon her. It was alarming to find that in this at least nothing had changed.

He came and laid his hands on her shoulders and pulled her to him, and then his mouth came down on hers. She wanted him so much; she was conscious only of that, how intensely she wanted him. Just for that moment he had her completely in his power.

But only for that moment. Almost at once she drew sharply back, pressing her hands to his chest to fend him off. 'No!' she cried.

He looked at once surprised and deeply mortified, even angry. Then he smiled faintly. 'Hannah —' His voice was gentle and pleading, but she tried to shut it out, and with a great effort of will pulled herself free and went to the door. She held it open and turned to look at him.

'I came to see thy mill,' she said. He frowned at her; but after a short while shrugged and strode angrily forward, leading the way down the stairs. By the time they reached the door into the mill he had himself under control again, and was all cool civility.

And then, as soon as they stepped through that door, Hannah forgot all about her feelings for Robert. She did not know quite what she had expected to find here. The mill of the boy Jack's account had taken the shape in her mind of something rather like her own mill, but much larger, with machines very like her own, only more numerous, and watched over not by grown men and women, but by children.

It was nothing like her little woollen mill. Two things struck her instantly with all the force of a blow, two inseparable and overpowering elements fused into the one essential quality of that vast room: the dust, and the noise.

Wherever she looked the air was full of a fine white dust, veiling everything in a kind of mist through which the deafening rattle of the machinery burst on her ears with a painful din. She drew in a breath, but it was cut short and she coughed, feeling as if her lungs were filling with the fine soft cotton fibres that floated everywhere. She fumbled for her handkerchief and pressed it to her mouth, glancing at Robert to see what he thought. He smiled.

'The cotton dust is a bit troublesome at first, but you get used to it.' His voice came faintly to her, as if from a great distance, and yet he was just beside her and she could see that he was shouting.

No wonder the child had a cough, Hannah thought; but she did not even attempt to speak to Robert. She did not want to risk removing the handkerchief from her mouth. She noticed that the dust was stinging her eyes too.

Robert gestured that she should go with him, and she did so, on into that white, clamorous fog. Slowly, one by one, great machines took on vast indeterminate shape, like monsters served by the small pale creatures – living creatures – coming and going in the mist, whose parchment faces and grave red-rimmed eyes stared at her before they disappeared again from view, as if she were some visitant from another planet. Somewhere, far beyond the machines, she could make out the whiter rectangles of long windows, or what she supposed were windows. Once, when she passed near them, she saw how thickly dust coated the panes, so that they could do little to lighten the pale gloom of the room, and gave no view of the world outside.

Now and then Robert halted by one or other of the machines, and signalled to her to come and observe what it did. She saw carding machines, much like her own she supposed, except that they were so huge, and in detail so much smaller and finer, teasing out the fine white insubstantial fibres of the cotton, until they were ready to be wound on to the bobbins of the spinning machines and spun into delicate threads so thin that, in the speed of the spinning, they almost disappeared altogether.

And everywhere there were the children, little creatures no bigger than Rachel, who leaned over the turning spindles and rollers and bobbins to guide the threads, to disentangle, to wind bobbins, remove spindles, tie broken threads; who, here and there, crawled beneath the machines, heads low to avoid the leaping churning mechanism that rattled on above them, struggling to loosen tangled threads, their small hands only just – with the speed of long practice – springing free in time from certain hurt. It made Hannah shudder to see it. She did not want to look in case some accident should happen before her eyes, and she should be helpless to prevent it. There was one tiny child with soft fair hair so close to the machinery that it seemed certain it would be caught up. It was all Hannah could do not to reach down and clasp the child in her arms and run and run with her away from this horrible place of noise and dust and constant menacing machinery.

There were a few adults there. She saw Henry Birley – who greeted her with scant politeness – and other men who stood watching the children, sticks in hands, not to protect, but to keep them at work; though she saw no child idling, only some who even so early in the shift were scarcely able to stand, from weakness and exhaustion, and others – many – who coughed and coughed as they struggled with some task in that constant dust.

It was a relief beyond words when Robert led her out at last into the hallway, and closed the door on the worst of the noise. A relief, and yet not a relief, because she had brought with her the vision of the children who worked on in there, who would go on working until after dark, and who would then snatch a few hours of exhausted sleep before starting again, day after endless day. Time went slowly for a child, she knew that. How desperately, unbearably long must the hours seem to these little ones who scarcely glimpsed the sun and the grass and the hills that had been her familiar friends from infancy, who never heard the curlew or the blackbird or the cuckoo, or the sounds of wind and water, for the din of machinery, incessantly at work?

She found she was trembling. She felt limp and drained of energy, but not this time from emotion, or not at least the unthinking and now somehow trivial emotion of before. She looked at Robert, noting that his skin and his hair and his good cloth coat all had their covering of white dust, as, she supposed, had hers. She expected him to be a little shamefaced, even defensive, certainly full of fluent excuses. She could scarcely believe her own ears when he smiled easily and said, 'There, you see – tidy, clean, well fed, industrious children. What is there to complain of in that?'

He was so unhesitating, so utterly sure of himself. Hannah did not know what to say. How could she begin to explain what she felt to someone who was apparently so astonishingly far from being able to see this place as it really was?

She had not found an answer to that when Robert went on cheerfully, 'Now you must see the apprentice house, and the weavers' cottages – only ten so far, but I'm to begin on the rest very soon.'

She went with him, abandoning her attempt to find words for what she wanted to say, the more readily as she was not quite sure what that was. She had a feeling that to say anything would be to waste her breath. In the end, all she did, as they walked together across the short piece of empty yard towards the apprentice house, was to say, 'Those children in there – how long do they stay at the machines at one time?'

'How many hours do they work? Twelve. Less on Sundays, of course, when they finish at midday. Sunday afternoons they have lessons – so you see their education is taken care of too.'

Hannah, who remembered the thirteen year old boy who could not read, was not impressed. Besides, how could such sick and exhausted children be expected to attend to their studies?

'On top of that,' Robert went on, 'they have an hour allowed for meals – one of which is taken in the apprentice house. Many mills require much longer hours – I've heard of sixteen in some places. Now *there* you'd have something to complain of. That's why I've never had any difficulty finding workers, of course.'

'I did not suppose they had any choice about coming here,' said Hannah sharply.

Robert looked a little surprised, as if he could not understand why she should have such a critical note in her voice. 'The poor law guardians are careful who they send the children to. They make full inquiries before anything is agreed. I have to meet certain conditions, you know. As I am happy to do, of course.'

Hannah asked about the food they ate – 'havercake and milk, porridge and so forth, the kind of thing we were brought up on' – and learned that all but supper were eaten at the machines. As Jack had said, the children were not allowed to leave the machines or sit down for their meals. 'It cannot be healthy to eat in all that dust,' Hannah said.

'Oh, they get used to it. It does them no harm. They don't ail much. There's the odd accident, a fever now and then, but they get the best medical attention, I'll have you know. You've cared for animals, Hannah. You know they only give of their best if they're well cared for. It's the same with children.'

How could he be so blind? 'Wouldst thou be happy for thy own children to live like this, if thou hadst children?'

Again, that surprise, that she should ask such a question. 'You know that is different. These are pauper children. If they weren't here they'd most of them be out in the streets starting on a life of crime. I'm sure you couldn't approve of that.'

'It is not the only alternative,' said Hannah, but she knew Robert was not listening. He was busy unlocking the door of the apprentice house, a tall grim building with high barred windows, set at right angles to the mill itself. 'There's a door through inside, from one to the other,' Robert explained. 'So when the weather's bad the children don't need to go outside. But this is more convenient for daily use.' He pushed the door open and ushered her through. 'Quiet now – we mustn't wake the sleepers.'

On the first floor he allowed her to peer round a door – also locked until he opened it – into a vast dormitory closely packed with small bunk beds, each one occupied by two boys, sleeping head to tail. The air was stuffy with the smell of so many none too clean young bodies, and disturbed by the odd grunts and moans of over-weary children whose sleep could not be truly restful. Did they ever dream of the things they could not have, Hannah wondered; of sun and fresh air and laughter, and the tenderness of loving parents? Perhaps few of them had ever known such things. Was it possible then to miss them?

Upstairs, in a near-identical room, the girls slept in similar conditions. On the ground floor again, Robert proudly showed her the kitchens and store rooms and the bare room with its hard benches where, on Sunday afternoons, the children had their brief experience of education. Henry Birley and the other overseers took it in turns to teach them, she gathered. What kind of education could such men be expected to give to children many of whom must be too tired to learn?

She followed Robert out again into the yard with a great weight of unhappiness settled about her heart. Such a little thing could make all the difference, she thought; the kind of parents who gave you birth, riches or poverty, a chance illness, an accident, whether you were born in some narrow city street or out on the desolate moor beneath the open sky. For these children, chance had brought a life of constant, exhausting toil; for her, a beginning apparently no more fortunate had led to a life rich in all that mattered most. 'It is so *unjust!*' she thought with a sudden burst of anger. What, after all, had she ever done to deserve her good fortune; what had these children done to deserve their misery, poor little innocents that they were?

They walked next to the weavers' cottages, but Hannah was not greatly interested in them. They were reasonably commodious and well appointed, with an obvious appeal for the men – and their families – who had come to live in them. But the people who lived here had chosen to come and were free to leave whenever they wished, not like the children who at six or so had simply been herded into some carrier's cart and transported at the whim, or the greed, of those who owned them to this place where no one thought of them as human beings or cared what became of them, so long as profits could be made by their labour.

'I think it is wicked!' The words, torn from Hannah by a passionate conviction too deep to be silenced any longer, came in a deep resonant tone, quivering with emotion. Robert, his exposition of the virtues of his cottages in full flow, came to a halt, abruptly silenced, and looked round at Hannah in astonishment.

'Wicked? What are you talking about? The cottages are —'

'Not the cottages,' Hannah broke in impatiently. 'The children – shutting them up like that day after day, year in year out, where they never see the sun or run or laugh and no one ever loves them or cares what becomes of them. It is wrong, Robert – wicked and cruel and evil.'

He frowned. 'Don't be foolish, Hannah. Have you heard nothing of what I've said to you?'

'I've heard it,' she retorted. 'All I know is that those little ones in there are God's children, like thee and me, made in God's image, and that the life they endure is not what the Lord meant for his children. If it is wrong to enslave negroes, so it is wrong to enslave children.'

'Don't preach at me, Hannah. I get enough of that in church on Sundays. Besides, what right have you to talk of right and wrong, from your heights of untouched virtue?' His tone was heavily sarcastic. 'And before you try to give me any more Quaker teaching, may I remind you that there are many good staunch Friends who run cotton mills without the least uneasiness of conscience, and employ children exactly as I do here. I've spoken of Miles Pickering already, haven't I? Why not go and preach to him? He ought to be ready to listen. I've heard him speak against negro slavery often enough. Though I think you'll find he sees no inconsistency in his behaviour. At least you could never accuse me either of inconsistency, or of hypocrisy.'

She had to allow him that, but it was small consolation. She stood still, her head bent, feeling depressed beyond words. Was her indignation merely an eccentricity, incomprehensible to anyone else? Was it Robert who would seem in the eyes of the world to be sane and right, a philanthropist providing for needy children?

'You could have had a say in what I do here,' said Robert, his tone unexpectedly gentle. 'You should have married me – you'd have a had a right to speak then.'

So she had told herself only a few days ago. But she no longer believed it. 'Thou wouldst not have listened.

Thou never did. Hast thou forgot that was the reason I did not wed thee?' She shook her head sadly. 'No, the only way to stop all this, to make things better for the children, is by the law, through parliament.'

He laughed. 'So you will be a politician now, is that it! I knew you were ambitious, but this —!'

'Do not mock,' she said gravely. 'It is parliament will end negro slavery, one day, if enough folks speak out. It is parliament will end this slavery too, if only men can be brought to see what an evil it is.'

He made an impatient exclamation. 'It's law and regulation that's held up enterprise so long in this country. That's why it's taken a new industry like cotton spinning to change things. The old trades, like wool, are so hemmed in by old ways and old restrictions, about wages and conditions and so forth, that they've stifled enterprise long since. Think of the old guilds that have been there for centuries, laying down the law about apprenticeships and the like – what purpose can they serve, in the seventeen nineties? And then there are all the Elizabethan statutes – *Elizabethan*, mark you – two hundred years old! It's less law we need, and more freedom, if this country is to thrive.'

'But what freedom is there for those children? Does their freedom not matter, only thine?'

'It's men like myself who create wealth. Hold us back, and you hold back the future. Then there will be neither freedom nor prosperity for anyone.'

She did not attempt to argue any further. What was the use? She had learned long ago that Robert would listen to no opinion that did not agree with his own. It was a pity that she had ever allowed herself to forget it.

She realised abruptly that Robert's expression had changed. It was soft, even tender, and he said in a tone that even now was able to stir some passion to life in her, 'All the same, Hannah, you should have married me. Never mind the mill. There were other things you could have had, things you'll never have with Samuel. Music, for instance – you could have learned to play an instrument, had singing lessons. We could have sung together sometimes.'

He could play on her still, as if she were an instrument, sensitive to his touch and the sound of his voice. In spite of everything, she felt the force of what he said. Yet she knew she must fight it.

'Those are trivial things, Robert,' she said severely. 'They are distractions from what really matters.' It was as if she were superstitiously repeating a charm in the hope that it might protect her from evil.

'Don't parrot those empty phrases at me, Hannah,' he retorted. (How did he know so well what she felt now, when before he had not come within miles of understanding?) 'If you want the religious argument, has it never occurred to you that you are denying God's gifts to you? Why else did He give you the voice you have, if not to use it?'

'I have other gifts,' she retorted stoutly. She had no intention of letting him see how moved she was by what he said. She was anxious only to get away before he could touch her irrevocably. 'I thank thee for showing me thy mill. I must go home now.'

She could see that he was startled by her sudden change of subject. He tried to mask his dismay (yes, it *was* dismay, and she, shamefully, was pleased by it) and said smoothly, 'Then you won't take that glass of wine with me?'

She shook her head. 'No, Robert. I have work to do at home.'

'You waste your time, Hannah. Your little mill is never going to come to anything.'

'It is not meant to come to anything,' she said serenely. 'Except to make life a little easier for the knitters and weavers. It does that already. That is all the success I ask for.'

'Wait till your children grow. You'll want more for

them then — more than your mill can give them, or Samuel. Then you'll wish you'd married me.'

'Thou canst not see, can thou? I do not measure success like thee — not in riches and luxury and worldly goods. There are greater riches by far I want for my children, riches no money can buy —'

'Music?' he asked teasingly, but she ignored him, saying only,

'I'll go, Robert. Thou didst intend otherwise maybe, but what I have seen today has not made me think better of thy mill. Only worse than I could have imagined.' She forced herself to turn away, but he put out a hand to grasp her arm. She felt the shock of his touch run right through her.

'Tell me, Hannah — you did hide that boy, didn't you?'

After a moment she said only, 'I hope I shall always be guided by my conscience.' And then she pulled herself free and walked away, leaving Robert standing watching her with a confused mixture of fury and frustration that made him long at once to shake her and embrace her. But she was already beyond his reach, as he knew a part of her always had been.

iii

Samuel did not think he had ever been so happy; except perhaps for those few days before his marriage, when he had let himself believe that Hannah loved him. Certainly today's happiness had a new quality about it, because this time it stemmed from something he had done all alone, by himself, without help from anyone, even against certain difficulties. Time and again they returned to him, those phrases heard today, to renew the glow of happy pride that had filled him when he first heard them. Yes, he knew it was all vanity, to be so delighted by mere worldly praise. It was his duty to suppress his delight and calm his excitement and set his mind on more important matters — and so he would, in time. But until then he would allow himself, just for a little while, to savour this unaccustomed pleasure.

At the mill he stabled his horse and went into the house with the mood of elation still hanging about him. In a moment he would be able to share it all with Hannah, which would be the climax of his happiness. After that, he promised himself, he would try to take a more humble view of things.

He found Hannah seated by the kitchen fire, with Agnes and Rachel. The table was set for supper, the pot keeping warm on the hearth, the three womenfolk (even the youngest) busily knitting as they talked, but quick to lay aside their work when he came in. Rachel slid off her stool and ran to him, letting her ball of wool fall to the floor, where it trailed behind her, to the delight of the cat. Agnes got up to return the pot to the full heat. Hannah ... Looking over Rachel's head as he hugged her to him, he saw that Hannah had risen to her feet but now simply stood there, her expression both abstracted and grave. He felt disappointed. He wanted so much to share his joy with her, but she did not look as if she would be readily receptive of his confidences.

Carrying Rachel, he went to kiss his wife and then, at her bidding, to come to the table. In a moment or two, as they sat relaxed over their meal, he would find an opportunity to tell her.

He waited, suppressing his impatience, until they had all been eating for a little while, mostly in silence. Then, trying to control his excitement so that he should not sound as if he were making too much of a small thing (it *is* only a small thing, he tried to tell himself), he said as quietly and slowly as possible, 'It was not for teaching -- that was not why Friend Whaley asked me to call. He has a tutor for his son already. No, it was to tell me how greatly he liked my book. He said that in his opinion it was "a work of surpassing interest".' He knew the excitement was breaking through, but he could not help himself. 'He talked of gathering a few others together, all those who share an interest in furthering botanical studies. Friend Lightfoot was there too, and he was full of praise for the idea. He said my book had been an inspiration to him. We talked a great deal. There were many proposals about our society, but in the end we were of the same mind. We are to meet at Friend Whaley's house on the second Fourth Day of each month – so we shall meet first next week.'

Hannah smiled and said how pleased she was for him, but he could see the little distance in her eyes. She had heard him, but she had not felt his happiness, not as if it were her own, not as he wanted her to do, so it should be complete. He went on talking for a little while, struggling to keep his fragile joy alive, giving all the details of the meeting today, of his hopes and plans. Hannah continued to smile, and Agnes made approving comments too, but it was not enough, and in the end he fell silent, trying not to feel hurt by it. He should not have allowed vanity to rule him. It was after all a very little thing, to have a book printed, and to be planning to meet with like-minded people – even for him, who had so little experience of such congenial gatherings. People were doing such things all the time, on a much larger and more important scale. He went on to ask Hannah about her day, and did not remember, until she mentioned it with great brevity, that she had been to Newgill this morning.

'Of course!' No wonder she was not much interested in what he had been doing! 'How was it?'

She looked very grave. 'As I expected.' Then: 'No, worse . . .' But after that, before he could question her further, she changed the subject and would not be brought back to it.

Later, Joseph woke as usual for his evening feed and – seeking an opportunity to be alone with her – Samuel followed Hannah upstairs, and sat with her as the baby sucked noisily at her breast. For a little while neither of them said anything, but Samuel was quite sure that was not because Hannah had nothing to say, rather that she was deciding how best to put it into words.

At last she looked up and said, 'Samuel, it is worse, that place, much worse than I ever dreamed. It is wicked, what Robert is doing.'

He said nothing, for he sensed what she was leading up to, and he did not want to bring her to that point any sooner than she would have come to it anyway. That he might somehow prevent her reaching it at all never occurred to him for a moment.

'Samuel,' she went on after a little silence, 'it is not right that we should meet with Robert and visit his house, nor that we should welcome him here – not while he is the cause of such suffering. Oh, Samuel, if thou hadst only seen it! The dust, the white little faces! Never to see the sun or breathe the air or run and laugh, like we did as children – as Robert himself did – oh, how can he let it happen, and think it right?'

He could see that there were tears rising in her eyes, and he was moved in spite of what he knew her indignation would mean to him. He sat near her and folded his hand about hers, where it rested on the blanket that wrapped Joseph. 'Robert has walked a long way from the light,' he said gently. 'I knew that, I think. But I hoped it was not so far that he could not turn back again, if he chose.'

'If he chose,' Hannah said drily. 'That's it – he does not choose, nor I think will he, not while things go well for him, as he sees it.' She shook her head. 'I do not know how he can sleep easy in his bed at night.' Then she raised her eyes steadily to Samuel's face. 'Give thy word that we shall have no more to do with him.'

Samuel looked away from those sad yet somehow relentless eyes. 'He is my brother, Hannah,' he said hesitantly. 'The only family I have.'

'Thou hast me. Is that not enough?'

'Of course, but . . .' It ought to be true, yet somehow it was not.

'Samuel, thou wouldst not eat at the table of a slave trader.'

'No. But . . .' For all the inevitable humiliations and awkwardnesses, he had been glad to be reconciled with his brother, as if an open wound had been suddenly healed. So life ought to be lived, at peace with all around, at odds with no one – least of all his own brother. It hurt him to feel that any part of his life was not as it should be. Yet how could he distance himself from Robert without giving an explanation and so, unfailingly, provoking a bitter quarrel. 'Perhaps,' he suggested uncertainly, 'we may meet without deliberate intent. I would not invite him. We would not accept any invitation from him. But if we were to meet in passing, then there need be no coldness, not like there was before. From me, I mean – for thyself, that is for thy conscience.' He felt that he was making a great concession to her, for even this degree of estrangement would cast a shadow over his life. But Hannah was right, of course. She saw the principles that were involved. He could not deny her this much at least.

Perhaps she understood what it cost him, for when she had given the matter some consideration she said gently, 'Let it be so then, love.'

He was grateful to her, but the last remaining trace of his happiness had gone, to be replaced by regret. It was not her fault, of course – if anyone should be blamed, it was Robert. Besides, no one ought to expect happiness, still less to demand it. If it came it was a gift, a glimpse of heaven, soon over, so long as life lasted. He should be grateful simply that he had been granted that gift, now and then.

Two weeks later they heard that the body of a child had been found in one of the loneliest hidden places on Thornside common. He was lying on a narrow ledge

412

below a steep rock face, where he must have fallen some time before. His leg was broken, and he was thin to the point of emaciation. It was said he must have lain there for some days before he finally starved to death.

CHAPTER EIGHTEEN

i

'I saw Eli this morning,' Sarah Dinsdale said. 'He had nowt much to say for himself.'

'No.' Hannah felt the usual twinge of guilt at the thought of him. Yet what else could she have done? There was no work for him here, had not been for weeks, and no money to pay him to idle his time away. A little cheese now and then, a few eggs, vegetables from their garden, oats from their own dwindling store – the occasional small gifts were poor compensation for lack of work.

She was growing used to the quietness of the mill, after all these weeks. There was as usual no sound at all from the floor above, where dust lay on the carding engine and the worsted spinning machine. Down here on the ground floor the jenny rattled spasmodically, with long pauses while George Holgate replaced the full spindles and filled up the emptied bobbins. Even then, they could hear no sound of water from outside.

George did not hurry, but did everything with leisurely slowness. There was no point in speed, when it took Hannah and Sarah Dinsdale so long to card the wool. Hannah had forgotten how laborious – and how tedious – hand carding was.

'Fair bit of cloud today,' George observed after a moment.

'High though,' said Hannah. 'And the light's wrong for rain.'

'It never rains for Thornside Feast,' Sarah put in.

'It did last year.'

Sarah grinned. 'Aye, but not to speak of.'

'It would be worth the speaking of if it rained so much this year,' said George gloomily.

All that could be said on that subject had already been said many times over during the long dry summer, so a little silence followed. Then Sarah said, rather in the tone of one suddenly taking courage to put into words something that had been in her mind for a long time, 'Mr Pickering from Carperby – he used to be a good customer of my husband. Said he wove the finest cloth in Wensleydale. But that were four years or more ago. He's bought none from him for a long time now. Yesterday Kit met him in the road – he walked right past with not a word nor a look.' She left the conclusion hanging in the air, to be drawn or not, as her hearers wished.

George looked at Hannah; and Hannah said quietly, 'Because he gets his yarn from me – is that what thou thinks?'

'It seems like it. Queer thing, otherwise.'

'He should say, if that's what he's doing – right out, to Kit's face.'

Sarah smiled faintly. 'Some folks are not as forthright as thee, Hannah Gayle.'

Which was perhaps as well, Hannah thought. She still felt hot with embarrassment when she remembered her visit to Miles Pickering's cotton mill shortly after seeing Robert's mill. It had taken all her courage to make the visit, but she had known she must do it, if only in fairness to Robert: if he was doing wrong, then for a convinced Friend to do the same was even worse. She had told herself that John Burton would not have flinched at the task, taught by John Woolman's example on such matters.

So she had gone, and asked to look round, and been kindly received by the Quaker mill owner. But when she saw in his mill conditions no better (and in some things worse) than those at Newgill, she had told him precisely what she thought. She had tried to speak calmly and in a kindly manner, as one Quaker ought in speaking her mind to another. But her indignation had shown through, and Miles Pickering had responded with something approaching a wholly un-Quakerly rage.

'Friend Hannah, I take in poor children who have no prospects and no livelihood. I feed and house and clothe them, I teach them a trade, I educate them. That is the Lord's work —'

'So I believe the slave owners would say,' Hannah had retorted, stung by an argument so like Robert's; at which point the outraged mill owner had made it clear that she was no longer welcome on his premises.

She had known her outspokenness had been wasted. Nothing would change at Miles Pickering's mill. 'But I have done what I could,' she had told herself, relieved that it was over.

But it had not been over. She had realised that the next First Day as she sat at meeting, with the stillness all around her and a restless, demanding clamour in her heart. At last, goaded into action, she had risen to her feet and for the first time in her life broken the silence, pouring out to everyone there the evils she had seen, the words coming in an impassioned flow that had surprised her as much as it had surprised her hearers.

There were those who had been moved to agree with her and voice their support, Samuel and Agnes among them. Others, sympathetic to what she said, had been unhappy with the means she had used, feeling that she had been tactless: a quieter approach would have been better, they felt. There were still others who saw her words as a personal and quite unwarranted attack on a convinced Friend whose philanthropy was well known. Even now, three years later, the divisions remained beneath the calm and courteous surface. Hannah's only consolation was that the numbers who agreed with her had steadily grown, outside the Quaker circle as well as within it, and there were already moves to gather support in the world at large, amongst those who had real political influence. Kit Dinsdale had been one of her supporters, as soon as he had heard of her stand, but then very likely he had not thought it would affect his livelihood.

'Does he blame me for it?' Hannah enquired.

'He thinks thou did right – thou knows that. And he's other buyers enough – more than enough this summer, with worsted so hard to get.'

That was reassuring, and Hannah knew Sarah felt no ill will towards her, yet she had herself never been entirely sure that she had done right. Perhaps indeed she had been tactless, putting off by her manner more people than she had won over. Certainly she was saddened by the divisions her action had brought. Yet she thought that if she had to begin again today she would do exactly the same. It was small acts of individual witness that had led at last to the great movement against the slave trade. Perhaps one day her little isolated action would become just one of many, part of a great wave of indignation that would sweep its way to London and force parliament to make laws that would protect innocent children from the slavery of the mills.

Into the silence that had fallen came the sudden sound of young voices, and feet running on the cobbles outside. Sarah grinned. 'The end of our peace,' she said. 'School's out for today.'

'Get thee home then,' said Hannah. 'The light will be going soon. Agnes will give a hand till then, and the children.' She laid the cards aside and made her way to the little office in the far corner of the ground floor where she kept her fast dwindling store of cash. With business so slow there was little coming in, too little to keep pace with what must go out. But there was just enough still to pay Sarah what she was due, and George too. It was as well perhaps that next week was Thornside Feast, when the mill generally closed.

Unless – 'I'll be in Monday if it rains,' Sarah said as she left.

Hannah smiled ruefully. 'I'll hope to see thee then.'

Betty Dinsdale, a slight ten-year-old, was with the other children in the yard. Most of them were girls, for the boys of Thornside attended the grammar school in the town, if their parents could afford it, or wished to take advantage of its rough and narrow regime. It was a long time since Samuel had taught mathematics alone, to paying pupils. He had given that up so that he would have time to teach their own children, but somehow, one by one, others had joined them, until now nine children gathered daily in the sunny parlour of the mill, Sarah's daughter among them. Those who could afford it paid a small fee; those who could not were taught free of charge.

The Dinsdales made their way along the lane with the other children, who were noisier than usual because of the impending holiday. Hannah went to Samuel, who was standing in the doorway with their youngest child John, two years old, in his arms, watching the older children at play. He looked contented, far removed from the anxieties that often kept her awake at night.

'I had in mind that Rachel and Joseph should give a hand with the carding,' Hannah said. 'But I think maybe I'll let them be.'

'Aye,' said Samuel, laughing as John tugged playfully at his hair. 'Why not send George home now and shut up early?'

She did not say, 'Because I cannot afford to lose a moment's work, the way things are.' She did not want to destroy Samuel's happy mood. Besides, what great difference would it make, to card wool for an hour longer? Unless it rained soon they'd have time enough to catch up on the carding next week, while the mill was closed.

'I'll do that,' she said.

Yesterday, as they came home from meeting, they had heard the strains of music breezily in the air, and knew the Feast had begun in earnest. The parish church was dedicated to St Aidan, whose festival fell on August 31, and at that time each year Thornside celebrated. On Sunday there had been church services, processions and more restrained festivities. Today, the town forgot all about the reasons for the Feast and celebrated with exuberant high spirits, welcoming back for the occasion many of its natives who had since moved away. It was a time for weddings and reunions and reminiscences and the deepest drinking of the whole drunken year. It was a time when, for the most part, good Quaker families stayed quietly at home.

But it was hot and there was still no sign of rain, and it was possible that there might be visitors to the Feast whose income had not been affected badly by the summer's drought, who would be pleased to buy a pair of Thornside stockings to take away with them. At the moment Hannah could not afford to miss any opportunity to make a little money, and there was still a small store of stockings left to sell. So that first morning the entire Gayle family drove the cart very early down to the meadows near the river, where today horse races would be run, and set up a stall in a prominent position not far from the track. Agnes and Hannah sat down with their knitting to wait for the crowds to arrive. There was not enough spare yarn for the children to knit, so they were left to play happily nearby, and warned to keep a watchful eye on John, who was inclined to wander.

The sun rose higher and the heat intensified. The horses' hooves churned up the dried grass of the meadows, sending up increasing clouds of dust as the day went on, until it hung in the air like a mist. Overhead, clouds thickened, hiding the sun; it grew heavy and dull, but hotter than ever. The racing began, the noise of hooves thudding beneath the roaring of the crowd. People pushed past the stall, some paused to talk, but few looked and no one bought anything. The children grew tired and irritable, and Agnes hurried away and returned a little later with three sugar mice, bought at another stall. 'I know it's to spoil them,' she admitted a little shamefacedly. 'But just this once . . .'

Hannah smiled through weariness and dust. 'Why not? If it keeps them quiet a little longer.' They stood watching as the children sat down on the brown and flattened grass and set to work on the sticky treats. Hannah thought that no one since the world began had ever had such lovely children, perfect even in their own distinctive imperfections: Rachel long and slender like her mother, but with her father's heavy brown hair and sweet solemn brown eyes and serious nature; Joseph, who was Samuel in miniature, though still retaining some of the plumpness of babyhood; John, who had nothing of Samuel in him at all, but was all Hannah, long limbed, blue eyed, with wild black hair. She loved them as she had loved no one in her life before, not even Robert, because they were a part of her as she of them, unequivocally, irrevocably. That was something no one, ever, could take from her.

'Where's Samuel?' Agnes asked suddenly. 'He was here a moment ago.'

'Oh, thou knows Samuel – he saw one of his botanical friends and off he went. We'll not see him again for an hour or more.' She glanced in the direction he had taken, but saw only the colourful noisy mass of the holiday crowd. And the next moment, emerging from it with heart stopping suddenness, not Samuel, but the tall elegant figure of his brother. She looked quickly down at her hands and saw how they trembled. She hardly ever saw him, she avoided him as much as she could, she neither liked nor respected him; yet still when she chanced upon him her heartbeat quickened and her colour rose and she could think only of him.

Would she ever learn to see him without agitation, clear eyed, as the man he really was?

She realised with astonishment and horror that he had come right up to the stall, and that just at the moment when their first customer of the day had engaged Agnes's attention.

'Good day, Hannah. A long time since we met, I think – too long for such close kin.'

She forced herself to look at him, trying to keep her gaze steady as if the blush that covered her face had nothing to do with her. Perhaps he would think she was simply too hot, as she was, of course; much too hot.

'You look well,' he went on, as blandly as if he had no idea what a turmoil he was setting up within her. Perhaps he really did not know.

Hannah, seeing him clearly at close quarters for the first time in months, realised abruptly that he had changed. He looked weary and careworn, and had lost the boyish youthfulness she had always thought of as an essential part of him. How old was he now? She was twenty-nine, and he three years older: thirty-two. Then she supposed he merely looked his age, but it was a shock all the same. It did not, unfortunately, reduce his power to disturb her, and he still had the same air of assured elegance. She ran her eyes over him.

'Ah!' he broke in. 'You are admiring my pantaloons, I see.' He stretched a leg forward, its shape smoothly outlined by the close-fitting garment in fine buff cloth, reaching from a high waist to the soft shining low cut boots. 'The demands of fashion, you see. They are all the rage in London. Breeches are going out fast ...' He paused, as if making a point, though she could not think what it might be. 'And stockings with them, of course. Soon the only people wearing them will be the poor and the old.'

'Someone will still have to supply them,' Hannah returned, her voice cool and firm. But all the same she felt a faint twinge of apprehension. She knew well enough how small a thing could affect her business. Last year disease and a cold spring had killed off many of the lambs and sheep, so that wool had been in short supply, and still was. This year there had been the drought. Where, before, prosperity had seemed certain, she now knew that nothing was certain.

'Another summer like this, and you'll not be in a position to supply anyone,' Robert said with a little smile.

'It is no worse for me than for thee,' Hannah retorted. 'Better perhaps, for thou hast two hundred workers to feed whether the beck runs dry or not.'

'Ah, but I have always worked for a good profit – I can better afford a little difficulty. Your margin for loss must be very small. Besides, after this year I shall no longer be at the mercy of the weather. I'm having a steam engine installed.'

'Then,' she said, 'if we're snowed in thou wilt run short of coal for thy engine.'

'Not if I get my stocks in well before the winter – as I shall, of course. Planning and far sightedness: two essentials for a profitable business. And the sense to see the way the wind's blowing, and go with it.' He gestured contemptuously towards the stall with its neat, untouched piles of stockings. 'All this is almost at an end, in the past. I warned you, but you would not be told.'

'Nor shall I now. And, past or not, I have customers to serve . . .' She glanced towards the two men who were now standing waiting nearby, and then back at Robert.

'And I,' he said, taking the dismissal with nonchalance, 'have a horse running in a short while. I must go and see that all's well. My black filly won the first race this morning. I hope you saw it.'

A little later he had disappeared again into the crowd, and Hannah, concentrating on her customers, tried to control her agitation.

Samuel had passed a thoroughly agreeable morning. Since the success of his book – and it had been a surprising success, even beyond the confines of the Dales – he found that wherever he went he was likely to be accosted by some admirer of his work, which would result in several minutes at least of congenial conversation. If that person happened also to be a member of his beloved (and now thriving) Botanical Society, then so much the better. Samuel, for most of his life a solitary man with few friends, now found he had many, and felt himself rich indeed.

By now about half a dozen men were gathered about him, and since only two or three of them were botanical enthusiasts the talk had moved on to more general and (to Samuel) less absorbing matters.

'Well, Toulon's fallen to our fleet, or so the papers are saying,' someone observed cheerfully. 'France must be nearly surrounded by now.'

'And seething with disaffection throughout, one gathers,' someone else added. 'Can't be long before the whole country falls to the Allies.'

Samuel shook his head sadly. 'War only brings sorrow, to one side or the other.'

'I suppose you'd sit back and let the French march into England and set up their guillotine by the Thames, dear brother —'

Samuel, colouring, looked sharply round as Robert strolled casually to join them. 'I think only that good cannot prevail unless it comes in peace,' he said quietly.

'Ever the idealist!' returned Robert. 'If that were true, then Friends would rule the world by now.'

'Not at all. Theirs is a kingdom not of this world. Thou knows that.'

Robert, softening a little, slapped him on the shoulder. 'How can you still keep your head in the clouds, after eight years of marriage and three children? You baffle me, Sam, I can tell you.'

'Your brother is a scholar of rare qualities,' put in

Ambrose Whaley, a prosperous and forward-looking landowner highly regarded by Sir George Scarr. 'One who lives in the world of the mind finds it easier to keep a hold on the true realities. We should all be thankful for such men.'

Robert looked startled. 'Do you really think so?'

'Indeed, yes. After all, our great men remind us that we are more than mere common clay.'

'Great men? Samuel?' There was deep derision in his expression and his tone.

Whaley seemed a little surprised that anyone should fail to share his view of the matter. 'Certainly. If not yet, then very soon.' He glanced at Samuel and smiled. 'But I see I embarrass you, my friend – and it is in any case time I was on my way. I look forward to our meeting next week.' As if by common consent the others went too, leaving Robert and Samuel alone together.

'Pompous fool!' Robert said, as soon as they had gone. 'I hear he gives his support to your call for mill regulation – or perhaps I should say Hannah's. I thought he'd have had more sense.'

'Thou knows we must differ on that,' said Samuel quietly. He had suffered Robert's anger on that point often before, and knew he had no hope of persuading his brother to share his view. 'I am puzzled,' he went on. 'Once thou didst say the revolution in France was a blow for liberty. Now thou art opposed to it. What has changed thee?'

'*I've* not changed,' said Robert. 'If you read the papers instead of botanising all the time, you'd know – it's the revolution that's changed. Besides, I'm a patriot – no foreign rule for me, nor foreign ideas. A pity you can't see the danger. But then Quakers always did put patriotism a poor second.'

'The Kingdom of Heaven before any earthly kingdom. Of course – why not?'

'Do you *never* doubt all that?'

Samuel hesitated. 'Not in that, no – on other things perhaps, sometimes.'

'Ah, then marriage has brought you down to earth after all! A man can't keep his illusions long, with a wife in his bed – still less with children under his feet, I would suppose.' There was just a trace of bitterness in his tone. Instinctively Samuel glanced behind him to where he could just glimpse through the crowd the stall where his wife and children were gathered. Robert followed his gaze, his expression unrelievedly grim.

'There's still time enough for thy wife to bear children,' Samuel said gently, his voice warm with sympathy.

Robert swung round on him, stung by the hint of pity to a bitter anger. 'Oh, don't humour me, brother! My wife's barren. That's a fact, and I've no choice but to put up with it. If I'd known ... Well, it's too late for that now.'

Samuel looked deeply troubled. 'Four years is not long, to be sure of such a thing. And even if it be true, a man and a woman can still find great comfort together, without children.'

Robert's glance was derisive. 'God, what can you possibly know about it? You speak from your own experience, is that it? I well remember what comfort you and Hannah had in one another, when you first married.'

Samuel coloured hotly. 'That was different.'

'Aye, I suppose it was. After all, she wasn't barren, was she?' He was silent for a moment, studying his brother's face; and then something new, something speculative, touched by a hint of amusement, came into his eyes. 'When all's said and done, maybe I'm better off this way. After all, if you've got children, you can never be sure, can you?'

'Sure of what?' Samuel asked, puzzled but unwary.

'The children – that they're yours. You've only your wife's word for it, after all.'

Samuel said with dignity, 'I do not need her word. She is my wife. That is enough.'

'It wasn't enough once, was it?'

'She was not my wife then.'

'Ah, but how can you be sure it has never happened since? You wouldn't have known about the first time if I hadn't told you. Hannah would never have said anything.'

Samuel's colour rose. 'We have no secrets. She is as true as any wife can be.'

Robert laughed harshly. 'I've never had much of an opinion of any woman's loyalty. Dear brother, you should beware of your natural innocence. I would have thought you'd have learned after the first time. Once bitten twice shy, after all —'

Samuel turned sharply away. 'I have no wish to hear such talk —'

Robert hurried after him and laid a hand on his arm. 'Wait! We must not part in anger like this.' It was the only argument that could have made Samuel stay and hear him. 'It is for your own sake that I speak as I do. Once I thought it best – but now . . . No, you should be told.' He looked away from Samuel's apprehensive face through the gap in the crowd to where the three Gayle children were visible, sitting laughing together on the ground. 'Has it never occurred to you – that youngest boy of yours: John, isn't it . . .?'

Samuel stood very still, grave and a little pale. 'What of him?'

'How old is he now? Two?'

'He was two in May.'

'So he was conceived nine months before, of course – at the end of August perhaps, or September. Hard to be quite sure about these things, I understand.' His eyes never left Samuel's face, just as Samuel appeared mesmerised by him, unable to look away. 'Has it never struck you, that was just about the time Hannah came to see me at Newgill? A whole morning alone in my

426

company – and afterwards, every sign of a guilty conscience. See how she's avoided me ever since.'

'Because of what she saw at the mill. Thou knows it was that!'

'Do I? It's what you believed, I'm sure. You told me so, after all. It's what Hannah wanted you to believe. But how can you know she told the truth?' His gaze moved again to the little group by the stall, coming to rest this time on John's small figure. 'He's not much like the others, is he? They both bear some resemblance to you. But not that one. He's not like the others, and he's not like you, not in the least.' He laid a hand on his brother's shoulder, so suddenly that Samuel jumped. 'I say no more. I can't be sure, of course. But that's just the trouble, isn't it? Neither can you. Still . . .' His face softened as he glanced again at the child. 'I should like to think that somewhere a part of me was to be carried on, into the future, long after I am gone . . .' The hand on Samuel's shoulder rose and fell again. 'But I must not take up any more of your valuable time. I know how busy you scholars are. If you want to talk further to me, don't hesitate to call on me. I know how consoling talk can be in a time of trouble. Meanwhile, please carry my good wishes to your lovely wife.'

For a long time after he had gone Samuel stood where he was in a kind of daze, seeing nothing and not even thinking of anything very much. Eventually, he gave himself a little shake, drew a deep breath and set off resolutely towards the stall, and Hannah, and his children – *his* children? He halted again; and then, abruptly, swung round and walked back the other way, through the crowd and on, out of the field, along the road, up on to the fell.

iii

'It feels like thunder to me,' Agnes said, towards the end of the afternoon. She was only putting into words what Hannah had been thinking for some time, but had

427

not dared to say, as if saying it aloud might somehow make it less likely to happen. Now, Hannah added the further thought that must have been in the minds of almost everyone in the field this afternoon: 'It might rain.'

The thunder began, a low distant growling, just as they were packing up to go home – before the races had come to an end, so as to avoid the last rowdy and drunken hours of the day. Samuel had not come back to them, but Hannah simply assumed he had become wrapped up in some botanical enthusiasm and gone to investigate it. Someone said they had seen him walking briskly through Thornside, making for the fell road. It was Hannah and Agnes, helped by the children, who packed up the unsold goods, dismantled the stall, loaded the cart and made their way home. They reached the mill just as the first heavy drops of rain began to fall.

The children, shouting with excitement, rushed to the centre of the yard and stood there, hands outstretched, faces turned to the sky, laughing at the feel of the rain on their hot skins. Even Hannah and Agnes made no move to rush for shelter, but stood looking up, smiling with relief and thankfulness.

'At last! At long last!' said Hannah. It would be too late for the hay and the barley and the oats, too late for the animals weakened by poor food and too little water; too late for those who would go hungry this winter, because the crops had failed and prices would be high. But it was over at last. The rain had come.

It was still raining, pouring down in a heavy relentless stream, when Samuel came home. They were sitting at supper, the children noisier than usual from happiness and excitement. The moment she heard him at the door, Hannah looked up, smiling to draw him at once into their joyous circle. The children scrambled from their seats and ran to meet him, chattering animatedly, John, as usual, pushing his way through a space to come to him first, eager for the first hug and kiss. Samuel, looking oddly abstracted, laid a hand on the heads of the two older children, frowned and said gravely, 'Don't push so, John.' Then he looked briefly across at Hannah, appeared to hesitate, and turned and walked from the room, closing the door behind him. A moment after they heard his foot on the stair.

Hannah glanced at Agnes, seeing her own puzzlement and anxiety reflected there. 'I'll go to him,' she said.

He was in their room, removing his saturated clothes with a look of grim determination that confirmed the impression she had gained downstairs that something was very wrong. She closed the door and went to him, putting her arms about him with no thought for the wet. But he stiffened and shook himself free. Had she offended him in some way? She could think of no possible way in which she might have done. But she did not attempt to move closer to him. Instead she went and sat down on the bed, watching him.

'Sam – Sam, what is it? What's wrong?'

He looked at her then, but with such reproach in his eyes that she was startled. When he said nothing, she repeated, 'Tell me what's wrong!'

He turned away from her, so that she could not see his face, and went to hang his wet clothes rather inefficiently over the back of a chair. Then he pulled on a dry shirt and breeches and went to the window, where he stood and stared in silence out at the rain. Hannah gazed in concerned exasperation at his back, narrow and angular beneath the heavy folds of unbleached linen, the thin shoulders a little hunched, the brown hair darkened and lank from the rain. He looked both dejected and rejecting, and somehow vulnerable too.

'Samuel,' she prompted again. This time he did speak, but so indistinctly that she could not make out what he said, except that John's name was in it somewhere.

'What was that, love?'

'John —' he said, quite clearly this time, but since that was all she was none the wiser.

'What about him?' There was a long silence, during which Samuel looked both uncomfortable and unhappy. At last Hannah, impatient, burst out, 'Samuel, what has John to do with this? Has he done wrong? He is very young, thou knows.' And he had been in her care all day, while Samuel had scarcely seen him. Had something happened yesterday, or the day before, or some time ago? Had some harm come to him, that she had not known about? Her anxiety increasing still more, she resumed, 'Tell me!'

Samuel turned round at last, though he kept his head bent, avoiding her eyes. 'No, no it is not that. It is nothing he has done, poor innocent.' He paused, and then went on, 'That day, Hannah – the day thou went to the mill —'

She stared at him. 'But I go to the mill every day.'

'No, not this mill – Robert's mill, the cotton mill.' He was looking at her now, his eyes accusing, his voice hard and fluent. 'Thou went to see it for thyself. Robert asked thee.'

'But that was years ago!'

'Three years – to the day, near enough. In 1790. I worked it out.'

It still made no sense at all. What had that long ago visit to the mill to do with John, who had not even been born then? Hannah wondered fleetingly if Samuel had somehow lost his wits. 'I do not understand,' she said.

'No? Tell me then, what happened there that day?'

'I told thee at the time – all the things I saw. It was for that we did not go to Robert's house again. But thou knows that.'

'That's not what I mean. What else happened? Thou wert alone with Robert, I think. For a time . . .'

She had not forgotten, of course. But it had not

430

seemed of any importance afterwards, except to herself, that Robert should have kissed her and made it clear how much he loved her still. What she had seen that day had convinced her of the impossibility of ever reviving their love, as she had for a little while fooled herself that they might do. The kiss had become a minor incident, which she would have preferred to forget, except that — like everything that had ever happened between her and Robert — she had not been able to do so.

Samuel must have read something in her face, something that bore out his evident suspicions, though what precisely he suspected her of she still had no idea. Now, he bent and grasped her arm and said sharply, 'What happened between thee and Robert? I must know!'

She shook her head, annoyed with herself that her colour rose as it did. 'Nothing, nothing at all.' She tried to sound calm and matter of fact, but she knew that she only sounded faltering and flustered and painfully guilty. Besides, the flat denial only made it clear that she knew quite well what kind of happening he had in mind, and was anxious to protect herself from all suspicion. It was hardly the action of innocence or a clear conscience.

She could see from Samuel's expression that this was his view too. He stood looking gloomily down at her. 'Thou knows what I had in mind, I see,' he said. He swallowed hard, and then added, 'Robert says . . . He told me there is reason to believe John is his son.'

Embarrassment, anxiety, guilt all fled in a moment of shock and anger that took Hannah's breath away. She felt the colour drain from her face, but her mind seemed empty, numbed, filled only with an inarticulate horror. Then she thought, How could he think that? And the next moment knew that he did not think it, that it was only the latest manifestation of Robert's spite, against her or against Samuel, she was not sure which. She wondered even if Robert quite knew himself who he hated most, who he most wanted to hurt.

But whatever his reasons, he had aimed to hurt, and he had hit the target. She thought of Samuel, and the way he had looked at John tonight, when the child came for the kiss that was his right; and fury seized her. 'He lied, Samuel – it is not true, it could not be true! John is thy son, thine and mine.'

She could see that the vehemence of her response had some effect upon him, but that still he doubted her. 'Thou lied to me, when thou said nothing had happened.'

She felt ashamed now of the small lie that had made it possible for him to believe the greater one. She knew that now only the complete truth would do, so with bent head, feeling as guilty as if she had indeed done what Robert accused her of, she said, 'It was not nothing. He kissed me. That was before I saw the mill. Afterwards, I would not have allowed it.'

'Thou wert private with him then?' She guessed how much anguish lay behind the quiet words. It had taken a long time for Samuel to regain his trust in her after the first terrible betrayal. He would always be more ready to believe that she had failed in love and loyalty to him, simply because he did not, even now, quite believe that he was worthy of her love. It was a bitter irony that in one sense he was right, because however close she came to contentment with him it was still Robert who obsessed her, in spite of all she had done over the years to try and free herself of that obsession.

'For a time,' she admitted. 'In his office. But it was not for long.' She wished she could control her fluctuating and betraying colour. 'Samuel, I am not lying to thee. I have told thee all of it now. There has only ever been that one time we have been together, before I wed thee. I have been true to thee always since then. John could not be Robert's son, *could* not. He is thy son, in every way.'

Samuel frowned a little, and said doubtfully, 'I want to believe thee. But John is not like the others. He is not like me either, not at all.'

'No, he is like me. Except that he has thy sweet nature. One person he does not resemble in the least is Robert. Look at him, talk to him, hear him – how canst thou doubt that he is thy son, thy very own?'

Samuel was silent for a long time. That he wanted to believe her, she was sure, but close though he was to doing so he could not yet quite allow himself to take that final step. When he did speak at last, it was in a low voice, almost a whisper. 'But why – why should Robert say that, if he knew it to be untrue?'

It was the question she had already asked herself, to which she had no very satisfactory reply. 'I don't know. Unless – unless it is because he is jealous of thee.'

'Jealous of me!' Samuel stared at her in amazement. 'How could he possibly be jealous of me? What have I got that he hasn't?'

She tried not to smile at that. 'Children,' she said, after a moment's thought. 'He has none, and I think that will hurt his pride a little.' Samuel, clearly impressed by that argument, nodded slowly. 'Then,' Hannah went on, 'thou hast something more that he has not – the respect of thy fellows, even their admiration.'

'He has all his fine rich friends.'

'That is not the same. He is useful to them, and they are to him, but that is not friendship. Maybe some of them like him a little too, but that's not the same as respect – not such as thou hast. Then – then there's . . .'

'Thee. Yes, he would envy me that, I think. I thought he had ceased to love thee long since; but when I look at it, maybe he does still, in his own way.'

She could not repress a small tremor of pleasure at

the thought, but it was not a comfortable one, and she wished it had not come to her. 'I don't think Robert knows what it is to love,' she said drily, though even as she spoke she wondered if that was true; or indeed if she really wanted it to be true.

'Even if thou art right, and he is jealous of me,' Samuel pursued, 'I do not see what purpose it would serve, for me to think thee false to me.' Hannah realised that Samuel found it impossible to believe that anyone could do something purely from vindictiveness or a wish to hurt. It shamed her that she could understand so easily – but then, unlike Samuel, she did know what it was to feel that kind of anger and hurt, even if she did not often give way to it. That was, after all, the chief reason for her coming here to Thornside – to fight the man who had tried to destroy her marriage.

Samuel too must have been thinking of that far-off unhappy time, for he said thoughtfully, 'Dost think . . . Was that why he told me of . . . what had happened before we were wed? Because he was jealous?'

'Why else would he want to?'

'I thought he only wished me to know the truth. I thought he meant to deal honestly with me.'

'Oh Samuel!' Hannah shook her head. 'No wonder Robert can hurt thee so! Thou art too trusting and too innocent. Thou dost think all men behave as thou would.' She laid a hand caressingly over his. 'Don't trouble thyself about why or how – just believe that if Robert speaks ill of me, or hurts thee, then it is he that is at fault, not me nor thee. I have never wronged thee, not since I agreed to be thy wife. Thou must believe that, love.'

His fingers closed about hers, and his eyes looked steadily into her own. 'I do, Hannah. I promise thee.' But she knew all the same that he would always be incapable of certainty, about anything that concerned her feelings for him. It was something she must take into account in her dealings with him.

Hannah said nothing more to Samuel on the subject; there was, she thought, no more that could usefully be said by either of them. But that did not mean that she was able to put it from her mind. On the contrary, she could think of nothing else, and anger at what Robert had done kept her wakeful long after she had gone to bed and Samuel's quiet slow breathing told her he was deeply asleep.

Why – why had Robert done this to them? Why did he want so badly to destroy their carefully acquired happiness? Did he really hope to achieve anything by it – and, if so, what? That he had tried to do it before was no clue. She had understood then that his anger and hurt at her rejection of him might have driven him to hit out at her and Samuel – though that he should bide his time so as to make the disclosure when it would be sure to do the greatest possible hurt suggested an unusual degree of cruel calculation. But lately they had hardly met, and there had been nothing between them to make him angry or stir his jealousy to life; or nothing that she could see. What now could make him want to destroy the contentment of their marriage? Was the fact of that contentment, and the children born to them, explanation enough?

Whatever the reason, he had made the attempt, and by so doing suddenly forced himself once more to the forefront of her life, as he had done at intervals ever since she broke with him, as if to remind her that there was in the end no escape from him. How could she ever have believed there might be, however much she might have longed for it; or tried to tell herself that she did?

But this – this latest, cruellest attempt to hurt her and still more to hurt Samuel, angered her the more for the damage it might have done. Indeed, she could not be certain even now that there had not been some permanent damage done to the love between Samuel and his youngest son. She knew Samuel's self mistrust and self doubt only too well to underestimate its enduring power.

The rain ceased in the night – Hannah heard it fall away to a gentle sighing, before it stopped altogether – but in the stillness that followed the swift powerful rushing of the beck could clearly be heard. Next morning, even before she thought she could reasonably expect them, George Holgate and Abraham Wood and Sarah Dinsdale arrived to begin work at the mill, and Eli Johnson came soon afterwards. For all of them Thornside Feast was of no importance, against the coming of the rain and the possibility of normal work again. Within less than an hour the mill wheel was turning as if it had never ceased.

Hannah should have been delighted, her whole attention absorbed by the longed for return to normality. But she could not drive Robert out of her head, nor the intention she had formed in the long dreary hours of wakefulness. As soon as everyone was hard at work and she knew that there was nothing in particular that she could usefully do, she pulled a cloak about her against the wind and set out at a brisk pace along the lane.

The trees dripped overhead with the weight of last night's rain, but the ground beneath Hannah's feet was hard still, under a thin coating of dust that was scarcely wet enough even now to have turned to mud. Out on the highroad there was little to show for the rain at all, beyond a slight dampness. It would take more than a few hours drenching to soak the ground again so that the grass would grow. All the downpour had done was to fill the becks, with the usual suddenness of a storm. It was enough for the moment, and very likely more rain would come; but not today, Hannah thought. It was cooler, and there were more clouds than she could remember seeing for a long time, but the sharp wind kept them moving and dried the puddles to nothing.

She had almost reached the cotton mill when she

came to a momentary halt, struck by doubts that had not once troubled her until now. Indeed, she had never given any further thought to what she intended to do, since the moment when she had made her decision. It had seemed the only right course, and she had been driven simply by the need to put it into action. Now she asked herself what possible purpose it would serve for her to stride up to Newgill to confront Robert in a mood of righteous indignation. She had never been able to influence his behaviour before; there was no reason to think that she would be able to do so now. Better, surely, to pretend the incident had never happened, and let Robert think his malicious lies had missed their target after all. To go and confront him was to admit that she and Samuel had been hurt. It could surely only give him greater satisfaction than ever.

Common sense was not enough to make her turn round and go home. Fired by her anger, she had come this far, and that anger could not be calmed unless it found an outlet. It might do no good to tell Robert precisely what she thought of him, but she had to do it.

Newgill was working again too. She had heard the noise of machinery as she approached and now, as she climbed the stair to the office (trying not to think of the last time she had done so), the sound was overpowering. She reached the door at the top and raised her hand to hammer on it with all her force. And then she waited, breath held, heart beating fast, braced to confront him. Would he open the door to her, or simply call from inside in that voice whose resonance disturbed her so?

He did neither. After what seemed a long time, with all her senses strained, Hannah knocked again. Nothing. She tried again, but she knew with certainty that he was not there. With a profound sense of anticlimax and disappointment she turned and made her way slowly back down the stairs. He might be in the mill itself, she knew that; very likely he was. But she could not confront him there. She wanted to pour out her anger in private, and where he could hear every word, not in front of the watchful eyes of a hundred children where the machines drowned every sound. And somehow she could not bring herself to go and summon him to her, by gesturing from the doorway. She would have to be sensible after all, and walk quietly and meekly home again, without a word.

Half way back towards the road she saw a horseman turn off in the direction of the mill. She knew who it was at once, even before she was able to see him with any distinctness. There was still, in spite of everything, some impulse in her that responded instantly to the most distant hint of Robert's presence.

She stood still, not sure whether she was glad or sorry that they were to meet after all. Perhaps she was neither; perhaps she felt a little of each.

He was still some way off when he removed his hat. She could see his smile now, full of a comfortable self satisfaction that fired her to renewed fury. She made no attempt to return the smile. The expression that greeted his arrival was cold, even grim, full of unequivocal hostility.

'What an agreeable surprise, my dear sister!' The mockery in the tone was so slight that she wondered if indeed it was really there, or if she had simply imagined it. With one swift graceful movement – the response of her body acknowledged its power – he swung to the ground and stood beside her, and bowed briefly. 'What a good thing I decided to call in after all! You will come and take a glass of wine with me, I trust? Then you will be able to tell me to what precisely I owe this honour.'

She frowned slightly, not simply to mark her disapproval of him, but because in spite of everything the effect his nearness had on her was still at odds with everything she wanted to think and feel. 'We can talk quite well here, I thank thee,' she said stiffly.

'As you wish,' he said, with something approaching

her own coolness, though he was smiling still, rather as if he knew quite well how uncomfortable she was, and was rather enjoying the situation. He clearly intended to give her no help by questioning her further. He simply stood watching her, waiting for her to speak.

It was much more difficult than she had expected. It was not that her anger had evaporated, but it had certainly faded a little from its first fury, and was further tempered now by the confused sensations his presence aroused in her, though that only made her more angry with him, in a different way. In the end, she could only come straight to the point, though the voice that emerged was far less sure and more breathy and tremulous than she had intended. 'Why didst thou tell those lies to Samuel?'

'Lies?' he returned blandly. 'I recall no lies.'

'Don't play games with me! Thou knows full well John is not thy son, nor ever could be.'

'John? Is that the little boy's name? Very like you – and nothing like my brother. But that means nothing, of course. Who's to say who his father is?'

Hannah coloured furiously, all her confusion swept away in rage. 'Only one man could ever have been his father, and that is Samuel.'

He shrugged. 'If you say so.'

'Thou knows it. Thou knows there was never anything between us like that!'

'Ah, but there was. You cannot have forgotten Uncle Samuel's mill, and the sacks . . .'

She coloured still more. 'That was long ago. There has been nothing since, nothing at all.' She felt helpless against his imperviousness, the feelings (if there were any) masked by that blandly smiling face, the refusal to admit that he might be wronging her. 'I see what it is!' she burst out. 'Thou canst not get children of thine own – so thou must claim thy brother's!'

He went white. The smile vanished. 'You bitch!' She felt sure that he would have struck her if he had dared;

but that would have been to admit too clearly how much her words had hurt him. Besides, he was not the kind of man, even now, to forget himself so much as to strike a woman.

Success gave her courage and confidence. 'Be sure of one thing, Robert Gayle. Do anything ever again to hurt me or mine and thou wilt answer for it – and in such a way as shall make thee rue the day that we met.'

It was clear that the venom of her attack astonished him. It was a moment or two before he said, a little unsteadily, 'Well, well – where is the quiet, peaceable little Quakeress I used to know? What would they say at meeting, to hear you use such un-Christian language?' He gave a short laugh, which sounded almost nervous.

'I am not at meeting; I am talking to thee. And I warn thee to take note, for thy own good. Thou knows I never speak lightly.'

He had himself under control again, enough to perform a deep bow, accompanied by a flourishing gesture of the hand that held his hat. 'I take note, fair Hannah.' But she knew that for all the assurance of the words, he was more affected by what she had said than he would allow her to see.

It was with a strong sense of satisfaction that she gave him a last cold and haughty glance and turned quickly round and walked away from him, towards the road and home. She might not have achieved anything very much by her words to Robert, but she felt much better for having delivered them. It was even possible that he might indeed think twice in future before hurting her or Samuel again.

iv

'Samuel . . .?' Sleepily Hannah reached out a hand, but met only emptiness. The sheets beside her were still warm, but Samuel was no longer lying in them. Some sense of his absence must have caused her to wake. She turned her head and opened her eyes. It was night still.

The room was in darkness, though where Samuel stood by the window there was some kind of light against which his figure was blackly outlined. The dawn was not far off then, a glowing dawn, red gold . . .

But the dawn light should be grey and colourless. This must be sunrise; except that it was too dark still for sunrise. Hannah sat up.

'Samuel, what art thou doing there?'

'Come and see.'

She slid out of the bed and went to join him. As she came near, he put his arm about her. 'There, see. It woke me.'

It *was* still night, and the dawn must be many hours away. The eastern sky was untouched with light, in the distance at least. This light was near at hand, just beyond the screening trees, down the road about half-way to the river. The branches showed black against it, tossed by the wind against the dramatic fiery backdrop of leaping red and gold . . .

Fiery; for it was a fire, a great wild conflagration fanned and fed by the wind that had so swiftly dried up all traces of the long awaited rain. Then Hannah realised where it was. 'Sam! It's Robert's mill, it must be!'

Samuel's grasp tightened. 'Aye.'

Robert's mill, where she had been only this morning, near which she had stood and warned Robert to leave them alone. And now it burned with a ferocity as great as her anger, and the revenge she had threatened, almost as if the force of her words had set it alight.

She shivered. That was pure superstition, the kind of nonsense that should have no place in her thoughts, ever. Yet she stood there watching in horror and could not shake off the thought that in some way her anger and her will had taken shape in those wildly leaping flames.

'Robert may not know. He will have been at home, I'd guess. Dost think we should send to him?' Samuel's

441

words made their way only slowly through the fog of Hannah's thoughts. She heard him say next, 'They'll have sent for him, maybe. But they'll need help. I shall go, I think . . .'

And then in an instant one thought only shot into Hannah's mind. She turned and clutched Samuel's arm. 'The children! All those children! Oh, thou art right – we must go at once!' How could she have wasted a moment on her own self indulgent reflections, when that agonising reality demanded all her attention? She would lose no more time on such things.

They dressed, woke Agnes to tell her where they were going and why, and hurried together out into the night. There was no need of a light. Even in the lane under the trees the red glow of the fire reached to show the way. Out on the road the light was intense, with an eerie, evil clarity that was almost like daylight and yet was not. Others had been woken by it too, for the road was busy with people hurrying down from Thornside towards Newgill.

They saw, long before they reached it, that the whole mill building was well alight, though not yet, not quite, the apprentice house beside it. 'Cotton waste fair flares up,' said Kit Dinsdale, coming up with them just as they turned into the mill road. 'And with all so dry . . .'

Noise and heat engulfed them well before they reached the mill, a chaos of roaring and crackling, the crash of falling timbers, men shouting and running, and the horrible, searing sound of children screaming and crying. Hannah heard someone cry out close by, and only realised when Samuel took her hand and looked at her anxiously that it was she who had done so.

Someone – Henry Birley, perhaps, but he was so blackened with smoke that he was scarcely recognisable – was organising a chain of men and women and children, anyone to hand, anyone willing, to carry buckets of water from the beck. But it seemed a hopeless enterprise, doomed to failure against the power of the fire.

Hannah went and clasped his arm. 'The children, in there!' She pointed to the apprentice house. 'Are they safe?'

'God knows!' the man shouted above the din. 'Someone went to see.' He glanced round him. 'Is Mr Gayle here yet?' She knew he meant Robert; they must have sent for him then. But she could see no sign of him, and did not waste time in looking further. The fire had already reached the corner where mill and apprentice house met.

The outer door of the apprentice house stood open, but Hannah knew before she reached it that there were children trapped in there, for she could hear them, shouting and banging. There was no sign that anyone had come to help them – and they would need help, for she remembered now that the dormitory doors were kept locked. She ran up the stairs to the boys' room and rattled the handle, uselessly. She looked round in anguish, and saw Samuel there, just behind her. 'It's locked! I'll go for a key.'

'I'll get something to break it down, in case it comes to that.' He disappeared, and Hannah ran back to Henry Birley, who brushed her away with, 'Keys! With all this going on! Get out of my way, woman!' She wasted no time – yet how much time had passed already! – but hurried to the apprentice house, reaching it just as a great rush of noise and heat and scattered burning fragments engulfed the end of it. Hannah felt the fire scorch her, singe her hair. But she did not pause. She picked up a large stone and ran up to the first locked door and banged and banged on it, in the desperate hope that she might weaken it, that it might suddenly give away. But it was solid, a good door to keep out intruders, to prevent escape. To her relief, Samuel reappeared, carrying an axe. He put his head to the door. 'Stand back!' he shouted, in case any child should be too near, and then he swung the axe above his head.

How long it took they did not know, but it seemed hours before the door fell inwards, and a rush of children scrambling and shrieking poured towards them, just in time before a sheet of flame shot with a great explosion of sound across the dormitory.

'The girls, upstairs!' Hannah shouted.

'Get the boys out – I'll go up,' Samuel said. For a moment Hannah hesitated. Then she saw how the weaker and smaller children were stumbling, trampled by the larger ones, and she turned to take charge and direct them to safety as best she could, leaving Samuel to run, axe in hand, up the further stair.

'How many are there of you all?' she shouted to one boy as she descended, with a very small and frightened child sobbing in her arms.

The boy shook his head. She had no means of knowing, then, if she had all of them safe; she could only hope. She gave her charge into the care of a calm-looking boy and turned to go and check for any others. And then she stopped. The fire had reached the stairs.

'Samuel!' she screamed. The ground floor was well ablaze, the first floor following fast; in a moment the second floor would go too. And how in any case could Samuel get out, with only the burning stairs and the high barred windows to offer an escape? She stood where she was, staring at the flames, numb and horror struck. Then she thought: 'Water – I must get water, for the stairs.' She hurried the children with her, to safety and the care of some of the Thornside women, eager to help. She called three of the older boys, unhurt and excited, to come with her for water. But there were no buckets unused, and Henry Birley would not let her take any. 'We need them for the mill. We might save something yet.' She supposed he meant the machines, though how he could think that anything would have emerged unscathed from the inferno within the shell of the building she did not know. And what did machines matter, against children's lives, and Samuel's?

Hannah ran back in agony towards the apprentice house. The fire had reached the roof, at the mill end at least, and the window spaces glowed fiercely in the blackened walls. A man came towards her: Robert, she saw, without any emotion except hope, for Samuel's sake.

She caught his arm. 'Robert, Samuel's in there! Make them bring water – please!'

To her relief he asked no questions, but ran himself to bring a bucket, and direct others to do the same. And just as they reached the burning stairway, a black figure staggered out through the flames.

'Samuel!' Hannah ran to him. She would not have known him, if she had not seen him go in. Hair and skin and clothes were blackened and charred. He held a child in his arms, a small girl as burned and blackened as he was, screaming with fear and pain. Someone took the child, and Samuel collapsed into Hannah's arms.

v

'Mr Gayle!' Robert, his hand on the door of Thomas Bell's workshop, turned impatiently to see a prosperous looking gentleman, whom he knew slightly by sight but could not name, stepping eagerly towards him. Robert knew what was coming even before he spoke again.

'What news of your brother?'

Damn Samuel! It was Robert whose livelihood had gone up in flames that night, and who had somehow to start again from nothing. Yet it was Samuel who had all the sympathy. No one ever asked how Robert was doing now, or offered help or showed concern. But he knew better than to let his feelings show. He forced a pleasant smile. 'Only good news, I am glad to say. He is out of danger and well on the way to a full recovery.' He took care to speak authoritatively, in the manner of a man with the latest information at his fingertips. It would never do for anyone to suspect that he depended on hearsay as much as any of them, or that he had not once called on his brother since the fire. He knew he could not expect them to understand (or to care) how incessantly busy he had been, first with the unpleasant, and unexpectedly difficult, matter of raising finance, and then with the wearisome and depressing task of setting the rebuilding in motion. Samuel, so he had heard, was nearly better; it would take months at the very least before Newgill was working again. And he had planned to install steam power this winter! If anyone had told him he would instead be starting all over again, he would not have believed them.

'Thank God for that!' said the man. 'It would have been a tragedy if such a brave action had cost him his life. You must be very proud of him.'

Robert smiled and bowed and was relieved that the man seemed satisfied with that and went on his way. Far too many people wanted to go over and over the incident with him, until he was almost tempted to tell them how heartily sick of it all he was.

Even Thomas Bell wasted valuable time inquiring after Samuel, before Robert was able to move him on to the important business of discussing the new machines he wanted built, on the pattern of the old. By the time he left the workshop and mounted his horse and turned its head towards Newgill, Robert was in a thoroughly gloomy mood. He would have to call at the mill this morning, to check that the builders had started work as instructed; but it gave him no pleasure to go there, not as it once had done. Most of the stonework was still standing, but it was unsafe in places and blackened and stank of smoke, a smell he thought he would never again be able to clear from his nostrils; and the horrible debris of what had once been the most prosperous enterprise in the dale had only just been cleared away in the last few days. After that, it would be home, to the elegant house he could scarcely afford to maintain any longer, and his constantly miserable wife, moping for the child she had proved incapable of bearing, useless woman that she was.

Just out of Thornside he met Hannah, driving up the hill with the cart piled high with yarn. She looked preoccupied, even harassed, and did not appear to see him until he had almost come up to her. Then she looked up, startled, and coloured in that gratifying way of hers. Robert felt better at once.

'Hannah! What an unexpected pleasure!' He removed his hat and bowed from the waist. 'I thought you were still tied to the sickbed.'

She reined in the pony and brought the cart to a halt, but she did not smile. Her face had the prim, rather shut in look which he knew meant she was trying very hard to hide the agitation of her feelings. 'Fortunately, Samuel no longer needs constant nursing. In fact he hopes to step outside this afternoon, if the rain holds off.'

'Ah yes, who would have thought a month ago that we could grow tired of rain?' She shot him a look which seemed to imply contempt for the triviality of the remark, so he said quickly, 'But I am gratified to hear Samuel is so well recovered.'

'Thou wouldst know it for thyself, if thou hadst troubled to call,' Hannah retorted sharply.

He felt angry at the accusation, resentful of the injustice of it. 'You have not called to ask after me,' he returned.

She stared at him, as if she had no idea what he meant. 'Thy life was not in danger, that I heard.'

'More than fifty children died in that fire,' he reminded her, and at once saw her expression soften.

'Aye,' she said quietly. 'Aye, I know. That has been the worst thing for Samuel, to think of those he did not save. It must be harder still for thee, to feel thyself responsible —'

'Responsible! For their deaths? It was hardly my

doing! You must know yourself how quickly a fire can start with spinning machines.'

'But if they had not been locked in —'

'Was it my fault that some fool lost the keys? What I regret is that I wasn't there at the start, to take charge. Maybe then I'd not have lost everything. Someone must have been careless, to let it take hold at all. But then you can't trust anyone. If you want something done, do it yourself. It's good advice.' He felt impatient suddenly, anxious to be on his way. Instinct told him he would get nowhere with Hannah today. So he bowed again and said a curt goodbye and rode on.

Hannah was relieved that he had gone. She had far too much to do to waste time with Robert. Samuel's illness had kept her by his side just at the time when at last the mill was producing good quantities of yarn again. She was only now free to make the deliveries to knitters and weavers that were so urgently needed, and even that would be a long business, for everyone would be full of questions about Samuel. She did not resent that exactly, for she too was proud of his courage, and she too had feared a far more tragic outcome; but it all took time, when she had no time to spare.

It was well into the afternoon when she returned home at last, the deliveries made. She realised at once that Samuel had yet another visitor, even before Agnes told her, for there was a strange horse tethered by the back door. She went upstairs, pausing outside the bedroom to listen to Samuel giving his usual modest account of the events of that night.

'It looked bad from outside, I'm told, but the stairs hadn't caught – they were stone stairs, thou knows. It was only the door that burned. That was the worst thing, but soon passed. I didn't give it a thought, not until afterwards. I wanted only to be out of it.' Hannah knew quite well it could not have been so simple. She knew too how often Samuel cried out at night as he relived that terrible time in his dreams. She knew how the thought of the children who had perished haunted him. But in daylight he said little, even to her, of what he had been through.

Hannah opened the door quietly. Ambrose Whaley, seeing her, soon took his leave. She would have pressed him to stay, except that Samuel's eyes pleaded with her to rescue him. She knew how it wearied him to go endlessly over it all, time and time again. He looked tired now, his face a little grey except where the burn scar on his cheek showed red.

'Maybe thou'd best stay in today. Tomorrow will be soon enough to go out, if it's fine.'

Samuel smiled and shook his head, reaching up to take her hand in his. 'I've waited all day for this. I'll not give it up now. Besides, it'll likely rain again tomorrow.' He spoke so firmly that she was convinced.

All the same it took a long time for him to negotiate the stairs, even leaning on Hannah's arm. In the hall Agnes came to meet them, offering her arm on his other side, and the children skipped about him, until Hannah sent them to play in the wood, well away from their father. He loved them, and he was much better, but there were limits.

Agnes had set a chair ready in a sheltered corner by the mill, where Samuel had a good view of the trees across the yard and along the lane, in all the loveliness of their autumn colours. The two women installed him there, well wrapped in rugs, and then Agnes went to see to the children, leaving Hannah and Samuel alone.

They were quiet for some time. Hannah watched Samuel, seeing how serene he looked, but frail too, more frail than he had seemed indoors. Somehow the stronger light only emphasised the haggard lines of his face and drew attention to the scars, not only on his face but on his hands too, as they lay unmoving on the thick folds of the rug. It was a moment or two before he

449

realised she was watching him, and then he caught her eye and smiled cheerfully.

'It's good to be about again. Give it a day or two and I'll be running down those stairs.'

She stroked his cheek, but said nothing.

'Hast seen anything of Robert since ...?' he asked after a moment, with a hesitancy that faltered into silence.

'Today. For the first time.'

'What has become of the children – the other children – dost thou know?'

'He did not say. But I heard some had gone to other mills, and some had gone back where they came from. A few stayed, I think.'

'Then he means to open the mill again?'

'The work's started already. But he'll not want the feeding of the children when there's no work for them – not after doing it all summer.'

Samuel was silent again, gazing thoughtfully towards the lane. After a while he said suddenly, 'Someone's coming.'

'Another well wisher,' Hannah commented without enthusiasm. She knew that Samuel had been touched and delighted by the extent of everyone's concern, but even he had begun to weary of it by now.

But there was nothing they could do, except wait patiently for the man to come fully into view, emerging from the lane: a big red-headed man.

'One of thy botanical friends, I suppose,' said Hannah.

Samuel shook his head. 'I don't know him.' Then he added, 'He wears a plaid – a shepherd?'

'A drover.' Hannah thought perhaps she had seen him before, with his cattle on the drove road, but she could not be sure. There had been so many drovers over the years, greeted in passing, and always with the thought of her unknown father uppermost in her mind.

The man came towards them, purposefully at first, then faltering a little as he saw Samuel. Hannah went to meet him.

'Hannah Gayle?' She nodded. 'Ye asked a question of me many years back.' She looked puzzled. 'If I knew of a Hector MacDonald.'

Hannah caught her breath, but could say nothing, only nod again and wait. 'To tell the truth, it had clear gone out of my mind. Then just the other day, at Appletreewick Fair, I met up with two fellows I'd not seen in years ...' He paused, studying her face; then he went on, 'We got into talk together. There was one of them a Highlander, touchy the way Highlanders are. We were joking. I said "Ye know the Highlander – smile in your face, stab you in the back." He took it badly, and we near came to blows, but that's not the point. He had a string of tales about Highlanders he'd known, heroes all. The other fellow matched them with tales of his own, to prove the opposite. It was then they fell to arguing who it was had done such and such a thing – I don't rightly mind what it was now, only that one said it was Hector MacDonald did it, the other not. In the end, they agreed it was some man else. But I caught the name, and I remembered, just like that. So I asked. They'd neither of them known him – before their time, they said, and they'd no knowledge of him now, what had become of him. But they'd heard tell he was from Moidart, from some wee place called Achnagar, they said; they couldn't be sure. But I thought I'd call here on my way home, and let ye know what I'd heard.'

Hannah swallowed hard, and then said carefully, 'I thank thee for thy trouble. Wilt thou take supper with us?'

He smiled and shook his head. 'Thank ye kindly, missis, but I'll be on my way. I've a few miles to cover yet tonight. I'll bid ye good day.'

She stood where she was, watching him go, feeling

451

dazed and more than a little strange. Then Samuel spoke suddenly behind her. 'I heard that, Hannah.'

She turned and went to him. What did it matter, after all? It took her no further forward; and besides it was Samuel who was important, and Agnes and the children and their lives here at Thornside. The man whose chance passion had given her life was of no importance to her any more. 'It was kind of him to remember,' she said casually. 'I had forgotten it myself. It was so long ago.' Then she asked, 'Art thou ready to go in again now?'

CHAPTER NINETEEN

i

It was late June, and sheep clipping was over, and Hannah had done the rounds of the nearby farms and selected the fleeces that met her needs, agreeing what seemed a fair price with the farmers. Now, daily, the carts brought the wool to the mill, coming to rest below the first floor entrance, where two of the workers waited to catch the wrapped fleeces thrown up from the yard and pass them to others behind for sorting.

Hannah herself did most of the sorting, separating long staple from short, while her hands grew grimed and oily from the wool, and soft creamy particles covered her steadily from head to foot like dirty snowflakes. She was glad – as they all were – when the midday break came and they could make their way to the kitchen to sit down with the family and eat the meal Agnes had prepared.

She felt exhausted, with none of the sense of excitement she had experienced in previous years at this time, knowing that the coming of the fleeces to the mill assured her and many others of another year of work, of shelter and food and clothing. What was wrong with her? Had all the difficulties of the last year made her too anxious about the future to find pleasure any more in her small but useful enterprise? She did not think it was that, for she was not conscious of worrying very much about anything. Perhaps it was simply that she was no longer as young as she used to be, and tiredness came more easily. But she was only just thirty; compared to Agnes, who never seemed to tire, she was just a girl. Besides, beneath her weariness there was a curious kind of sensation fizzing away, as if a fierce hidden energy lay scarcely suppressed, waiting for the moment to explode. She did not want rest and quiet; she did not want the tranquillity of the family circle, the quiet companionship of Samuel, nor even the livelier dependency of the children. She wanted to run from them all, to break free, to be alone, with no demands upon her at all, in a glorious irresponsibility.

The talk around the table came and went in her consciousness, stirring no interest.

'. . . I've heard Miles Pickering's mill's better than it used to be.'

'But doing badly, they say.'

'It would. Cotton's not a trade for the Dales.'

'Newgill's doing all right – would have been doing even better, if it wasn't for the fire.'

'Hast heard, Samuel – thy brother's calling a meeting to set up a militia.'

'Whatever for?'

'Defend us against the French, I suppose.'

'But we're miles from France.'

'They've just beaten the Allies, over in Belgium. It was in the papers yesterday. Only a matter of time before they overrun Belgium, it's said.'

'Robert Gayle just wants to show how far he's gone from Friends' testimonies,' put in Agnes, a little sharply. 'Setting up a toy army's the best way he knows.'

Hannah was mildly surprised that Agnes could speak so disapprovingly – and perceptively – of Robert; once she had seemed blind to his faults, as they had all been of course. But though her attention had been briefly caught, Hannah said nothing. That would have required too much effort, and a greater interest than she felt. When they went on to talk instead of trade, and the weather, and then (once Samuel's enthusiasm had been fired) of plants, she felt like screaming. It was agony to sit still, to listen, to keep calm and quiet, even more of an agony than the restrained activity that soon caught her up again, back in the mill once the meal was over.

That night, lying awake in bed, she tried to make herself see how blessed she was. She had Agnes and Samuel and three healthy, beloved children; she had a comfortable home, a prospering business, an income sufficient for her own wants, with a little left over in case of need, whether their own or a neighbour's. She had useful work to do and a secure future, and all this in spite of a life that had begun in the most difficult circumstances. True, there was a side of her nature that Agnes could neither know about nor understand. True, Samuel was not a passionate man, and aroused no passion in her, and since the fire had become quieter and more reserved than ever. True, there were times when the ties of motherhood became burdensome, the demands of her work an intrusion. But she supposed that no life – even the happiest – was without its more difficult times. She had no right to expect that she alone should be spared the common lot of humanity.

She wanted to be grateful and satisfied, but she was not. All this, all that I have, is not enough, she thought. She remembered suddenly what Robert had said to her on the day of that memorable visit to Newgill, when her thoughts were full of the dreadful scenes she had witnessed: 'Why else did God give you the voice you have, if not to use it?' She had brushed the words aside, as those not of God but of the Devil. Now she wondered if perhaps Robert had been right after all. Was that what was wrong with her – that a part of her, some wild inexplicable, creative side, given to her to be used to God's glory, was daily being ignored and crushed in the practical routine of her life? Surely that was nonsense. Other people gave up such things, all the time, amongst Friends in particular, and they did so without a constant struggle to accept what must be, what was so clearly right. In youth, perhaps, men like John Woolman had found the struggle hard and often failed, but in the end, in maturity, they had found serenity and a sense of purpose. Why should she be any different? What was wrong with her that she found it so hard, that she should fall again and again into this mood of passionate rebellion?

'I *hate* myself!' she thought as, all outward obedience, she rose at dawn and dressed, ready to go to her daily work at the mill. 'Mary Harker was right – I have bad blood in me. What else could make me as I am? A true daughter of Agnes and John Burton would not have turned out like this.' She could not blame it on her natural mother, either. She was quite sure that Christian Lambert, given the blessings her daughter had, would have accepted them with humble gratitude. No, she must owe all her angry rebelliousness to the wild Highland blood of her lost father. They said Highlanders were a primitive and unreliable people.

It was a beautiful morning already, even before the sun had risen. The light was clear, the air fresh, a little breeze brought sweetness from the moors. Hannah ached to walk on past the mill, along the lane, up onto the fell. But she did not do it, of course; or not then. Later, there was a little lull. All the day's fleeces had been delivered and sorted; the carding machine was working under the now expert supervision of Amos; Eli was contentedly at his combing, George controlling the worsted spinning; Sarah downstairs with the jenny. Hannah could have found something useful to do without too much difficulty, but she did not try. She seized her chance and slipped unnoticed from the mill and set out almost at a run along the lane.

By now the sun was high in a sky of burning blue over which tiny clouds raced, driven by a brisk wind. On the drove road crossing Thornside common the wind was no longer merely brisk but fierce and cold and uncompromising. It pleased her, for she could push forward against it, forcing her pace to an energetic speed, feeling her face glow. Her cap blew off, and she did not replace it but carried it in her hand, shaking her head to loosen the last heavy strands of her hair until it was lifted and fingered by the wind, blown behind her in a great cloudy mass. She held her head high and laughed; and then she began, defiantly, to sing.

It gave her a wonderful exhilarating sense of release, to let her voice flow out in all the fullness of its power, allowing it to rise and fall where it would, to follow this melody or that, repeat a line she liked, embellish a simple phrase with trills. Sometimes her voice found a familiar tune, sometimes one she might have heard but could not be sure, sometimes it made patterns of its own, running, like her feet, along unknown paths on a journey of discovery, which might equally well bring disappointment or delight, but was worth while simply for the excitement felt along the way.

All her troubling thoughts took flight. She felt strong, alive, happy. 'I am myself,' she thought: 'I am free.' She made no conscious choice which way to go. She left her feet free, like her voice, to find their own path. She met no one, saw no one even in the distance. The moors were empty. She was alone with the wind and the curlews and the larks and her own liberated voice. Alone, that is, until a thudding of hooves behind her, not heard until it was almost on her, made her turn sharply, her voice abruptly silenced. She made a self conscious move to replace her cap; and then saw who it was, dismounting there just a yard or two away from her, like a living embodiment of her mood. She saw too the look in his eyes, and the way they lingered on her flushed face and wild hair, and she had no time and no room for any other thought or sensation but a sudden flaming of the senses, a thudding of the heart, a drumming of blood in her ears, a melting away of all power in her limbs.

'Hannah —' His voice was hoarse, as if for once he too had lost all control of his feelings. He came to her, hands outstretched, and without a moment's hesitation she laid hers in them. To do so seemed the most natural, inevitable thing in the world. 'I could not believe it was you I saw, singing like a wild thing. But I knew it must be. This is how you should always be, always.'

She smiled at him, breathing fast. 'What brings thee this way?' The words meant nothing; or, rather, their meaning, beneath the apparent triviality, lay in the softness of her voice, and the things she did not say which Robert could read clearly enough in her eyes.

'You, of course,' he said, and then gave a little laugh. 'No, that was not why I came. But I must have known, somehow. It seemed only that I had to get away, at once, before it all drove me insane.'

'I too,' said Hannah. She could not speak in more than a whisper, breathless as she was.

'You see – it is as I've always said: we are two of a kind. Why else should we meet like this, quite by chance, because at the same moment we felt a need to escape from the imprisonment of our daily lives? Our spirits colluded, if our bodies and minds did not.' He must have felt how moved she was, or perhaps it was simply, as he said, that he shared her feelings so completely that she had no sooner to think or feel than he was there, at one with her. When he spoke next he seemed to be using the exact, anguished words that might have been wrung from her. 'Oh, Hannah, why are you not mine? It was never meant to be like this!'

She could not even think of an answer to that now, nor did she want to. At this moment it seemed inexplicable; or rather, not inexplicable, but untrue. For she was his. Deny it as she would, as she had tried for so long to do, she could not escape the inescapable. He was in her blood, a part of her as she of him. It was that single inevitable fact that explained everything: why she had come here today, why she had let him take her hands, why she could never be at peace with Samuel. Why, the next moment, she felt a profound sense of relief and rightness as he pulled her near, never taking his eyes from her face. She saw that they looked very black, deep and dark and soft, with none of the bright mockery she knew too well. These were the eyes of the boy who had kissed her long ago in the byre at Low Farm, while the candlelight glimmered on the mirror that had shown her what he had seen. Her Robert, hers, as she was his, complete only in him.

'Hannah, you should have married me. I know now. All I have, all I want – they are nothing. If I could have had you, they would not have mattered to me at all. I would give them all up now, every one of them, if it could bring you back to me.' He paused, and his hands moved up her arms to hold her closer still. 'I wish I could live my life again. I would not let you go a second time.'

'You would give up your cotton mill?' she asked wonderingly.

'I don't know . . . I don't know. I only know it would not be like this, a second time.'

'We have no second time,' she reminded him sadly.

'No. Yet . . .' He broke off; and then, slowly, carefully, he bent his head and brought his mouth down on hers. She reached up to draw him nearer, knowing as his arms closed about her that she was once again where she was always meant to be. This time she would not struggle against it.

After a moment, a long entrancing heart-stopping moment, Robert drew back a little and said in a soft breathless voice, 'Can we not find somewhere else? It's too open here.'

About fifty yards away the land sloped down into a little hidden valley, so small it was more of a hollow, edged with a windblown thorn tree. With the same sure instinct they both looked towards it, then at one another, and then began to hurry – neither walking nor running, stumbling a little – across the tussocky grass.

The valley was open to the sun but sheltered from

the wind, a place of warmth and golden light. On its edge Hannah paused – she did not quite know why – but Robert, halting too, tugged at her hand. 'Come!'

She had no power to resist, nor did she wish to. It was as inevitable as everything else that had happened here today, like a dream in which some power beyond her control directed and ruled her, though whether from inside or outside herself she did not know. She knew only that her whole being, all her senses, all her instincts, were centred on Robert, in a universe in which he alone was real. She went with him and they fell together on to the bank where they were hidden from all but the larks way above them; and there her wild spirit found peace and completion at his coming, while the horse grazed quietly and the wind bent the grasses, and far off a drover sang as he rode behind his lumbering herd.

Hannah had wanted him. She had felt no hesitation and no doubt. Her hunger had been satisfied. Yet into the languid contentment of satisfied desire flowed not happiness but a horrible turmoil of emotions. It was like waking from a blissful dream to find that reality had become a living nightmare. Shame, dismay, even a kind of grief, clawed at her; and fear – fear that she would indeed bear Robert's child; fear that Robert would tell Samuel what had happened today. Most of all she felt a deep hopelessness, because it was Robert her body craved, and without him it would never find peace; yet with him no other part of her would know any peace at all, ever again. She was torn in two, racked by guilt, tormented by a passionate regret. Bad as it had been before, it had not been so bad as this.

She scrambled to her feet and stood looking down at Robert. The mockery had returned to his face, or at least some kind of gently ironic amusement. He lay relaxed on the ground with one arm crooked beneath his head, his eyes brightly returning her gaze, careless and contented.

'Well, Hannah – you've given in at last. It had to come, you know. We both wanted it.' Perhaps the new grimness in her face warned him she needed convincing, for he rose then and put his arms about her, holding her loosely, yet near, though she made no move to respond to the embrace. She bent her head and would not look at him. 'Don't deny it any more. I am not asking you to leave Samuel. Nor shall I leave my wife. God knows,' he added ruefully, 'I couldn't afford that. But that need not stop us meeting – up here, in my office at the mill, anywhere you choose. There are a thousand secret places. No one need ever know. If you bear me a child – well, that will be our secret too. Any likeness to me would be a matter of family resemblance, to anyone who saw it. Samuel will never know, never – because only you and I will know of it, and I shall never tell. I give you my word on that, Hannah. I would swear a most solemn oath, if I thought that would make you understand how completely you can trust me.'

Hannah looked up and saw that Robert was entirely serious. The sparkle had gone from his eyes again, giving his expression an unusual gravity. 'Thou knows thy word is enough,' she said mechanically, though even now something warned her that to trust Robert was complete foolishness.

'So you see,' he went on, 'we'll all be happy. You and me, because we have one another. Samuel, because he has you and the children. Harriet, because she has me. No one will be any the wiser – and you and I will be the better spouses because we are happy.'

Oh, she was tempted! It sounded so simple, so reasonable, so perfectly in tune with all she felt. This, the one thing that was missing from her life – its absence, surely, the cause of all her restlessness – to have this too would be to find completeness. Samuel, her friend and companion; the children; and Robert: wholeness at last. Standing here with Robert's arms about her, it did not feel wrong. On the contrary, it felt absolutely right, the solution to everything. How could she deny him, and so deny herself?

Yet . . . She felt his hand press against her mouth.

'Say nothing, Hannah. Not now. You'll be riding this way soon, won't you – to make your deliveries? I'll watch for you. I'll see when you go, and meet you on the way, by chance as it were. There will be no need for plans, or explanations, or lies. We should avoid them at all costs. Much the best that way – it avoids awkwardness, and makes discovery much less likely. Now . . .' In a kind of daze she saw him bend down and retrieve her cap from the ground. 'Let's make you look all good and Quakerly again. You can go meekly back to Samuel and he will think only that you have been out to take the air.'

She allowed him to push her hair back beneath the cap and then to lead her to where his horse grazed quietly beside the road, and there he held her and kissed her once more, and then stood watching, saying nothing, as she walked away. She felt the warmth of his mouth as if it was still on hers all the way down the hill.

She had left the mill this morning in a mood of restlessness and confusion; she was going home in a state of turmoil far worse than anything she had felt before. Yet for that one moment as she fell into Robert's arms it had seemed as if everything was about to be resolved, for ever. Now, though her body still felt heavy with contentment, though some restless part of her had been stilled, yet in satisfying that she had stirred some other, hitherto quiescent part of herself into painful life. How could she be at one and the same time so contented and so thoroughly discontented, so fulfilled and yet so ashamed, so much at peace and yet so troubled?

And at the end of it all there would be Samuel – dear, loving Samuel, her friend, whom at last in truth she had betrayed, just when she had thought she was safe from

462

any danger of it. She felt that she had taken a single, irrevocable step across some great gulf, to a far lonely place from which there was now no returning to the warmth and sweetness and safety of what she had left behind, which until now had seemed so stifling. She had escaped, but it was a sense of imprisonment rather than of release that filled her now – the imprisonment of the exile, the criminal judged unfit any longer for decent society, transported to a desolate land open to the bleakest winds, the bitter cold of judgement, where she was free but not free, because there was no going back. Alone, isolated as the drover on his long journey – except that he had a dog and a herd for company. What had she? Robert? It was Samuel who was her chosen companion, not Robert who could answer no need for friendship in her; and she had taken the step to Robert's side that must cut her off from Samuel for ever.

She told herself this was all foolishness, a superstitious fancy. No step in life was wholly irrevocable. There was always the hope of forgiveness and reconciliation, which would allow her to take a step back into something approaching the innocence of the past, and start again, with new hope and new strength. She could not tell Samuel what had happened today – the very thought of how crushed he would be to know of it made her shudder – but that did not mean she had to do what Robert wanted, to meet him and to yield to him again. Nothing could compel her to agree to what he had put before her up there on the fell, even though at the time all her senses had responded to what he offered with a jubilant affirmation.

How could she have done what she had done today? It was not simply her betrayal of Samuel that shamed her; it was also the thought that – in spite of all she knew of him, with her eyes opened by long experience – she should so readily have given herself to Samuel's brother. This was the man who used children worse

463

than animals, who when they burned had thought more of his lost livelihood than the sad young lives destroyed; who could boast of his part in the slave trade, who would charm and wheedle and threaten to get what he wanted, with no second thought for those he hurt on the way, who saw the making of money as the only worthwhile end of life. Sometimes she had thought she hated him. Hate – like adultery – was a thing of darkness, alien to those who walked in the light; yet it was surely a more healthy, more acceptable response to what Robert was than the persistent, ineradicable passion that had drawn her to him. How could she love such a man? Surely indeed she did not love him, unless it was possible to love someone neither liked nor respected.

No, for that was not love but desire, the most basic animal impulse that should have no place in her life unless it was transformed by love. Better the passionless emotions – friendship and respect and tenderness and companionship – that linked her to Samuel, than this lust for a man who had done so much to harm her and Samuel and all those she loved. It ought not to be beyond her power to drive so dark and ugly a passion from her life. Indeed, she had thought she had done so, all but the last lingering traces; only for this to happen.

I was wrong, I was weak, I sinned, she thought; and I am most deeply sorry. But it is over. It will not happen again, as long as I live.

But what if Robert does indeed come to find me, as I take the yarn over the moors – what then? Will it indeed be over? Or shall I fall again, as easily as a ripe apple from the tree?

No, no! Next time I shall be ready for him, armed against his attack. I shall not allow that strange mood to take hold of me again, to weaken my resistance. I shall be obedient Hannah Gayle, going about her lawful business, prepared to deal firmly with anyone inclined to take liberties – in particular an undesirable like Robert Gayle.

But how can I be sure I won't suffer that mood again, or something like it? How can I be sure that what he offers – secret meetings without fear of discovery, all the sweetness of bodily fulfilment, while yet remaining Samuel's loving wife – will not prove too great a temptation, too easy, too safe in the little, occasional, short lived escape it offers? Enough perhaps to make me content for ever with the unexciting routine of life with Samuel ... If only that were possible, without guilt, or fear, or subterfuge. Perhaps indeed it was. Unless she tried it she would never know ...

There, just at the point where the lane turned off the road towards the mill, she came to a halt and gave a little moan and pressed her hands to her face. 'Oh, what shall I do? What shall I do?'

She knew what she ought to do. It was clear and uncompromising, the true path; and it led by a swift and direct route right away from Robert.

But if she did not take that path, might she not be happier in the end? Might they not all be happier?

She heard cartwheels jolting over the ruts just round the corner, and moved quickly, on along the lane. She did not want anyone to see her in such distress of mind. After all, any little clue unthinkingly revealed might in the end form part of a whole series that would give her away – if she chose Robert's path, that is ...

In the kitchen, everyone had already gathered for dinner. Samuel came to meet her, his expression a little anxious. 'Is owt wrong, love?' he asked in a low voice.

She shook her head. 'I wanted to be alone a while,' she said, and hoped that her guilt did not show in her face.

Samuel merely nodded, as if her answer satisfied him completely. 'I understand,' he said, and they went together to take their places at table.

'That's the last of the worsted then,' said George Holgate, tying the skeins of fine strong yarn into a bundle – a cop – ready for delivery to one of the weavers. 'I reckon that's taken care of all the orders for tomorrow.'

'Aye,' said Hannah, a little abstractedly. Her head throbbed. George's words seemed to come to her from a long way off, meaning little – except that the one word 'tomorrow' echoed mockingly round and round in her head. Tomorrow, when she must drive the cart over the fell to deliver the yarn, and Robert would ride after her, casually, as if by accident, to have his answer. The very thought of it gave her a sickening sensation in the pit of the stomach.

She had made no decision yet. But she knew that by deciding nothing she would in fact have made her choice, because it would all be left to her feelings, those powerful, treacherous feelings, to make the decision for her. And she knew they would take her straight to Robert's arms, once she was confronted with him again. If only she had been sure that she wanted to resist, then she could have done so. But she was not sure.

She had been short tempered with everyone today; they all seemed like intruders into her private pre-occupations. Tomorrow, when it's all settled, then it will be different, she told herself, trying to make herself believe it. She was glad that the day's work was over, and she could hurry the workers away from the mill and go home; glad too that Samuel was out tonight, at his Botanical Society meeting. She had found it very hard to bear his nearness during the past days. All her feelings of friendship for him, her pleasure in his company, her sense of security, seemed to have been submerged by the ripples spreading out from her meeting with Robert. Through their distorting pattern she could see only the surface of Samuel, the unexciting features that had little attraction for her, that not only failed to quicken her pulses but even, with Robert's presence filling her senses, disgusted her. She saw his shapeless mouth, his insignificant chin, the little scar on his cheekbone, his soft child's eyes behind the spectacles, the pale complexion and lank hair, the thin body somehow always a little bent, as if fearful of an impending blow; and they all repelled her as they had never done before. It was a relief not to have to look at him across the table tonight, or to force herself to talk to him as if everything was exactly as it had always been.

When he came home at last, she pleaded tiredness so that she would not have to listen to his animated account of the evening, and went up to bed before him. He followed very soon afterwards, and she knew the moment she looked at his face what that softening of his expression meant, and that in a moment he would come and put his arms about her.

She walked briskly and purposefully away from him, to the far side of the bed, and continued her undressing there. 'Oh, I am tired!' she said, trying to make her voice sound slow and heavy with weariness. It was as well, she thought, that Samuel was not on the whole very perceptive.

Unfortunately, he must have been more awake than usual tonight, for he was not apparently in the least fooled by her pretence. He followed her round the bed, put his hands on her shoulders and turned her, very gently, to face him. Close to, she could see even more clearly the desire that gave his insipid features an unusually purposeful look, one she disliked even more than his customary hesitancy. 'Hannah, all the time I was riding home I thought of thee,' he whispered. She felt his hands move caressingly up and down her arms. She jerked herself free of him.

'Not now, Samuel,' she said, trying (with little success) not to rebuff him too harshly. 'I only want to sleep tonight.'

He stayed where he was, watching her. A little anxious frown had appeared between his brows. The look of concern in his soft eyes made her want to scream with exasperation.

'Thou hast not slept well these past nights,' he said.

'How wouldst thou know?' she retorted, turning away from him to climb into bed. 'Thou wast snoring away contentedly enough.' That was hardly fair, for Samuel never snored, but she was in no mood to be fair.

'I felt thee turning about.' He hesitated a moment, and then went back round the bed and slid beneath the covers on his own side, though he instantly moved close to Hannah. She curled up with her back to him, shutting him out as best she could, though she could not shut out the feel of his thin body, bony yet somehow insubstantial, against her unyielding back. She tried not to think of how it felt to lie close to Robert, a hopeless endeavour, for the thought of him was now more than ever an inseparable part of her, from which she felt only death would ever free her.

'Hannah . . .' Why could he not be quiet and leave her alone? He might not be very perceptive, but he was, on the whole, sensitive enough to respond to her moods. 'Hannah, what's wrong?'

'Nowt. I am tired, that is all.'

'Please! It's more than that, I know. Thou hast been in a strange mood for days now. Something must be wrong . . . Thou art not with child again?'

Please God, let me not be! 'No, of course not. I'd tell thee if it was that.'

'What would thou *not* tell me about then? What's on thy mind? Hannah, I know thee well enough to see when something's wrong. I am not blind – and I love thee. I cannot be happy while thou art troubled.'

'Then thou canst be happy now, because there is nowt wrong.' Oh how she hated herself, this creature of darkness who could repel Samuel's tender concern, who could see something irresistible in Robert Gayle!

Samuel was silent for a little while, as if trying to decide whether or not to accept her assurance. She was not sure what he had decided, for when he spoke again he appeared to change the subject.

'Hannah, I have something to tell thee.'

'Mm ...' she murmured, trying to sound at once encouraging and sleepy.

'I have had in mind for a time ... thou knows the study I made of marsh flora? I read a paper on it to the Botanical Society.'

She could not remember with any clarity, but she murmured 'Mm ...?' again, questioningly this time, and he went on,

'At our meeting today there was a guest, a Scot – Craig, his name was. He was interested in the whole subject of upland marshes. He thought a study of the marsh flora in the Highlands of Scotland might be rewarding, a comparative one perhaps. He suggested that my knowledge and interest could be put to good use. What is more, he is a wealthy man, and would finance such a study.'

'That is good,' said Hannah, her tone neutral.

'Aye.' Rather to her surprise there was a hint of reluctance in his tone. 'The only thing is, it would mean going away from home – for some weeks, many weeks perhaps.'

She almost cried out with delight. To think of meeting Robert, knowing that she need not go home to Samuel afterwards! It was not that their meetings would be made easier, for they had more to fear from the eyes of neighbours, and of Agnes, than from Samuel; but it would take away all the torment of living two lives. For as long as Samuel was away there would be only one man in her life, and that the one she most wanted. A few weeks, many weeks, of freedom ...

Very carefully, she said, 'Thou must do whatever is right.' She hoped that there was no tremor in her voice, from the fierce excited thudding of her heart.

But it was not a wholly pleasant sensation, for there was fear in it too, which she did not want to examine too closely.

She felt Samuel's hand touch her again, cautiously, coming to rest on her shoulder. This time she forced herself to let it lie there. 'Hannah – I suppose thou couldst not . . . Thou art always so busy with the mill, of course.'

She knew quite well what he was trying to say, but she had no intention of letting him see that she understood. 'Aye, it takes all my time. But thou knows that. That is why it does so well.' Had he not said, more than once, 'My father would have been proud of thee'?

'Aye.' He fell silent, for so long that she thought he had at last decided to leave her in peace. Indeed, she had begun to feel drowsy in earnest when his voice reached her again, unsure, almost questioning. 'It was a thought I had, that we could travel together – just the two of us . . .'

She came sharply awake, turning her head half way round towards him. 'Thou knows I could not. It is not just the mill – there are the children too.'

'They would be content with Agnes.' Then: 'But thou art right, of course.' As always, said his tone. Illogically, his way of deferring to her, in this as in everything, suddenly irritated her beyond words. She clenched her teeth as he began to speak again. 'I had a thought, though – it is proposed that I should make this study in the Highlands of Scotland. Thy father was said to come from there. I thought perhaps . . .'

He had never raised his voice above a whisper, but the impact of his words on Hannah was that of a great shout, its noise exploding in her brain. She lay very still in the silence that followed. For the first time in days she had no thought at all of Robert. Her father – that shadowy figure, the dark creature of legend, wrapped in his plaid beneath the stars . . . 'We could find him?' she whispered at last.

'Aye, or try to. We could make inquiries at least. He may be dead.'

'I know.' Her heart was thudding more than ever, but there was a different beat to it now. She felt excitement still, only it was unmixed with fear. There *was* another emotion, one she did not immediately recognise. Disappointment? Surely she ought to be disappointed; yet beneath the excitement was something extraordinarily like relief. For Samuel had offered her a way out, an acceptable, obvious, unequivocal way out, one she could take without hesitation or doubt or any sense of loss.

Slowly she turned over in bed to face her husband. 'I think I should like to come,' she whispered. 'I think I could do it.'

He reached out to draw her close, and she let him have what he wanted, and felt only a lingering sense of loss.

Later, she thought: There is still tomorrow. She said softly, as one thinking aloud, 'There will be so much to do. If only I did not have the yarn to deliver tomorrow. It is a whole day gone from the mill.'

As if she had coached him in his reply, Samuel said at once, 'I can do it for thee. I will give my pupils a half holiday.'

Hannah slept soundly that night, without dreaming, as she had not slept for days. Next morning she knew, with relief, that she was not pregnant.

iii

'I am going to settle the account with Tobias Wheeler,' said Hannah, putting her head round the door of Samuel's study. 'I shall not be long, then I will help thee to pack.'

Samuel looked up and smiled, with the faint look of abstraction that was usual when he was sitting, as now, among his books.

'I hope thou dost not intend to take all of those

with thee,' Hannah added, with a smiling glance at the volumes littering his desk.

He shook his head. 'Indeed no. But I want to be sure I take the most useful ones. A pity,' he went on thoughtfully, 'we could not have gone a little earlier in the year. So many plants will have finished flowering.'

'Thou shouldst have put it off until next year,' Hannah retorted, with a trace of irritation.

'I thought it better we should go now. It will be good for us to be alone together for a time. Sometimes I think, with so much busyness about us, we grow a little apart.'

Hannah was startled. She stared at him for a moment and then, confused, looked away again. Did he suspect far more than she had realised?

As she walked up the hill towards Thornside, Hannah's senses were alert for any sound of horse's hooves, any glimpse of an approaching rider or vehicle. Often she glanced behind her, to make sure that she was not being followed. It had been like this ever since she had made the decision to go away with Samuel. She wanted feverishly to make her escape before Robert knew what was happening, and that meant that she must not meet him. Her eagerness to avoid him at all costs had led her into the most uncomfortable and ridiculous of situations. Once she had even found herself hiding behind a wall, because she had seen him coming. Crouched there, for all the world like a small animal hiding from the huntsmen, hearing his horse thud by on the road, she had wished momentarily that she had stayed where she was and faced him; yet at the same time she had prayed that he would not see her as he passed. He had not, and she had fought an unreasonable sense of disappointment as she had returned to the road, with as much dignity as she could muster, and continued on her way, glancing about her at every small sound, real or imagined, in case he should have changed his mind and retraced his steps.

She reached Thornside and Tobias Wheeler's shop without difficulty, settled the account and took her leave; and stepped out into the street again, head bent as she considered what other errands required her attention.

A hand clasped her arm. 'Hannah!' The voice was soft, but she did not need to hear it to know whose voice it was; the clasp had already told her that.

She looked up, through a wild rush of feeling. She did not want to see him; yet – oh, she was glad, so glad! She could not speak.

His face was sombre, his expression accusing. 'You have been avoiding me. Why?'

She found she could not bear the sharpness of his gaze. She lowered her eyes. 'I thought it best.' Why should she sound so guilty about it? Why indeed should she feel guilty?

'They say you're going away, you and Samuel.'

She did look up again then, trying hard to keep her gaze steady. 'Yes. To Scotland. Just for a month or two.'

There was a little silence, while Robert seemed to be trying to read her thoughts in her face. 'I imagine that will put a strain on you, being so much alone with him – in the circumstances. Or have you told him?'

She coloured. There was no need to ask what he meant. 'No.'

'Ah!' She was not sure whether it was relief or disappointment that lay behind that sighing exclamation. Or was it rather (terrifyingly) the realisation that a weapon still lay in his hands, for him to use as and when he pleased? She might be stupidly besotted with Robert, but she had no illusions about him. If she had met him as he had intended, he would perhaps have kept his word and remained silent about their meetings. Now that she had made it clear – however subtly – that she would not do what he wanted, he would feel free to use the knowledge of what had happened between them exactly as he chose, whenever it suited him to do so. Through a sudden surge of fear, she thought: I must think what to do about it. She thought perhaps she would be safe until she and Samuel returned from Scotland. Robert would take pleasure in biding his time, knowing how the thought of that shared knowledge would haunt her. But afterwards, when they came home again . . .

He was silent for a long time, frowning a little, as if trying to decide what to do next. Then he said in a low hurried voice, 'Meet me once before you go.'

The shake of the head came automatically, but it was harder, much harder, to frame the single word 'No.'

He frowned still more. 'You were not so sure the other day.'

'No,' she said steadily. 'But I was wrong.' She wanted to stay, for all her apprehension. 'I must go.'

He glanced about him. She thought perhaps that if there had not been so many other people in the street he might have made some gesture of tenderness towards her, even perhaps kissed her. But instead he stepped back and made the little mocking bow she knew so well. The frown had gone now, to be replaced by that surface brightness. 'Good day then. Make the most of your journey, then you will be refreshed to face whatever awaits you on your return. Though of course you may wish to change your mind about meeting me then . . .'

Was it a threat? She thought so. But she walked away from him with apparent calmness. Underneath, it was another matter. How could she at one and the same time be afraid and angry, and yet swept by regret that he had not been able to take her in his arms and kiss her? It made no sense at all; but then good sense had never had anything to do with what she felt for Robert.

CHAPTER TWENTY

i

'I never thought there could be such beauty!'

Samuel's voice was hushed with awe, as if to speak any louder would be in some way a desecration. Hannah said nothing, but simply reached out and closed her fingers about his, without taking her eyes from the loveliness before them.

It was not the first time that they had stood like this in some high place and exclaimed at the beauty of it all. Far from it, for such moments had become a daily occurrence ever since they crossed the Highland line, that dark ridge of mountains first glimpsed five weeks ago as they set out at sunrise from Stirling, where they had spent the tenth night of their journey.

Their first days away from home had been dreadful. It was only as they were leaving Thornside in the hired coach that Hannah had realised, with a jolt of apprehension, that for the first time in her married life she was to be completely alone with Samuel for whole days together. There would be no Agnes to stand in the way of their privacy, or provide an excuse for not talking of intimate things. For two lovers, deprived for too long of the solitude they craved, it would have been wonderful to be setting out on this journey together. For Hannah, who had so much in her thoughts that Samuel must not know, it was appalling.

They had not talked a great deal as the coach jolted north over rutted roads through a rain drenched landscape. At first Samuel had tried, now and then, to interest Hannah in what they saw, or in the prospects before them, but she had responded with so little enthusiasm that he gave up at last. The days had dragged by, hour after hour of wearying, uncomfortable travel, while Samuel tried to read and Hannah knitted busily, as if by constant movement of her fingers she could keep her guilty thoughts at bay.

They reached Edinburgh, where Samuel had letters of introduction to various scholars, and a dreary social round occupied their time. Five days, while Hannah tried to take an interest in the long hours of scientific talk, but all the time was haunted obsessively by the thought of what would be waiting for them when they returned to Thornside.

She had hoped to put that anxiety from her mind while they were away, but she realised now that, on the contrary, she would have to bring herself to face it and somehow resolve it well before their three months' absence was over. When they had left Thornside the day of their return had seemed very far away. Now, each hour brought it nearer. She would find herself lying awake at night shivering at the vision of Robert coming to the mill to tell Samuel what they had done. However bitter her regret, she could not undo what had happened. But, she told herself, that did not mean she had to accept the worst that Robert could do without preparing herself for it. Trying to look at it all as calmly as possible, she saw quite well that she had two choices.

The one was to decide that the moment she returned home she would give Robert all he wanted, and share a secret life with him behind the facade of her marriage to Samuel. But the very thought of such an existence revolted her, and she could not understand any longer what madness could have made her yield to Robert as she had done. She might not feel any very passionate attachment to Samuel, but even had he not existed it made no sense at all to want to link herself with Robert in any way.

So that left only the other choice, to steel herself

somehow to tell Samuel what had happened, before Robert could do so; which meant before they returned home. As each day of their absence passed she felt increasingly sick with fright at the prospect and wondered how she would ever bring herself to do what she must do.

And then they left the towns and the scholars behind, and abandoned the coach that had carried them from Thornside. The main roads into the Highlands, built half a century ago to ease the military suppression of the rebellious clans, were excellent, but left untouched all but a tiny part of the wild mountainous land. Samuel and Hannah, each with their own quest that must take them inevitably to the remotest places, were forced to hire ponies – much like the sturdy galloways at home – to carry them and their luggage the rest of the way. The journey, until then little short of a nightmare, suddenly turned into an adventure. They were exploring a new land, stranger by far than Hannah had expected, and there was no longer any room in her thoughts for anything but the discoveries they shared. And they did share them, for now that they were truly alone Samuel proved himself to be the most delightful of travelling companions. Without fail, it seemed, he shared her every joy, her every excitement, understood how she felt without the need to put anything into words. In those early days she had feared to be alone with him; now she realised that there was nothing she wanted more. She ceased to think of Robert at all.

Today they had ridden through a soft fine rain over some of the most desolate mountains they had as yet encountered. Here and there they had passed a settlement, like many they had seen on their journey, made up of a few tiny low single-storey dwellings, too small and poor even to be described as cottages, built of rough unmortared stones and thatched with turf or heather according to what was most readily available. Usually it would be empty of inhabitants, except perhaps for a

477

few men attending to the poor strips of cultivated land, because at this time of year the people drove the animals to the summer grazing grounds, where they lived in makeshift shelters, and spent their days making cheese and butter and dancing and singing and talking. They wore rags and went barefoot and had a wild uncouth look which their lilting incomprehensible language did nothing to relieve. Hannah had somehow not excepted such strangeness, in this land where she ought to have felt at least a little at home. If they had not found a guide to accompany them, a lively Highlander named Angus MacNeill who had been with them for two days now, they would not have been able to communicate at all, still less to find their way. Yet the people were hospitable enough, once the first approach was made, inviting the travellers with incongruous courtesy to share their meals and sleep in their pungently odorous huts, and entertaining them with long tales that kept Angus translating far into the night.

But today the travellers had not paused, for Hannah wanted only to reach their destination before nightfall. They did not even stop so that Samuel could examine the marshy places on their way, to see what kind of plants grew there. They had not halted at all until they reached the top of the mountain that marked, at last, the approaching end of Hannah's search.

Below them, swathed in a grey curtain of rain, lay a grey sea merged into a grey sky; but only for a moment. The next instant the sun broke through, sending long silver shafts of light on to the now glittering surface of the water; and then the clouds parted in earnest and Hannah and Samuel, enchanted, caught their breath.

The land sloped down to a wide bay, edged by gentle green pastures on which sheep grazed. Small knots of woodland ran, here and there, down to the shore, delicate with silver birch and rowan; and beyond them, lapped by little waves, was the whitest sand they had ever seen, pale and smooth as moonlight. The sky was blue now, the intense and yet fragile blue of a sky threatened always by the next rain, and beneath it the sea stretched sunlit and silver to a horizon broken by the dark rugged shapes of rocky islands. At the far side of the bay, a little stream ran down to the sea between a denser wood, scattered with oaks, in whose shelter lay the inevitable huddle of houses, made charming by distance.

Hannah stood looking at the little settlement. Samuel must have known what she was thinking, for she heard him ask Angus, 'Is that it then?'

'Aye,' Angus said. 'That is Achnagar.'

The houses – hovels – seemed to come sharply into focus, while everything around them grew misted and insignificant. That was Achnagar, from which her father had set out thirty-one years ago on the journey that had ended in her conception. What kind of man was he, who had come from so remote and primitive a place to do business with hard-headed cattlemen in a foreign land? He must have family here, people perhaps who spoke only the Gaelic, who could not read or write, who had never seen the world beyond the mountains that sheltered the bay. Yet he had not been like them. What had made him different? And would she find an answer to her questions – these and so many more – by following the tiny winding track down to the bay? From here there was no sign of life, not even a twist of smoke from a roof (few Highland houses had chimneys, they had found), or a chicken scratching in the midden. She wondered where the summer grazing ground – the shieling – was. It might even be close to where they stood.

For the first time she began to think of her father as a human being, as real as her mother. What would he be like, what kind of man? Her heart was beating so fast and so furiously that it seemed to consume all her energy. She was trembling, and she was glad when Samuel suddenly put an arm about her, for she thought that otherwise she would surely have fallen.

'Let's go down,' Samuel said gently. They remounted the ponies and set out slowly and with care down the steep slope.

'It's the first time I've seen sheep in any number,' Hannah commented, trying to speak casually, as if there was nothing out of the ordinary about what they were doing. 'I'd begun to think they don't keep sheep in the Highlands, except the poor thin little beasts we've seen at the shielings.'

'Aye,' Samuel agreed. 'These are a different matter altogether.'

It was much further than Hannah had thought, a mile perhaps once they reached the foot of the slope, across a landscape more undulating than had been apparent from above. Often they lost sight of the settlement, as the track dipped into a hollow or threaded its way through a tangle of trees, or rounded a miniature headland jutting out on to the shore. Down here the sun felt hot, and the air was warm and sweet with the smell of the sea. To live here, with that loveliness constantly before the eyes, the sound of the sea always in the ears, the soft sweet air in the lungs, must be wonderful, Hannah thought.

In the end they came on the township suddenly, sooner than she had expected. And they saw at once what had not been evident from above, that it was not just uninhabited, but had clearly been deserted for many years. A strong smell of damp and decay rose from it; roofs and walls had fallen in; the midden had long since rotted to a rich and odourless humus, lavishly covered with weeds; the little fields that edged it had returned to grass. The only living occupants were the sheep grazing heedlessly among the ruins.

Hannah sat still on her pony and stared at it in dismay. She felt close to tears. All this way – for this! All her hopes, all her dreams, the years of longing to know the truth, had crashed in ruins as surely as Achnagar itself had done.

'Art sure this is the place?' she heard Samuel ask.

'Aye.' Angus's voice had a faintly puzzled note. 'It is many years since I was here, you understand.'

They dismounted and wandered about a little, perhaps in the vain hope that they might find some sign of life after all. But there was nothing. The people who lived here once had gone, taking everything with them, leaving only the remnants of long dead fires, a discarded cooking pot, a broken stool.

Samuel came and put his arms about Hannah, and she bent her head on his shoulder and tried to find comfort there.

They were interrupted suddenly by the sound of thudding hooves. Samuel released Hannah, and turned to look behind him. This was no primitive Highlander on a shaggy pony, but a respectable and well-dressed gentleman on a good horse, who somehow looked entirely out of place in so remote and wild a spot.

As soon as he was near enough he drew rein and doffed his hat, all smooth politeness. 'Good afternoon. I believe I have the honour of addressing Mr Samuel Gayle?'

Samuel, astonished and wary, said cautiously, 'Aye, that's right.'

'Then you must allow me to shake you by the hand!' The man dismounted and came striding towards them and clasped Samuel's hand with obvious enthusiasm. 'When I heard you were in the district, I had to come and seek you out. I am so glad to have found you. I am a great admirer of your work. A remarkable book, of enduring usefulness to mankind, I am sure.' When Samuel appeared to be unable to think of any appropriate reply, he went on eagerly, 'It would give me the greatest possible pleasure if you would consider honouring my house as my guest – you and your

481

charming wife both, of course – this is Mrs Gayle,
I take it?' He bowed towards her, smiling happily.
'Your servant, ma'am. I fear accommodation in this
region leaves a great deal to be desired, by civilised
standards. If you have made no arrangements for
tonight, I should consider it an honour to give you
a true Highland welcome beneath my roof.' It was
apparently only then that he began to realise that
his hearers were still gazing at him with a mixture of
bewilderment and doubt. He threw his hands in the
air, as if astonished at his own stupidity. 'Forgive me,
I have not introduced myself; MacDonald is the name,
James MacDonald of Achnagar. My house is just two
miles from here, across the bay.'

At the name, Hannah felt Samuel's eyes stray momentarily to her face. Then, sure that it was what she
wanted too, he turned back and said to the man, 'We
accept thy invitation, and thank thee for it.'

They mounted again and went with their host back
across the bay and then up a steeply rising path –
wider and smoother than the one that had brought
them down – through a wood that clung insecurely
to the mountainside. As they went, James MacDonald
talked as fluently as ever, in a pleasant voice so lightly
accented that his Scottish birth was not immediately
apparent. 'You are making a study of our Highland
flora then, Mr Gayle?' he inquired at last.

'That is one of the purposes of our journey,' replied
Samuel. Then he glanced at Hannah for her approval
before adding, 'But we came to this place for quite
another reason.'

'Indeed?' The man sounded genuinely interested.

'We are anxious to have news of someone of thy
own name – perhaps he may even be kin of thine. He
was called Hector MacDonald.' He said 'was' Hannah
noticed, as if he no longer had any expectation of
finding him alive. She wondered if she did not share
his pessimism.

482

Their host smiled. 'You do not know the Highlands well, Mr Gayle, or you would know that we Highlanders are all kin to one another. But I fear kinship is no guarantee of acquaintance. There are as many MacDonalds as there are grains of sand on the shore. I do not immediately recall a Hector MacDonald, but I will give it some thought. Perhaps you can furnish me with further details. I may even have some information among my records. I am the laird, you see, the chieftain, as you may have realised. This is all my land.' He gestured sweepingly towards the bay, and then at the mountain above them. 'If anyone knows its people and their ways, I do. And its flora, too, for that is, as I indicated, one of my enthusiasms. You must tell me what plants interest you in particular, and I will direct you to the best places to look for them.'

Achnagar House was long and low, built of stone, and looked as if it had stood for many years, perhaps even centuries; but it was unmistakably a gentleman's house, as far removed from the hovels they had passed today as any Dales farmhouse. Trees and a walled garden, carefully laid out, surrounded it, a groom took their ponies and led Angus away to where their host assured him he would find a good dinner, and the doors of the house were opened to them by a servant, who then showed them to a well appointed guest room with a view across the bay, and warm water, and the promise of supper as soon as they were ready.

The food was simple but abundant, the surroundings unbelievably comfortable (especially after the austerities of the past days) without quite being luxurious, and it was clear that their host's enthusiasm for Samuel's book was very real. He produced a well-thumbed copy and eagerly turned to this page and that, commenting on differences and resemblances between the plants of the Yorkshire Dales and those that grew on the mountain near his home. When he had said he would be honoured to have Samuel in his house, it had evidently been no mere polite formula.

Hannah knew Samuel was in his element here, absorbed in his favourite kind of talk, but what she wanted was somehow to bring the conversation round to her own search. She was glad when – trying perhaps to move to some topic more obviously interesting to her – their host began to speak of his family. 'We've been here for centuries. We are connected to all the other MacDonalds, of course, but I always think of the Achnagar MacDonalds as a little clan in their own right. Our history is no less violent, I fear.' He said that as if he took considerable pride in it, and there was almost a note of regret in the way he added, 'Those days are long past now, of course. But my father was of the old breed of Highlander – an unrepentant Jacobite, who fought for the Young Pretender and went into exile for his pains.' He gestured towards a portrait on the wall behind him. 'I never knew him. An aunt brought me up, and fortunately I was able to regain the family estates as soon as I came of age. Fine heroic gestures are all very well, but they have no place in the modern world. The Highlands, like everywhere else, must drag themselves into the eighteenth century or perish. That was the principle I worked on from the outset. There was everything to do – you cannot conceive what it was like when I took over: land largely uncultivated, and what crops there were quite insufficient to feed an excessive population. An economy based on cattle – a hardy native breed, but offering very poor returns. At first I set about to improve them —'

'Then thou didst send cattle south, to England, on the drove roads?' Hannah broke in eagerly.

'Naturally.' He smiled. 'Some of my beasts may well have passed your doors in days gone by. But not in recent years.' He shook his head. 'It was an unprofitable business. This is simply not good cattle country, and the long journey to market hardly improved the quality.

Then in 1781 we had the cattle plague. In that year many of we landowners faced bankruptcy. It was just about that time I had a chance visit from an old friend, who told me of an experiment he planned to undertake on his own property. I still thank God for that day, and that friend's advice.' He paused to give emphasis to his words before he explained, 'His solution was sheep.'

'Ah, we saw sheep by the shore!'

'Indeed you will have done, Mrs Gayle. And not, you may have noticed if you have an eye for such things, the poor feeble creatures beloved of our poor Highlanders, so fragile they must be protected from the least breath of cold air. No, my sheep are Cheviots – a tough and hardy breed, excellent both for wool and meat.'

Hannah nodded. 'Thou didst make a wise choice.'

He looked a little amused, as if he thought such an expression of approval eccentric, coming from a woman. 'So I have found. They have been the salvation of Achnagar.'

Hannah began to feel that she too had met a kindred spirit in this man. 'There is nothing better for poor upland pasture. And it must be better for the people, to have wool to spin and knit and weave. They will be able to live more comfortably.' She paused, struck by a sudden realisation. 'Is that what happened, by the shore – to the people who lived there? Have they moved to better houses? It must be hard to bring up healthy children in such places as they must have been.'

'Indeed it is,' their host agreed. His voice had a dry note. 'The conditions there were as squalid as you will find anywhere.' He shuddered visibly. 'However, I fear the will of the inhabitants to self improvement left a great deal to be desired. They always undertook a little spinning and so forth, for their own needs. But anything more than that, anything requiring perseverance, that was another matter. Once their simplest needs were met, they called a halt and retreated to their squalor to tell stories and sing songs as if they had not a care in the world. I have always taken my duties as a landlord seriously. As I see it, it is for the man of enlightenment and education to direct those who are less well endowed with gifts of mind and body into wiser paths. But so long as they could wallow in their dungheaps here, my tenants had no interest in improvement. An indolent people, indolent and feckless beyond belief.'

Where, Hannah wondered, had she heard talk like that before? ". . . There is no order, no routine, no purpose . . . they have no wish to improve . . . They will never improve at all, if someone does not show them how . . ." Robert; Robert talking of the benefits his mill would bring to the Dales and to the people he so despised. But here it was different, of course. She had seen for herself how the people still lived as they must have done for hundreds of years, in the most appalling poverty, sharing their cramped living space with their animals. To want to help them to improve their lot must be a good and natural response.

'What didst thou do then?'

'I encouraged emigration. There is abundant land, good land, in Canada and the United States of America. Once shaken out of his natural apathy, the Highlander proves himself resourceful and independent. Many have made a great success of such a move.'

And my father among them? Hannah wondered bleakly. Is he thousands of miles away across the sea, where I can never hope to meet him or have news of him? 'Then . . . then Hector MacDonald, the man we were inquiring about – he has emigrated?'

Their host looked at her blankly for a moment. He had clearly forgotten their earlier conversation. 'Ah, yes – now, that I don't know. As I said, I do not immediately recall . . . No, wait a moment! I do believe that was the name of the second son of old Hugh MacDonald – yes, I am sure of it. Aeneas was the elder, drowned at sea. It was Hector who was left.

But the man you speak of – you say he came from the township? It cannot be he, then. Hector MacDonald lived about a mile up the glen, where my shepherd lives now. You cannot see the house from the bay.' He looked curiously at Hannah. 'May I ask what is your interest in him?'

What would he say if she were to reply, 'He was my father'? Hannah wondered. She did not say it, of course. She and Samuel had agreed before they ever set out that only Hector MacDonald himself – should they find him – would ever learn that fact. Carefully, she said, 'He used to drive cattle through the Dales some years ago – many years ago. Someone at home has reason to want to find him, or at least have news of him.' It was, she supposed, quite true, in its way. 'We never knew him, or anything about him. All that we heard was that he came from Achnagar.'

'Ah, if he was a drover, then it may be the same man. It would be getting on for forty years ago now, I suppose. But that was certainly one of the things he did, for a time – before his brother died, and they had need of him at home. His father was my tacksman.' When he saw that the word meant nothing to her, he explained, 'A tenant farmer is the nearest you would come to it in England; but with the people of the township as tenants under him. It is a peculiarly Highland institution. It meant something when the clans were organised on military lines. A primitive arrangement. Hector took over when his father died, for a short time.'

So he had not been simply a drover, nor come from the poor settlement near the shore. It gave Hannah a strange indefinable feeling to realise that she was at last talking to someone who had known her father, who could tell her about him, and fill out the shadow in her imagination into a complicated human being, living a distinct life very different from her own. 'What was he like?' she heard herself asking, as if in a dream.

'Oh, agreeable enough, on casual acquaintance. But

compared to his father, or his brother ... Perhaps you have met that kind of thing in a family, where there are two sons: the eldest is all anyone could wish, the second something of a ne'er do well. I am not saying,' he added hastily, conscious of some kind of indignation in Hannah's face, and even, he thought, in Samuel's, 'that Hector MacDonald was so bad as that. But he was not single minded enough to do well at anything – no staying power, I suppose. A bit of a hothead too, while his health lasted —'

Hannah's heart seemed to turn right over. 'Then he's dead.'

'Oh, now that I don't know. He may be. Certainly his health wasn't up to the rigours of the journey to Canada. I believe he went south, to the Lowlands perhaps, but what became of him I do not know. Come to think of it, though, there was an old woman – an aunt perhaps, I'm not sure – she went to her daughter over in Glen Shiel. I do believe I have her address somewhere. I'll give it to you before you go. It's just possible she knows something, if you think it worth the effort of seeking her out. Of course, she may be dead herself by now.'

Upstairs, alone in their lovely room filled with the sound of the distant sea, Samuel said, 'We shall go and find this old woman tomorrow.'

Hannah, standing at the window to gaze out on the bay, lit now by the moon, turned to look at him. 'But what of thy studies? Thou hast done little enough work these past days.'

'This is more important. Besides, I had set myself four weeks for my studies, and thou hast been patient for five already. If there is time, I shall do more; if not, then I have what I need already.' He smiled suddenly. 'To tell truth, I think I am as anxious as thou to find thy father.'

She looked at him, standing there in the candle-light in his shirt and breeches, a thin gentle figure gazing at her with love; and all of a sudden she felt an overpowering tenderness flow through her. For a moment she stood very still where she was, aware of Samuel as she had never been aware of him before, with all her senses alive to him, and all of them responding to him with a delight that was wholly new. She had never felt quite like this before, with anyone; but it was a wonderful feeling, because it was unmixed with hesitation or doubt or shame. She went to him then, and put her arms about him and kissed him very slowly and gently; and then, neither leading, neither following, they went together to the bed and turned into one another's arms. For a long time, while the candle burned down and faltered to extinction and the moon rose higher until it shone right in through the open uncurtained window, they lay exploring and caressing, finding new delights to give and to share, anticipating and yet holding at bay the lovely final moment when they came together at last in a wholeness so complete that Hannah wept afterwards with happiness.

ii

'This must be the place,' said Samuel. Hannah dug her heels into her pony's flanks to catch up with him. This morning, when she had told him that before they left the bay she would like to see the house where her father had lived, Samuel had understood at once. So they had followed the line of the burn up from the ruined settlement through a pretty tree-lined glen, and come at last, where the glen widened out a little, to a simple, sturdy stone house, which reminded Hannah a little of High Farm, though it was built in quite a different style. At right angles to it were a stable and outbuildings, sheltering a small vegetable plot. A dog barked at their approach, but there was no other sign of life.

They sat there on their ponies, side by side, looking

at it. Hannah tried to imagine her father, a little boy, splashing in that lively burn, or running down the glen to the sea, which was just visible between the trees. Had he played with the children of the township, chattering away to them in their strange language? Had he gone with them in the summer to the shielings, and joined in the singing and dancing? It was very quiet now; hard to think that the glen might once have been loud with the laughter of children. Even this house, still inhabited, had a solitary and deserted look. But then it was raining steadily today, and the peculiarly tormenting midges they had come to know only too well were already biting ferociously. 'Let's go,' Hannah said.

They found the old woman, but not until close on dusk, at the end of a day made miserable by incessant rain and stubborn midges. She lay in a box bed in the single smoky evil-smelling room of a hovel on the shores of Loch Shiel, the sole remaining resident of a township deserted for the summer, except for the weary-looking daughter who looked after her, and who greeted the visitors with open mistrust. It took Angus some time to convince her that they meant no harm.

Inside the cottage, it was too dark to make out any detail of the features of the woman in the bed, except to see that she was very old and very ill. Neither she nor her daughter undertood any English. Angus had to explain everything to them at length in Gaelic, and even then it was some time before either of them showed any sign of grasping what he wanted.

Then the old woman, until now motionless and apparently semi comatose, came to sudden life. She began to talk, on and on, moaning and weeping as she did so, in an unending lament that tore at Hannah's emotions and set her nerves on edge. It made it worse that they understood none of it; and it was not for a very long time, until the old voice subsided into near incoherence and the woman appeared to be almost asleep, that Angus was able to tell them something of what she had said.

'She is weeping for her sister's son, Hector Mac-Donald, and for Mairi and the little ones – Mairi was his wife,' Angus added, sensing the question on Hannah's lips. 'She curses the day they went away from the land of their people. She has no knowledge of them, whether they are living or dead. But once only she had a letter – she has it still, beneath her mattress.'

The daughter, prompted gently, slid an exploring hand under the mattress and drew out a tattered and dirty sheet of paper. They took it to the doorway, and turned it about in a vain attempt to read what was written on it. 'I suppose it's in Gaelic,' said Samuel; though even had it been written in English it would have been scarcely more legible. But there was what appeared to be an address at the top of the page, and Samuel took out a notebook and copied it out as best he could. 'I *think* it says Catrine. Is there a place called Catrine? It sounds more like a girl's name.'

Angus, applied to, could not help. They had to be satisfied with what little they had. They lingered just long enough to express their gratitude to the women for their help, and then left as soon as they decently could, preferring the rain and the fast approaching night to the prospect of being invited to sleep in such a place.

iii

Catrine proved to be a village, growing fast round a busy cotton mill, inland some way from the little port of Ayr in the western Lowlands. The address was more accurate than they had expected, and Samuel and Hannah quickly found the small workman's cottage to which it referred. It reminded Hannah depressingly of the cottages Robert had built at Newgill.

But there was no Hector MacDonald there, only a large widow, just home from the mill, with a house full

491

of noisy children clamouring for attention, their day's work also at an end. She could not help them, but a neighbour, overhearing, remembered the MacDonalds well enough. 'They left – oh, four years back, I'd say. There was nothing for him here any more. Glasgow, I think he went to.'

Samuel and Hannah gazed at the speaker in dismay. 'But how shall we ever find him there?'

The woman shrugged. 'Try the cotton mills. That was the kind of work they were after. Someone might know.'

They travelled north to the prosperous, expanding city on the banks of the Clyde, and found a clean and respectable inn from which to set out on their search.

The laird of Achnagar had been right to claim that MacDonalds were as numerous as the grains of sand on the shore. Hannah and Samuel began to think that most of them must be employed in the cotton mills of Glasgow; but not one, it seemed, a Hector MacDonald.

'Perhaps,' Samuel suggested, after two days of fruitless inquiries, 'we should call on all the MacDonalds we can find, whatever their first names. One of them may be his wife, or his son, or his daughter.'

And, thought Hannah, he may be dead; that may be the reason why we cannot find him. But she did not put the fear into words.

Then at last, at a mill missed the first time round, they were given the address of Hector MacDonald, mule spinner, temporarily at home following an injury. They left the mill, triumphantly bearing the paper on which the mill manager had written the address. And it was then, faced with the imminent prospect of meeting her father at last, that Hannah began to be swept by doubts. She came to a halt. 'Samuel,' she said, 'what if we do wrong to seek him out?'

Samuel frowned a little. 'Why should we do wrong?'

'He has a wife and a family. He knows nothing of me – or I suppose he does not. Perhaps he was not even married when he met my mother. It is likely he has not told his wife what happened, if he remembers it at all. What will she feel – what will they all feel – if I turn up at the door and say, "I am thy daughter"?'

After a moment's thought, Samuel took her hands in his and said earnestly, 'Shall I go ahead and make inquiries first, without thee? When I have seen for myself, then we can judge what best to do.'

Hannah considered the matter and then shook her head. 'No – no, I think I had best do it myself. I should like thee to be there, of course. But let me do the talking. I shall let him think we come only from friendship. We must say nothing until we are sure we can do no harm.'

They knew as soon as the door of the lodging house was opened to them that their search was not, after all, at an end. Hector MacDonald, mule spinner, was a thin lame young man in his twenties, whose family (so he told them) had lived in or near Glasgow ever since his grandfather came to the mainland from Skye fifty years ago.

Depressed and exhausted, Hannah turned to go, Samuel following; and at that moment the young man called after them, 'Hold on!' They looked round. 'There's a man with my name, lives not far away. Someone came looking for me, and found him by mistake. I don't recall his address, but I can take you there.'

It seemed hard to put an injured man to such trouble, but he seemed unconcerned and they set out with him along the street.

Young Hector MacDonald came to a halt before one of many high tenement blocks in a grim street about ten minutes walk from where they had started. 'You should find him up there.' His head jerked upwards. 'I'm not so good on the stairs, so I'll leave you here. As I remember it's the third floor, on the right. But anyone will tell you.'

Hannah just remembered to thank him before he left them. She heard Samuel say, 'I suppose he may not be at home. He may be out at work.' She said nothing, but felt Samuel take her hand and lead her up the dark and stinking stairway to the third floor, and a door much like any other they had passed on the way.

She had expected to be excited and full of emotion, but this was worse than anything she had imagined. She was trembling so much that she could not control her limbs. She stared at the door, thinking: 'Knock – I must knock,' but quite unable to raise her hand. When she did raise it at last it shook so much that she was afraid it would make no sound upon the door. And then, just as she was about to bring it down on the stained surface, she stopped.

From the far side of the door came suddenly the most unexpected sound, breaking into that gloomy place like a thin silver shaft of light: a high clear sweet rippling line of music, from some kind of flute or pipe. Hannah stood quite still, enraptured. The sweetness of it seemed to pierce her heart and stop her breath. She was momentarily transported away from here, from doubts and anxieties, from her body with all its troublesome needs and demands. The next moment, alongside that ethereal sound came a human one, as lovely in its way – a child's voice, pure and true, following the line of the music with effortless sureness; and then breaking off abruptly in a sudden harsh paroxysm of coughing. The piping stopped too, and someone spoke in a low voice. The coughing continued. Hannah was returned firmly to the squalid landing of the Glasgow tenement. She glanced at Samuel and then, her hand still shaking, knocked on the door.

She felt Samuel's clasp tighten about her and knew he too was tensed, waiting for some sign that they had been heard. The voice fell silent. The coughing ceased briefly, before beginning again, intermittently now.

There was a slow shuffling sound, as of uncertain

footsteps, and they heard the latch lift. The door edged open, a short way, and then all at once to its full extent. A man stood there, tall, but so frail and so bent that he did not seem tall. From a gaunt pale face framed with a shock of tangled hair a pair of deep blue eyes, shadowed and deep set, looked back at Hannah.

She had no doubt then. This was her father. They were her eyes that looked back at her; her eyes, were she to be eaten up with anxiety and ill health and poverty. She stood gazing at him – the hair, black once, now lavishly streaked with grey; the fair skin stretched too tight over the fine bones of the face; the shabby nondescript clothes (no dashing plaid here) hanging loose on the thin body, which was held more or less upright only by a great effort of will, the long fingers crooked painfully about the latch, so thin that she thought she would be able to see the light through them, were there any light bright enough in this damp and dingy place. My father, she thought, stupidly, painfully. Does he know, as I do, that his own flesh and blood stands here? Does he see the likeness?

Apparently he did not, for his expression had the blank politeness of a weary man faced with the necessity to be courteous to a stranger; no recognition, or wonder. He just looked a little puzzled, that was all.

He turned his head aside briefly while he coughed, and then he returned his gaze to Hannah. He was clearly expecting her to explain why she had come, but when after some time she continued to stand there in silence he said, 'Is your business with me?' His voice was soft, a little hoarse, with the musical Highland lilt to it that was quite unlike the robust Glaswegian speech.

Hannah could not find her voice. It was hard enough even to breathe through the obstruction in her throat, the choking sensation that clutched at her chest. A movement in the dimness of the room beyond her father's shoulder caught her eye. There was a child there, sitting curled up on a folded rug on the floor in the furthest corner. Hannah could just make out a frail thin body in a well mended dress, the same tangled black hair framing a delicate white face, her own blue eyes again. My sister, she thought with a sudden renewed sense of shock; that must be my sister. She knew she was trembling more than ever.

She wanted to talk to her father – that was, after all, why she had come – but still she could not frame the sentences that, gently and tactfully, should lead her to the moment of disclosure. She could not think clearly. She could only feel, or rather her being seemed somehow at the mercy of a whole universe of sensations that whirled about her and caught at her so that no clear sense of what she felt emerged. The worst of it was that she could see in her father's face the exhaustion of a sick man kept too long on his feet, and increasing bewilderment as to what she was doing there and why.

At last, prompting her with gentle courtesy, he said, 'You were wishing to see me?'

She tried to gather her thoughts. 'Aye – aye, that's it. I should like to speak with thee.'

'Then you had best step inside,' he returned quietly, and stood back to let her pass.

She took a step forward, dimly conscious as she did so of a voice murmuring behind her, 'I'll go now. I'll come back for thee in an hour.' Samuel, said some part of her mind; but she was scarcely aware of what he said, still less of his subsequent departure.

She knew that a chair had been pushed towards her, and the door closed as she sat down. Then everything seemed to come into focus, and she saw with sudden clarity the small crowded room, the bed on which her father now sat, the table whose surface was piled with the family's meagre stock of bowls and spoons and kitchen utensils, the washing draped on a line strung across the corner above the head of the little girl; and also the roughness of the furniture, the general air of damp and cold, which obvious attempts at cleanliness and tidiness could do nothing to lessen, the tiny glowing knot of coals in the grate that gave out little warmth. This was home for a family, mother, father, children, the only place in all this great city which they could call their own. It did not even offer privacy, for every sound from the adjoining rooms, above, below, on either side, came clearly, mingled with the noise of traffic and people in the street.

She glanced at the child, who was watching her gravely from those too-large eyes; and then at her father, and found that he too was watching her, still puzzled and uneasy. What should she say now? Should it be some dramatic announcement: 'Thou art my father. I am thy daughter'? No, she thought; that was no way to do it. It must be done carefully, cautiously, the whole subject approached with great tact and subtlety. Yet where, in her present confused and emotional state, was she to find the calculating sensitivity that the moment required? Perhaps after all she would have to leave without revealing anything, contenting herself simply with having met her father and seen – as far as she could – what kind of man he was. Better that than to risk destroying what there was left of happiness and security for a family that had, clearly, already suffered too much.

But if she was to say anything, she must begin to say it soon. For all she knew they might be interrupted at any moment, perhaps by the return of his wife from wherever she had gone. As it was, she had been fortunate to find her father alone; it would be foolish to squander such an opportunity to talk of things she would have found it much more difficult to mention before his wife.

'Thy wife . . .' she began tentatively. She saw his gaze sharpen. 'She will come home soon, perhaps?'

He shook his head. 'Never again. She died when this little one was born.' He laid his hand on the head of the child. 'Seven years ago. We were at Catrine then . . . So it was her you wished to see?'

'No, only . . .' Hannah, with a sudden sense of panic, wondered what on earth she could say now, except, gently, 'I am sorry to hear it – that thou hast lost thy wife.'

'Aye, well; it happened.' It was, Hannah thought, the resignation of a man who had long ago ceased to expect any better of life. She realised he was once again looking at her questioningly. 'I do not understand —' He broke off, but she knew quite well what it was that puzzled him. Her behaviour must seem extraordinary and inexplicable, and probably very tiresome to a man with so many cares to burden him.

She decided then that subtlety, tact, sensitivity were beyond her. She had to say something to explain her presence, and if she was not to be subtle then she must be direct. She drew a deep breath, and then – quietly, carefully, with a sense of being somehow suspended in the stillness at the heart of a storm – she said, 'I am Hannah Gayle. I was Hannah Burton. I was raised from birth by John and Agnes Burton. But my natural mother was Christian Lambert.'

She saw that his expression had not changed at all. It showed only courteous interest, and a hint of bewilderment. It was clear that the name meant nothing to him, or not yet at least. 'She is the daughter of the host of the Drovers' Inn, on Hollinthwaite Moor in Swaledale in the North Riding of Yorkshire.'

This time there was a faint look of recognition on Hector MacDonald's face. He even smiled slightly, a gentle and transforming smile, hinting at the charm that had won her mother. But Hannah realised very soon that it was simply a smile of uncomplicated reminiscence. 'Aye, I remember that inn. It was a cheerless place enough. But I stayed there sometimes. I was a drover once . . .' He looked at her more closely, the smile vanishing, as if he realised that there must be some connection between that apparently trivial fact and her visit. 'But you know that, perhaps?' Then he shook his head. 'It would be before you were born. You cannot remember it.'

'I believe thou didst pass that way last in 1763, in the sixth month, in what thou wouldst call June. Two nights, I think, thou wert there. Nine months later, Christian Lambert gave birth to me.' Her gaze held his. She knew he had begun to grasp what she was saying, some of it at least. The rest followed slowly, its meaning taking unambiguous shape before him. 'Dost remember Christian Lambert?' she prompted gently, after a moment.

She saw him colour, faintly, though any increase in colour made a dramatic difference to his pale face. 'No, not . . . I remember something . . . Not the name.' He was clearly making a great effort to bring it all to mind.

Hannah's memory was clear enough. She could still see her mother facing her across the table in the inn kitchen, talking of Hector MacDonald with the light of her recollection melting away all the bitterness from her expression. How could something that had meant so much to Christian Lambert mean so little to the man who had shared it with her that now he could scarcely bring it to mind at all? Had he ever known Christian's name? Could a man father a child and not even know its mother's name? There was something inexpressibly shocking about the whole thing. Poor Christian, who had suffered so much and yet was denied even this tiny acknowledgement of her humanity. What had she been to Hector? Simply a convenient body in which he could satisfy his need, much as a handful of oatmeal would satisfy his hunger?

Hannah looked at him, angry and deeply hurt, for Christian's sake; and met his bewildered, unhappy blue eyes, set in that haggard face. How could she be angry for long with this sick and broken man?

After a moment, he said quietly, 'What you are saying, I think, is – that I am . . .' He halted, though whether from a scruple at speaking aloud in front of the child, or from a fear of making the thing more real by putting it into words, Hannah could not be sure.

She nodded, and when she came to reply found that she could speak only in a whisper. 'I have always wished to know thee. It was something missing, all my life.'

There was a little pause; then he said, 'You are sure?' He too spoke in a low hoarse voice.

'Canst look at me and doubt it?'

He did look at her then, with close attention. She knew he was taking note of her features, her colouring, all the indications that, in spite of the differences of age and sex and health and fortune, she was his flesh and blood. At the end he looked very tired, as if the acceptance of the truth had taken more from him than had been apparent. He sighed. 'You had best be telling me everything.'

So she did, gently, wasting no words, but choosing them with care, mindful always of the child. She told him all her mother had told her, of the meeting on the moor, the long months of terror and concealment, the lonely agony of giving birth, the anguished decision Christian had made to abandon her child; and what had come afterwards, the happy childhood and the eventual marriage, all distantly observed by the innkeeper's daughter.

'And now I have found thee,' Hannah concluded. 'It is the end of my search.'

Her father leaned forward to rest his head on his hands. She could not see his face, only the long thin fingers thrust into the springy grey-black hair. He said nothing, but she knew that was not because he felt nothing. On the contrary, he was feeling more than he could put into words.

'I am sorry. Perhaps I should not have come.' She knew as she spoke that they were empty words. She regretted any hurt he had suffered, the more so because it was clear enough that life had been little kinder to him than to her mother. But she was not sorry for coming, nor did she feel she could have done anything else. It had been necessity that brought her here, not a whim. But the words were a gesture towards him – of consolation, of sympathy – and as such they clearly reached him, for after a moment he raised his head, and she saw on his face the unmistakable look of a man exhausted beyond subterfuge or concealment.

'I had no idea – none at all . . .' He paused, but then, before she could say anything, added, 'I do remember . . . something . . . so little. But you, coming here —' He gestured briefly with his hands and a smile hovered about his lips and then was gone. 'As you see, there is nothing for you here.'

'I want nothing. I have all I need, now I have met thee.'

He bent his head on his hands again, more from weariness than emotion, Hannah thought. In the silence that followed, she looked about her, trying to think of something to say. Her eyes came to rest on the small silver pipe that lay upon the table, beside the stacked wooden bowls. 'It was thee I heard play then, before I knocked on the door?'

'Yes.' He stirred, raised his head, relaxed a little. 'You have a liking for music perhaps?' It was his first gesture towards her, expressing an interest on his part in what kind of woman his daughter was.

She coloured, more deeply than the simple question merited; but then for her it was not a simple question. 'Aye.'

'You play an instrument perhaps? Or sing?'

'Sing, a little,' she whispered.

'Can you sing "Fear a' bhata"?' Hannah looked round sharply at the little girl whose question had come so suddenly between them.

'I do not know it,' she admitted. 'Perhaps thou canst sing it for me.'

Effortlessly, unselfconsciously, the child did so, the high clear notes soaring up into some realm where poverty and dirt and ill health were unknown, some remote place of unalloyed loveliness like that tranquil bay visited just a short while ago, which seemed so far from where they were now. Hannah felt her heart follow the notes, with delight and, increasingly, a longing to go with them, sharing their sweetness. The next moment her father had picked up the pipe and was playing a lilting accompaniment, adding exquisite harmonies to the simple line; and Hannah could restrain herself no longer. The music had already wound itself into her mind; that the words were incomprehensible to her did not matter. She simply opened her mouth and began to sing, pouring out the lovely lilting melody to run alongside her half sister's heedless singing.

She had never felt a delight like this. The three of them were linked together in a pattern of sound, creating from three separate strands – the high ethereal piping, the child's sweet clear treble, Hannah's richer and fuller soprano – a wonderful whole, which seemed somehow to bring completeness to each one of them, so that their music became not three sounds but a unity. To be a part of that was a joy so intense that Hannah felt like laughing and crying at once, but more than that she wanted to go on singing, on and on, for ever and ever.

The song ended. She sensed the end coming, and reached the final haunting note precisely as the others did, so that it hung on in the little silence that followed like a wistful ghost. Hannah sighed, from the depths of her contentment.

Then she glimpsed her father's face as he put the pipe down on the table, and saw that there were tears in his eyes. 'It was my mother's singing that I heard then,' he said huskily. 'It is her voice that you have, my daughter.' She felt his fingers, cold and bony and trembling, close about her own. Then he turned to the child. 'Isabel, this is your sister – your father's daughter, as you are.' He reached out towards the child, who rose slowly to her feet and came, blushing shyly, to lay her hand too about Hannah's; unlike her father's, it felt hot and sticky, too hot for health. 'Isabel was our last born, of course,' he explained. 'She is at home because she is sick and cannot work.'

'There are others then?'

'Hugh and John and Margaret, the ones who are left of the seven my wife bore. They are at the mill.'

'And thee?'

Again came that ghost of a smile. 'It is long since I have worked. I shall not again. It is no grief to me.'

Hannah thought of the incessant noise and dust of the cotton mills, the long exhausting hours of dreary and dangerous work, without respite. It was no wonder father and daughter looked so ill, if they had worked in such conditions. And then she remembered the bay at Achnagar, the breathtaking loveliness, the clear air, the tranquillity, the sturdy house by the burn, spacious enough for a large family to live in reasonable comfort. 'Why didst thou come here? Why didst thou ever leave Achnagar?'

All trace of the smile left his face. She felt the clasp of his fingers slacken, as if a revived hopelessness had drained all his strength in a moment. 'You know Achnagar?'

'We went there, seeking thee. The laird told us thou hadst gone away. I supposed it was because there was no living to be made there. But thou hadst land – would it not have been better to stay there and live on what there was, however little?'

'It was not so little. And indeed it would have been very much better. Better to starve in the glen of your ancestors, than this . . .' His eyes, sombre now and very dark, settled on her face. 'He did not tell you then why we went away – the laird, I mean?' He said 'laird' as if the word came close to choking him. 'My cousin, James MacDonald.'

'Thy cousin?'

'Second cousin. But what does it matter? It has long ceased to matter to him. And as you say, he is the laird, though we knew him as our chieftain. By the laws his father knew, the land was the people's; by his law – Sassenach law – it was his. There was no profit in the people any more, or the cattle we reared. And he must have profit. So the people had to go.'

'He *drove* thee out!' Hannah's voice was sharp with indignation and horror.

Hector's smile hovered again and then fled. 'He did not set the dogs upon us or burn the thatch about our ears; not quite. We had always paid a little rent, since he came to Achnagar. Some found it hard, but none would starve while there was food to be shared amongst us. Then he asked for more, and more, until we could not pay – even I, who had more than most. So we left, and now the Sassenach farmer pays a great rent for my house and tends the sheep who feed on our grazing grounds. James MacDonald is a rich man, I hear. His people are scattered, across half the world – those who did not die in the leaving. As for ourselves, we went to Catrine, and I worked at weaving for a time. But I had little skill at it, and my wife died, and we came here. The mills give us bread. It is not living, that is all. We have only the music left, and the old tales. It is my great sadness that the children do not even remember the place of their birth, indeed that Isabel has never been there. Perhaps one day they will go back.' The sadness left his eyes, and only anger remained, and bitterness, the glowing ashes of a spirit long crushed out of him by the cruelties of life. 'It is progress, he used to say. It is what must be, for it brings prosperity. His father would not have spoken so. *He* considered himself rich – but rich in people. He would not have understood his son's mind. I tried to fight it, when it seemed we must go, but I was alone, because the people trusted their chieftain, and did not believe he would turn them from the land. They would not hear what I said; and nor would he. Now there are no people at Achnagar, only sheep . . . There is a song that was made when we came away.' He began suddenly to sing, in a voice that was hesitant and husky but true, with something left still to show what it must once have been. The words were incomprehensible, of course, but Hannah understood it all the same, for the pain and the sense of loss were all there in the desolation of the music and the haunting cadence of its ending. The sound of it brought a lump to her throat.

In the little silence that followed there came a gentle knock on the door. Hector made a move to stand up, but Hannah intervened. 'May I?' He sat down with obvious relief, and she went to open the door. It was a moment or two before she recognised Samuel there. Somehow he seemed very far removed from the world which she had just glimpsed; for a moment it was almost as if he had never existed. She felt an odd reluctance to admit him to intrude on the intimacy and emotion within the room. But she heard Hector welcoming him, and so she said, 'This is Samuel, my husband,' and stood back to let him come in.

They went every day for a week to see Hector Mac-Donald. Samuel would come with Hannah, and then leave her there, coming back later to collect her. Sometimes he would stay a little, talking and listening with his usual gentle courtesy. Hannah ceased to resent his intrusion, and learned to be grateful for his sympathy. What he did not learn directly from Hector she told him later, when they were alone at the inn, or walking together through the streets of Glasgow.

They could not prolong their stay indefinitely. They had promised to be home by the beginning of September, and August was almost over. When there were two days left, Samuel said to Hannah, as they walked one morning to call on Hector, 'It has been in my mind, that we cannot simply leave him, as if it was all at an end, for ever. That would be to make use of him for our convenience, with no thought of his needs.'

It had been in Hannah's mind too, though all she said now was, 'I shall write to him, and ask him to write to me.' But she looked at Samuel, wanting the other thing she had to say to come from him first.

'We are not rich, but neither are we poor. We could find room for him, and for his children, at Thornside. He will need care, it will take time, but . . .'

Hannah smiled at him and took his arm. 'I hoped thou wouldst say that,' she said. 'I think it right too.'

But Hector, when they put the proposal to him, was moved but unyielding. Shaking his head, struggling for words, he said huskily, 'It is too far – it is too late to begin again.' Then his expression changed, as if something new had occurred to him. He glanced at Isabel. 'The child there – she needs a woman's care, small as she is. Margaret does what she can, but she is just a girl herself. Isabel was very sick last winter, and she coughs so badly even now. I have wished that she might have good country air to grow in. Perhaps if you would take her with you, raise her with your own little ones . . .'

Hannah knew how fond he was of his youngest child, and how much it would hurt him to part with her, and it moved her that he should be so ready to put her interests before his own. In that, she reflected, her natural parents were alike.

They refused to leave Glasgow until they had found better lodgings for her father and his family, and made sure he had the medical care he needed, though it was clear enough that there was little any doctor could do for him now. To spare his sensitive Highland pride, they left money with Margaret, a sensible, kindly girl of seventeen, and promised to send more from time to time so that the family need never want for anything again. 'It is what any daughter would do for her father,' Hannah pointed out, to forestall any future objections from Hector. When the time came to leave, she and Samuel were able to console themselves with the thought that they had given the little family peace of mind. It was perhaps all that they had to give.

CHAPTER TWENTY-ONE

i

They reached Moffat in the late afternoon on the second day of the journey home, and halted at the comfortable inn where they had stayed on their way north nearly three months ago. Once supper was over, Hannah coaxed a weary Isabel to bed and sat by her until she was asleep, glad that the child already seemed to regard her presence as both natural and comforting. Downstairs in the parlour, she found Samuel busily writing up some long neglected notes. He glanced at her as she came in, with the vague expression that warned her his thoughts were with his plants and that only a great effort on her part would drag him away from them. She went to him and dropped a kiss on his head, and then murmured, 'I am going for a walk.' He made some indistinct noise by way of reply and she pulled a cloak about her and went out.

It was a still evening at the end of a gentle, sunny late summer day, the sun slanting low over the green Lowland hills. Until today Hannah had felt detached from her past, in a lovely interlude shared with Samuel that had seemed unending; indeed she had not wanted it to end. But in two or three days they would be home, and she could no longer put off the decisions that must be made.

She walked quickly out of the little town, leaving the clustered grey houses behind her and hurrying up the hill to the north, past sheep grazing with the single minded persistence of animals who had only an hour or so more of daylight left in which to feed. It was fresh but not cold, with a little breeze blowing from the south west.

It seemed a long time since she had been alone. She had not wanted solitude during the past weeks; on the contrary she had rejoiced in the deepening intimacy that had grown up between herself and Samuel, as if they were discovering for the first time the people who lay beneath the too-familiar surface. By the time that intimacy had been broken by Isabel, Hannah had realised that her feelings for Samuel had irrevocably changed. She thought that – paradoxically perhaps – that was why she and Samuel had been able to accept Isabel's presence not as an intrusion or a distraction, but as an enrichment in which they both shared.

But all the joys and discoveries of the past weeks were about to end, and Hannah was forced now to face the fact that happiness founded upon a deception was not really happiness at all. It could not last, but more than that it was in any case a delusion, possible only because she had closed her eyes to what lay beneath it.

She reached the summit of the hill and there, breathing fast, sat down on a rock and closed her eyes, and tried to collect her thoughts and clear her mind of its intrusive lumber of emotion, so that she could look coolly at where she found herself.

Her first thought, when the agitation of pulses and breathing had stilled, was a wholly joyful one: she had found her father. It was a little like finding exactly the right notes to conclude a line of music; everything had fallen into place and was now complete, in a way it could not have been before. She knew as much perhaps as any human being could hope to know of the different elements that had gone into making her what she was, and the process that had begun so painfully at that first appalling meeting with her mother had proved in the end to be both healing and enriching. The only pain in meeting her father had been in finding him in such distress, and she could console herself with having been able to do a little to alleviate that distress. She ought perhaps to have felt some anger towards him for the casual thoughtlessness that had led to her conception, but she found she could not do so. If her mother could forgive him for it enough to carry the thought of him with her as the one brightness in a bleak existence, then who was Hannah to judge him more harshly? And it was not as if he had tried to evade his responsibilities; he had simply been unaware that he had any. She had not perhaps found in Hector MacDonald a father of whom she could be proud (if such things mattered), but she had found one she could love. She rejoiced that in Isabel she would have a lasting link with him.

Isabel: that brought her, abruptly, to the other thing that had for so long been lurking uneasily in her mind. She could no longer evade it.

She and Samuel, from a common impulse, had invited the child to share the secure happiness of their home. Hannah knew quite well that Samuel had no doubt at all that they were offering her all the things that until now she had scarcely known, not simply materially, but emotionally and spiritually too.

But Samuel did not know what Hannah could never forget, however hard she tried; what indeed she must not allow herself to forget, or it would force itself upon them in a way that would with certainty utterly destroy all the security and happiness they had promised to Isabel. He did not know that once they were back at Thornside Robert would come to him with an accusation against Hannah that was not only worse than anything he had heard before, but was this time completely, horribly true.

Would Samuel believe him? Hannah wondered. After last time, he might refuse to do so. But at the very least his doubts would come to life again, to gnaw at him and eat away at the peace of mind that their time together during the past weeks had brought him. And if he were to ask her outright for the truth, could she openly and deliberately lie to him? She had at times been less than honest with him, but this was a different matter.

No, she saw now what she had always seen: that there was only one way to prevent the disaster with which Robert threatened them; and that was to forestall him, by confessing everything to Samuel herself. Except that she feared that in doing so, she would simply bring disaster on them the sooner.

She remembered – and shrank inwardly at the recollection – how devastated Samuel had been by Robert's first disclosure, how desperately long it had taken for him to overcome his horror at the thought of it, and then only when another grief, greater than the first, had brought them together again. This time it would be worse, for she had been deliberately and knowingly unfaithful to him. That would be much harder to forgive, but – worse than that – it would hurt him far more and strike a far greater blow to his fragile self esteem than that earlier deception had done. Indeed, she was by no means sure that this time she could either expect or hope that he would forgive her, or that their marriage would not be utterly destroyed by it. And what, then, would Isabel do? Better by far to have left her in the care of her dying father than to have taken her from him to a house of bitterness and misery.

For a long time Hannah sat there on the hill, gazing without seeing it at the glow of the setting sun and torn by anguish at the impossible dilemma that faced her. Whichever way she looked, she could see no way out, nothing that would not lead, inevitably, to disaster. Yet she had to make a choice, and soon, before she found herself once more in Robert's power and beyond taking matters into her own hands.

Would the damage be less, ultimately, were she to leave it to Robert? If Samuel refused to believe him, then all might be well. But it was a dangerously uncertain prospect, offering a reprieve that would never quite be complete, for the possibility of discovery would always be there, haunting her for ever. On the whole, confession seemed the only wise course, the only right one; if she could bring herself to do it.

She tried to still the turmoil of her thoughts, to lay herself open to the quietness that might show her the way; but quietness eluded her, surrounding her but always beyond her reach. Far off, the sun sank below the dark line of hills in the west, touching with a last faint glow the distant waters of the Solway Firth. There was still a little light on the hilltop, but darkness had already filled the hollows and crept up the slope towards her, and would soon reach her where she sat on her rock beneath a sky of pale green-blue dotted with stars. She was dimly conscious of the cold that seeped in with the night, chilling her until she felt she would never be able to move again; but that was a trivial discomfort against the anguish of her mind, and she took little notice of it. Only when she had made her decision would she rise to her feet and descend the hill again.

'Hannah!' She heard the voice, sharp with anxiety, long before Samuel's dark shape emerged from the shadowed depths just below where she sat. The moment he saw her he broke into a run. 'Hannah! Oh, thank God – I was afraid . . . Thou hast been gone so long.' He bent towards her, hands outstretched, ready to help her to her feet; and then evidently saw something in her face and her bearing that halted him. 'Hannah, what is it? Thou art troubled.'

She did rise to her feet after all, though with difficulty, and Samuel had to put out a hand to steady and support her. Her limbs were numb with the cold, stiff and cramped. She stood beside him, shivering, feeling as if now the cold had reached her mind too, chilling it into the same ineffectual numbness. She was no nearer knowing what to do for the best than she had been when she set out from the inn this evening. Yet what better opportunity was there likely to be than this, if she were ever to make her confession to Samuel?

'Thou art frozen,' he said anxiously, rubbing her arms. 'Let's go down – there's a good fire in our room.' He put an arm about her and turned her as if to descend, but she swung round to face him, clasping urgently at his coat.

'No, Samuel. Wait. I . . .'

He waited, attentive, ready to hear her, but nothing came. She stood with bent head, held by his arms, shivering, troubled, but speechless. 'Hannah . . .' he prompted gently.

For a little longer she remained still, and then suddenly she raised her eyes to his face and said earnestly, 'Samuel, it has been good, this time we have had together, on our own.'

'Aye,' he agreed readily enough, but with some puzzlement. 'I have felt it too.'

'I have learned much about thee,' she went on. 'Things I did not know. I have learned to love thee more, to care for thee as I have never done before.' Suddenly the words so long sought were flowing out, though how or why, or where they would ultimately lead her, she did not know. It was as if something outside herself, beyond her control, had taken charge, and she could do no more than allow it to sweep her along. She saw that Samuel – moved, happy – was about to speak, so she quickly pressed her hand to his mouth, 'No, listen! Thou knows, I think, that thou hast always been my dear friend and companion, but that my first love was Robert. Perhaps, too,' – here she bent her head again, and her voice dropped – 'thou hast guessed that . . . what I felt . . . did not end when I wed thee. That he . . .'

She felt his mouth come to rest on her head. 'I know,' he said softly. 'Robert is like that. It is not easy to break free. I hoped perhaps . . . But I knew thou must love him . . .' That he guessed a little of it did not make

513

the knowledge any less hurtful; Hannah could hear the hurt in his voice. Left to herself she would have faltered, even given up the struggle, but the words resumed as if with no will of her own behind them.

'It was not love as thou knows it, Sam – not once I knew what he was. It could not be. They used to talk of evil spirits. In the Gospels, they tell of possession – it was like that, Samuel, as if I was possessed by Robert, as if I could not break free. I wanted to. Sometimes I thought I had. But—'

'I know, I know,' he murmured soothingly. But he did not know, and she must tell him, now, before they went down the hill to the inn and the fire and the sleeping child.

'There has been temptation, Samuel, more than once. Some thou knows of, but not all. I have not always been strong.'

There was a little silence. She sensed that he was allowing her meaning to reach him, trying to face that meaning. She held tight to the folds of his coat, as if willing him not to be hurt, not more than he could bear, not so much that it would destroy all hope for their future together.

'I think – I believe – that I am free of him now. I have not thought of him for many days. I have been glad to be with thee. I have felt no desire for any other man, nor any other companion. I do not want any other – in truth, I have never wanted any other from the day I wed thee. It was not the wanting, it was something I did not want. But,' – here she looked up again into his shadowed face, whose expression she could no longer read – 'I cannot be sure until we are home, until I see him again. Only, I think that even if I am not free of him, then I can be strong now. No, I don't think it only; I am *sure*. I think if thou knows my weakness, if I can tell thee of it and know thy love is there still, then I can surely be strong.'

'God's love is always there, and His strength.' The

514

words came automatically, as if Samuel was thinking of something quite different, and struggling with that thought beneath the calm surface, whilst at the same time making the response that his upbringing had taught him was the right one in the circumstances. Hannah waited quietly, inwardly bracing herself for the moment when he would show her what he really felt and thought.

When, after what seemed an interminable time, he neither moved nor spoke, she said quietly, 'I love thee, Sam, as I never loved thee before. I love thee as I have never loved Robert; with all my heart, with all my self.'

His grasp tightened about her, held her close for a moment and then relaxed. 'Let us go down,' he said. 'Soon it will be too dark to see our way.' His voice was quiet and steady, but husky with emotion.

She knew it was not the moment for her to say any more. She had said what she had to say, as much as she needed to say, and now it was up to him, to question her further, argue, upbraid, make whatever move he thought was right. It was out of her hands. She felt apprehensive, and yet also calm and relieved. The decision had been made for her, and she now had only – only! – to face the consequences, whatever they were.

They moved in silence down the hill, into the deeper shadows of the valley, though even there it was not yet as dark as she had thought, looking from above. It was a clear night, and there was still some lingering trace of daylight that seemed to hang about the landscape as if reluctant finally to go.

They came at last to the point where they could see the town laid before them, all black outlines and glowing rectangles of light, with here and there a lantern hung over a doorway, drawing them on to light and warmth and comfort for their chilled limbs. It was there that Samuel halted and turned to Hannah and held both her hands in his. She could not see his face, except as a faint blur in the darkness, but she knew he was looking at her with great earnestness. 'Let us leave it there, Hannah. I have always loved thee. Thou lovest me. That is enough for the moment.' And then he began to walk on again towards the inn. It was not a final statement; it was not quite a beginning, nor an end; but it was infinitely better than what she had feared, and she was content to go with him, comforted, and almost at peace.

ii

In these first days of September the weather was fine and warm, so at Brough they left the coach behind and hired ponies to take them the rest of the way.

'We'll go back over Hollinthwaite Moor,' Samuel said to Hannah; and then added, 'If that is what thou wouldst wish.' It was, as he knew quite well.

Isabel, riding pillion behind Hannah on that bright Monday morning, enjoyed the fresh air and the sunshine and the wild countryside. As they went, Samuel pointed out to her the birds and animals and plants she might otherwise have missed, and she was by now sufficiently at ease with them both to find a wholehearted pleasure in his gentle guidance. Hannah, watching him, was reminded of how he used to do just the same for her when they were children together.

They followed the drove road on to Hollinthwaite moor, moving steadily nearer to the place where, long ago, he had given her the first small token of his love, and the first hint that she was not the child she had thought she was, thus setting her on a long journey of discovery that was only now at an end. And they were coming nearer, also, to the place where the second stage of that discovery had taken place.

The Drovers' Inn looked little more welcoming today than it had in the wilderness of snow all those years ago. Hannah felt a twinge of apprehension. Was it wise to come here like this? She had explained nothing to

Isabel, and she had no idea how Christian would react to so unexpected a visit.

They left the ponies in the stable yard and went into the inn parlour. It was deserted, but from the kitchen beyond came the sound of clattering pots. 'Wait here,' said Hannah softly. 'I'll see her first.' She stepped forward and pushed open the kitchen door.

As usual, she saw the delight shine from her mother's face, to be followed by the inevitable moment of hesitation. She was, Hannah knew, checking her natural impulse to rush and hug her daughter with a fervour fed by emotions that had no other outlet. Only then did she come, slowly and carefully, to put her arms about Hannah. Ashamed of all the years of coldness, when a little more affection would have cost her so little, Hannah returned her kiss with a new warmth that made her mother give a little cry and then hug her fiercely.

'I thought thou wert still away,' Christian said, her voice unsteady with unshed tears. 'When didst get home?'

'We have not been home yet,' said Hannah quietly. 'We are on our way there. But I wished to see thee first.'

Christian drew back a little so as to look into her face. 'What's happened, lass?'

Hannah took her hand and led her to the settle, and they both sat down.

'I have seen my father.'

'Hector MacDonald? Thou hast seen him?' The questions came in a whisper. At Hannah's nod, Christian's plain face crumpled with emotion. She looked plainer than ever, her colour uneven, her mouth trembling. Yet Hannah felt none of the repulsion she had so often felt before. She stroked the trembling hand held in her own, and was conscious only of tenderness and sympathy for all that her mother had endured. 'Where – ? How – how didst thou find him?'

There were so many questions unasked behind the two that had been put into words, that Hannah did not know where to begin. Instead, she answered none of them, but said, 'He asked me to tell thee, he is sorry for all the pain he brought thee, and thankful that thou canst still think kindly of him. He said thou art a part of his youth, and such happiness will not come to him again, so for that reason thou art precious to him. And' – here her voice became husky, so that she had to pause and clear her throat – 'he thanks thee for thy daughter, and the care thou didst take of her.' As she spoke, she was back in the simple sunlit room in Hector's new lodgings, on the evening before they left Glasgow, watching his face as he gave her the message, and seeing how moved he was. She did not know what had made him choose those words, but she was sure he had given them a great deal of thought, trying in that small way – the only way open to him – to make some amends for what had happened to Christian.

If that was what he wanted, he had succeeded; Hannah could see that before ever she finished speaking. There was a rush of colour to her mother's face and tears filled her eyes, and she smiled tremulously, quite unable to say anything. After a moment or two Hannah went on to tell her how she had found Hector, and something of what she had found, softening a little the hardships he had endured and omitting altogether the fact that he had not even remembered her name. Some things were better left unsaid.

After that, she told Christian about Isabel and took her to see the child, and then they all sat down to havercakes and milk, saying little but held together by a companionable warmth that Hannah had never known before in this place. When they came to leave, she felt that yet another happiness had been added to the riches gathered in the past weeks. She would bring Isabel here again, she decided, and her own children, who had rarely come with her; and she would come more often than in the past. It was time that her friendship with the lonely woman who was her mother became something to be openly acknowledged, as far as it could without revealing her long concealed secret. As for that secret, there was one person, long ignorant, who must be told. It was not Christian who had insisted that Agnes should not know it.

In the mill yard the cat was stretched in the evening sun with a new litter of kittens playing about her. Isabel, slipping wearily from the pony's back, saw them and laughed with delight and ran to them, her exhaustion forgotten. Hannah glanced round at Samuel and he smiled and put his arm about her. Then they went to greet Agnes and the children, who had run out at the sound of the ponies.

'This is Isabel,' said Hannah, when the first embraces were over. The child had come to her side, carrying one of the kittens, and she put out an arm to draw her nearer. 'She is going to live with us.' Then she added to the puzzled and astonished Agnes, 'We'll tell thee later.' And they went indoors.

CHAPTER TWENTY-TWO

The adults sat up late that night, long after the children were asleep, their new 'sister' sharing Rachel's bed, an arrangement that had begun in bashful silence and moved quickly to happy giggling.

'A waste of candles,' Agnes usually said, if anyone sat up long after dark without good reason, but tonight she made no protest. There were, after all, too many questions she wanted to have answered before she could hope to sleep.

At first it seemed as if no one was going to answer them, and somehow Agnes was unable, either, to put the questions into words. In the end it was Hannah who broke the long silence by saying baldly, 'Isabel MacDonald is my sister.'

Agnes stared at her. 'Thy *sister*?'

'My half sister. Her father Hector MacDonald is my father. I . . . I learned long ago who my mother is.' And then, as simply and as briefly as she could, she told Agnes the whole story, and the old woman listened in a silence broken only now and then when, for the sake of clarity, she asked a question.

At the end, Hannah reached across the table and took Agnes's hands in hers and said huskily, 'One thing I know. Whatever may have been true in nature, it was thee and John who were my true mother and father, and who gave me all that I have in life that is good.' Agnes wept a little, and then asked a few more questions, which seemed designed, more than anything, to assure herself that Hannah had not suffered in any way from the long search for her parents. After that, she seemed to think that there was no more to be said on the subject, for after a suitable pause she said in the brisk tone of one putting emotion behind her, 'Now I have news for thee – news about Gayles this time, not Burtons.'

Robert! thought Hannah. There was some response inside her, yet it was nothing like the agitation she remembered, more a faint acknowledgement of the fact that there was still her brother-in-law to be confronted, and the threat he posed to the real happiness that lay before her.

'Sir George Scarr is dead. Last month, of an apoplexy.'

Samuel frowned a little. 'I am sorry, for Harriet's sake. What does that mean for them – materially, I mean? She was not the heir, I know.'

'For that she should count herself fortunate,' Agnes said drily. 'They have troubles enough without inheriting any more. It seems he was not, after all, the wealthy man we all thought – or at least, not at the end.'

'What happened then?'

'He left debts, terrible debts. Money owed all over the county, and in London too, they say. The creditors had kept quiet while he lived, thinking he had money still, and that it would only be a matter of time and they'd get what was owed. But then he died and they found he had not a penny left, just debts.'

'How terrible!' murmured Hannah. She left it to Samuel to ask,

'What of Robert? He has his own means, I know, and the mill is profitable, I suppose. But did his father-in-law not have money in the business?'

'Aye, and more than we knew, I think. It seems there's nothing left of what he came home with – that went long ago. And the mill hadn't done as well as he led everyone to believe, so I hear. Then there was the fire. It was his father-in-law's credit supported him lately, it seems. So when the old man died, the creditors closed in on him too.'

There was a brief appalled silence. Then Samuel asked, 'How is he? What will he do?'

'The mill's up for sale already. But there's not much interest, I'm told. The other cotton mills in the dale are in trouble, Miles Pickering's among them. It's being said they're all too far from the main routes. Transport costs too much, and they can't sell cheaply enough. And now that many mills are going over to steam, water power can't compete. The successful ones are in the towns, where there's plenty of labour, and canals to take the goods to market. Bringing in pauper children doesn't pay either, if there's others can get in daily labourers.'

'I'm glad enough of that,' said Hannah. 'But what will Robert do?' She thought it was the first time in her life that she had said his name without a tremor.

'No one seems to know. He's sold his house and the land and bought a small property near Hawes; I forget the name of it, but it's half way to Bainbridge – twenty acres and an old house. Not much, after what he's been used to. As for his wife, she's never known any but grand ways. It'll come hard for her ... I think,' she added in a low voice, 'there's some trouble between them too.'

Hannah felt Samuel's hand close about hers, as if to reassure himself, and her, that they still had one another. 'Poor Robert,' he said, with real distress. 'Has he been to see thee?'

'I've seen neither hide nor hair of him since the news broke,' said Agnes. 'They say he's ashamed to show his face. But maybe he's just too busy, what with the debts and the selling and all. And the mill's still working of course, for the moment, while they've cotton left to spin.'

'What about the mill children?' Hannah asked. 'What will become of them?'

'If the mill's bought as a going concern, I suppose they'll stay. If not, then ... well, they'll send them back where they came from maybe, or put them to some other work hereabouts, if any can be found for so many.'

'I shall go and see Robert in the morning,' said Samuel with determination when, much later, he and Hannah went up to bed. 'He is my brother after all. Who else can he turn to in trouble, if not to me?'

Hannah could not think of any objection to that, though she felt a little uneasy about it. As for the rest, it was all too much to assimilate as yet, coming on top of everything that had happened in the past weeks. She did not quite know what she thought of it all.

As it happened, Samuel did not need to go and call on Robert; they were still at breakfast when he rode into the yard.

Samuel went to open the door to him, Agnes summoned the children to come with her to feed and unbar the hens; Hannah rose to her feet, so that when Robert came in she looked as if she was on the point of leaving – as in fact she was. She glanced at him, as casually as she could, and at once met his eyes. She felt something, she was not quite sure what, except that her principal emotion was a sense of shock. She had never seen Robert like this, so crushed and exhausted. He looked years older than when she had seen him last and – yes, that was it – she had never before seen him look so like his brother. Perhaps Samuel's increased air of confidence only added to the resemblance.

She heard Robert say, 'I heard you were back,' and Samuel return gently, 'News travels fast,' and then she murmured some excuse and – unnoticed by the two men, she thought – went out into the sunlight. At a time like this, it was right that the brothers should be alone together. She refused to consider that there might be awkward consequences for herself. In any case, she suspected that Robert would have other things on his mind this morning than a wish to revenge himself on either of them.

The children's laughter was carried to her on the still air from a far corner of the garden. Hannah smiled, and paused to listen for a moment, and then she went on her way to the mill.

It was as if she had never been away, except that the workers greeted her a little more volubly this morning. She went from one to another, talking to them, asking questions about how things had gone in her absence; and feeling a revived pleasure in watching the skilled hands at work. 'I can see I'm not needed here,' she said to George Holgate, who had been nominally in charge in her absence.

He grinned. 'That's right,' he agreed cheerfully. 'We never noticed thou wert gone.' Then he added, 'Mind, nowt went wrong. If it had now . . .' She was grateful to him for that concession to her self esteem.

She went to her office and looked at the books for some time, studying sales of yarn, both kinds, orders for knitted goods, payments made and received. It was all better than she had expected. Cotton mills might be doing badly in the Dales, but wool was another story. But then, as she had told Robert long ago, wool was a part of the Dales, and always would be. Odd to think that, now she had proved that she had been right and Robert wrong, it no longer mattered to her that she should do so, except that no one could grieve at the passing of the cotton mills and all they meant. But as for that old rivalry, it had been based on a passion that was over now – for ever, she thought. She would continue to find satisfaction in her work, because the mill served a useful purpose, but it was no longer a means with which to prove her superiority to Robert.

She ran her eyes over the columns of figures again, confirming her first impression. They might not be wealthy, by the standards Robert had set himself, but they were doing very well indeed. It was time to review the wages paid to the workers without whom she could have achieved nothing. But first, there was Robert, who might need help to pay his creditors, and even to live. His own brother could not refuse him that, if he asked for it. Hannah laid the books aside and went back to the house.

Samuel and Robert sat on opposite sides of the kitchen table, Robert full of gloom, staring at the scrubbed surface on which his finger idly followed the knots and whorls in the wood; Samuel all grave sympathy. They were neither of them talking as Hannah came in, but at first they did not seem to notice her pull up a stool and sit down near them.

Then Samuel did look at her. 'Hannah, Robert has come to put a proposal to us.'

'Oh?' She forced herself not to look at Robert.

'I told him it was for thee to say, not me.'

'I see who's the man in this house,' Robert put in, with something of his old mocking jocularity of tone. Hannah, furious, turned her angry gaze on him, but Samuel only said mildly,

'I told thee – it is Hannah who manages the mill, not I. Thou knows it is what our father wished. Thou knows too that I am not fit for business. So it is Hannah who decides.'

Hannah frowned, instantly on her guard. 'What has the mill to do with this?'

Robert straightened, assuming something approaching the air of bright assertiveness she knew so well; only now she knew too how hollow it was, simply a mask for what pride would not allow him to reveal. 'I came with a proposal which my dear brother is too self effacing to consider for himself. I shall put it to you then, knowing your good sense – and your compassion.' His eyes were on her with the look that once would have melted her and bent her to his will. Now she felt only pity and – to her surprise – a faint disgust. If there was any attraction as well, it did not amount to much. 'I am selling the cotton mill, as I gather you know already. Once it's all settled I should have enough to pay off those leeches of creditors, and still have a little over. That's by the by . . . I need some other means to live, of course. Now, unlike my dear brother here, I have an excellent head for business, as even you must acknowledge, whatever our disagreements may have been over the use I put it to. It was only my damned bad luck with the fire stood between me and a fortune.' He waved a hand airily. 'What I propose is that I put my business sense at your entire disposal. You've a good little concern here, a credit to your caution and common sense. But what it needs – and I'm sure you must agree with me, if you think about it – what it needs is a little imagination, some new ideas, a fresh eye to be cast over it. I propose to supply that new eye. Never fear, I know you don't want cotton mills. I can tell you, I'm done with cotton mills too. But there's room for expansion in your little business here. Two heads are better than one, they say.'

'Wilt get to the point please, Robert,' Hannah put in briskly, to his obvious surprise. 'What precisely is thy proposal?'

He coloured faintly. 'That you should take me on as a partner – an equal partner, mark you. Half shares all round. You supply the common sense, I supply the vision. What do you say?'

'No,' said Hannah quietly, without hesitation; with so little hesitation in fact that he did not at first realise she had turned him down, and went on,

'It can't fail. I —'

'No, Robert. I said no.'

He stared at her in total disbelief. 'But – why? It makes good sense.'

'It makes no sense at all, not to me. I know thee very well; thou knows how well.' There was a little silence then, while she met his eyes steadily, without flinching. I am no longer afraid of thee, she was saying, beneath the simple words; do thy worst. After a moment, she

526

went on, 'If thou art in need, thee and Harriet, then we will help thee all we can. We would not think of doing otherwise. But never as long as I live wilt thou have a part in Thornside mill. I know thy business ways, and they are not mine. Thy 'vision' can never have any place in anything I do. Whatever thou might think, I have my own vision, and it is that I'll be guided by, not thine.'

Robert gave a furious exclamation and pushed back his stool, getting to his feet and leaning across the table towards Samuel. 'Damn you, Samuel, you're not going to sit there and let your wife speak to me like that – are you?' He crashed his fist down on the table. 'Speak, Samuel! Never mind Hannah, say what *you* think! The law says you own the mill, not your wife. You must see the sense of it, you must – and the justice. Father would have wanted it, of course he would, his two sons working together in harmony. He would have asked for nothing more. It's what you've always wanted too, that we should be friends. What better way is there than this, tell me that?'

Hannah held her breath. She knew Samuel as she knew Robert; she knew what Robert's appeal would mean to him, working on the unease he had always felt about his father's legacy, and his lifelong conviction that, set against Robert, he had nothing, was nothing. She saw how Samuel sat in silence, his eyes held by his brother's. Like a rabbit held in thrall by a stoat, Hannah thought. One leap, and it would all be over; there would be no escape for Samuel. But she said nothing, only waited. This time Samuel must answer for himself.

He did so at last. He shook his head slowly, his expression almost melancholy. 'I am sorry, Robert. Hannah is right. We will help thee, and gladly. But there is no place for thee at the mill.'

'Damn you, puny milksop that you are – can you never go against Hannah? Have you no will of your own?'

'It *is* my will,' Samuel put in, but Robert swept heedlessly on,

'You owe her nothing, if you would only see it. She's not worth it – a slut, a whore. You know she's —'

'Be silent!'

Robert, astonished, shut his mouth. Hannah too was amazed to hear Samuel intervene with such force. She was the more amazed when he did not leave it there.

'Thou wilt not speak of my wife so in my house, not ever! I want no ill words from thee ever again, concerning her. Thou hast heard what we have to say. That is it. We are agreed, and there is no more to be said. If thou hast need of our help, then stay, and thou art welcome as my brother. If thou hast only harsh words for us, and idle proposals thou knows full well we can never accept, then I must ask thee to go, at once.'

Robert, swallowing hard, trying to hide his dismay and retain something of his air of superiority, stammered, 'But you have not heard —'

'Nor do I wish to,' returned Samuel with dignity, rising to his feet. 'I have listened to thee already more often than I ought. Thou wilt never again have the power to come between me and my wife ... Now, sit down again in peace – or go. It is as thou wilt.'

'Oh, you need have no fear – I'm going!' He paused a moment, as if drawing breath for one final devastating thrust. But in the end he said no more, only turned and strode out of the house, slamming the door behind him.

Hannah stayed where she was, quite still, and suddenly afraid. This new, decisive Samuel was so unlike the man she knew so well, and loved so lately. She did not love him the less for it; on the contrary. But she did fear him, because this was a man who knew quite well what Robert had threatened to reveal and who might now turn from protecting her to demanding a full confession of all that had happened between his brother and herself.

Then she heard him move, and felt his hand close about hers. Like hers, it was trembling. She looked at him. His expression was grave, his face pale, but there was tenderness in his eyes. 'When I was a lad,' he said quietly, 'I always used to walk up on the fell, the moment I was home from school. There has been no time for that since we came home this time. Wilt thou come with me now?'

Before them, Wensleydale lay spread out in the September sun. The distant hills were hazy but for the gleam of Semerwater; nearer, the trees that filled the hollows and topped the smaller hills and clustered round sturdy farmhouses were already touched with bronze and red and gold. The river shone silver and blue as it wound its way along the dale.

Here, the incessant little wind, never quite still even on the quietest day, cooled cheeks hot from the exertion of the climb, and blew loose threads of Hannah's hair across her face.

They stood side by side, hands linked, saying nothing, utterly still. It was not the silence of awkwardness or estrangement, but rather of absorption, in private thoughts which in neither case excluded the other.

This is where I belong, thought Hannah. It is my home. That is something no one can take from me; nor yet the truth that I belong to Samuel, as he to me.

She had come a long way to reach this place, further by far than the short distance from Thornside, tucked into the hillside just out of sight below them; further even than the hundreds of miles to the mountains where her father had been born. A lifelong journey, which would go on into the future, but yet had now reached a place of healing and repose from which she could set out again when she chose with her strength renewed.

It was, she thought, a little like the moment of full recovery after a long illness. She was whole as she had never been before. It was not simply that she had at last discovered all the different threads that had gone to make her what she was. It was also that she had realised that they did not matter, not in the end. She was not a creature made up of wayward and conflicting impulses, at the mercy of qualities drawn from so many disparate sources, over which she had little control. She was herself: Hannah. Not Hannah Lambert, or Hannah MacDonald, or Hannah Burton or even Hannah Gayle, for those were just names, attachments to make recognition easy. Nor was she merely Christian's daughter, Samuel's wife, Rachel's mother, Robert's one time sweetheart. No, she was, simply, and yet gloriously, Hannah: a woman approaching middle age, with faults and virtues, needs and desires, strengths and weaknesses, unique and precious as was every human creature, but no more strange than they, no more liable to temptation or to passion, no less able to find the strength to do what was right, and the vision to show her the way. She was not an outsider, but one among many, sharing the common lot of humanity. She did not need Robert to give meaning to her life, for she knew now that it had a richer meaning by far than anything he could ever have given her.

She turned her head to look at Samuel, and he smiled. Hannah; and Samuel: two people alike and yet unlike, separate and yet joined irrevocably, not by law but now, in truth, by love. Hannah no longer felt that she must remind herself constantly how kind he was, how gentle, how courageous in his own quiet way. What point was there now in listing his good qualities, in the hope that they might make her love him better? She loved him, and that was enough. Love had no use for 'how' and 'why'.

Samuel moved closer to her and put an arm about her, and she laid her head on his shoulder.

'Samuel,' she said at last. 'Thou knows there may be children from Newgill with nowhere to go?'

'I know.'

'Dost think – could we not take some in?'

'To work in thy mill?' Samuel sounded astonished, and appalled.

'No – no, of course not. To be cared for – taught to read and write, and to knit. I could teach them, and Agnes.'

'And I. But they would need to have time to be children too – time to play and to laugh.'

'And sing perhaps, a little,' Hannah added, with a smile.

'We shall look into it,' Samuel assured her.

They began to descend the hill, hand in hand. Thornside came into view, all crowded roofs and curling smoke, and beyond it the woollen mill in its sheltering trees.

'I am glad we are home again,' said Samuel, his voice warm with contentment.

LOVE AND MONEY

Ruth Harris

SISTERS AND STRANGERS. HEIRESS AND PAUPER. THEY SHOULD NEVER HAVE MET . . .

Deedee Dahlen even smells rich. Hailed from birth as the 'million dollar baby', she reigns at the top of a vast pyramid of wealth. She is New York's leading socialite. She lacks nothing. Except love . . .

Lana Bantry is born on the wrong side of the tracks. She grows up embittered and deprived. She inherits nothing. Except a burning ambition to make money . . .

They are sisters. Their father kept them apart. Their lover brings them together. The result is shattering . . .

GENERAL FICTION
0 7474 0319 8

INHERITANCE

Judith Michael

IT WAS LIKE A DREAM COME TRUE. SHE HAD DISCOVERED LAUGHTER, LUXURY, AND THE LOVE OF HER LIFE. AND THEN THE NIGHTMARE STARTED . . .

When the fabulously wealthy Owen Salinger died, he left an inheritance to Laura Fairchild. But Laura already had a legacy – a hidden secret from her past. And the Salingers used that legacy to destroy her life – and claim her inheritance.

Laura didn't want revenge, she wanted the fruits of power, passion, worldly success – and her lost love regained. And so she built an empire – an empire that stretched from fashionable Boston to the fabulous haunts of the European jet-set. But the past is forever present – and the stakes are perilously high . . .

Also by Judith Michael in Sphere Books:

DECEPTIONS

POSSESSIONS

PRIVATE AFFAIRS

GENERAL FICTION
0 7474 0298 1

<u>FALSE PRETENSES</u>

Catherine Coulter

IT BEGAN WITH MURDER . . .

Elizabeth Carleton, beautiful and talented concert pianist, looks certain to be convicted of her millionaire husband's murder; until a mystery witness provides her with an unshakable alibi . . .

Newly acquitted, she struggles to rule her husband's financial empire, confronted on all sides by her vicious and scheming in-laws. In the hostile world of Wall Street, Elizabeth battles against all odds. And when she meets Jonathan Harley, both success and happiness are within her grasp. But her husband's murderer still stalks . . .

GENERAL FICTION
0 7474 0459 3

<u>RIVALS</u>

Janet Dailey

FLAME BENNETT is a woman of contrasts; as fiery as
her copper-red hair, yet as cool as her clear green eyes.
Ambitious, successful and sought-after, she moves in
the most glittering San Francisco circles. And she is
looking for love . . .

CHANCE STUART, multimillionaire real estate
magnate, has come a long way from an unhappy,
poverty-stricken childhood. His dark good looks,
electric blue eyes and devastating charm have made
him supremely sure of himself. And now he is sure of his
love for Flame. The attraction between them is
immediate and intense . . .

Their passion deepens and develops – and then erupts
into a white-hot hatred. For Flame and Chance are the
unknowing inheritors of a vicious family feud; a quarrel
that spans a continent and stretches back for a century.
They are the heirs of a turbulent story of intrigue and
betrayal, of a history that is about to repeat itself.
Locked into a deadly battle of wills, they are destined to
become the bitterest of RIVALS

Also by Janet Dailey in Sphere Books:

THE GREAT ALONE
THE GLORY GAME
HEIRESS

GENERAL FICTION
0 7474 0292 2

All Sphere Books are available at your bookshop or newsagent, or can be ordered from the following address: Sphere Books, Cash Sales Department, P.O. Box 11, Falmouth, Cornwall TR10 9EN.

Please send cheque or postal order (no currency), and allow 60p for postage and packing for the first book plus 25p for the second book and 15p for each additional book ordered up to a maximum charge of £1.90 in U.K.

B.F.P.O. customers please allow 60p for the first book, 25p for the second book plus 15p per copy for the next 7 books, thereafter 9p per book.

Overseas customers, including Eire, please allow £1.25 for postage and packing for the first book, 75p for the second book and 28p for each subsequent title ordered.